MAX NOWAZ

Get Rich or Get Lucky

Other Books by Max Nowaz

The Arbitrator
Timbi's Dream

Plays

Cheating Death
A Holiday to Remember

MAX NOWAZ

GET RICH OR GET LUCKY

Matador
9 Priory Business Park,
Wistow Road, Kibworth Beauchamp,
Leicestershire. LE8 0RX
Tel: 0116 279 2299
Email: books@troubador.co.uk
Web: www.troubador.co.uk/matador
Twitter: @matadorbooks

ISBN 978 1785899 317

British Library Cataloguing in Publication Data.
A catalogue record for this book is available from the British Library.

Printed and bound by CPI Group (UK) Ltd, Croydon, CR0 4YY
Typeset in 11pt Aldine401 BT by Troubador Publishing Ltd, Leicester, UK

Matador is an imprint of Troubador Publishing Ltd

ACKNOWLEDGEMENTS

I would like to thank everybody concerned in publishing the book and especially:

My friends and family for their continued support and encouragement.

My writers group for pointing out specific factors and for their general criticisms and suggestions for improving the book, which were invaluable.

All those people who read my first novel The Arbitrator and commented on it, thus lifting my spirits to continue further.

CHAPTER 1

The builder was early. He knocked so hard on the old door that Adam thought the door would fall off its hinges.

"Coming," shouted Adam, as he struggled to put on some trousers and rush down the stairs, almost tripping down them in the process. He was not sure if the man had heard him.

Just as Adam was about to open the door, he knocked again. A burly, sour-faced man greeted him.

"Sorry, I wasn't sure if you heard me, mate," he said. "I'm in a bit of a hurry as I'm starting on another job this morning, so I'm a bit early. Where's the job you want the estimate for?"

"Come in," said Adam. "This way."

The man followed him into the kitchen. "I see you got your work cut out here." He smiled.

"I've got to finish the work in four weeks. My future depends on it." Adam knew instantly that it was the wrong thing to say to a builder.

"What would you like me to do?"

"I want these new units put up and the old ones taken down. As I already said, I'm in a bit of a hurry." Adam regretted repeating himself, but the monkey had already slipped the cage.

"What's your hurry?" asked the man.

"I've got a survey to get through in four weeks," said Adam, regretting giving this information again. What was wrong with him? He was leading himself to the slaughter, but he felt tired; tired of all the incessant building work he had gone through lately.

"The earliest I can do it is in two weeks. It will cost you £700," the man said without blinking. "A very fair price, if you ask me."

"Can't you do it this week?" Adam asked hopefully. He knew it was daylight robbery, but he was desperate.

"It'll cost you an extra £500." The man smiled again. "Time is money."

It was on the tip of Adam's tongue to tell him to fuck off, but he controlled himself. He knew he was being badly ripped off.

"Why? Don't you think it's a bit steep?" he heard himself pleading.

The man told him that he had a lot of work on at the moment. He shrugged his shoulders, throwing his hands up in the air, but he would like to help Adam out, and as a concession he would do it for an even £1,000.

Adam protested that it was still too much, and £700 was not exactly cheap. He said he didn't think he wanted to pay any more than that, at which the man grimaced and said that he'd be lucky to get anybody else at such short notice. He was trying to do Adam a favour and he was sorry, but that was his price, so Adam could take it or leave it. His beady eyes gleamed as if he knew he had Adam in a corner.

"I think I'll leave it," said Adam, much to his own surprise, but his hackles were up. Adam had never liked being pushed into a corner. "I'll do it myself."

The man's expression almost turned into a scowl; he was himself surprised. "You're wasting my bloody time." He looked almost threatening.

"Not at all, it's my time that you've wasted," said Adam with much satisfaction, even though he wasn't looking forward to the job. Later that afternoon as Adam tried to take down one of the old kitchen units, part of the wall behind it collapsed, revealing a bricked-up doorway to a hidden cellar.

There had been no mention of the cellar in the fact sheet

of the house he had received from the estate agent. Even the surveyors had missed it during the survey. Those surveys were not worth the paper they were written on, he thought.

The next thought that crossed Adam's mind was one of misgiving. What extra problems did he face now with this semi-derelict house he had burdened himself with – the prospect of a damp, or even a flooded cellar?

The cellar was in fact quite large, and it was dry and there was a small metal box on a shelf cut into the wall. The box was securely fastened by a rusting iron clasp and an old lock. The thought of hidden treasure sent his pulse racing, and Adam wanted to get his hands on whatever was in the box.

Adam forcefully prised it open, eager to find out what was inside, but instead of treasure, he was disappointed to find a book. It was bound in tatty brown leather, untitled and gave off a horrific smell. *What a waste of an evening*, thought Adam.

It was his night to go and play badminton, but that was in London. He was a long way from there at present, in Littledon. The house was his latest acquisition, and a first outside London. He had bought it in a moment of madness at an auction. Badminton would have to wait for another day, and also his weekly drink with Charlie, after club night. However, his thoughts drifted to Charlie.

★ ★ ★

"You could probably be a good badminton player," said Charlie. "You have a lot of natural ability."

Adam was having a drink with him after club night. It was over two years ago that he had joined the badminton club in a desperate bid to improve his social life.

"I need to play more often to manage that, and unfortunately I've no time for it at present."

"I suppose you've got family commitments," Charlie acquiesced.

"No, I'm not married, but I'm doing up a house," said Adam. "This is much worse. The house was in a very bad state when I got it and I have to do a lot of the work myself."

Charlie remarked that it must be good to be a handyman, and Adam told him that he was self-taught. If Charlie had seen his first house after he had finished with it, he would have laughed at his handiwork. Still, he had made a good profit on it.

Charlie was intrigued, and asked Adam what he had done to it. Adam told him he had converted it from a two to a three-bedroomed house.

"You must've had a lot of capital to begin with, to embark on such projects." Charlie sighed. "I can't even get enough money together for a deposit to buy a flat."

"Not really," said Adam. "I went to the bank and borrowed a load of money to buy a car and used it as a deposit for the house." Adam blurted out the information without thinking, and realised that maybe he was bragging about the wrong thing.

Charlie asked Adam what made him take such a risk. It seemed to surprise him that anybody would undertake such a risky endeavour.

Adam told him that he had been desperate. Three years ago his then-girlfriend ditched him because he was a complete non-achiever. He was thirty and didn't even own a good car, so he had no choice but to improve his fortunes.

Adam didn't tell Charlie, however, that he had been obsessed with the idea of making it rich for some time, though for a time after college he had wanted to be a writer. But after a stack of rejections, his sense of insecurity had kicked in and all his literary aspirations had gone out of the window.

He had analysed it himself, after assiduously reading a good many books on psychology, including Freud and Jung amongst others. He had concluded that his insecurity stemmed from the fact that his father had left him and his mother when he was twelve and just about to reach his teens. They had then tail-spun into poverty from a fairly comfortable standard of living.

His mother had failed to keep up with the mortgage payments for the house and they had moved into mouse-infested rented accommodation. His insecurity had multiplied steadily over the years as his mother complained incessantly about a shortage of the filthy lucre, without which life had slowly ground them down.

He had been lucky though, and had managed to claw his way into a second-rate university and get a degree in business studies. He still owed quite a bit on his student loans, even though he had worked steadily all the way through college in various low-paid part-time jobs.

But the thought of poverty haunted him, and had also been instrumental in the downfall of the few relationships he had had with women. His parsimonious ways had been the main problem, and though he did attract some women, he still suffered from a lack of confidence because of his feeling of insecurity about his finances.

Adam had adapted to a very frugal lifestyle as he struggled to save the money he needed to fulfil his ambition of owning his own house. This, however, proved costly nonetheless, as all his relationships with women nosedived because of a lack of funds to support a reasonable lifestyle.

Finally, out of frustration he had resorted to the desperate but simple scheme to buy his first house. Adam hated the crass, bourgeois nature of his scheme and his failed literary spirit rebelled against it, but he had to accept he was stuck with it if he was to prosper in the worship of Mammon.

"You still don't have a good car," laughed Charlie.

Adam told him that he had been pretty stretched with all the money he was having to spend on the new house, and would get a better car when he sold it.

"So you are a property developer."

"Hardly, but a wise man told me a long time ago that unless you have a really fantastic job, it's impossible to become rich doing nine to five."

★ ★ ★

The next week, when they went for a drink again, Charlie surprised him.

"I'd like to invite you to a barbecue this weekend. I've already asked my friend Dick and he said to bring you along." Charlie told Adam that his friend Dick had a big house in Highgate Village. Adam knew it was a posh area.

"Dick's house is worth a million pounds. You should see the girls that turn up to his barbecues." Charlie seemed very proud of having such a friend.

"Oh, really?" Adam was interested.

"He's a big shot in advertising and the girls are real babes."

"Have you had any luck with them?" But Adam already knew the answer to that question.

Charlie explained that unfortunately these girls were more interested in their own types. One needed a good car and an expensive pad to impress them, and again, unfortunately for Charlie, he possessed neither at present.

A slightly downbeat Charlie went on to elaborate that he lived in a rented studio flat in Tottenham, a not-very-desirable area. Adam asked Charlie why Dick bothered to invite him.

"We went to school together." Charlie cheered up. "Isn't it marvellous what he's achieved?"

"I suppose so."

"He's such a successful man, don't you think so?"

"It seems like he's doing well." Adam took a good look at Charlie, a shabbily dressed, thin, wiry individual. "Why would he be interested in me?"

"I told him you're a budding property developer."

Adam found out soon, much to his utter disappointment, that Dick indeed worked in advertising and the girls were usually from a similar background and normally disinterested in the likes of Charlie or himself. His efforts were further undermined when Dick invariably mentioned that Adam drove an old Skoda. Charlie had never learnt to drive.

★ ★ ★

After giving the outside of the book a thorough clean by spraying it with leather furniture polish, which had the effect of diminishing the unpleasant smell somewhat, Adam flicked through the book. It was in German, and just out of sheer curiosity he read some words aloud.

The whole house then began to shake, and the lights started popping one by one. He closed the book promptly, and then it stopped.

The next morning when he awoke he found the bulbs to be intact. He had a feeling then that there was something strange about the book.

He wanted to investigate further but there were far more pressing problems to worry about at the time. He had bought the current house with the help of a sizeable bridging loan at an extortionate rate of interest, before he could sell the last house. He suddenly found that he was barely able to cover his expenses, and there was now a sudden housing downturn and the old house was not selling.

He needed to remortgage his current house quickly to repay the bridging loan as he was running out of money fast. However, before he could do that, there were many jobs that still needed to be finished. The survey for the remortgage was due in four weeks. In his mad dash to get rich quick Adam had over-extended himself.

It had rained quite a lot the night before and the roof of the house had seen better days. After spending several hours the next day trying to move slates and taping up the gaps to the best of his ability, he decided to break for lunch. As he sat down with a cup of tea and bit into the sandwich he had made, his thoughts turned to the book.

It was certainly very strange what had happened, but he was not even sure it *had* actually happened. No, he must have imagined the whole thing.

It seemed impossible that reading aloud from a book would cause the whole house to shake, unless the book had hidden powers. But that was nonsense, of course. No, there had to be another explanation for what had happened.

That evening Adam checked the internet to see if there had been any seismic activity in the area, but there had been none; neither had there been any mention of an earthquake in the news on the television. It was all very strange.

★ ★ ★

As the book was written in a Germanic script it took him many days to make any sense of it. But he brushed up his schoolboy German, and with the help of a large dictionary he acquired, he deciphered a few verses.

He then checked the verse which had caused his house to shake. The paragraph before it gave a warning not to invoke the spell in an enclosed space, lest one should literally bring down the house upon oneself. As far as he could make out, the verse read:

I summon thee, the invisible force that blows the air around the world, to give me the power to raise winds from the air that surround me, to gather rain clouds and make rain at my command.

It was an ancient rain-making spell, and that could point to only one thing: it was probably a book of magic. *What nonsense,* he thought; he was the last person on earth to believe in hocus-pocus. It was just so much hogwash. However, he decided that he would try out the spell again, now that he had patched up the roof somewhat, to see if he had imagined the whole thing or not, just for his own peace of mind.

Next day he had a quick look outside the window and saw that it was quite a sunny day. There were no signs of any clouds anywhere. *Perfect,* he thought, *let's see if I can ruin a few people's day.* He took the book out from its case and made his way into the back garden.

After making sure that he was not being watched, he opened the book and looked for the spell. Last time he had only muttered a couple of lines of the spell and had then closed the book in a hurry. This time he decided to recite the whole spell, making sure he pronounced all the words carefully.

For a while nothing happened, then suddenly he heard the sound of thunder at a distance. Then some very dark clouds started appearing not too far away, as if suddenly materialising out of thin air. Adam decided he would rather watch the show from inside the house. He closed the book and hurried back inside.

All of a sudden the sun disappeared completely, and it got quite dark. The sky was covered in black clouds. When the rain came, it was very heavy. The water fell in sheets, reducing visibility to a few feet from the house.

Adam burst into spontaneous laughter; he could not help himself. The spell was working, and he could not contain his joy. It was like winning the lottery. What other secrets did the book hold? Was it going to make him rich or famous, or both? Could he have a career on television, as a magician? He wouldn't need any conjuring tricks; his magic would be completely authentic.

Adam managed to stop himself from getting totally carried away. For a start he would have to keep the book a secret, for one could only imagine what would happen if news of the book got out. He would have to be very cautious and only try out some little spells at first, to get the hang of things, before trying any really big stuff. What would happen if the spells did not work out or worked badly – could he set things back to normal? Only one thing was sure: the roof was leaking again.

Adam knew he had to be very careful but he had to tell somebody, otherwise he would go mad. He definitely could not tell his mother, or his ex-girlfriend Linda; they would immediately assume that he was crazy and laugh at him. If he actually demonstrated that it worked, his ex would probably try to report him to the authorities for practising the black arts and his mother would probably support her.

★ ★ ★

Adam had met Linda when he was in the process of selling his second house. He still remembered that night at a barbecue at Dick's, when he walked in with a large crate of beer.

"Ah! The delivery is here," laughed Dick, and his very even teeth gleamed.

"Help yourself," said Adam, putting down the crate.

"Nobody drinks beer these days, except you and Charlie," Dick roared again. He had that polished, practised laughter, which was sort of infectious.

"Leave him alone," said Rachael, Dick's new, blonde girlfriend. "I'll have a beer."

"They'll have to go into the fridge first," said Adam. He liked Rachael, the blonde bombshell, Dick's latest acquisition. She had a sense of humour.

"There's a few cans in the fridge already, if you'd really like a beer," said Dick, perplexed. "I thought you never touch anything but shots and red wine."

"One can always have a change," retorted Rachael.

"Join the plebs, eh?" Dick smiled. "You've always got a soft spot for Adam, our budding property developer." It seemed to Adam that he was always a source of merriment to Dick.

"Come with me," said Rachael. "I want to introduce you to Linda, a friend of mine who's looking desperately for a husband."

"And you think I might suit?" asked Adam, amused.

"Sure, an upwardly mobile property magnate like you might just be the right person. She's not in advertising."

Linda had turned out to be a petite brunette, busy in conversation with some other men. Rachael ignored them and grabbed Linda and pulled her over.

"This is Adam, Linda, I told you about him. He's a bit shy with women, can I leave him in your good hands?"

"Hello, Adam." Linda smiled. "Don't worry, I'll take good care of him."

"Hi, Linda, I hope I'm not imposing on you." Adam smiled.

"Not at all," said Linda. "Rachael told me a lot about you."

"All good, I hope?"

By this time his house was in a fairly good condition, and Linda had no idea that Adam was selling it to buy another rundown house to renovate.

Linda was a legal secretary in her early thirties, and was of similar age to Adam, but looked older. Adam soon got to know that she was actually desperately looking for somebody to have some children with and Adam almost fitted the bill, so he decided to roll with it. Maybe it was time for him to settle down.

"You should get yourself a better car," Linda had advised Adam on their second date, and then she had given him strict instructions not to park his Skoda directly in front of her rented flat when he went round to pick her up on a date.

Trouble started when Adam sold the second house and moved on to the next one, which was the last house before the present one.

Sure, it was in a better area, but it needed some major overhauling. By this stage Linda had been ready to move in with Adam, but she baulked when she saw the new house. Adam assured her that it would soon be ready, but she was not buying it.

"I can't live here," Linda had complained. However, she had moved in, reluctantly as she had already given up her flat, but she was not happy at all.

★ ★ ★

No, he could not breathe a word to Linda, not after all that had taken place between them, so whom could he invite to come down to look at the book?

Adam thought of the people he had worked with until he had been let go the previous month. Could he tell Vera, the boss's wife, for whom he got the sack, and tempt her back to him? No, it was too dangerous even to think about it – she would tell her husband immediately and that would be that.

There was no point taking a chance with things; better to go slow. It was best to invite Charlie and Dick and give them a little surprise. They were probably also the wrong people as things went, and of course they would never believe him. He would have to provide a little demonstration for them. It would be fun.

Yes, it would be greatly amusing to see their faces when he performed a little trick for them. They, who had always instinctively doubted his ability to achieve anything much, would soon at last see what he was capable of. *Yes! Yes!* thought Adam; he was going to be both rich and lucky.

Adam decided that he would invite them down on the following weekend as this would give him enough time to practise a suitable spell to impress them with. Something not too difficult but suitably impressive, so that they finally got the message that he was somebody worthy of their attention. It was time to change the pecking order.

CHAPTER 2

"What was so urgent about meeting here today?" Dick almost hissed as he screwed his eyes up in that familiar fashion which Adam absolutely detested. Dick, who was a large, well-built man, looked almost threatening when he did that. Charlie said nothing; he was busy sipping his beer.

They had already had lunch at Adam's expense, and Adam had given them a lift from town in his car. Dick had made his usual jokes about the Skoda but he was quite happy to leave his own car at the station and gulp down a few large glasses of red wine during lunch. The plan was that Adam would take them back, after viewing the house, to Ironbridge Spa station.

Adam said he had something to show them, but wanted to get out of the house first. Adam was nervous, as he ushered his two friends, a tenuous relationship at times, out through the back door and into the garden. He had good reason to be nervous; he needed to get them outside. He had decided to cast the rain-making spell after all, having failed to find a suitable alternative spell because of lack of time.

It was the beginning of spring. Most of the trees were bare, but the back garden, which was large, was overgrown. To the right of the property the hugely overgrown rosebushes, which were turning treelike, nearly obscured the garden from the neighbour's house. On the far left side of the garden ran a narrow stream which was about two to three feet wide, with very little water flowing through it. The stream could be reached down a small incline, but the garden was overgrown and Adam had not ventured down to it.

"I thought we were here to see the house?" said Charlie.

"I will show you the house, but there is something else first," said Adam with a mysterious smile, trying to hide the feeling of foreboding he felt. Adam held a package in a plastic bag under his arm.

"This is the third time you've moved house in as many years, and each time the new place is worse than the last one," commented Charlie, but as if he were trying to appear grateful for the beer, he added, "Where do you find the energy?"

Charlie fidgeted. He was about the same height as Adam and was dressed more shabbily than normal, in jeans and a sweatshirt. Dick, always a well-dressed individual, was wearing a jacket and tie.

"I think I'm going to stay here for a while." Adam was defensive.

"That's what you say every time." Charlie laughed.

"Well, he's made a pile each time," Dick muttered. "But I think you've taken on a bit of a handful on this occasion – the house is derelict."

Adam protested that it was not that bad. He hated it when Dick criticised him, especially when he was exaggerating things. He did not mind Charlie so much as he thought nobody paid a lot of attention to what Charlie said, at the best of times.

The house was big. The old part on the right, as one faced it, was built out of solid stone, but there was also a very large brick-built addition to the left side of the house towards the stream. He told them it was four centuries old. Well, at least the stone part was. He was trying to defend his decision to buy the place.

Dick commented that this time he thought Adam had bitten off too big a mouthful with this house. Adam always had a sneaking suspicion that Dick envied him making money from renovating houses, but he never spoke about it openly. Was Dick worried that Adam might end up more affluent than him? Adam couldn't tell.

"You've got to admit…" started Charlie. *There he goes again*, thought Adam, who was convinced that Charlie always tried to look at things logically, except his viewpoint always seemed irritatingly illogical to his friends. However, Charlie seemed totally oblivious of the hostility, which Adam knew others felt, to what he thought were his matter-of-fact interpretations of events.

"You got to admit," resumed Charlie, "that this place is miles from anywhere, miles from the nearest station. You're not going to be able to resell it very easily, and the fact that it's derelict doesn't help."

Adam looked at the ramshackle house, though once in its younger days it must have been quite pretty. Charlie did have a point. Years of neglect had taken its toll, and the window frames were rotten; one had actually fallen out when Adam tried to open it. Part of the roof had also caved in slightly and was letting in a lot of water. Still, he had things under control. The new roof would go on in a few days and the new windows had already been ordered.

"You just watch me," insisted Adam defiantly; he was loathed to concede the point. "Since when have you become a property expert?" He took the opportunity, as he always did, to contradict Charlie. "You just wait and see. I haven't made a loss yet."

"Yeah, but look at your lifestyle," sneered Dick. "You live on a building site most of the time."

Adam tried to defend himself by stating that he had to make some sacrifices otherwise he would get nowhere in life. He wanted to be rich by the time he was forty, and that was not too many years away.

Dick reminded him that he could have settled down in his last house and had a nice life. He should have married Linda, his last girlfriend, when he had the chance. As he still hadn't sold the house yet, maybe he still could. Dick smiled in that sardonic way which really riled Adam. It was a sore point, but he had put a few tenants in it recently to ease his financial situation a bit, so selling it was out of the question.

"Well, I did want to, but she wanted a nicer house in a nicer neighbourhood. Anyway, she left me for an older man she met on the Tube, because she thought he was loaded. Not everybody's got a good job like yours." He did not mention Dick's good-looking wife Rachael, a fact which made Adam much more envious.

"Come on, Adam, that's not true," said Dick. "People don't care how much money you make." Adam could tell he was lying. Dick always blinked very rapidly when he was trying to convince other people of what he did not believe himself. As for having fun, he said he had more fun with his wife than he ever had before he got married, and he also had a relationship he could depend on.

He's such a sanctimonious sod, thought Adam. But he was a successful man, and like all successful men, he loved giving advice, *gratis*, much to Adam's annoyance.

"Anyway, I didn't call you here just to show you the house," he said aloud. "There's something else."

"You've got three tarts coming down to see us!" Charlie tried to sound logical. "That's why you said no wives or girlfriends. It would be a great way to spend the Saturday." A big smile filled his face.

"No," said Adam. "Sorry, but I don't know anybody in the village well enough."

"Then what is it?" asked Dick. "I've got to get back. There's a wife waiting for me, you know."

It would have been annoying for Dick if he had managed to conjure up some women, Adam thought wryly, but there was not much chance of that happening.

"I've found a book in the cellar. I believe it's a book of magic," muttered Adam, almost not believing the statement himself. He tapped the package.

"You what?" they blurted out simultaneously.

"You're cracking up," said Dick, making his funny face.

"He's right." Charlie shrugged. Then, as if trying to defuse the situation, he continued, "But I do like the house, and especially the pond there." One could just make it out through the overgrown grass. "Have you got any fish in it?" Charlie pointed in the direction of the pond. He was trying hard to deflect the conversation.

The little pond was situated on the lower flat bit of the garden. It was an oddity, with the stream running past it not far away. Adam had seen it from his upstairs window, but had never investigated it.

"I haven't checked," retorted Adam. "I've got the book right here."

"Let's have a look," said Dick, rolling up his eyes again. "I mean the pond, see if there's any fish," he laughed.

"Don't you see the difference this could make to our lives?" asked Adam, annoyed. He was ready to share his find with them and couldn't understand why they were being so dismissive.

"I happen to like my life," said Dick. "I don't need any mumbo-jumbo to improve it."

"Same here," agreed Charlie.

"Where did you find the thing again?" asked Dick, as if the information given earlier had somehow been ignored as irrelevant.

"It was in a cellar underneath the stairs, the doorway to which was bricked up."

"So how did you find it if it was bricked up?"

"The wall collapsed when I was trying to hang up a kitchen unit." He had since then had a door put in leading to the cellar, to replace the collapsed wall.

"And you think it's a book of magic! What nonsense!"

"I can prove it. Don't you see what this means?" Adam said with all the conviction he could muster. He started unwrapping the packaging he had covered the book with in his zeal to preserve it. He felt angry; they never paid any attention to anything he said, even though their reaction was totally reasonable.

There was the time when he said the share market was too high and would collapse. He had been right, but they had pooh-poohed the idea and lost money. He could think of any number of occasions when he had been right, but Dick had always contradicted him and Charlie always followed Dick, even though he had been proved wrong time and again. He was sure that Charlie believed subconsciously that with his large build Dick fitted the image of a natural born leader, but he was going to really show them this time. He was not somebody to be trifled with.

As Adam struggled with the package in his haste to get the book out, the other two looked stupefied, but then, shrugging to each other, they made their way to the pond, which was set in the slightly overgrown lawn and was about six feet square.

Adam started to look in the book for a suitable spell. He decided he did not want to repeat the rain-making spell after all, as this could just be explained by coincidence, especially as it was a slightly overcast day. They would just laugh at him and claim it was just a hoax. No, he would have to do something much more convincing.

As Adam flicked through the book, he realised that he was not very convincing. For a start, his German was rusty, on top of which the book was old, so it contained a lot of strange words and phrases. What would convince them? Maybe he should turn one of them into a frog. He had come across a spell which mentioned *der Frosch*, German for 'frog', and was for that exact purpose.

His thoughts were interrupted by the present; Charlie was calling him.

"Coming," said Adam.

What could he do to show them? He cast aside any thoughts of turning one of them into a frog. It was far too dangerous even to contemplate it. He had worked on a spell to transmute an apple into a pear, but would that satisfy them? They would probably say it was some sort of a conjuring trick. Anyway, he did not have an apple. No, it would have to be something more drastic to impress them.

His mind was racing. Maybe after all he should turn them into bloody frogs; his thoughts returned to the subject again. It would certainly teach them a lesson; it would serve them right for disbelieving him.

He had looked up the spell, though he hardly remembered what a frog was in German until he had come across it the other day. He thumbed through the book looking for the spell again. There it was – how to turn somebody into something else; a frog was just an example, it seemed, maybe for the benefit of the fairy tale. No, he dismissed the thought again; it was a step just too far to take.

It was a lovely warm day, if slightly cloudy, and the sun was quite hot for early April, but he felt a little shiver down his back. They were standing next to the pond and Charlie was pointing at something.

"Hey, Adam," he shouted. "Did you know you've got some crayfish in the pond? The water is unusually clear."

"If you had a barbecue we could fry them," said Dick.

"Yes. There are exactly three of them, one each," said Charlie. "What about it?"

"Forget the barbecue, there's something else I'm going to do first. I've got the book right here," Adam said. He still could not believe that they were not interested in sharing his find.

"You're not serious," laughed Dick. "What, turn us into frogs?" as if he were reading Adam's thoughts.

"Why not a crayfish?" piped Charlie. "We can join those other three, I hope they are females."

"You don't believe me then?" asked Adam seriously. "I'm telling you, this is real magic."

"Sure." Dick smirked. "And I'm a bloody crayfish."

"Right," said Adam. "What's the German for crayfish?" He thumbed through the dictionary.

"Fucked if I know," said Dick.

"Right, here it is, it's *der Flusskrebs*," said Adam. "Who wants to go first?" He could not believe what he was suggesting, but they were asking for it. Even though it was not very likely to work, he felt frustrated.

"You're kidding," said Charlie, looking slightly apprehensive.

"I'll go first," said Dick. "Charlie's a chicken."

"Alright then," said Adam, apprehensive himself. "You're sure?" he asked Dick.

"I'm sure." Dick was derisive. "Are you?"

"No, I can't do it," Adam blurted out suddenly. "I won't take the chance."

"Here, let me." Dick snatched the book out of Adam's hand. "My German's better than yours."

"I don't want to try it," said Adam.

"Who's a chicken now?" Dick laughed. "Looks like it's going to be you after all, Charlie." Dick winked at him.

Charlie winced in horror, but as Dick read out the spell, instead of mentioning Charlie by name he shouted out Adam's name. It took Adam by surprise and he was frozen for a moment; however, nothing whatsoever happened. Adam was baffled.

"This is a piece of garbage," snarled Dick. "You've just brought us here to waste our time."

"Wait, let me try," said Adam.

"So you think it's going to work for you?" Dick stared at him. "Go on. Try it on me, then."

Adam read the verse aloud, mentioning Dick by name and filling in the blank space with *der Flusskrebs*. For a moment nothing happened, but then suddenly there was a clap of thunder and Dick disappeared, and then they noticed there was a large crayfish wriggling on the grass before them.

Charlie fainted. Adam picked up the crayfish and looked at it. It peered at him through its two dark eyes, which seemed not to comprehend what had happened to it.

"That'll teach you," he said to it. "You won't doubt me again." But suddenly panic engulfed him. "Oh God, what have I done? I hope I can get you back, Dick."

But why had it worked when he had done the spell and not Dick? There was something strange going on, but he did not have time to find out.

Charlie woke up and eyed the crayfish. "This is a trick, isn't it?" asked Charlie. "Dick's hiding somewhere."

"No, this is Dick. I told you not to test me." Adam tried to exert some control over the situation, but his whole body shook uncontrollably as he spoke.

"Bring him back," shrieked Charlie. "I thought you were just kidding."

"I didn't think it would work either," protested Adam. "After all, it didn't work when Dick tried the same spell on me."

"Well, get him back."

"I can't." Adam was looking desperately through the book. "I can't see the spell for that. I'll have to put him in the pond while I find it."

"Oh my God," cried Charlie as Adam slipped Dick into the water.

"What are we going to do?" asked Charlie again.

"Let me think. What if I reverse the spell by swapping the words 'Dick' and 'crayfish'? That should work."

Adam opened the book to the same page and read out the spell again with the words 'Dick' and 'crayfish' the other way around, but nothing happened. He tried it again, thinking he might have missed something the first time, but drew a blank again.

Something was wrong. Obviously just reversing the words wouldn't work.

Charlie wanted him to find the right spell and Adam flicked through the book, desperately looking for it.

"There must be a spell in here, but I can't find it," said Adam, exasperated.

Two hours went by in silence, while Charlie walked nervously up and down the garden, most of the time staring nervously at the crayfish for any change to happen. However, Adam saw nothing in the book he could use. It was beginning to get dark, so finally Adam closed the book.

"My German isn't good enough," he said with disgust. "I need more time."

"Do you really think you can change him back?" asked Charlie.

"I'll have to find the right spell to change him back, but I could do with a drink while we look up the spell." He needed a drink badly to steady his nerves and calm Charlie down. "Unless you want to become a crayfish as well and join him?" Adam smiled in an attempt at a joke to take the edge off the proceedings.

"Shut up, for goodness' sake," snapped Charlie, but he relented. "I think I could do with a drink too, but where can we leave him?"

"I expect he'll be alright in the pond for a while. Where can he go? Look, he's got company."

They noticed the other three crayfish were gathering around Dick, who seemed to be the biggest crayfish in there.

"Well, we should be able to tell easily which one he is. He's bigger than the others."

"That's right," Adam tried to assure him. "We'll get him out once we've found the spell. Let's have a quick drink to calm our nerves, eh?" Adam moved towards the house and Charlie followed.

CHAPTER 3

"Better not say anything to anybody," said Adam as they left the house an hour later after more fruitless searching for the right spell. Adam carried the book with him, so he could have a further look in the pub.

"You think I'm crazy?" Charlie smiled. "Who's going to believe me anyway?"

"I suppose so. There's a pub just around the corner. It's called The Three Witches."

"Yeah, I saw it on our way here. It's a bloody unusual name."

"You don't get many of them, that's for sure."

"We could do with one of them right now," said Charlie ruefully. "If only it would help to bring Dick back."

"I'm sure we'll manage. It must be in the book," Adam said to reassure Charlie. "Ah, there's the pub. Not a word to anybody now."

Charlie nodded. They walked in silence, Adam contemplating the matter. The event had been almost too stupendous to take in. One or two people nodded to them on their way to the pub. They were villagers out and about on their own business.

They entered the pub, which was fairly crowded. It was an old country pub with exposed beams. Adam ordered a couple of pints and looked around apprehensively. He didn't know anybody in there, so they settled at the bar.

A few minutes later, as he was ordering their second pints after gulping down the first, there was tap on his shoulder. It was a busty middle-aged blonde. Adam thought he had seen her somewhere before.

"Hello." She smiled.

"Hello," said Adam, his mind turning somersaults trying to remember who she was. But he didn't have to wait.

"You don't recognise me, do you? I'm Wendy, your next-door neighbour," said the slightly plump woman.

Adam remembered her now. "Where is your husband?" he asked nervously. The husband was a big, burly beast of a man.

"He's parking the car." She smiled again. "We went to a car boot sale. He'll be here any minute."

"Can I get you a drink?" asked Adam.

"That'll be nice, a large gin and tonic, please."

Adam winced and turned around to order, leaving Charlie to hold the fort. He was just about to order the drinks when there was another tap on his shoulder. It was the husband. Charlie had already moved away with Wendy to an empty table.

"I'm Jack, by the way," said the large man with a slightly greying beard and a large grin. Adam had seen them around, but he had been busy, so had not introduced himself so far. In any case, he craved as little attention from the neighbours as possible.

"I'm Adam. I'm ordering, so what would you like?"

"A pint of bitter, please. Where's your other mate? I thought there was three of you."

"Oh, he didn't feel like a beer," Adam lied, but he didn't feel too guilty. Technically he was right. Dick probably didn't much feel like a beer at the moment.

Adam and Jack moved towards the table with the drinks. Charlie was in deep conversation with Jack's wife.

"You've started work on the house, then?" asked Jack, but Adam was not listening. He was more concerned with what Charlie had been telling Wendy.

"He has been telling me all about you," quipped Wendy.

"Has he now?" Adam stared at Charlie, who gulped. "I hope it's nothing bad."

"So you're doing up the house to sell it on again?" asked Wendy.

"I think you've picked the wrong house for that," guffawed Jack, who seemed confident of what he was talking about. "They couldn't sell it for years the last time they tried."

Adam cursed Charlie under his breath. Adam always made it a point to tell people that he was moving in to any houses he bought. That way the neighbours were always friendly. In his experience nobody liked to hear that he was making money by buying and selling houses, especially when they found out how much profit he was making, which they invariably did. There were always nosy neighbours who knew how much he had bought the house for, and it was easy to find out from the estate agents what he was selling it for.

Adam had his stock answers for such people. He had just lost his job and couldn't afford the mortgage, or his parents were getting too old so he had to move in with them; those were two such good reasons why he had to sell. But his favourite was that his girlfriend had given him an ultimatum: either he moved to where she was, near her mother, or she was leaving him. That always got a lot of sympathy. But one could never tell them one was in the business of doing up houses part-time to make money. Then they classed you as a parasite on society.

"I think I'm going to stay here," Adam lied. He tried to sound definite.

"You'll have to, mate." Jack smirked. "Did they tell you that house has a bad history?"

"What's this?" asked Adam.

"Ha," hiccupped Charlie drunkenly. "You didn't know, did you? Three women disappeared from that house once."

"No, I didn't know that," said Adam, hoping Charlie hadn't spilled the beans, but it was too late.

"Charlie said your friend's disappeared," chirped Wendy.

"No, he hasn't." Adam denied it. "He's in the house. Now, look, what's all this you've been telling them?"

"Nothing, I haven't told them anything." Charlie looked drunk.

"He said you've turned your friend into a crayfish," insisted Wendy.

"He's always making little jokes like that, and you fell for it. How am I supposed to do that, for heaven's sake?" Adam was angry.

"With your little book you found. What's that under your arm?"

"It's something I'm reading, so mind your own business," shouted Adam. Everybody in the pub looked round.

"Hey, don't get upset. Who can't take a joke now?" laughed Wendy.

"Yeah, steady on, mate," guffawed Jack again. "Who do you expect to believe a cock-and-bull story like that?"

"But if you've got crayfish in your pond maybe we should catch them for a barbecue," said Wendy.

"That's a good idea," said Adam reluctantly.

"Why not after we've finished our pints?" suggested Jack, who seemed to Adam not to want to buy a round.

Charlie slurped his drink, and Adam was stuck for words. But suddenly there was a loud clap of thunder and it started raining very heavily outside. Everyone was caught by surprise and Adam could hear Jack muttering that he could have sworn that there was not a single cloud in the sky when he had walked into the pub. Adam breathed a sigh of relief; there was no chance of a barbecue.

"Are you getting them in, then? Looks like we're going to be stuck here for a while," said Adam happily.

"I suppose so," said Jack reluctantly. "Though your friend looks like he's had enough."

"I'm sure he'll be able to manage another one," insisted Adam. "Then he'll be able to tell you some more interesting stories."

"Are you sure?" Jack looked unconvinced. He did not seem too eager to spend money that he did not need to.

"Oh, he'll sober up in a minute." Adam positively beamed. He wasn't going to let Jack get away without buying a proper round, and he certainly didn't want to let him go fishing for crayfish.

Jack reluctantly made his way to the bar as it started raining even more fiercely. Then it suddenly occurred to Adam that it had also rained heavily every time he had used the book of magic, for example when he was practising turning an apple into a pear, but he had not paid much attention to that fact.

He needed to consult the book. However, at that moment, it was out of the question for him to look up the spell he needed to change Dick back, with Wendy's eagle eye upon him. Just as well the book was in German so most people would not understand it, and hopefully Wendy did not speak the language. Before he could think any further, Jack caught his eye, signalling that he had been served and needed a hand. Adam gave Charlie a nudge and asked him to help Jack. He didn't want to leave him behind with Wendy again.

As a tipsy Charlie made his way reluctantly to the bar, Wendy eyed Adam as if to size him up. Adam looked at her. She was a rotund woman with a slightly worn look, on the wrong side of forty. Like most forty-something people she was searching for that elusive something. Maybe it was that unfulfilled dream or the flourishing of a second youth which would most likely manifest itself in an illicit affair before settling down to the disappointments of older age.

"So you are thinking of staying?" she ventured.

"Maybe." He wanted to discourage her. "I'll definitely have to stay until I finish the house." He never liked getting too friendly with the neighbours.

"That'll be quite a long time, I think." She smiled as their eyes connected. "Judging from the state of that place." She was eyeing him up, but Adam was not sure for what.

Adam told her it was not as bad as she thought. He was piqued. It seemed everybody was an expert when it came to doing up properties. It did not matter who they were, they all wanted to give him gratuitous advice on the best way to spruce up a property, even though some of them had never bought one, let alone sold more than a single property in their lives, and others maybe none at all.

It was one of those peculiarities of life that made everybody an instant expert as soon as they set foot in a house. He remembered one time when some Middle Eastern refugee who had turned up at one of his parties had given him advice about the right choice of wallpapers for a quick sale. He had turned out to be a gatecrasher who Adam had taken great satisfaction in throwing out.

"Well, you'll have to invite us round," said Wendy. "After all we're only next door."

"Sure," said Adam. "Soon as it's ready."

The others came back at that moment with the drinks and Adam felt immense relief that he did not have to talk to her anymore. Jack eyed him; he seemed suspicious.

"You two were having a good old natter."

"Adam's going to invite us round to have a look at his house."

"I didn't quite say that." Adam felt obstinate.

"If you want any help with the building work, I'm your man," Jack said, ignoring his comment. It was obvious he was angling for some work. Adam had come across his type before. There were always people who lived off the land and turned their hand to anything as soon as any little opportunity offered itself. They were always self-made experts in everything, especially building work. "I've done loads of work for people around here; you can ask anybody. Jack's the name, building work's my game."

"Oh, he's ever so good," interjected Wendy.

A strange warning bell started ringing in Adam's head. He knew he was headed for trouble with these two.

"Wendy's very good at decorating, she's done our house. You should have a look at it."

Wendy told him that she was more of an interior designer. Colour schemes were her forte. Adam nodded in acknowledgement and smiled. He was positive that, from the clothes she was wearing, exactly the opposite was true. With that sort of colour co-ordination the only way he was going to let her loose anywhere in his house was at the point of a shotgun.

Charlie, who had been peculiarly quiet all this time, spoke up all of a sudden, lurching towards Jack in a drunken manner and jabbing him on the chest with his forefinger. "You told me your game was car boot sales at the bar. You said you had a handsome day today, as it happens."

"So we have, so we have, but it's only a hobby," protested Jack, annoyed.

Charlie was going to say something else, but Adam stopped him. He knew Charlie was heading for trouble. Like a lot of men, once the drink got hold of him, the normally timid Charlie was somebody to be reckoned with, and was a pain in the backside.

"I think we should be making our way back. Dick will be wondering where we are."

"No, he won't. Anyway, the rain hasn't stopped and he's probably enjoying the rain," commented an inebriated Charlie.

"No, he isn't. Come on, let's go, you've had enough to drink. A little rain won't hurt."

A very reluctant Charlie got up and they departed, leaving a somewhat surprised Jack and Wendy behind them. Adam stuck the book under his jacket to stop it from getting wet, for it was not just a little rain, but a deluge. The sky had opened and it was chucking it down, as if the Great Flood was upon them.

When they got home they were quite drenched, and a little worse for drink. Adam decided he was in no shape to look up the spell that evening and suggested they tackle the problem in the morning. So under protest from Charlie, they decided to call it a day and go to bed.

★ ★ ★

Adam had trouble going to sleep that evening, for his mind remained very active. It was still raining when he finally fell asleep. He was having a really vivid dream about his ex-girlfriend Linda, who had ditched him several months ago, when she had got fed up of continuously living in what she termed were building sites Adam was renovating.

However, just as he was getting to the part where she was about to beg him to take her back, he was awakened by a loud knock on the door. As it made Adam jump up in his bed, he therefore made his way downstairs to answer it. A nasty surprise awaited him. It was Jack, and he was holding a small fishing net.

"I've come for them crayfishes," he bellowed, as if they belonged to him.

"I don't think that's a very good idea." But before he could finish, the telephone rang. "Just hang on, let me answer that phone. I'll be with you in a minute." However, as Adam moved in to pick up the phone, he heard Jack shout something behind him, which did not register immediately. As he picked up the phone a sexy voice purred on the other end of the line. It was Rachael, Dick's wife.

Adam had always secretly fancied her, but when she had made a pass at him at a party, before her marriage, while Dick was in a drunken stupor and soundly asleep downstairs, he had, much to his surprise, refused. It had been a close thing, but he had been worried that she was only teasing him. She always came across as a bit of a man-eater to Adam. Therefore, when she had tried to grope him in the upstairs bedroom he had chickened out, much to his annoyance later on, though he was under the sneaking suspicion that she was only testing him.

One of Adam's secret ambitions had always been to pull a real peach like Rachael, but unfortunately he never managed to get his hands on such women. Oh, he got on alright when it came to girls, but it had always been Dick who had picked the real lookers. And though nobody had expected it, Dick had suddenly decided to settle down with Rachael.

She had moved into his big house in Highgate and now lived in real style, which was not surprising, given the salaries they both commanded. Everybody aspired to be like them. They were the absolute personification of an ideal couple, so her actions had been even more astonishing to Adam, who could only think that she would have laughed her head off if he had gone for it.

"Hello, Adam," the voice purred again. "Could you please put Dick on? He's not answering his mobile."

"Hello, Rachael." Then it dawned on him who it was, and he suddenly became very flustered. "Dick? He's not here… I mean, he's outside. That is, he should be. Can you hang on a moment, or better still, I'll call you back. I mean, I'll get Dick to ring you. Bye."

He hung up in panic; also, he had just realised what Jack had been shouting behind him when he went to answer the phone. Jack was going on ahead, letting himself in through the side gate. Adam bolted for the back door and flung it open. From a distance he could see Jack was standing next to the pond and scratching his beard.

"Hold on a minute, Jack, don't fish them out," Adam shouted as he ran towards him.

CHAPTER 4

"Fish what out? I can't see those crayfishes anywhere."

"Crayfish," snapped Adam.

"I thought you said there was more than one."

"That's right, and it's still crayfish."

"I get it. What, you an English teacher or something?"

"Yes," answered Adam tersely. He was well pissed off with Jack by now.

"A gentleman and scholar then, well, here's a little problem for your scholarship. There's no bloody crayfish in the pond." Sarcasm lit up Jack's face.

"What do you mean, there's no crayfish? You must have fished them out." Adam grabbed the big man by the lapels of his shirt. He was very angry by now.

Lucky for him, Jack actually seemed quite timid when it came to punch-ups, as big as he was. Like a lot of big men he relied on his size to keep him from being challenged, so it came as quite a shock when it happened.

"Hey, take it easy," he cried. "I haven't got your crayfish. You can search me if you like."

Adam let go. There was a little stream of water running from the pond to the stream. It really had rained the day before. Jack made a funny face and left.

Adam ran up and down the length of the stream that was within his property, falling down as he did so. He climbed over the fences downstream, and searched as best he could to see if he could locate the crayfish. It was not such a big stream, with hardly any water in it. They were bound to be somewhere in it; he even got down to his hands and knees, but there was no sign of the crayfish anywhere.

After over an hour of searching Adam decided to give up. His trousers were muddy and ripped where he had caught them on a nail in a fence, his knees were bruised and he had cuts on his hands. The crayfish were gone. Remorse filled him – what had he done to his friend Dick? It was definitely his fault, trying to show off his book of magic. What was he going to tell Charlie?

Adam thought he was going mad. Even if he found some crayfish in the river, would one of them be Dick? In any case, he didn't even have the spell to transform him back.

★ ★ ★

The morning slipped by in a haze after that. Adam made himself a cup of tea and started to think about what had just unfolded. The enormity of the situation slowly dawned on him. The crayfish were gone. Dick was gone. Now it did not matter if Adam found the spell to turn Dick back to his original self, because there was no Dick around anymore. What was he going to do?

Adam felt too dejected to have breakfast or even to look in the book. What could he tell Charlie when he woke? The catastrophic event engulfed him completely, grief overcame him and he felt sick. It was all his fault – why had he left Dick in the pond instead of bringing him inside the house? But there had to be an answer somewhere, and it had to be in the book.

He was on his third cup of tea when Charlie staggered into the living room, nursing a hangover. What was Adam going to tell him? He knew Charlie was prone to panic and that was the last thing Adam needed. He needed to get Charlie out of the way and then concentrate on the book to find the answer.

"What was all that commotion about this morning?" asked Charlie.

"Oh, nothing," lied Adam.

"Shall we go through the book to see if we can change Dick back?"

"Didn't you mention you had to get back to London to finish a job?"

"It'll have to wait, this is more important. Got anything to eat?"

"Sorry, can't offer you any breakfast, I haven't got any food here," Adam lied. His first priority was to get rid of Charlie as soon as possible. The less Charlie was involved, the better for him.

"Maybe we can get started on the book then. Christ, I'm hungry, though."

"I can call you a cab." Adam was desperate to get rid of Charlie.

"What about Dick?" asked Charlie.

"I can deal with that myself, if you don't have time," ventured Adam. "I need time to concentrate and find the right spell." He did not want to take Charlie to The Three Witches again, if he could help it.

"I haven't got too much cash on me, so maybe you can give me a lift, after we have a quick bite at the pub. Christ... I'm hungry, are you sure you haven't got anything to eat?"

This was exactly what Adam did not want to hear. He wanted Charlie gone before he found out that the crayfish Dick had disappeared.

"I need to go through the book to get Dick back."

"What do you mean, get him back?" Charlie enquired.

"I mean, change him back. Okay, let's go to the pub." Adam did not want to explain any more to Charlie right then. He felt distraught, but Charlie was the last person he wanted to discuss the situation with, before he had time to think things through.

"Shouldn't we do it now?" There was an anxious note in Charlie's voice.

"It'll take time to find the right spell. Best to drop you off at the station first."

So it was down to The Three Witches again for Sunday lunch with Charlie, and of course Jack and Wendy were there, as if waiting to ambush them. Adam tried to avoid any questions from Jack about that morning by offering him and Wendy a drink, and sent Charlie to get the drinks.

Charlie obliged willingly, as he did not want to be left alone with Jack and Wendy, and it seemed he could almost read Adam's mind in this matter. Adam composed himself for the question that was coming.

"Where's your other friend?" asked Wendy.

"Yeah, what was his name now?" said Jack.

"Who, Dick?" asked Adam nonchalantly. "He went home this morning, you know, the pressures of having a young, attractive wife…" He left Jack to imagine the whole thing. Adam was quite sure he didn't have a clue about the matter, after taking one quick glance at Wendy.

"Yeah, I can imagine," said Jack.

"But we didn't see him go," protested Wendy. "We were up pretty early."

"That's right," said Jack, recovering from his momentary effort of concentration, trying to imagine what Dick's wife looked like.

Adam insisted that they must have missed him. He must have slipped past them while they were distracted in some way. Adam almost chuckled, thinking about the crayfish Dick slipping past them. He commented that he didn't know they were keeping such a close watch on him. He was annoyed.

Jack said that they were in the neighbourhood watch and it was their duty to keep a lookout for things. As his was the last house on the road, nobody could walk past without them knowing about it, especially when they were working in the front garden, as they were that morning. Jack smiled knowingly.

Adam suggested that maybe they had popped in for a cup of tea. His annoyance was beginning to show. He stressed that it was not up to him to know how they had missed Dick. He did not like Jack and Wendy much, but now he was starting to positively dislike them.

Jack was about to say something, but Charlie saved the day by turning up with the drinks at that moment. This brought a momentary halt to that line of interrogation, to Adam's great relief, and gave him time to deflect any more prying questions from the couple. He decided to offer Jack a little bait. He said that maybe Jack could do something for him after all.

Did he have some work, then? Jack's eyes lit up. Adam said that he was thinking of renewing the fence between his and Jack's property and putting in a more secure side door to the garden. Jack could probably do that for him.

"No problem whatsoever, Jack's the name, building work's my game." He seemed to like repeating the phrase as if to drive the point home. "Just ask Wendy. Didn't I put the fence up at the back of our garden?"

"That's right." Wendy beamed widely. She seemed to be Jack's main source of reference for his work. Adam winced visibly. He had seen the fence which was Jack's handiwork. He would have to keep a good eye on Jack if he did any work for him.

"Come and see me tomorrow. I'm working on the patio. I've got to dig it up and level it. They are coming to concrete it on Tuesday."

"Maybe I can give you a hand with that as well," suggested Jack.

"No need, it's only a small job. Besides, I must do something myself to save a bit of money, the budget is pretty tight, you know. I've got to pay for a new roof and new windows to be put in."

"I suppose so," Jack agreed grumpily. "I can understand your position, it's not easy to do up a house like that." He gave Adam that knowing smile.

"Isn't Charlie staying to help you?" asked Wendy.

"No, I'm afraid not," Charlie said quickly. "I've got a lot of things to do, so I've got to get back. Besides, I'm no good with building work – got delicate hands, you see." He showed them his hands. "Need them for my line of work."

Adam grimaced, but did not say anything.

"What line would that be?" Jack enquired.

"A freelance draughtsman," said Charlie proudly.

"I thought it was all done with computers now," Jack offered.

"A lot is," said Charlie. "But there's still demand for a good man."

"Charlie's the best," offered Adam, trying not to show his sarcasm.

"What about you, what do you do?" asked Wendy.

"Well, at the moment I'm not doing anything much as I'm fixing up the house. The last job came to an end, so I thought I would concentrate on the house before looking for another job."

"You're not on the dole, are you, while working on the house? That would be a bit naughty, wouldn't it?" Jack smiled.

"No, I won't be unemployed long enough for that – maybe a month or so to get the basic work done and out of the way. You can always get work in my line." Adam smiled, hoping he would not have to eat his words in a month's time.

He had got the push from his last job for making a pass at his boss's wife at the last office party. It was all her bloody fault as far as Adam was concerned. She had insisted on showing him how to dance the salsa. Whilst doing this, their bodies had somehow managed to come into closer contact than was advisable when dancing with the boss's wife at an office party with just about everybody watching. He had in fact ended up grinding her slightly, and in the heat of the moment his right hand had slipped a bit low onto her buttocks. Whilst she did not seem to mind it or protest, it had not gone unnoticed by his boss.

The following week, though not immediately, he found himself in his boss's office being given some weird and wonderful reason for which he was to be let go.

"What do you actually do?" asked Jack.

Adam snapped out of his mini-daydream about his ex-boss's wife. "I'm an accountant," he ventured, fully expecting a look of horror in the eyes of those present.

"Not an English teacher, then?"

"Sometimes, for a bit of a change," said Adam.

"Good with figures then?" Wendy smiled.

"Well, I am, I suppose." Adam sounded slightly smug.

"There's always a job for an accountant," said Charlie ruefully.

"That's right," said Adam, sounding almost pleased with himself. But this was far from the truth. He hated accountancy and was really a failure in his profession, as he could never hold down a job too long. Number-crunching was boring, but like Charlie said, there was always a job available if one wanted it. He was in fact filling in as an English teacher for foreign students in his last job.

He was sure people detested accountants; they were boring. In fact, he had put down his profession as an airline pilot on the form he had filled in for a dating agency. He had considered being a deep-sea diver: it was romantic, working on the rigs to bring the oil in. It might have been more romantic, but not practical. North Sea divers had to spend a long time on the rigs, and had to be away rather a lot, which was very inconvenient. As an airline pilot you could be away just the right amount of time, when you needed a break from your love life, without facing awkward questions from her when you got back. In fact, Adam knew somebody who had successfully carried on like this for several years, until the man had retired from the airline industry to get married. Then he suddenly became an accountant. All he needed now was to get his hands on a uniform.

★ ★ ★

That afternoon Adam felt depressed and very guilty again. It was really all his fault, he thought as he took Charlie to the station after lunch. They did not converse much on the way. Jack and Wendy seemed too embarrassed to bring up the missing crayfish. Adam was not even sure that Jack had mentioned it to Wendy.

Adam spent several hours going through the book after getting back to the house. It was slow, frustrating work and he wasn't getting anywhere fast. He even walked down to the stream to see if he could locate any crayfish, but found nothing.

Dick's wife, Rachael, had not rung him again. In the end Adam decided to get busy digging the ground out for the patio and levelling it for the concrete that was to arrive soon for its floor. He needed a break from the book to think things through. He had to keep calm if he did not want to be blamed for Dick's disappearance. He had to act normal and the best way was to carry on as if nothing had happened while he searched for the answer, and deal with Charlie when the situation arose.

Adam finished levelling off the patio and went in to have a bath. Bathing was a long, drawn-out affair with the old water heater playing up on him. Eventually, however, he filled the bath and he got into it to ponder over the day.

Things had not gone at all well that day, or when he got back from dropping off Charlie. He had the need to do some physical work, to rest his mind after the recent overactivity. Not dwelling on what had taken place gave him a chance to relax so he could think clearly about the next steps to take. He was going to look through the book again later that evening, and if necessary spend the whole night on it.

Adam tried to relax in the bath; he wanted to have a soak and time to think. They were coming to do the roof the next day, or at least start on it. Things were moving along, but surely he needed to cancel the building work and concentrate on finding Dick. Panic gripped him again – Christ, he could not just give up on Dick. However, Adam knew bankruptcy was definitely staring him in the face if he could not finish the work in time and remortgage. He was going to end up poor again, so what was his choice? Adam decided he must carry on with the building work while he looked for an answer; there was no other choice. He had to be strong if he didn't want to be poor.

There's got to be an answer in that book, he thought. He had to look for it as soon as he finished his bath. He must look through the book until he found it.

At that moment, there was a loud knock on the front door of the house. Adam could hear it as the bathroom door had been left ajar. The current bathroom was still situated downstairs, on the other side of the old central staircase next to the kitchen, in the newer part of the house.

It must be bloody Jack, thought Adam, *come about the job*, and he decided to ignore the knock and stay in the bath. There was that knock again; whoever it was sounded impatient.

"Go away, I said tomorrow," cursed Adam, and did not move.

He was sure it was Jack – who else could it be at this time? But then he heard the side door to the garden being opened and somebody walking around the back of the house. He was going to be burgled, thought Adam, and he decided to get out of the bath. At that very moment, a woman poked her head through the open window of the bathroom. It was Rachael.

Adam was frozen on the spot with one leg in the bath and one outside of it. One of his first priorities when he had moved in had been to put a new bathroom upstairs, in the room above the current bathroom, but it was still waiting to be connected up. Everything was there: the bath, the sink, the toilet and the fittings, all except the pipework. So there he was downstairs, in the old bathroom.

"Ah, there you are," said Rachael. "Don't you think you should put some clothes on and open the door?" she said matter-of-factly. Adam reached for a towel as fast as he could and jumped out of the bath. He wrapped the towel around his waist and, still dripping, made his way to the back door.

As soon as he managed to open the door, Rachael marched straight in, before he even had time to finish saying, "Hello, Rachael."

Rachael was about the same height as Adam, but looked taller in her high heels. She was a well-built, muscular woman, who obviously liked to work out but maybe was becoming a tad lazy about it. However, she oozed confidence out of every pore and was power-dressed in a no-nonsense greenish suit which projected her personality even more.

"Where is he?" she asked without a hint of politeness.

"Where's who?" Adam replied, fully knowing who she meant.

"Don't play games with me, Adam," rasped Rachael. "He's still here, isn't he, shacked up with some local talent, no doubt?" She flicked her long blonde hair back with her expensively bejewelled hand.

Why did it always still surprise Adam when women thought of Dick in such glowing terms, as if he was some super-Casanova whose ability to seduce other women was no less formidable than the original? No women would ever run down all this way to check up on him if he ever went missing for a day, and certainly not one as attractive as Rachael. He felt disgusted; Dick had always inspired such feelings in women, and he of all people should be used to it by now.

"Well, he's not here," said Adam tersely.

"Well, where is he? You must know where he is."

"No, I don't," repeated Adam in an almost tremulous voice, but he managed to control it. "Now, can I get some clothes on first before we continue this conversation?"

"Sure, I'll wait here," laughed Rachael. It was the 'I've seen it all before' look of a very confident woman. Her laugh was infectious; not too loud, but soft and sensuous. Adam had often wondered if it was natural or much-practised and developed, but it was perfectly formed and in any case there was no way Adam could tell the difference.

"The lounge is over there. It's a bit basic at the moment," Adam apologised. He gestured towards the lounge, which was in the older part of the house, past the kitchen. Why was it that he was always unprepared when he met a gorgeous woman? In fact, his whole life was a work in progress, which did not seem to progress when it came to women.

"I'll be alright," said Rachael. "By the way, you're quite a muscular little man, aren't you?" This was Rachael's way of paying a compliment, while putting Adam down at the same time. Her designer perfume filled the air and as Adam breathed it in, he felt a sense of heady intoxication. Rachael winked and smiled again. What was wrong with her? It was no way for a married woman to behave. No, there was absolutely nothing wrong with her, Adam decided; she was just having her little joke.

When Adam went upstairs to put some clothes on, his mind was working overtime on what to tell Rachael. He was trying to think of a good line, but in the end decided to keep things simple.

It was best to say that Dick had left early in the morning and stick to it. However, when he came downstairs he had another shock awaiting him.

"His coat is still here." Rachael pointed it out to Adam as soon as he had entered the room. "He wouldn't have left without his coat."

Adam looked at the stylish beige coat hanging from the rack. He had forgotten that Dick had been wearing a coat when he came to the house. He had not had any luggage with him as he had not intended to stay the night, but he had a coat.

"He must have forgotten it," Adam protested.

"He's gone somewhere local, hasn't he? That's why he did not need a coat." Adam could see that Rachael was a bit perturbed about the matter; in fact there was a note of desperation in her voice. She was desperate to locate Dick as she could not imagine this could be happening to her; Dick disappearing with a bit of local talent was more than her competitive personality could tolerate. She sounded like a jealous schoolgirl.

Adam could feel the beads of perspiration breaking out on his forehead and on his back, while he was trying to think of the answer that would satisfy Rachael. But try as he might, he could not. He couldn't imagine Rachael ever losing a man to another girl, but that was how it looked to Rachael and he was in no position to divulge the real reason.

"I don't honestly know why he left his coat," was all he could say. "I mean, it has been pretty warm lately." This was the truth, but would she buy it?

"Well, he must be coming back here. Do you mind if I wait for him until he does?" asked Rachael.

"Not at all," he heard himself say. "Can I get you a drink or something?"

"A cup of tea would be nice," Rachael said, with good grace for a woman feeling scorned.

That was the last thing he needed; there was going to be no chance of studying the book of magic to find a spell to try to bring Dick back that evening, if that was at all possible. He needed time to think, so he took his time to make the tea and they made themselves comfortable.

She looked quite appalled about the state the house was in; Adam could see it in her face. Rachael was used to the finer things in life, coming from a well-heeled middle-class family in rural Oxfordshire. She had a plummy accent which she suppressed to fit in with the likes of Adam.

Adam surveyed his living room, probably for the first time, and it was a mess. The living room, which occupied the stone part of the house, was quite large in itself, but it had a solid floor, which was quite uneven, with flagstones covering it in a very rough fashion. They looked like paving stones which had been nicked from some road job. Because of the ongoing work, the floor had not been carpeted.

As if reading his mind, she said, "You like living in tips, don't you?" She smiled and crossed her legs, Adam thought, in a deliberate fashion, so he could catch a glimpse of her knickers, which were red. Was it an invitation to make a pass at her, or was he just imagining things?

But Adam suppressed the thought. "I'm doing the place up."

"You are always doing places up. No wonder Linda left you." She was being very bitchy, lashing out at the nearest object, which happened to be Adam.

"One has to try and make a living. We're not all on Dick's salary. I did quite well with the last house and this was a bargain," retorted Adam. "It's got four bedrooms, though I'm going to turn one into the upstairs bathroom."

"Very impressive, I can see that." She smiled again, but sarcasm showed on her face. "What do you do for entertainment around here?" Why was she keeping up the small talk? Adam's life was hardly interesting for her, but she probably needed a distraction from thinking about Dick's disappearance, Adam surmised.

"There's a pub called The Three Witches in the village. Other than that, there's not much else to do."

"So you are going to live like a hermit for six months until you spruce up and sell this place, I suppose?"

"No, I'm going back to London. I still have a flat there, which I am renting at the moment, but it should be empty soon. I'm going to keep it for myself until I sell this place."

"You're quite a man of property." Rachael smiled and uncrossed, then crossed her legs the other way. He was now almost sure she was teasing him. She knew he secretly fancied her; most men did. She was having a bit of fun making him suffer. "Well, you'd better get me a drink – that's if you keep anything here. It looks like it's going to be a long wait." She smiled again.

She seemed to be taking things quite calmly, he thought. But it was necessary to get rid of her if he was going to have a look at that book.

"Don't you think I should give you a lift to the station? It's getting quite late," he said aloud, hoping she would agree.

"I'm not going anywhere until he turns up." She was adamant.

He gave up. "I've only got some rum. Is rum and Coke okay?"

"That'll do. A large one, please," she said. Adam had noticed Rachael liked a drink, but she was never drunk – she could hold her drink.

"Right you are," he said, and went to get the rum and Coke. Inwardly, he told himself to relax, as there was nothing else he could do. He poured her a large measure and did the same for himself.

She accepted the drink from him in silence and took a large gulp. As Adam sat down, he noticed she was staring at him.

"You men always stick together, don't you?" she said finally. "You were always the quiet one. I bet I could get Charlie to spill the beans without too much trouble."

Adam smiled, but he was glad now that Charlie had left. "I am telling you the truth. I don't know where Dick is, and nor does Charlie."

"You could be telling the truth. I searched his coat, his car keys aren't there." Rachael seemed resigned about the facts.

Christ, thought Adam, why had he not thought of that himself? But he said nothing.

"Well, you'd better get me another drink," said Rachael, gulping the rest of her drink down. "I'm not going until he turns up, so you'd better find me a bed, unless you want me to sleep in your bed." She smiled tauntingly.

"That won't be necessary, I have a spare bed. Charlie slept in it last night." Adam knew straight away that he had said the wrong thing.

"And where did Dick sleep last night?" Rachael's eyes lit up.

"Ah… he slept in my bed and I slept on the sofa here, before you assume anything," Adam lied. "I'll change the sheets on Charlie's bed and get it ready for you." Things were becoming very frustrating; he wanted to get back to the book, but there was no chance of it while Rachael was there. For a moment he was tempted to come clean, but immediately dismissed the idea as suicide.

"Don't bother. I'll take your bed if Dick slept in it. You can have Charlie's."

"If that's what you want."

"If it's okay with you?"

They made small talk and had another few drinks. Rachael mainly talked about herself. She had only known Dick for a short while before they got married. It had been a whirlwind romance and had taken everybody by surprise. According to

Rachael, she had given up a promising career in modelling for Dick.

However, Adam did not quite believe this, as some facts pointed to things being different. Rachael was not nearly tall enough, on the wrong side of thirty and though she had a pretty good figure, it was getting slightly plump around the edges. But she was a real looker. Yes, she was very pretty; indeed she was beautiful.

Finally, it was time for bed. Adam showed Rachael his bedroom above the kitchen and wished her goodnight. He himself was in what was the master bedroom next door, above the living room. It was full of his junk as he was using it as storage until his friends came down to visit him.

Adam was just dozing off when there were footsteps across the corridor. His bedroom door opened and Rachael slipped into his bed.

"I'm sorry," she said, "I can't sleep. It's a bit spooky in there. I think you have rats in your loft."

"Pigeons," said Adam. "The roof on the other side of the house has holes in it." As Rachael's naked breasts pressed against his back, he realised that she was wearing nothing but her panties. It felt strange and very tempting, but Adam felt guilty as hell, though he could feel the sap rising. But he resisted the urge to turn around and grab her. The fact that he was instrumental in Dick's disappearance weighed his conscience down like a huge boulder, and he could not bring himself to try anything.

★ ★ ★

However, the next morning he regretted his decision as Rachael got out of bed. Adam could not keep his eyes off her breasts as she pulled the sheets back.

"What do you think of them?" she teased.

They were perfect: nicely rounded, on the large side but not too large, with semi-erect long nipples pointing up. He could look at them all day.

"They're lovely," he said sadly. "Dick's a very lucky man." Adam wanted to grab her, but the moment had already passed.

"You're a gentleman," she said. "Most men would have tried to take advantage of the situation. Anyway, keep this to yourself. Dick would not understand, he is the jealous type, you know."

Who could blame him? thought Adam. He put it down as another missed opportunity, one of the several that had come his way and then gone straight past him. That he had missed out on so many occasions he put down to bad luck that dogged him as far as women were concerned.

Rachael departed early with Dick's coat, bemoaning the fact that he was still absent. Dick was in for it in a big way when he finally turned up, if he ever did! Adam drove Rachael to the station. Rachael was very quiet most of the way, but she opened up at the station as they waited for the train.

"I feel a bit let down," said Rachael. Her eyes were sad.

"Hope it's nothing I've done," said Adam.

"I feel let down by Dick, his disappearing like this." She tried to smile.

"Maybe he has an explanation." Adam tried to soothe her.

"I've been humiliated by him, having come here to look for him."

"Maybe it was not his fault," Adam tried to protest.

"Doesn't matter whose fault it is, or what his explanation is, he will have to pay." Rachael looked grim, and her eyes nearly brimmed, but she controlled it. "I thought we had the perfect marriage."

"Don't do anything foolish," said Adam. He decided to give her a little hug to console her, but it was a huge mistake. Rachael grabbed Adam very tightly, and as Adam felt those large cups press against his chest, something stirred in his loins.

"So you're not totally irresponsive to me." She smiled as if to confirm the obvious. "Let me know when Dick turns up."

Meanwhile, she said, she had things to do. She was a high-powered executive and had a board meeting to attend. Adam saw her off and sighed in relief. He realised that he had a busy day ahead too as he waved goodbye to Rachael as her train pulled away.

Somebody always had to pay, and he was glad it was not going to be him. Meanwhile he had managed to ruin the perfect marriage by turning Dick into a crayfish and making Rachael think that he had run off with another woman.

CHAPTER 5

As he drove back to the house, Adam's mind was racing. He had to find a solution to this problem. He had to get Dick back, before things got out of hand. There must be a way to do it. The answer must be in that book of magic, and he had to find it. But he needed time to sit down and study the book and look for the answer. He had not had a single moment to spare since Rachael had arrived, and there proved to be none when he got back either: the roofers were there, ready to start work. One of them had a small truck and Adam could see a little terrier running around inside the cab, yapping at people through the slightly open windows. Jack was also there waiting for him. He was the last person Adam wanted to see.

"If you were going to get your roof done, you could have seen me first," said Jack.

"Why is that?" asked Adam.

"I could have got you the best deal, mate. I know a lot of people in the game. There are a lot of cowboys out there, you know," said Jack within earshot of one of the roofers, who looked daggers at him. "No offence, mate," Jack said again quickly as he caught his eye. "I didn't mean you." The man said nothing.

"You'll have to excuse me, Jack," said Adam impatiently. "I have to get these guys started. I'll talk to you later about the fence."

"Sure, sure," replied Jack. "I was just making a point. By the way, who was that attractive woman to whom you gave a lift this morning?"

Adam had a good mind to tell Jack to mind his own business, but instead he just said, "That was Dick's…" Then, realising his mistake on the point of saying 'wife', he quickly interjected, "Well, a friend. What's it to you?"

"Nothing," said Jack, smiling. "When you said a friend, you mean Dick's friend? I noticed she was wearing a ring. Dick's wife?"

This time Adam was angry. "Please, mind your own business," he said shortly.

"Sorry," said Jack. "Bit touchy this morning, aren't we? Say no more, I've got the picture."

Adam turned his back on Jack and asked the builders to follow him.

"That neighbour of yours is a fucking irritating bastard," said one of them. "If he doesn't watch his mouth I'll punch his face in."

"You'll be doing me a favour," said Adam. "But it's probably best to ignore him."

"I'm Daley, by the way," the man introduced himself. He was the man with the truck and the little terrier. He was slightly taller than Adam, with a strong, wiry build.

"I spoke to you on the phone." Adam nodded.

After that, they got down to the business of repairing the roof. The roofers wanted to strip down the whole roof to start with and then start replacing it, but Adam was having none of it after the last rains. He wanted them to start with the brick building first and then the rest of the house. In the end he got his way, though it was going to cost him another £100 to do so, because they'd have to get an extra skip later, or some such reason. Adam agreed as he had other things to think about at that moment, things which were more important.

However, he soon realised, as they were putting the scaffolding up, that they were bang on his new patio, for which he was expecting the concrete the next day. He ran out to stop them just in time, and after another half an hour of arguing he managed to get them to skirt around the bit of ground he had levelled the day before. Whilst all this was going on, he could see Jack peering over the hedge with a funny smile on his face.

He's quite an inquisitive bastard, thought Adam. *I'll have to watch him.*

As the roofers started work, Adam retreated to his lounge with the book. He had to find a solution. However, it was not easy to concentrate in all the commotion that was going on. It was bedlam with the people running up and down the scaffolding, carrying the old slates down and taking up wood to replace some old joists which had rotted over the years.

Adam dozed off. He was jolted back from his dream by the phone ringing. He got up and sprinted to pick it up, because for some reason he did not want to miss it.

There was a strange voice at the other end. It was a woman.

"Hi, this is Susan," she said. "Is that Adam?"

"It's me," he said, puzzled.

"Got your number from Inroads," the voice said again. "Would you like to meet up?"

It suddenly clicked that Inroads was the dating agency he had joined earlier to spice up his social life. What had particularly attracted him was that they didn't use computers. Apparently they were the biggest hand-matched agency in the world.

Adam was caught by surprise at this new development. He had completely forgotten that he had applied to this particular introduction agency during a period of vulnerability when he was feeling very low about not having a girlfriend. Events had since overtaken such things and he had a humungous problem on his hands: he needed to work on Dick's disappearance to see if he could somehow alter the situation.

But Adam was still frustrated, and he also needed badly to get Rachael out of his mind. It was totally outrageous for him to get involved with Rachael while Dick was gone. He was Adam's friend, and Adam needed to try to get things back to normal, but he was not sure if he could. But he needed to see this woman to take his mind off Rachael; after all, he had that night to look through and research the book.

"Sure, why not?" he replied. "When can you make it?" He might as well go ahead with it, he thought, as he had paid for the agency's services already. After all his frustration with things generally and then on top with Rachael, he could do with some other distraction.

"Tomorrow evening is good. Where would you like to meet?"

"What about at a Tube station somewhere? Where can you get to?"

"After work? How about Camden Town? About six o'clock."

"Okay by me," said Adam. "Shall I meet you near the ticket office? I'm about five foot eight and I'll have a black leather jacket on. What about you?"

"About the same height. I'm Asian with dark hair. I'll have a green coat on."

"Okay, see you then. Thanks for ringing."

Adam put the receiver down. *That was amazingly painless*, he thought. She sounded really nice, but immediately he felt guilty. He needed to spend time with the book to find an answer, but maybe he could manage that tonight. No, he would ring her back and cancel, he decided. But as Adam started dialling her number there was a loud knock on the front door.

"We've stripped the roof and put the felt on," Daley said. "We're just off to get some more wood and the tiles and a bite to eat. Be back soon, guv."

With that they drove off. Adam went up to check their work. They had definitely stripped the roof. He went downstairs and put the book away, and decided he would go for some lunch himself at The Three Witches, and a drink as the roofers could carry on with the work when they came back, without waiting for him. Susan had slipped from his mind.

★ ★ ★

He regretted it as soon as he entered The Three Witches when he saw Jack and Wendy sitting there. There was no getting away from them, thought Adam. He bought a drink and ordered a sandwich before joining them.

"I see they stripped half your roof." Jack smiled enigmatically, as if it was a mystery.

"That's right," replied Adam. "They're supposed to come back to finish putting the tiles up."

"Well, the weather is pretty good at the moment, but you need to get that finished as soon as possible before it rains."

"I know, hopefully they'll get started this afternoon," answered Adam.

"The weather's been a bit funny lately," said Wendy.

"Yeah, remember last time you were in here with Charlie?" said Jack.

"Yes."

"Well, it was a bright day like today, but it suddenly pelted down like it was the start of the Great Flood."

"It certainly did," agreed Wendy.

Adam remembered that day well. That was when the crayfish disappeared.

"That doesn't mean it is going to rain today."

"Of course not, but it's good to have reliable workers to finish the job," said Wendy. Jack nodded and carried on his knowing smile.

Adam insisted the roofers would be back. He was getting annoyed, but he was also feeling a little glad that he had not allowed them to strip the whole roof. He tried to change the subject, for he did not want to talk about his house anymore. He asked Jack why the pub was called The Three Witches, biting into his sandwich as it had turned up.

Jack told him that, according to a legend, there were three witches living in this village. In fact, they used to live in Adam's house. But they all disappeared suddenly, all three of them, a little bit like Adam's other friend.

"What do you mean?" asked Adam indignantly. "Dick certainly hasn't disappeared." This unexpected information had caught Adam completely unawares.

Jack commented that he wondered why, then, was Dick's wife down there looking for him? He smiled knowingly.

"How do you know it was his wife?" Adam asked rather sharply.

"You said so." Jack smiled. "She had a ring on her finger. She was either looking for him or you are having an affair with her, or both."

"It looks a bit suspicious, if you ask me," said Wendy.

"Nobody's asking you," said Adam. "I'd be grateful if you could keep your noses out of my business." He got up to go.

"Don't get annoyed." Jack laughed. "We're only joking, have another drink."

But Adam was not in the mood. "I'd better get back and check on those roofers," he said, and got up.

"What about the fence?" Jack asked as he was leaving.

"We'll sort it out when the roof's finished."

★ ★ ★

But there was no sign of the roofers when he arrived back at the house. He waited another hour and then rang their number. The girl at the other end assured him that the men had already left and were definitely on their way. However, at about five o'clock there was still no sign of them. Adam cursed and rang their number again. This time there was no answer. There was an answerphone message asking him to leave his name and number and they would get back to him. They had gone home.

Great, thought Adam; that was all he needed. He prayed that there would be no rain, but he was worried. Nothing was going according to plan. He decided he would go up there and remove anything that he could to the other side of the house, in case it rained. He was halfway through rolling up the carpet when the telephone rang. He ran downstairs to answer it. It was Rachael.

"Dick still hasn't turned up," she said. "I'm getting a bit worried. I think I will have to report it to the police."

"Give it another day or two, please." Adam tried to convince her without sounding desperate. The last thing he needed was for Rachael to involve the police. "Look, I am coming down to London tomorrow night. Why don't I come to see you and we can discuss the matter before you do anything?"

"My mother thinks he's run off with another woman. Tell me the truth, Adam," she begged.

"Rubbish," replied Adam. "I'm sure there is a reasonable explanation for all this. He'll be back before you know it."

"I hope you are right. I'll see you tomorrow," she said finally.

"I'll be a little late," Adam said in the best soothing voice he could muster. "I've got something else to do first." There was no point in cancelling the date with Susan; he had to go into London anyway now.

Rachael rang off. Adam decided he must concentrate on the book. He had to find the answer. He made himself a cup of tea and got down to business.

Several hours and several cups of tea later, he had not even managed to get through a quarter of the book. It was a struggle.

The dictionary helped, but he was getting nowhere fast. So far he had found nothing that would help him to find Dick.

Exhausted, he made himself a cup of soup and then went to bed. He would have to stick to his task the next day.

★ ★ ★

His sleep was very disturbed that night. He was worried that the roofers had disappeared with his deposit, and the bank was chasing him to foreclose on his property because he had run out of money. In the end he suddenly woke up dripping in cold sweat.

He lay awake in bed until morning and then forced himself to get up. People were due to arrive that morning to bring the concrete for the patio; that's if they turned up. However, they did turn up around midday, but not the roofers. It was another nice, bright day and there was no sign of a cloud in the sky. Adam rang the roofers twice that morning, but the answerphone was on and there was no reply.

The concrete people dumped the concrete within an hour, but as their hose would not reach the place where he wanted it, they used the roofers' wheelbarrow to shift the concrete to the patio area. Adam had to pay them extra for it.

Just as well the roofers were not there, he thought. He managed to smooth the concrete with the aid of a broom, which he ruined in the process. Several hours had gone by, and after managing to lose both his shoes in the concrete, he decided to wash the wheelbarrow and have a bath to get ready for the evening. There was going to be no chance to look at the book that day. Adam felt guilty about going to see Susan and thought about cancelling the appointment, but he had to go to London anyway. His immediate need was to calm Rachael down and then start again on the book the next day.

While he was still in the bath, an idea suddenly came to him. Yesterday he had seen a spell in the book which would summon somebody to him or to a desired place if he spoke of him or her by name. As he knew the main roofer's name, he decided to try the spell on him before he left for London. Yes, he wanted John Daley to come and finish the roof, and even though he could not compel him to do the work, it would make him turn up at the house. As it was a handy little spell he decided to make a copy and stick it in the top pocket of his jacket. If it worked he would try it to find Dick.

When he had finished casting the spell, he felt a bit more satisfied and headed out for London in his car to meet the latest woman in his life. As he was leaving, he had a sneaking suspicion that some clouds were forming in the sky. However, he thought nothing more of it as he drove through the traffic to London; to Camden Town, in fact.

★ ★ ★

After a lot of manoeuvring through the back streets because of traffic, he finally reached Camden Town and parked the car. He was fifteen minutes late and the thought occurred to him that she must have gone by now, after getting tired of waiting for him. However, since he was there he decided to go and check. There was nobody there, so he decided to ring her on her mobile.

"I'm sorry," she said, "I'm going to be another twenty minutes, I'm running late."

Typical, he thought; after all the effort he had expended to get there more or less on time, she was late anyway, but as he was there already he decided to wait. He bought a paper from a kiosk and looked through it. There was nothing very interesting in it except an article about a little town that was preparing for the Queen's visit soon.

He had actually passed the place on his way to London. That was where the train station was; where he had dropped Rachael off the other day. He wondered why the Queen was even going there, as the place did not seem to be of much interest to anybody. Sure, it was a nice enough place, for what it was, but he could not think of anything significant which the Queen would actually go to visit.

These things were not something he worried much about, and though it puzzled him at that moment, he soon forgot about it and started looking through the property pages, which were much more interesting to him.

A few minutes later, he looked up at a figure in a green coat approaching him. It was an Asian woman of slightly plump proportions who looked forty plus. Adam was not too impressed, but tried not to show it. She was short, but had high heels on.

"Susan?" he enquired, hoping he was wrong, but she nodded and there was no escape.

"You're Adam?" she asked.

"That's right," said Adam. "Nice to meet you."

"You look a lot younger than I thought you would be," said Susan.

"Is that right? Thank you." He did not articulate what he actually thought though, namely that she looked a lot older than she had claimed.

"What would you like to do?" she asked.

"Shall we go for a coffee somewhere and get to know each other?" Adam ventured.

"Well, I thought we could go for a meal," she suggested. "I'm a little peckish."

"Fine, why not?" He was a little hungry himself.

"I know a nice little place around here," she said. "It's a Chinese restaurant. Do you mind Chinese food?"

"Not at all," said Adam. In fact, he quite liked Chinese food.

With that, they walked towards the Chinese restaurant. Adam followed her lead in silence, trying to think of things to say, but he found himself struggling. His first instinct was to run away and leave her, as he did not fancy her a jot, but he resolved to go through with the experience.

A moment later they were at the restaurant, which was a fairly modest affair, decked out in green, with a fair sprinkling of dragons everywhere on the walls. They picked a table away from other people so that they could have a chat in private. After ordering a few dishes too many and a bottle of the house plonk, they settled down to the formalities of the introduction.

Just as Adam had feared, she turned out to be over forty, and recently divorced with three small kids. In fact, everything Adam had told the agency he did not want. As the evening progressed, he became more and more depressed listening to her. Her ex-husband was stalking her and had beaten up the last man she had tried to go out with. However, because the children still wanted to see him, it was difficult for her to ditch him completely.

Adam listened to all this with a bemused smile, cursing under his breath. In the end he could contain himself no longer and asked her what she was doing out on a date.

"Well, I have to start somewhere," she retorted. "I can't just sit and rot at home just because I've got three children."

"That's another thing," said Adam. "I told this agency I strictly did not want to meet anybody with children."

"Why? You got something against children?"

"No, that's not the point. I'm sorry, but I just don't want to look after other people's children at this particular stage in my life."

"So what are people like me supposed to do?" she asked, exasperated.

Adam was nearly at the point of saying that he did not have the answer, but decided otherwise. He did not want to get involved in some ludicrous argument, which was of no benefit to him whatsoever. Better to cut his losses and run.

"Tell you what. Why don't we both tell the agency that we never met, that way we will both get an extra person to try out?" said Adam.

What a disaster, he thought. He could have been studying the book all this time, but then he did have to come to London to see Rachael anyway.

★ ★ ★

He reached Rachael's half an hour later, still not knowing whether to feel angry or bemused by the encounter with Susan. He decided to have a word with Inroads the next day, in fact, a few strong words. But, then again, it was probably better to keep quiet and get another date.

Rachael invited him in and asked him if he wanted to eat anything. He said he was not very hungry, so she offered him a drink. She was already on her third whisky by this time. Rachael was drinking heavily, and from experience this was always a bad sign.

"Well, not a word from Dick," she said finally. "Have you heard anything?"

"I'm afraid not," said Adam, "but I'm sure he'll soon surface." He had to try hard to stop himself from smiling at his unintended pun. The drinks were beginning to have an effect on her.

"He was always a callous bastard," said Rachael, "leaving me like this without a word. If he thinks he is going to get away with this, he's got a surprise coming."

"Now, now, Rachael, I'm sure there is a good explanation for all this." Adam tried to sound soothing.

Rachael suddenly started sobbing uncontrollably, and Adam hesitatingly put his arms around her to comfort her. As her sobs subsided a little, she suddenly grabbed Adam and started to kiss him. Adam tried his best to push her away.

"I have nobody to turn to, Adam," she complained. "Dick's left me, and you don't care much for me either."

"I do like you," Adam tried to reassure her, "and I'm sure Dick hasn't left you."

"Where is he then?" she cried. "You don't think I'm attractive either, do you? Just like Dick."

"You are very attractive," Adam stammered.

"Prove it." She grabbed him again, and before he had time to resist, she was kissing him again. Adam tried to resist but it was difficult; he was caught up in the moment, taken by surprise.

"Rachael, I don't think this is a very good idea." Adam tried to protest and break away, but it was too late. She had a good hold on him by now, and he was going nowhere.

"Not bad for a little man like you," she said. "There seems to be something different about you lately." Rachael smiled.

CHAPTER 6

Next morning Adam left early, saying goodbye to Rachael, who told him that she was not going to go to the police to report Dick missing for a couple of days, much to his relief.

Adam felt guilty as hell, but tried to convince himself that it was not his fault. Still, at the same time he was guilty. He was guilty of making Dick disappear. He needed to bring him back somehow.

He drove back like a maniac as he was in a hurry, but when he did get back he had a shock waiting. It had been raining the night before. The ceiling on the upper floor of the brick building had collapsed and the carpet was absolutely soaked. There was a little puddle of water on the ground floor of that part of the house. Adam cursed the roofers as he opened the back door to see if there was any damage to the concrete outside.

There was a narrow channel running from the house, right through the middle of his patio floor. Worse still, there was the toe of one of his shoes sticking out from one side of the channel, as if somebody had been buried under the concrete.

But even worse was still to come, as he noticed from outside that the bathroom window was open. Adam ran upstairs to check his bedroom. Everything was strewn all over the room. He immediately realised that he had been burgled, and that the suitcase with the book in it was gone.

Adam searched the room desperately to see if by any chance the book was still there. His faint hope was that they might have thrown it aside, thinking it was a piece of junk. But there was no such luck: the book was gone.

Adam could have cried, but stopped himself from doing so. He sat down on the bed and tried to think what else was missing.

He decided to call the police, and to make a list of things that were stolen. They had left his chequebook but had taken the £500, which was his next instalment for the roofer, who wanted to be paid strictly in cash.

By the time he had made the list he was regretting calling the police. Hardly anything else was missing except the money to pay the roofers, the book and a leather jacket. It was unlikely the insurance company would pay him back the £500, as there was no proof he had it there. There was no value attached to the book and he could not prove it was his. Also, the £250 excess of the insurance policy meant his loss of the value of the leather jacket was not covered. He had not lost his credit cards as he had them with him.

The police said that they were coming round in two to three hours with a fingerprint expert to go over the place for any clues. He had been told not to tidy up, so there was nothing Adam could do but wait.

While Adam was making himself a cup of tea, there was a knock on the door. It was Jack. He was holding Adam's lost suitcase.

"Found this outside my house," said Jack. "Does it belong to you?"

"Yeah, it's mine alright. I had a burglary last night and they must have thrown it on their way out."

"Lose much?" asked Jack.

"Not too much, just some money," said Adam. "Luckily I had my credit cards with me. By the way, you didn't happen to see anything, did you?"

"No, sorry, I can't keep a watch all the time. Anyway, it was raining really hard last night. The weather has been really funny lately."

"How's that?" asked Adam. *So much for neighbourhood watch*, he thought.

Jack told him that this was the third time it had happened. "There was not a single cloud in the sky all day and then all of a sudden, it really comes down. Funny thing was that a couple of miles away from here, it was bone dry."

That was indeed strange, thought Adam. Unless, of course, it had something to do with the magic, for yesterday was the fourth time he had used the book.

"Very strange," he said aloud. "But I don't think it will be happening again soon." Unless he could find the book, he thought.

Jack seemed suspicious. How did Adam know, unless he had something to do with it?

It took Adam by surprise, and he was almost caught out, but he protested his innocence and said he didn't have a clue. He asked Jack why he had thought Adam had in some way influenced the rain.

Jack said his friend Charlie had talked about a book of magic Adam had found, and maybe he was into witchcraft. Also, there was the disappearance of his friend.

Adam told him Charlie had been talking nonsense, and his friend Dick hadn't disappeared. Was there anything else? Adam asked tersely, grabbing the suitcase from Jack.

Jack said no and he turned to go.

"Thanks for bringing this back," said Adam, waving the suitcase, and shut the door quickly before Jack could change his mind.

As he was putting the suitcase away, there was another knock on the door. Adam cursed, thinking it was Jack. But when he came downstairs and opened the door, it was John Daley, the roofer, standing there. He had an insolent grin on his face.

"Where have you been? Have you seen the state of my house?"

"I'm sorry," said John Daley, "but I never thought it would rain like that. Funny, it hasn't rained a couple of miles out."

"It's brought the ceiling down," said Adam. "And it's your fault – if you had put the slates up when you said you would, there would be no damage."

"Look, I'm sorry." John Daley sounded very apologetic. "That ceiling was about to collapse anyway."

"You're bound to say that."

"I'll tell you what," said John Daley again, "I'll put a new ceiling up for you free of charge. How's that?"

That took Adam by surprise. Last time he had a talk with him he wanted cash for any little thing he could think of, but now he was trying very hard to please. The change could not be more astonishing. Then Adam remembered: the spell must have worked; Daley was back.

"I can't pay you anything today. I've had a burglary and the money's been stolen," said Adam.

"That's alright, pay me when you can. I'll get on with the job," Daley acquiesced. There was no stopping the man.

"You'd better stick to the outside of the house. The police are coming to get fingerprints," said Adam.

"It's okay. I don't need to come in. Anyway, I bet they don't find anything," he laughed.

"Why's that?" asked Adam.

"Nobody's going to be fool enough to rob a house without wearing gloves." Daley smiled.

The man was right. It was just a waste of time to have the police nosing around. Adam closed the door for the second time as Daley turned to go.

★ ★ ★

At about one o'clock a police van and a car turned up, and a policeman in uniform knocked on Adam's door. It was a fairly large man in a rather tight police uniform standing in front of him. He had a large stomach and a bright red nose, and a little notebook in his hand. Adam opened the door wider and let him in. It was difficult to guess his age, but Adam could tell that he was partial to a drink or two and large portions of food.

"You've reported a burglary," the policeman said. "I'm Constable Stevens from the local police station. I'd just like to ask you a few questions and have a look around the place, and then my colleague will dust for any fingerprints."

"Okay," said Adam.

"When did you discover the burglary?"

"This morning... I wasn't here last night. I stayed at a friend's in London."

"Right," said the constable, noting it down. "Did you lose much?"

"Not many things; about £500 in cash."

"Why did you have so much cash?" asked the policeman.

"I was keeping it to pay the roofer."

The policeman doubted if he would see the money again, and it was unlikely that he would get it back from the insurance. He asked Adam if he had any insurance.

"Yes, of course," said Adam. "But I don't think I'll make a claim. I only lost a leather jacket and a..." Adam hesitated.

"And... what?"

"A book," said Adam. "An old manuscript."

The policeman asked him if he had any photographs of it. Adam replied in the negative.

The officer looked pessimistic and intimated that he doubted that they would ever recover it; however, he asked Adam what it looked like.

"Well, it's about this big, leather-bound and the script is in German."

"Have you got a receipt of purchase?"

"No," said Adam, "I found it here."

"Well, I doubt if you'll get anything from the insurance then."

"I didn't think I would," agreed Adam. "That's why I didn't want to claim. Is there any chance of recovering it, though?"

They would try, of course, and the officer sympathised, but Adam's best bet was to try the local antique shops and the Sunday market nearby. It might turn up there. Lots of things did. He asked Adam where he thought the burglar had entered the house.

"I think it's the bathroom window. I'll show you, I found it open." Adam gestured the policeman to follow him.

The policeman went up to the open bathroom window and peeked outside.

"I don't think they came in here," he said finally. "They must have just opened it to make you think so."

"Why do you say that?" asked Adam.

"The ground is pretty soft with all that rain, but there's no foot marks outside or in here."

"They could have come before the rain started."

"Maybe. What time did you leave the house last night?"

"About six."

"It started raining soon after, but I'll have a look outside. Is there any way out?"

"Yes, sure, please follow me," said Adam.

As they went outside through the back door, they stepped on what was to be the concrete floor of the patio.

"Is that channel through the middle by design?" asked the officer, smiling.

"No, the rain caused it," retorted Adam.

"Well, there seems to be the toe of a shoe sticking out of it. You haven't been burying any bodies underneath the concrete, have you?" He smiled again. He was a regular sleuth.

"Of course not." Adam was indignant. "I lost my shoes when I was smoothing out the concrete."

"Sorry, sir, just a routine question." He was trying to stop himself from smiling again. He was having a laugh at Adam's expense.

"Sure," said Adam. "Is there anything else?"

"No, that's it. I'll be leaving," he said with a smile. "I will tell my colleague to take over. Thank you for your assistance. I still think they didn't come in through that window, but probably climbed the scaffolding to get in."

With that the constable left, and a few minutes later there was another knock on the door. This time it was another man, not in uniform, holding a little box, which looked like a toolbox. It was the fingerprint expert.

He said it wouldn't take too long. He would start with the upstairs and then come down. The man was as good as his word, and had finished within half an hour. He pointed out some smudges on the bedroom wall, which looked like finger marks made by a man wearing dirty gloves.

"I think they came in through the roof and left by the front door, if you ask me," he said. "You've got no deadlock on the door."

"No, I'm waiting for it to be fitted," said Adam. "It's a new door."

The man suggested that he should do it as soon as possible, and also put some locks on the windows and the back door while he was at it. He shook his head in disapproval, incredulous at the lack of security.

Adam told him that he would get right on to it and showed the man out through the front door after thanking him again.

"Sorry I didn't find anything." The man shrugged as he left.

Daley had been watching them on and off, whilst carrying on with putting felt and battens on the roof to take the slates.

"Well, did they find anything?" he asked after they left.

"No," said Adam.

"I told you so," he laughed. "It's a bloody waste of time, if you ask me."

"They said the burglars came through the roof using your scaffolding." Adam eyeballed him.

"What are you suggesting? It had nothing to do with me."

"I'm not saying that," said Adam. "But it was your scaffolding. If you had done the slates earlier, they couldn't have got in."

"That's it, blame it on me," said Daley. "They would get in, mister, if they wanted to get in. They would just kick your door in as it has no deadlock."

"Alright, forget it," said Adam, "but you'd better finish the slates before you go today."

"Don't worry. We're starting today."

Daley left, leaving Adam deep in thought. He would have to check out all the antique bookshops in the area and also go to the Sunday market, just in case the book appeared in one of these places. Today was Wednesday, so he still had a few days before the market day to play around with.

★ ★ ★

It was amazing how a crisis could concentrate some minds while others went to pieces. Things had gone disastrously wrong in the last few days for Adam. His only worry before finding the book had been how to keep his girlfriend Linda without marrying her in the process. A contest he had lost.

Adam analysed his life. Without the book he would have been following the same old pattern he had previously followed. Going out to some dances at the same venues to meet the next female in his life, until he met her – *if* he met her. Well, he always did meet somebody, but nobody had turned out to be satisfactory. It was always a means to an end. Though he had never been as unfortunate as Charlie in his relationships with women, he had never been as successful as Dick either.

He was doing well now only because Dick was missing. The key to it was the absence of Dick. Now he realised where he had been going wrong in his life. He had always been in the shadow of people who were better at promoting themselves than he was. He had always tried to compete on their terms rather than his own, but it was a contest he could never win. The key to success was competing on a set of criteria which suited him.

He had never understood this before, but it was crystal clear to him now. Dick was always better off; he had a much better job and a much better house in a better area, even though these things did not actually mean that he was economically better off than Adam.

But Adam had always competed on Dick's terms and undersold himself. To most people his image was that of a lowly EFL teacher, not a budding entrepreneur who did up houses for vast profits. Most people did not even know what EFL meant. He had to explain that it was English as a Foreign Language.

Why was it that he could never say that he was involved in developing properties, and was quite successful in it, unlike Dick, who had failed in his first venture in that field? Sure, he had a nice house now, but it was mortgaged to the hilt.

Obviously what was needed was a change in the perception other people had of his identity. Rather than seeing himself as others wanted to imagine him, he should have been promoting how he wanted others to see him, which was as a very successful person in his own way.

It occurred to him suddenly that people who were socially successful were those who could project themselves as successful people in the first place. Obviously, good looks and being tall helped a great deal. But there were other factors, factors that were in his favour, but he had to let people know that these factors mattered.

Doubts filled him again. He was doing well in Dick's absence, but would he do as well if Dick were present? Surely the key factor, therefore, was Dick's absence. It was probably best if Dick was not present at all.

No, no, what was he thinking? He did not want to take Dick's place with Rachael. He was Dick's friend, and even though things had happened, he did not mean them to happen and certainly he did not want to continue in this fashion. Adam realised that he was in denial about Dick's disappearance. He wanted to absolve himself of any guilt or responsibility in the matter.

But at the same time, things were out of his control. The book was gone, and without the book, Dick was gone. He had to face facts – Dick was not coming back. Guilt overcame him and his whole body shook for a moment. Adam suddenly felt that subconsciously he had probably always wanted to get rid of Dick because he had always fancied Rachael, and now he had achieved his goal. It was definitely, however indirectly, his fault that Dick had disappeared, and he was certainly making the most of it while Dick was away.

He decided to get the piece of paper from his jacket pocket and try the spell once more, this time using Dick's name. Adam was not sure what to expect. Would Dick show up at his front door, or would the crayfish show up in the pond?

He got busy tidying the house and doing essential household chores, but his mind was not on it. He waited for the rain to start, but nothing happened and several hours went by. He even ran down to the garden to check the pond, to see if the crayfish was there, but there was no sign of it. In the end he had to conclude the spell hadn't worked. Dick was lost. The book was lost as well. He needed to pull himself together, otherwise he would be lost as well.

Adam resolved there and then not to see Rachael again. He had to find a new girlfriend to get away from her, otherwise ten years hence he would still feel guilty about deceiving a friend. But what if he never managed to get Dick back? No – he decided the decent thing to do would be to allow Rachael to have a different life, while he made his own way.

The book, which had been a total disaster for him instead of being a boon, had definitely opened his eyes. Whatever happened from now on he would approach life differently. Adam's mind began to wander; he did not want to think about Dick anymore. He needed to get some ideas for his new image and get a new circle of friends, friends who would appreciate his qualities more and would accept his new image more readily than his old buddies.

He had to follow a different path. A path geared to his abilities, where he could succeed. Dick was not coming back, and even if he did, Adam had to get on with his own life and make his mark with or without the book of magic.

Adam took stock. To survive the ordeal once the police got involved in looking for Dick, he had to act as normal as possible and somehow keep Charlie from blabbing.

To survive financially he had to finish the house quickly and get himself another teaching job, as he had got the sack from the last one, though not because of incompetence. Adam concluded he needed to make the best of the situation and get on with his life as normally as he could. There was no chance of getting Dick back without the book and there was very little chance of ever getting the book back.

He decided he would go back to London the next day and look in at the last English teaching college he worked in to ask for a reference, and then visit one or two others to see if they had any vacancies. He also had to let Charlie know the bad news about the book and that Dick was not coming back, and that his chances of getting the book back were the same as winning the lottery.

Adam started drawing up a list of things that needed doing to move his life forward. He had to become successful in something. It did not matter what it was as long as he was successful. He needed to take his mind off his current problem. Yes, he was sorry for Dick but he had to convince himself that it was not really his fault, and he had to stop feeling guilty about what had transpired, and get on with things.

He decided to give Charlie a ring before starting on the list. Life was quite straightforward if one had a path to follow. Most people just wandered through life aimlessly without thinking about the next step and were mainly the victims of circumstances, like he had been up to now, but he was going to change that. He rang Charlie.

When Charlie answered he seemed very excited.

"Did you know," he asked, "Rachael has gone to the police to report Dick missing?"

"Yes, she told me she was going to," said Adam. "So what?"

"Well, guess what she told them."

"What?"

"That we were the last people to see him, before he disappeared." Adam could almost hear the groan in Charlie's voice as he mentioned that fact.

"What does that matter? Just stick to the story and you should be okay," said Adam. "That's if they come round to see you at all."

"I'm sure they will." Charlie was adamant, and very nervous. "You have to get him back."

"I can't," said Adam.

"What do you mean, you can't? You're the one who is responsible," insisted Charlie.

"Listen, Charlie, I'm coming up there tomorrow. I'll explain when I see you. I don't want to talk about it anymore now."

"You've got to do something, Adam," Charlie pleaded.

"I'll see you tomorrow," said Adam, and put the phone down.

Adam was very worried, as he knew Charlie was going to crack under questioning. He was just too nervous. Adam needed to go and see him as soon as possible to try and placate him. But what would happen when he told him that the crayfish were lost and the book had been stolen also? He would definitely crack then.

He had to prepare himself, for the police were going to come round and see him for sure. What if they found out about Rachael? Surely she would not be stupid enough to tell them. He had to stop seeing her at all cost; he had been so stupid in getting involved with her. That was a good enough motive for doing away with Dick, or at least the police would think so. But how was he to know at the time that the book would get stolen and Dick would be gone for good?

What Adam needed was a girlfriend, and quickly, to establish an alibi. He almost wished that he had not given Susan the brush-off so quickly. Maybe he could ring her again, but then he put the thought aside. But he needed to get in touch with Inroads for another date. He was desperate; he just had to get away from Rachael.

There was a knock on the door. It was John Daley, who had parked his truck outside with his little terrier keeping guard in the cab. He said they would finish that side of the roof the next day, and he needed some money. He could then move the scaffolding to the other side and start on it.

"Listen, I don't want you to start on that side just yet," Adam said. "I've got some windows coming in on Friday and I want to get those done first."

"I can't do it for another three weeks, then. I've got other jobs to do, I'll have to take the scaffolding away." Daley sounded a bit pissed off.

But that suited Adam fine; he needed to think. "Just patch up the slates on the other side. At least that will get rid of the pigeons."

"Okay," said Daley. "Will you pay me tomorrow?"

"You said you would do the ceiling for me. I'll pay you when you finish that," said Adam.

"Okay, Monday then," said Daley unhappily. Adam was really surprised at how readily John Daley agreed to everything he demanded.

Daley left with that. Adam wanted to do something else before going out to do some shopping and clearing up. He rang his last workplace about the reference. He was told to go and see them the next day, which was Thursday.

In the end Adam decided not to bother with Inroads for the moment. He already had enough on his plate.

CHAPTER 7

Adam awoke to the banging on his roof overhead on the stone-built part, where John Daley was repairing the broken and missing slates. He had started early and was soon taking the scaffolding down, before Adam had a chance to get up there to have a look. However, it all seemed fairly satisfactory. Daley was going to come back on Monday to finish the ceiling and collect his money.

Adam looked out of the window, to the back of the house at the soaked carpet which he had hung outside to dry, but it was still very wet and the carpet was ruined. He decided that he would have to get rid of it and re-carpet the house when it was finished.

Daley and his boys disappeared about midday without asking Adam for further payment, which surprised Adam a little. Soon Adam was getting ready to go to London to see Mrs Cruz for the reference. His mind was still in a state of turmoil, and he needed to keep himself occupied or he would go mad, thinking about Dick and the stolen book. He had held the most valuable thing ever in his hands and now it was gone, along with his friend. Adam was in a state of shock.

Fortunately Adam had not been a great believer in buying unnecessary consumer goods for quite a while. Money had been tight while the mortgage was not sorted.

Adam decided he needed to look ahead. After his little episode with Rachael he was now convinced, more than ever, that he needed a change in lifestyle. He was definitely missing out on the good things in life.

He needed to kit himself out like Dick, with some designer clothes and a new car. The first leg of this journey to a new life was a visit to the clothes shop in the little town of Ironbridge Spa, as soon as he received his new loan. But to sort his life out, he needed a job desperately.

As Adam and his trusty Skoda made their way towards the town, he thought of Dick. As he entered the outskirts of the town, he thought of Dick again. He had just passed Dick's new BMW parked in the station car park. He did not know how Rachael had missed it. Well, he did in fact know, at least the time when he had dropped her at the station. He had taken a little diversion to avoid the car park and skirt around to the other side.

The car was still parked there, gathering dust. Just as well it was not parked in front of Adam's house, he thought as he drove past. Poor Dick – would he ever come back to drive it again? wondered Adam. But no, he decided it was definitely not all his fault that Dick got turned into a crayfish. He had asked for it.

Adam wanted to stay busy. He parked his car near the main shopping centre and decided to look at some new clothes. The guilt was still weighing him down.

Ironbridge Spa was an unspectacular town, which had neither an iron bridge nor a spa. The bridge had rusted away a long time ago and had been replaced by a concrete car park, which covered the narrow river. The spa had dried up. In fact, the whole place was unremarkable and it had an unremarkable shopping centre, with unremarkable shops.

After spending half an hour looking, Adam felt quite frustrated. He even tried on a couple of jackets and a pair of trousers, but found nothing that suited him. He hated shopping at the best of times, so he gave up easily and decided to walk back to the station to take a train up to London.

The only noteworthy thing about Ironbridge Spa was that it had a train station. That meant a lot of commuters lived in the vicinity of the town. In fact it was quite an efficient direct line, with trains which took half an hour to reach Liverpool Street station running every fifteen minutes. That was why Adam was sure he was going to make a killing when he sold his house again the following year.

However, the Queen was due for a visit here on Saturday. Adam could not think of any reason whatsoever why the Queen would want to come to Ironbridge Spa, other than maybe to commission a new iron bridge.

But where would they put it? Would they dig up the car park and site the bridge there on the site of the original one? Highly unlikely. He decided to find out why the Queen was coming.

★ ★ ★

When he got to the station, he found they were busy sprucing up the place. A plethora of workers had come out of the cracks and were busy polishing and painting. Normally one would be lucky to see a single face around for most of the time, except during rush hours.

"What's up, mate?" Adam enquired of one of the workers.

"Don't you know the Queen's coming down here, and the Duke and all? The royal train is going to pull up right at this station."

"What for?" asked Adam. "Why would she want to come to Ironbridge Spa of all places?"

"Dunno, mate." The man shrugged. "Something to do with getting to know the common people, and you couldn't get more common than here."

"You could be right there," agreed Adam, who could not think of anything exceptional at all about the place at that moment, or for that matter, at any other time either. "So the Queen's definitely coming here," Adam repeated to himself, still in disbelief.

"That's right, mate," the man said again. "We got to do the place up till it shines and get the car park cleared for the visit."

Adam saw another man in uniform approaching them from the corner of his eye. The workman quickly slunk back to his work as he saw the man. Obviously he was the supervisor, or some such higher species.

"Please stop disturbing the men, sir," the man said. "We got a job to finish."

"Yes, sure," said Adam. "I just wanted to find out what was going on here."

"The Queen's coming," the man said behind him as Adam moved off to the ticket counter.

Unfortunately for Adam, the supervisor had disturbed him at a vital moment. In the confusion he completely forgot what the other man had said earlier: that the car park had to be cleared. It was not until he was on the train that he realised the significance of this: Dick's car was still parked there.

Adam decided that there was nothing he could do about that now; he would have to see about it tomorrow. He had another day to shift it, or so he thought.

Adam dozed off several times during the journey and tumbled out of the train in a slight daze at Liverpool Street station. He was not used to commuting and hated travelling, which he considered to be a waste of time, unless he was going somewhere new. This was why he had always preferred the inner city despite its associated problems of noise, crime and grime.

However, he was enjoying his stay in the countryside at present. It was a big change for him and he decided he was prepared to put up with a bit of travelling discomfort for the benefits.

He reached St. John's College of English a little after two. It was based near Holborn on White Lion Street and occupied the three upper floors of an office building.

When he went upstairs, he found the college was unusually empty for a Thursday afternoon. He reached the reception, which was a large room on the first floor, to be greeted by Mrs Cruz.

"Hello, Mrs Cruz, how are you?" he said.

"Fine, thanks, Adam. Do call me Vera." She smiled in a friendly fashion.

"I'm here for a reference, Vera," said Adam.

"How have you been keepin'?" She was of foreign extraction and even though she spoke fairly good English, she quite often didn't pronounce her 'G's.

"Not bad," said Adam. "I'm living in the countryside now."

"A country square." She smiled again.

"Hardly that," said Adam. He didn't attempt to correct her, but it made him smile. "Though I do have a nice house."

"A country gentleman, then."

"I suppose you could say so," said Adam, trying to impress.

"Did you drive in, in your Lada?" she asked. "Are you still driving that?"

"It's a Skoda. No, I'm not driving it anymore," he lied.

"What have you got these days?" she asked.

Adam tried to think of a car and could not think of one, but finally remembered Dick's car. "I've got a BMW now." Adam was too embarrassed to admit he was still using his Skoda.

Mrs Cruz was impressed, and commented that Adam seemed to be going up in the world.

Adam replied he was trying to, but he needed to get another job to pay for the luxuries in life. What he needed was a reference, and was it possible for her to write one for him?

"As long as you don't tell Mr Cruz." She smiled. "You should call me sometime."

"Thank you, Vera. By the way, where is Mr Cruz? In fact, where is everybody?"

"Well, he's having a break as demand is a bit slack at the moment, so we have cancelled some afternoon classes."

"Oh, sorry to hear that," sympathised Adam.

"It's alright, I hate this place anyway," she said. "I wish he would sell it."

Adam was surprised; he had thought the business was booming.

She told him it was, most of the time. In fact Mr Cruz had gone to make arrangements for a visit to Turkey to recruit some students. He would be away all next week. She winked mischievously.

"When's he going?" Adam asked.

"Saturday," she said. "Why, are you thinking of asking me out?"

"Why not?" Adam heard himself say. "What about lunch on Sunday? You can come down to see my house."

"Only if you promise to behave yourself." She smiled.

"I am a country gentleman, remember," said Adam, smiling back.

"Better still," she said, "why don't we meet for a drink on Saturday evening? I'm doin' nothing."

"That sounds good to me," said Adam.

"Ring me late Saturday afternoon, about four. I'll give you my mobile number. If you just wait a minute, I'll do your reference now."

She was only a few minutes on the computer, and gave Adam a printed reference letter. It was perfect.

"It's a standard one my husband keeps on file. I just put your name on it and signed it on his behalf. Here's my number." She gave Adam another piece of paper.

"Thanks," said Adam, "I'll see you soon." Things were beginning to look up already. With a bit of luck he could wean himself off Rachael and maybe get his old job back. So Vera wanted some fun after all, while the husband was away. He needed to finish the house to get the mortgage, but he also needed a job to qualify for it. Mortgage companies did not give mortgages to people without jobs.

"Yes, soon," she said, giving Adam a big hug and a peck on his lips. Wow, things were suddenly looking up.

Adam left. He was due at Charlie's soon. Charlie, who lived in Tottenham, was a connoisseur of Greek and Turkish food. He lived in a little flat which had been carved out of a cavernous terraced house, originally with nine or ten rooms.

It was a garden studio flat, and Charlie was very fond of his little patio and small, overgrown garden full of very tall weeds, which looked like a miniature jungle. Charlie never attempted to clear the weeds, but was quite content to look at them from his patio, which was stepped up about eighteen inches from the garden. He had lived there for a number of years.

★ ★ ★

Charlie opened the door with a frown on his face. He was clearly in a disturbed state of mind.

"Hi, Charlie," said Adam. "You okay?"

"You must be joking," said Charlie.

Adam had been thinking about Vera coming round to his house on Sunday. He had decided he would borrow Dick's car to impress her. Dick had left his car keys on Adam's table, before he had disappeared. Adam still had them in the house, hidden away. Dick probably would not like it, but he was in no position to mind, unless he showed up before Sunday.

It was a good plan. He would park the Skoda in town and pick Vera up in Dick's car, and then back to his place for lunch and whatever else that followed. Later, after dropping her off at the station, he would park the car somewhere nearby and nobody would be any the wiser. Except he was supposed to see her on Saturday as well, but he decided it was too dangerous to borrow the car and drive it all the way to London. If Rachael had reported the car stolen as well, he could be picked up by the police. However, he was willing to take a chance around Ironbridge. Nothing much ever happened there.

Charlie asked if Adam knew that Rachael had reported them to the police. Adam tried his best to reassure Charlie and told him that she hadn't reported them. Most likely she had reported Dick missing, as Rachael had told him she was going to do it.

"Oh, she spoke to you as well?" Charlie sounded disappointed.

Adam told him that he went to see her on Tuesday night, as she had wanted to discuss the matter with him before she did anything.

"Oh, and what did you tell her?" asked Charlie, slightly miffed. He seemed hurt that Rachael could give more importance to Adam than himself.

"Nothing," said Adam. "Can I come in or are you hiding something in there?"

"No, no," said Charlie, "come in." He stepped aside to let Adam in.

"What are we going to do?" Charlie asked, when he had made the tea. "You've got to do something soon, Adam."

"I'm sorry, Charlie, I can't." This was as good a time as any to give Charlie the bad news. "When I got back home yesterday morning, I found I had been burgled. The book is gone."

"What do you mean, gone?"

"Stolen," emphasised Adam. "I don't think we can bring Dick back."

"You stayed the night at Rachael's?"

The significance of what Adam had said was yet to sink in with Charlie. He had just cottoned on to the other important bit. Adam hastily informed him that it was late and she had just offered Adam a room. Nothing else happened.

Charlie looked at him suspiciously for a minute and then said, "Don't worry, there's no way she would have anything to do with you. She's class, after all, you know. I mean, look at you."

"You're right," agreed Adam. "Like I said, she just offered me a room."

"What was that you were saying about the book?" Charlie tried to concentrate. Adam had noticed Charlie's lack of ability to concentrate after the tragedy, which Charlie referred to as 'the event'. Well, now it was going to get more tragic.

"I said it was stolen and we can't get Dick back," Adam repeated himself.

"You cannot be serious," cried Charlie, almost managing to sound like John McEnroe, the tennis player. Adam had seen a clip of him disagreeing with a line call, in the old days before touchline technology.

"I'm very serious."

"You should have been more careful," whined Charlie. He had always been a very careful person and almost despaired at Adam's risk-taking ventures, and had let him know this on many an occasion.

"Yeah, hindsight is a great thing," said Adam. "Listen, the important thing is we can't get him back. We have to deal with the situation."

"Have you told Rachael?" asked Charlie.

"How can I tell her that he's been turned into a crayfish and has been washed away by the rain?" said Adam. "Never mind the book." Adam decided to let Charlie digest the full horror of the situation.

"You mean he's disappeared from the pond also? You've murdered him," said Charlie, sounding hysterical.

"Stop that," said Adam. "I did nothing of the sort. He wanted to be turned into a crayfish. How was I to know that it was going to work?"

"We have to tell her something," said Charlie. "The poor thing is out of her mind with worry."

"Of course she is," agreed Adam. "But what can we do? She will come to terms with it herself. Meanwhile, we should say nothing to land ourselves in hot water."

"That's right, just think of number one, as always." Charlie could sound pretty self-righteous at times, normally without any justification, but Adam decided to let it go.

"Do you know the Queen's coming for a visit to Ironbridge Spa?" Adam tried to change the subject.

"Ironbridge what?" asked Charlie. He was still distracted by the turn of events.

"You know, my station," said Adam. "I picked you up from there when you came to see me."

"Yeah, I remember. Why would she want to go there?" asked Charlie, surprised.

"I don't really know," said Adam. "A man there said she wanted to get closer to the people."

"Yeah, but why at Ironbridge?" insisted Charlie.

"I don't know," Adam repeated himself. "Why don't you switch on the telly? It might be on the news."

Charlie duly switched on the tiny television set in his tiny room. The news had just started; it was six o'clock.

"The Queen is due for a historic visit to Ironbridge Spa on Saturday, to open a new spa house, which will form part of a new leisure complex in the area, and will provide much-needed employment locally," said the man on TV. "There is a report, however, that the police had to blow up a suspicious car in the station car park today. The car had been parked there for several days and the owner could not be traced. The police believe the car had been stolen last Saturday under suspicious circumstances, and could have a terrorist connection."

They showed the picture of a car parked by itself and a police robot approaching it, and a few minutes later, it being blown up.

"That looked like Dick's car," cried Charlie.

It was Dick's car, and Adam knew it. Could things get any worse?

"It did look like Dick's car," said Adam. "I'm sure it wasn't."

"But he parked it in the station car park when he came to see you."

"Did he? I can't remember," Adam lied. He did not want to unduly worry Charlie.

"We have to tell the police," insisted Charlie.

"Are you mad?" asked Adam, fully thinking that they were bound to be around sometime soon anyway. He had to get rid of the keys before they did turn up, in case they searched his house.

"Listen, if the police come to question you, keep calm," Adam said again. "Just stick to the story that he left and we don't know where he went, okay?"

"Sure," said Charlie, looking unconvinced and very disturbed indeed. At least that is what it looked like to Adam.

Adam said goodbye to him and made his way back to Ironbridge. There were police everywhere, with police cars rushing back and forth, one of which only just missed him. The Queen's visit had been cancelled.

CHAPTER 8

Next morning, Adam woke to find the windows man battering on his door. He and his assistant had arrived with a truckload of windows, and on time, much to Adam's surprise.

Adam had not slept well all night. He had kept thinking of Dick's car and having bad dreams about the police. In one scene he was in court being accused of Dick's murder, and Rachael was the chief witness. She accused him of murdering Dick in order to seduce her, as he had always coveted her secretly. The dream was so real that Adam woke up in a pool of sweat and had to change his clothes before he could get back into bed again.

He was just about to get to sleep when the windows people had shown up and rudely awakened him. He was still groggy when they started bashing his windows out. All this building work was beginning to get on his nerves, but he knew he had to hang on and get the job finished.

The plan was to take out all the windows downstairs first and then start replacing them one by one. Adam did not like this plan, as he preferred one window to be taken out at a time and replaced before moving on to the next one. But he was too sleepy to put up much resistance, so he let them get on with it while he busied himself with making some coffee for himself and also for the builders, who all wanted two to three sugars each. Adam had noticed this trend amongst builders. In general, they tended to have a lot of sugar in their tea or coffee. *I suppose they need the energy*, he concluded, and started heaping in the sugar.

After delivering the sugared tea and coffee, Adam hung back. He was becoming highly alarmed at the large gaps that were appearing in the walls of the house, and decided to intervene. He decided to call a halt to any more windows being taken out, and asked them to start putting them in. After a short argument, which Adam lost, the men carried on with their usual plan.

At this time, the phone rang. It was Rachael. She said Charlie had rung her to tell her about the car, which had been blown up. She had then watched the news and was fully convinced it was Dick's car. Did Adam know anything about it?

Adam managed to convince her that he did not. He could not remember what Dick's car looked like, as he had not seen it for a while, and he certainly could not remember the number on the car's plates.

Rachael decided she was going to ring the police and confirm what had happened and try and get the insurance to pay up.

"Are you sure you want to do that?" was all that Adam could say.

"Yes, I think so." Rachael sounded positive. "I am getting fed up with this situation. Something must have happened to Dick, or I'm sure he would have rung me by now. He was pretty punctual at keeping in touch, you know. This is the first time anything like this has happened."

"I'm sure things will sort themselves out," said Adam. What else could he say about the matter? As far as he could see, things always had a way of sorting themselves out. Not always for the best, as it happened, but sort themselves out they did.

"When are you coming to see me?" asked Rachael.

"I don't think that's a very good idea," said Adam.

"This is a big house," said Rachael. "I'm feeling very lonely and my mother can't come down until Saturday, so I need you."

"But the police might start thinking that we are involved in his disappearance."

"I haven't told them that you were the last person to see Dick, but I may have to when I talk to them about the car."

"It was myself and Charlie, we both saw him last," protested Adam.

"I know, I know, but it was your house. Look, if you come tonight I won't ring them till Monday."

"What will your neighbours think?"

"Let them think what they like, I don't care. In any case, I'm going to let the house and move out if Dick doesn't show up soon."

"You shouldn't decide on such things in a hurry," said Adam.

"That's why I want to discuss things with you," Rachael replied. "When are you coming?"

"How about around eight?" Adam gave in. "I've got some people working here putting windows in. They won't finish till late. I can't stay the night, as they are coming back early tomorrow."

For once Adam was telling the truth. He was also almost sure that some hitch would arise very soon, which would delay the windows for several days.

"Just park your car around the corner and walk up," said Rachael. "That Skoda of yours is a bit noticeable."

So she cared about the neighbours after all. But it suited Adam fine to park around the corner. He did not want to be associated with Rachael at this time, but he was helpless as he did not want to deal with the police just yet. But there was also the temptation, at the back of his mind, of seeing Rachael again, and he found her invitation too difficult to resist.

Surprisingly, the new windows went in without too much bother and the men fitted all of them downstairs; and soon the house began to look completely different.

The workers left about six o'clock, leaving Adam plenty of

time to prepare himself for the journey. It was better for him to go to her, as there was less chance of him being spotted there than if she were to turn up at his place.

Not only that, there was the small matter of getting rid of Dick's car keys. He had first thought of throwing them in the back garden, but had decided against it. He would get rid of them in London where it was much safer. Already he was beginning to think like a criminal, and hated himself for it. But he had little choice in the matter.

If Dick did not come back, and this was looking more and more likely, the finger of suspicion would surely point at him and Charlie, especially if they found out about him and Rachael. But she did not seem to care at all. She was only worried about not being lonely.

Well, why should she care? As far as she was concerned, Dick had left her for another woman. In fact, she was convinced of this, and wanted to get her own back. Who better to fulfil her need for assurance that she was still desirable than Adam, who happened to be there and available and also willing?

Adam was skating on thin ice and could foresee himself falling through at any moment. He had to convince Rachael that she had to stop seeing him, but how? He needed a plan, but it was too late for tonight.

Adam parked the car and dumped Dick's car keys in the nearest drain before walking around the corner to Rachael's house. It was a clear evening, and was still fairly warm. Spring was in the air, but Adam could not enjoy the spring weather as he normally did. Things were weighing down heavily on him. For a start, he felt very guilty about this whole affair.

He had been trying to convince himself that it was not his fault, but somehow this did not work. He was seducing a friend's wife, who he had a hand in getting rid of. Ouch! That sounded too final – maybe there was some way of bringing him back, but how? He needed some guidance in the matter, but from whom? Who could help him? He needed time to think.

Adam hesitated before trying to open the gate to Dick's house. This thing with Rachael, it had to end – but what if she did not want to listen to reason? Well, this was definitely not his fault; he decided she was seducing him and not the other way around. Adam knocked on the door.

Rachael was already opening the door before he could finish knocking. She had seen Adam through the window.

Rachael commented that Adam seemed deep in thought, after the normal greetings were over. Adam told her he was just worried about things he needed to do. He needed to get another job as he would run out of money unless he could refinance his house soon.

"Have you already finished the house then?" Rachael asked.

He told her that the major work was almost done, but he had to go through the bank survey and also show them that he was employed to get the money. However, even though he would be able to pay the instalments of the new mortgage from the rent he was getting, the bank wouldn't give it to him if he didn't have a paying job.

"I'm sure you'll work it out," said Rachael. "I suppose you're used to it."

"I suppose so." Adam shrugged. "It is hard work, but it's not as bad as people think it is."

"And the returns are pretty good," laughed Rachael. "You must be a millionaire by now."

People always exaggerated things when it came to property. Adam had accumulated a fair amount from buying and selling, but he was hardly even halfway to becoming a millionaire. But it was always so. Either people did not believe one was making any money, or if they did, it was assumed that you were made of money. Sure, he had assets, but he had no money; he was asset-rich and cash-poor.

Assumptions are never proportionate, thought Adam. They were always too much or too little. That was the way of things. For example, people almost always assumed you had money if you had a good car, or you were poor if you drove a cheap car.

"I'm doing okay," Adam said finally. "But far from being a millionaire."

"That's good," said Rachael. "Shall we have a drink first, or would you like something to eat?" She wasn't too interested in his financial plight.

Adam felt a bit awkward about the situation; he needed a drink to loosen up. "Just a drink, please, I've already eaten. I thought you wanted to discuss something with me."

"I wanted your advice on something to do with building work. You know Dick was planning to do some major renovations to the house and the builder's pressing me, and what with Dick's disappearance I don't know what to say to him."

"The house looks fine to me. Why were you renovating?"

"Well, Dick thought we could add value to it by doing a loft conversion. I'm not so sure."

"Don't do it if you're not sure. Do you want to live in a mess for six months? In any case, why not wait until Dick comes back?" All of this came as a surprise to Adam, as Dick had never mentioned anything about a loft conversion to him.

"Well, the builder says he's going to start another job if we don't start here soon. It's doing my head in as I've got so much pressure at work at present."

"Tell your builder to wait. They always say they've got another job to go to, just to pile pressure on you."

"You're so masterful with your decision-making. I've been worried sick about what to do." She gave Adam a little kiss.

"What was that for?"

"For helping me to decide. I feel so helpless with Dick not being here."

Adam felt sure that was far from the truth. She had never come across as a helpless woman to Adam. What was she playing at?

"Let me get you a drink. I've got some gin, or would you like rum?"

"Whatever you're having. I can't drink much, I'm driving."

Rachael came back a few minutes later with two very large gin and tonics.

"Wow! Those are big," exclaimed Adam. "I told you I was driving."

"It's mainly tonic. Maybe you can give me some advice on another matter." Rachael eyed him, and there was mischief in her eyes. She brushed up against Adam. "Let's sit down on the sofa, I'm tired from work."

As Adam sat down, she sat down quite close to him.

"What's the other matter you want my advice on?" asked Adam, feeling slightly uncomfortable.

"My boss wants me to go away with him this weekend." Rachael nonchalantly placed her right hand on Adam's thigh.

"Why are you asking me?" Adam was beginning to feel an involuntary stirring.

"With Dick not here, who else can I ask but you?" Rachael looked at him intently, but didn't move her hand away.

"Maybe you shouldn't go. Dick could be back any time," Adam lied, and gulped his drink.

"Then you have to help me. I'm so stressed out by the whole situation I don't know what to do. I need your help."

"Why me?" Adam gulped down the rest of his drink and put down the glass.

"See, it wasn't such a large drink. You are a discreet sort of a person who can keep a girl's secret. Not a blabbermouth like Charlie. Tell me, have you been missing me?"

"I suppose so," Adam obliged. "You are a very good-looking woman. Dick was – I mean, is – a lucky bloke."

"If he was so lucky, why did he leave me?" asked Rachael angrily.

"He hasn't left." Adam tried to placate her. "I'm sure he'll be back."

"Well, I'm not going to wait very much longer for him. Are you sure you don't know more about this? Because you keep telling me that he will be back."

"Well, I'm hoping he will," said Adam, trying to wriggle out.

"Are you sure?" asked Rachael, squeezing his thigh. "Fed up of me already?" She had already finished her drink and was ready for action.

"No, of course not," he protested. "It would just be nice to see Dick back."

"Liar," laughed Rachael, as her hand accidentally brushed the front of his trousers. "Something here disagrees with you."

That was the end of that conversation and beginning of another gruelling session for Adam, an event he was quite unused to even after the last time, in which not too much talking took place. Adam gave in. He felt ashamed that his resistance had crumpled so easily, but Dick was lost. With the loss of the book went any remote possibility of ever getting him back. He decided he needed comforting just as much as Rachael.

Rachael was one of the quiet types, Adam had observed. She hardly made a sound during the whole business, until she climaxed with a gasp and a few convulsions. Then she liked to rest as she still played with him, urging him on to the next session without too much delay.

"Our little friend is a little tired," she said. "Shall we give him a little more time?" she purred.

"I think I need a little rest as well," said Adam.

"Well, I think you'd better stay tonight then, I haven't finished with you yet. Come on, Adam, you can go tomorrow morning."

"I suppose so," sighed Adam, as he gave in. *One can't have too much of a good thing*, he thought to himself.

★ ★ ★

The next morning Rachael told him that she was expecting her mother on Sunday and she would then decide on what course of action to take. Adam felt very much superfluous. He had never been there to give her any advice, but to perform other duties. At least with her mother there, he would have a week's break, which would give him a chance to think of a plan to put Rachael off. At least he hoped he would be able to come up with an idea which would not offend her too much. It was just getting too dangerous.

"Want to come back again tonight?" asked Rachael as he was leaving.

"I'm sorry, I've got things to do," Adam said quickly, thinking of Vera, though he was not seeing her until the following day. He needed a distraction to get his mind off Rachael.

"So have I," said Rachael. "I'll be here, though, if you change your mind."

Adam nodded and said goodbye. He was flabbergasted with Rachael's sexual appetite, and highly impressed with Dick's ability to cope with it. He was exhausted after one night. But maybe, he surmised, after a couple of years of marriage things had probably quietened down to once a week instead of three times a night. He envied Dick, who had been a lucky man, but felt sorry for him at the same time.

Adam suddenly remembered that he needed another car, now that Dick's car was gone. After all, he could not very well go around and see Vera in his Skoda, after telling her he now drove something entirely different. He was still determined to see her, as he knew subconsciously that any relationship with Rachael was doomed to failure from the very beginning.

He thought of buying a car, but firstly he had no time that day and secondly, he had very little money left to do so. There was only one thing he could do: he would have to rent one.

As Adam drove past Ironbridge Spa through the meandering country lanes towards his house, he was overcome by the quietness and tranquillity of the countryside. It all felt so peaceful, yet his life had been anything but peaceful in the last few days.

He had moved to the hamlet of Littledon for some peace and quiet after his break-up with Linda. He had primarily bought the house to make money, because it was a bargain, but he was undecided about selling it now. He did not want to move again soon, but wanted to find out if he could settle there for a while. It was a great house, or would be once it was finished, and Littledon was a nice place to settle down in. People were fairly friendly, even though his neighbours were a little too nosy.

How weak he was, though, he thought, to give in to lust. Yes, he would destroy himself along with Rachael if he did not gain control of the situation. But it is never easy to give something up, especially something one enjoys. He had to wean himself off by using a different approach, for he was hooked. He had been without a woman for such a long time since Linda had left him, the temptation had been too much for him. At normal times he would have endured it, he told himself, but these were not exactly normal times.

He decided he needed Vera to get off Rachael, for he had a window of opportunity the following week when Rachael's mother would be visiting and Vera's husband would be away.

★ ★ ★

The double glazing people were waiting for him with another truckload of windows when he reached the house.

"Where have you been?" The man was annoyed. "We've been waiting for half an hour for you."

"You're not supposed to be here until half past eight, and it's not that yet," Adam protested. How he hated these moments. There was always one more thing to do to the house, and none of them were ever completely finished until the day he finally sold it. There was always something left to do. Anyway, within ten minutes they were working away on the upstairs windows, and he was making their tea with three sugars each.

He decided that he needed to sort out a car for the weekend if he was going to get anywhere with Vera. But was he jumping into the fire from the frying pan, getting involved with another married woman, whose husband had not disappeared but was only going away for a week? However, times were desperate and desperate measures were called for. If Vera was interested, so was he.

Adam needed a distraction if his mind was going to cope with the enormity of the situation, but he needed to get away from Rachael for obvious reasons. In the end he got the *Yellow Pages* out and started ringing around for a car, but being reluctant to splash out too much, he decided to settle for a cheap little Ford Escort. After all, it would only be the replacement car while his car was in the garage. He booked the car hire for the next two days and decided to pick it up next day.

He busied himself for the rest of the day, clearing the place up and looking for any other things Dick might have left behind, but found nothing else. Though Vera would not be coming round until Sunday, he wanted to make a good impression on her. He needed a job if he was going to stop his money running out and Vera could be the key, but Dick's disappearance was still bugging him.

Adam thought of the book again. He could not give up so easily on it; there must be a way of getting it back, and he had to look for it. He decided he would start by ringing up all the antique bookshops listed in the telephone book to see if they had acquired anything like that lately. He had a feeling that it was unlikely that the thief spoke German, so he would soon sell it to somebody as an old manuscript, for whatever he could get.

He soon found that there were a few antique shops in Ironbridge Spa, but a quick enquiry over the telephone yielded nothing. Adam decided he would pay them a visit the next day and speak to the proprietors in person to see if he could jog their memory.

However, Adam decided his priority was to impress Vera and get his old job back. He was sure that with her backing, her husband Mr Cruz would find it difficult to refuse him. He needed the job desperately to survive a financial meltdown.

The windows went in without any major mishaps. His luck was finally changing, he thought.

It was about five, and he had just paid the fitters off when the telephone rang. It was the police. They were going to send somebody round to have a word with him the next morning. It was just a routine matter they wanted to clear up and would not take very long. It would be Officer Stevens. Adam grimaced hearing that name, as he found the man totally odious.

Adam thought of Rachael's open invitation to go and see her again, but the prospect of the police coming round to see him the next day put paid to that thought.

★ ★ ★

Next morning Adam awoke early. Officer Stevens was due about ten o'clock. That left him enough time to get ready and clear up a little from the mayhem caused by the new windows. He also had to get hold of a plumber to put in a new bathroom and central heating.

The kitchen was not brilliant, but it worked and Adam decided he would leave it as it was for the moment. He had replaced some of the units himself, including installing a dresser unit on wheels, which he used to hide the door to the cellar. He only wished he had installed it earlier so he could have hidden the book there instead of in his suitcase on the day of the burglary, but he had been lazy.

Adam was getting fed up of building work and wanted a break from it, and had been planning a good week or two of holiday away from it all. But he wanted to finish the main jobs in the house, and most of all wanted to make it secure. Having a burglary had caused him to feel more vulnerable than he would otherwise, and he decided that he would install an alarm system as well.

About five past ten a squad car pulled up in front of the house and PC Stevens got out. Adam had already spied him through one of the windows and so opened the door to let him in.

"Hello, Officer Stevens," said Adam. "What is this all about? Have you caught the man responsible for the burglary?" But Adam already knew Stevens was not there because he had solved the burglary.

"I'm sorry, we haven't caught anybody yet," said Stevens. "I'm here on a different matter." His small eyes squinted as he broke into an enigmatic smile.

"Oh," said Adam, feigning surprise.

"It's about your friend, a Mr Drummond," said Stevens again. "Do you know he has disappeared?"

"I heard something about it from his wife," said Adam.

"Well, maybe you can help me with that, sir. According to Mrs Drummond, you were the last person to see him."

"Why do you say that?" asked Adam, slightly irritated.

"As you probably already know, the car that was blown up in

the Ironbridge Spa station car park was Mr Drummond's. Mrs Drummond identified it from the TV footage."

"I didn't know that. Why did you blow it up?"

"We thought the car had been stolen and was being used for terrorist purposes. As we could not get in touch with Mr Drummond at the time, there was no other option."

"That does not mean I was the last person to see him," insisted Adam.

"Well, he came to visit you last Saturday, did he not?" asked Stevens.

"That's correct," agreed Adam "He came with another friend of mine called Charlie Watts. Dick – Mr Drummond – left early the next day to go somewhere else, I don't know where. Charlie stayed behind. So, strictly speaking, we both were the last people to see him."

"I suppose so," agreed PC Stevens. "But you didn't drop him back at the station in Ironbridge?"

"No, I didn't. Charlie and I wanted to go for a drink, so Dick decided to catch the bus. I told him where to get it from."

"And you don't know where he was going?" asked the constable.

"Back to his wife, or so we thought," said Adam.

"And you didn't know that it was his car that had been blown up?"

"Not until I talked to Rachael, I mean, Mrs Drummond," said Adam.

"When did you talk to her?" asked Stevens.

"On Thursday. I was in London and popped in to see her," said Adam. He decided it was better to admit that now before they found it out. Maybe they already knew. Who knows what Rachael might have told them.

"So, you know her quite well, then?" PC Stevens eyed him suspiciously.

"Well, Dick and I are old friends, so I've known her for

a while. She was worried about Dick." Adam tried to sound casual.

"Alright, sir, that will be all for the moment," said Stevens, to Adam's relief. "By the way, did any of your neighbours see him leave?"

"I don't know," replied Adam. "You'd better ask them."

"Don't worry, I will. Goodbye, sir." With that, PC Stevens departed.

CHAPTER 9

On his way to pick up his rented car, Adam dropped into a couple of the antique shops in Ironbridge Spa, mainly to convince himself that he hadn't given up the ghost as far as Dick was concerned. But if he was expecting any success in finding the book, he was disappointed.

They were musty old places full of bric-a-brac and broken old furniture, but hardly any books and certainly not the book he was looking for. Both places seemed to be run by wide boys, who were more into clearing houses than buying genuine antiques. Though the word 'antique' featured prominently on their shop signs, they sold job lots of old junk cleared from houses where, the owner being deceased, the relatives just wanted to clear the old furniture after having their pick.

Adam enquired of both if they had come across any books recently, but more or less got the same reply. In any case, he decided to leave his name and telephone number, so that they could contact him in case they came across any old books in German.

Adam made his way to the garage to pick up the car. He parked the Skoda around the corner and went in with his documents to pick up the Ford Escort.

After a slow drive, Adam reached London about 1.30pm and decided to stop for lunch and to window shop for some clothes. There was plenty of time to ring Vera, who had stipulated that he not telephone her before 4pm. Adam decided it was prudent to ring after then, to make sure her husband was definitely on his way.

As Vera lived in Winchmore Hill, which is in North London, Adam had decided not to go to the West End to do his shopping, but stay in North London itself. As Adam's flat was located in Wood Green, which had a very large shopping centre, he decided to visit his tenants, who owed him a month's rent, and to buy some clothes at the mall, which offered quite a good choice in fashion.

He had a first-floor flat in one of the terraced houses in the area behind the Underground station. The location of the flat made it very handy for him to get to as well as to let. Adam had actually lived in the flat every now and then, in between tenancies. He had even stayed there with Linda, his last girlfriend, before moving to his last house with her.

The previous owner of the flat had let it to some punks, who had promptly painted it black and purple all over. They then had half a dozen people living in the flat instead of the two who rented it, trashing the place in the process and falling behind on the rent.

After a lot of complaints from the neighbours, the man decided to repossess the flat through the courts. But he had had enough of renting property and had sold off the place at a bargain price to Adam instead.

Adam rang the bell, but there was no answer. For a moment, he thought nobody was in, but he decided to ring again and was rewarded by footsteps coming down the stairs. A girl with bright red hair opened the door. Adam did not recognise her.

"Is Graham in?" he asked.

"I'm sorry, but he's gone back to Australia."

"What do you mean, he's gone back to Australia?" asked Adam, slightly irritated. "Who are you?"

"I'm a friend of his, just come back to London," she said, smiling. "I live in the flat."

"I can see that, but who gave you permission to live here?" asked Adam.

"Graham did, of course," she replied matter-of-factly. "Graham took a month's rent from me before he left."

"Brilliant," retorted Adam. "He owes me a month's rent. I'm the landlord and I want you out."

"That's not fair, I paid for this place," the girl protested. "You've still got his deposit, haven't you?"

"Only two weeks. So, what do we do now?"

"Well, I could take on the flat, once I get a job. If you throw me out you are going to lose two weeks' rent anyway. So, why not let me have it and I'll give you a new deposit?"

"And what happens if you disappear in two weeks' time?"

"I won't, I'm here to work." She smiled. "I'm also waiting for a friend to join me here."

"Can I have a look around the flat to make sure everything is okay?" Visions of black and purple paint appeared in Adam's mind.

"Have you got any ID, since I don't know who you are?" the girl asked.

Adam produced his driving licence, which he happened to have on him as he had rented the car. "Satisfied?" He was a bit miffed at the thought of having to produce ID to enter his own flat. But at least the flat was alright, much to his surprise. He decided that it was probably best to cut his losses and sign her up, and they agreed to meet in a week's time to sign a new contract with her and her friend.

Her name was Mary, and she came from Bournemouth on the south coast. She did not give him her parents' address. At least she was not from Australia. Adam vented his anger against Graham the Australian, but then remembered he had had a few other Aussie tenants and they had been perfectly fine. There was nothing else to do but write off the two weeks' rent.

He left Mary and headed for a pub around the corner to have some lunch and a quick pint. Before ringing Vera, he needed to get over the disappointment of not collecting the month's rent, which meant he had to withdraw more money from the bank.

Adam sipped a pint of the local ale, brewed in the premises of The Rat and Gherkin. He also chewed a mouthful of his steak and kidney pie – a habit which he persisted with, despite his fear of mad cow disease. As he did so, he could not help but ponder again on the turn of events.

He was the unluckiest man alive, he concluded. He had lost a priceless book of magic after having found it in the first place. How unlucky was that? It was magic that had actually worked, except he was too slow to realise its value, being caught up in more mundane matters until it was too late.

He had also lost a friend, and was not sure if he would ever see him again. Dick had his faults, of course, but Adam missed him; he missed the little skirmishes he had with him, but most of all Dick's strange humour, even though most of it was directed at him.

Of course he had been compensated in the form of lovely Rachael, but that just made him feel guiltier. In any case, Adam knew it was at best very temporary. Rachael only considered him a diversion, and would be off as soon as she found Dick's replacement. In fact, this outcome was so inevitable in his mind that Adam resolved for the second time that he would not see her again, in case he got more tangled up in that situation.

That left him with Vera. This was another departure for him: an affair with a married woman whose husband was still around. Adam had largely been rather conservative in his ways when it came to women. Normally he had shied away from any involvement with married women, and girlfriends or even ex-girlfriends of his friends. But it seemed a bit odd to Adam that she seemed to be encouraging it. He put it down to boredom.

Lately he had had a very lean time as far as women were concerned, ever since Linda had left him. He was still feeling a bit desperate. There was not much chance of seeing Rachael anymore, he thought, now that the police had become involved, but there was Vera, and also the possibility of getting his old job back.

Adam was about to leave the pub and make that call to Vera, when he happened to notice that one of the two men sitting at the corner of the pub was eyeballing him. The Rat and Gherkin was one of those rough pubs which were frequented by local toughs who took great pleasure in baiting any strangers and occasionally giving them a good beating.

This looked like one of those occasions to Adam, as the man seemed intent on some mischief, the way he was looking at him. Seeing as there were two of them and one of him, Adam decided it was politic to beat a quick retreat. Adam was not by nature a coward, but he was not feeling very lucky this particular day and it was by far the best decision to make, he thought.

However, before he could make it out of the door one of the men caught up with him.

"Oi, you! I want a word with you," said the man.

"What about?" asked Adam, backing away. "Do I know you?"

"You've been visiting our Mary. What's that all about?"

"What's it got to do with you? Are you following me?"

"We saw you coming out of the door at Mary's. We're Graham's friends and know her quite well. Why are you hassling her?"

"Well, go and ask her then." The man was beginning to wind him up, and as Adam tried to move past him, he was annoyed.

"I'm fucking asking you!" The man stood his ground.

From the corner of his eye Adam could see the other man getting up from his chair. It was time to go. Adam headbutted the first man who was blocking his way, and then kneed him in the groin for good measure. As the man doubled up, Adam pushed past him.

"Next time, mind your own fucking business," said Adam as he left. He was definitely having a bad day. Perhaps it was his imagination, but in the back of his mind he thought he had seen the second man somewhere before.

★ ★ ★

Having reached his car without any further problem, Adam drove off and then rang Vera. She said she could meet him around the corner from her house, to avoid the neighbours. She did not, however, seem very impressed when Adam described the car he was driving, though he quickly explained it was a replacement car for the weekend.

"At least it's not your Skoda. I wouldn't want to be seen dead in that," she quipped.

Twenty minutes later Adam pulled into the turning she had mentioned and Vera got in within a few minutes.

"Where would you like to go?" he asked her.

"Somewhere away from here," she said. "There are too many nosy neighbours around."

Adam drove up to Muswell Hill and decided to stop for a drink. "I have to be back by ten," Vera said. "My husband is going to ring me." She was looking around furtively to see if she had been recognised or if there was anybody in there she knew. Luckily, she did not know anybody.

"You seem a little worried." Adam smiled, trying to defuse the situation.

"You don't know my husband, he's the jealous type," she said, still looking around. "I'm sure he has me followed sometimes."

"I didn't spot anybody," Adam tried to reassure her.

"It's probably alright," she replied, bordering on paranoia, "but I'd better be back before ten."

There was plenty of time, Adam said soothingly. They could have a couple of drinks and go for an early meal. "I'm sure you could be back by half past eight or nine o'clock."

"Okay, I'll have a martini then." She relaxed a little. Adam got up and went to get the drinks. *I've got a right one here,* he thought; why did he even bother? Anyway, as he was already here, he decided he would try to make the best of the situation. He had to think about the job. It had not been a good day so far, so he had no great expectations for the evening, but maybe he would get Vera to give him back his old job.

After the first drink, Vera started to relax a bit. She even broke into a little smile by the time they were on the second one.

"You are a little devil in disguise," she said. Adam knew she was trying to justify her own behaviour. "I never thought you could get up to somethin' like this."

"We haven't got up to anything yet," Adam retorted, slightly irritated. "We're just having a drink." Adam could not understand why she was on the verge of paranoia one minute and then being flirtatious the next. Maybe the drink was loosening her up, but she was definitely shit-scared of her husband. He had an amazing hold on her.

"I know," replied Vera. "But it is a big step for me. I've never done this sort of thing before in my life."

Adam guessed she was probably being a bit economical with the truth, but decided to play along with it. "It's the first time for me as well," he said, smiling.

"Good." She smiled. "Tell me – how are things with you? Have you got another job?"

"Not yet, but maybe in the summer." He didn't want to sound desperate. "How is the college?"

She said the college was doing okay, but things could be better. That was why her husband had gone abroad on a recruiting mission. Adam remarked that the place looked full when he used to be there.

"A lot of competition these days." Vera shrugged. "But we are okay."

"Oh, good." Adam was relieved. "I was thinking of going into the business myself."

"Don't bother." She dismissed the idea totally. "If you are really interested, my husband is thinking of getting out. You could buy into our place. It's too difficult to start up on your own."

"I'm not sure I can afford that."

"Maybe you can have a chat with my husband sometime. It'll be a lot cheaper than setting up by yourself."

Adam, who did not think it was a very good idea, agreed to have a think about it.

As it was already past six by this time, they decided to move on to a restaurant down the road to eat.

The Chinese restaurant turned out to be fairly dimly lit, with little private alcoves, which suited Vera down to a tee. The woman was a voracious eater and loved the food. Adam was enjoying the meal as well and ate rather more than he intended, all washed down with a nice bit of warm sake.

With a few drinks inside her, Vera had loosened up quite a bit and was even playing footsie with him under the table. Adam decided she was just another tease, but enjoyed it all the same.

About eight, he duly paid the bill and they walked down to the car. It was dark by this time and Vera had lost her fear of being recognised and walked along beside him, even though she refused to take his arm when he offered.

Adam drove back silently through the dimly lit streets. It had not been such a bad evening after all, and he had quite enjoyed the meal.

"Shall I drop you around the corner?" he asked her as they neared her place.

"That'll be fine," Vera replied. "Thanks for a lovely evening."

"I enjoyed it very much as well," Adam said genuinely as he parked the car.

"Tell you what," Vera said suddenly, very much to Adam's surprise, "why don't you pop in for a coffee or somethin'? But give me a few minutes to get in first."

"Are you sure?" Adam asked, still surprised.

"It's quite dark, I'm sure it'll be alright." Vera's apprehension had all but disappeared by this time. "Anyway, you could be a friend of the family calling round." Vera gave him a big smile and got out.

Adam gave her ten-minute head start. Vera had told him that it was the third house on the second turning on the left after he had turned right into the road.

The houses on the street were large and semi-detached, so fairly secluded. Vera was waiting for him and she opened the door to let him in.

"I thought you might have changed your mind." She gave him a huge hug, which surprised him. "I've been controlling myself all evening," said Vera, as she led him into the sitting room. "I've often thought of you since our dance at the college party."

"For which I got the sack."

"Well, my husband's a very jealous man, but I really like you."

Adam decided there was no point wasting time in case she changed her mind, and made his move on Vera. As he grabbed her she did not offer any resistance.

After playing around for a while, Adam got her clothes off and moved in. At this stage, however, he suddenly found his movements were rather restricted by his tight trousers around his ankles, as he had not had time to take them off.

He was finding it difficult lying on the sofa with his movements restricted. He was almost there but not quite, so

Adam decided to get up and untie his shoes and take his trousers off properly. But just as he stepped out of the trousers the phone rang, and Vera jumped up with a start and pulled her own clothes back on, to Adam's utter amazement, and ran to answer the phone.

"Hello, darling," Vera said into the phone as Adam stood there contemplating his navel. "You're early, it's only nine o'clock. No, no, I'm not busy. It's because you said you'd ring at ten."

Adam moved up to Vera and grabbed her from behind. She gave out a little squeal and nearly dropped the phone.

"No, I haven't got anybody here," Vera said into the phone as she gave Adam a squeeze with her free hand. As Adam moved his hand down, she gave out another little squeal. "Can't a girl have a little fun by herself? I'm really missing you."

However, if Adam thought he was going to get lucky after the call, he was mistaken. The call had brought back all of Vera's apprehension. As soon as she put the phone down, she decided it was time for Adam to leave.

"I think he suspects somethin'," she said. "You shouldn't have done that."

"Done what?"

"Grabbed me from behind."

"What was I supposed to do? Just stand there?" He was irritated.

"You could have waited a little until I finished talking," she said, and then added unreasonably, "Just put it away, will you?", pointing at his now limp *corpus delicti*.

Adam did as he was told and asked if she was coming to his house for lunch the next day, but she was not sure. Her husband was going to ring the next morning and she had to be in the house.

Adam left a few minutes later, totally frustrated. It had been an awful day after all, he decided, with good reason. There had been some good bits, but on the whole it had been almost a total waste of the day.

★ ★ ★

When Adam got back to the house, he was still reeling from what had taken place earlier. He was still in a state of shock when he climbed out of his car and made his way in.

There were a few messages awaiting him on his mobile, which he had ignored earlier, as he was busy with Vera. The first one was the distraught voice of Charlie, who sounded desperate.

He said he needed to see Adam as soon as possible. The police had been to question him that day. He didn't think they believed anything he said, and they wanted to see him at the police station next week. He didn't know what was going on, so could Adam give him a call back as soon as possible?

Adam ignored the plea and carried on listening. The next message was from his mother, who complained that she had not seen him for some time, so could he drop in soon, as his dad wanted to see him? Adam made a mental note to ring her the next day. It always meant trouble when she said his dad wanted to see him.

The last message was from Rachael. She wanted to come down to his place the next day, as her mother's visit had been delayed for a couple of weeks. This revelation threw Adam into a state of panic. Vera was due for lunch the next day; that's if she turned up. But he could not afford to have them bumping into each other. He needed to put her off. Anyway, it was certainly not a very good idea to be seen with Rachael at present. What would the police think if they found out? He decided to ring her immediately, but she was not in. Adam cursed the woman and decided to go to bed. He wanted to get up early and make it to the Sunday market in Ironbridge the next day.

He spent a restless night, tossing and turning in his bed all the time with recurrent bad dreams. At one time, he was in bed with both Vera and Rachael, and police burst in on him. Another time, it was Vera's husband and Dick who had ganged up together to get even with him and were chasing him up some narrow alleyway which seemed to lead nowhere.

By the time he awoke, Adam was exhausted. It was half past nine and the phone was ringing. It turned out to be Vera.

"Hello, Adam," she said. "Hope you haven't forgotten about our lunch date." She sounded really sweet, and it was totally unexpected after the evening before. However, never one to look a gift horse in the mouth, he decided to play along.

"I'll see you at the station at twelve," he said. "I haven't forgotten."

That would give him time to kill two birds. He could go to the Sunday market in Ironbridge first to look for the book and then meet her for lunch.

As soon as he put the phone down, it rang again. It was Charlie. It was urgent that he saw him, he screamed down the phone. Adam decided he would take Vera back to London and drop in and see him. Charlie seemed to be cracking up and Adam knew that it could spell trouble if he did not manage to calm him down.

"Don't worry, I'll be there," he assured him. "Just keep calm."

Adam busied himself to get ready, but as he was about to leave, Rachael rang him.

"I'm thinking of coming down to see you this afternoon," she said. "Can you pick me up?"

"I don't think that's a very good idea," Adam blurted out.

"Why ever not?" asked Rachael. "Are you trying to avoid me? I told you in my message that my mother is not coming down for a couple of weeks."

"I've got very nosy neighbours. What will happen when Dick gets back?" He tried to put her off.

"They don't know Dick," she said. "I need to talk to somebody."

"Listen, a policeman came to see me about Dick. They might be keeping an eye on the place." Adam was desperate to stop her from coming.

"Surely they don't suspect you of anything?" Rachael was incredulous.

"No, of course they don't," Adam reassured her. "But they might start thinking the worst if they see you here."

"Well, then you will have to come here, unless you've got something to hide."

"Alright." Adam gave in. He said he was going to see Charlie later and would drop in afterwards to see her. But he couldn't stay too late.

Rachael assured him that she had things to do the next day too. She sounded very convincing.

Adam left for the market. This was shaping up to be another difficult day. *What the heck*, he thought; it could not get any worse than the day before.

★ ★ ★

He parked his car near the market and decided to have a quick look around for books. The market was set up on a fairly long street called Church Street, because there was a church at the end of it, though it no longer functioned. It was now an entertainment complex with cinemas and a nightclub.

Well, at least it was pulling in the punters these days, and more than the church probably had in recent years. It was a sad demise in some ways, as the church building was very beautiful architecturally. Like many other such buildings it had suffered that fate because of the dwindling population of worshippers, the rest having defected to worship Mammon.

As Adam walked past some stalls, he bumped into none other than his old pal John Daley, who was walking around with some artefacts. When he saw Adam, he tried to shy away without acknowledging him, but Adam caught up with him.

"I didn't know you were interested in antiques," said Adam.

"I'm not, I just want to get rid of these," said Daley, sounding irritated by his failure to avoid Adam.

"What are those things you're getting rid of?" asked Adam.

"Mind your own business," Daley said sharply, "unless you want to buy something. It's just some junk I picked up." He tried to sound more conciliatory.

"Have you got any books?" asked Adam. Daley's jaw dropped a little bit, but he recovered quickly, a fact that didn't go unnoticed by Adam.

"No books," he said. "But there's a great stall down the street. See you tomorrow. Got to rush." And with that Daley was off, leaving Adam to stare at his receding backside disappearing at a distance.

Adam made his way to the bookstall, further down the street. If he was expecting some grubby little stall full of second-hand paperbacks, he was mistaken. There were a fair number of decent old editions there. Adam thumbed through the books, but there were none in any foreign languages. He decided to buy a copy of Shelley's poems, a 1916 edition in fairly good condition.

"Do you have anything in foreign languages?" he asked the proprietor, who was a short, stubby man in a worn-out grey suit. Why he wore a suit to run a Sunday stall was beyond Adam, but he was not really interested in that.

"No, don't get much call for it," the man replied.

"Nothing in German?" Adam asked again hopefully.

"No, sir," he said. "But we have a shop in Cambridge and they have a foreign section, I believe."

"Can you give me their address?"

"Sure," the man replied, and produced a little card with a smile.

Adam put the card in his pocket and paid the man £5 for the Shelley, which he thought was a bit steep. Still, he decided it was worth it. He would have to look in at the shop at the first opportunity. But meanwhile, he had other things to do and as it was nearly twelve o'clock, he decided to make his way to the station to see if the delectable Vera had turned up.

CHAPTER 10

Vera was waiting for him at the station when Adam got there, and she was dressed to kill in a short, sexy, black number that exposed the sides of her thighs rather tastily. With her fishnet stockings and a mock fur coat, she looked a picture and Adam could hardly take his eyes off her.

She grabbed him and gave him a kiss on his lips, which he rather enjoyed, as it really got everybody's attention in the station. What a change from yesterday, thought Adam, when she had seemed so apprehensive about it all.

"You look absolutely stunning." Adam tried to compliment her.

"You like it, then?" she asked. "I bought the dress some time ago, but don't get much chance to wear it."

"You look a picture," replied Adam, but all he could picture was her supine body without a stitch of clothing. "Shall we go for some lunch?"

"That would be nice." She smiled very seductively.

"We could either go somewhere here or down to my village pub."

"Well, if it's not too far let's go there. After all, the point of this exercise is to see your country residence." She smiled again, knowingly.

"Yes, of course," Adam agreed. "For a time, after yesterday, I thought you weren't coming."

"Well, you made me a bit cross yesterday." She gave him a mock look of anger.

"Sorry," said Adam, "I got a bit carried away." Adam was worried about a possible *faux pas*.

"We both did," she agreed. "Let's not worry about that. Listen, I've got some good news for you."

Adam was very surprised. What news could she possibly give him that was better than her turning up to see him? However, he was intrigued.

"Oh yes?" he asked. "What is that then?"

"I spoke to my husband again," she said. "He's agreed to let you have your job back."

Well, that was news indeed, and Adam was really surprised. He was not really sure why she had taken the trouble to come and see him to give him this piece of news, when it was perfectly possible to convey it over the phone. She seemed to be playing a game with him, but Adam didn't want to look for ulterior motives. He didn't really care if she had another agenda; he needed to get away from Rachael, as that relationship was positively unhealthy for him. But, wasn't he complicating things by getting involved with Vera, the boss's wife? Then again, maybe this was the way she wanted it. He could also do with a job. He asked when he could start.

"Monday, two weeks' time, if you want," she replied.

"Well, it would help if you could put that in writing. While I trust you, I'm not so sure about your husband," said Adam. "Why the sudden change of heart?"

"I convinced him," she said. "He wants a new partner and if you could buy into the business, it could be a lot of fun."

"I'm sure." Adam nodded. So that was it: she was softening him up. Adam was not ready to commit the money to buy a share in the business, but decided it was best to play along with her. He needed the job offer to get his mortgage.

"I'll send you a job offer tomorrow by post. Don't forget the added benefit: me!" She winked. "Any time you need a bonus, you only have to ask."

"Maybe I could have a sample today," suggested Adam. A faint glint of hope lit up his brain.

"Maybe you could." She smiled playfully. "If you are very lucky, but I think you said something about lunch." With that she grabbed his arm and they made their way to the car.

Adam drove back in silence; he was deep in thought. Something kept nagging him all the way to Littledon. It was the scale of the change that had taken place in Vera's attitude that strangely worried him, but he could not quite put his finger on why she needed to go to this length to convince him to buy into the college. Was there something more in it? As he meandered down the country lanes towards Littledon, quietly listening to Vera's comments about the wonderful countryside, Adam could not help becoming a little alarmed. Finally, he could contain it no longer.

"Why did your husband change his mind about me? I didn't think he liked me much."

"Well, he's realised that you were a good teacher and the students liked you," she explained. "The party thing was such nonsense as we were all a bit merry. I assured him there's nothin' in it."

"And he believes you?"

"Why not? I'm normally very faithful to him." She patted his thigh and kept her hand on it. "A girl's got to have a bit of fun sometimes, though."

Adam did not feel satisfied by the answer, but let it go for the moment. They had reached the village by now and he parked the car near the pub.

"Let's go in and have some lunch," he suggested. "You can see the house later on."

"That suits me, as I do feel a little peckish. What a quaint little spot. How did you ever find this place?" She viewed him with wide-eyed amazement, and it was impossible for Adam to tell if the look was genuine or not.

"Had a bit of luck really. I overheard somebody talking in a pub in London and then I looked it up from an advert in the local paper." Adam ushered Vera into the pub and ordered some drinks after finding out what she wanted. He then booked a table in the restaurant section of the pub for half an hour later. They were in luck. It was still early and there were tables available. As he was going through this process, he could not help noticing all the envious looks he was getting from the local lads.

Just when he was beginning to think that he had made a mistake in bringing Vera there, he was given a breather by the entrance of Wendy and Jack into the pub. This was probably the first time Adam was glad to see them, assuaging his trepidation as it did.

"Hello, hello," said Jack, "who's this then?"

"Oh, this is Vera," said Adam. "I used to work with her in London." He was really glad to notice that Vera was not wearing a wedding ring. "She's just visiting."

"Very nice," said Jack.

"Hello, Vera," said Wendy.

After the introduction to Vera, Adam did not bother offering Jack and Wendy a drink, which they seemed to be expecting and looked quite disappointed. It was becoming a bad habit to offer them drinks automatically, in his bid to become friendly with the neighbours. Adam decided he did not really want their company today but, unfortunately for him, nobody had told Jack and Wendy.

"The police have been asking questions about you," Jack blurted out after joining them without asking first, when they sat down at the table with the drinks.

"Why is that?" asked Adam, feigning innocence.

"It's about your friend Dick. He's disappeared, hasn't he?" Jack smiled wickedly as if he knew something.

"Has he really?" Adam decided to front it out.

"Well, that's why his wife was down here looking for him."
Jack looked highly suggestive; he had a little smirk on his face.

"There's a perfectly good explanation for that," Adam insisted
without elaborating any further. Mercifully for him, right at that
moment they called out his name, announcing that his table was
ready.

Adam excused himself from Jack and Wendy, and got hold
of Vera's hand and ushered her away from the pair towards the
restaurant area.

"These provincials," he said in Vera's ear. "They can never
mind their own business. Those two are always nosing around
for gossip."

Vera did not say anything but took to her chair silently, and
Adam had a sinking feeling that he had blown it again. She was
not oblivious to Jack's insinuations.

"So why are the police questioning your neighbours?" she
asked, while they were waiting for their first course.

"I don't really know," Adam lied. "Look, all I know is that
a friend of mine has disappeared and his wife has reported him
missing."

"But why was she down here to look for him?" she persisted.

"Well, he came to visit me. He and another friend called
Charlie, except after he left us, Dick never went back home. I
don't know where he is and that's the truth," Adam reassured
her.

"Why was your friend Jack going on about her?" asked Vera.
"He had a filthy smile on his face."

Adam told her he had no idea. It was best to deny it. He knew
from previous relationships that once one admitted anything at
all, one was lost. As Nietzsche so aptly put it, one may confess
one's sins to forget them, but the people one confesses to never
forget. With a bit of luck he might just salvage the situation still.

Most of the meal was finished in silence. Adam decided not

to linger in the pub a moment longer than was necessary. They got back to the car and drove it around to the house, and he invited Vera in for a coffee.

But much to Adam's annoyance, Vera was suffering from another change of mood. She, of course, remarked on how pleasant the house was, and she was really impressed by his choice of everything. But every time Adam made a move to become more intimate, she rebuffed him. Finally she blurted out, taking him by surprise. "You have something going on with your friend's wife, haven't you?" Vera sounded irascible.

"Not at all." Adam denied it instinctively. But it was no use, she had made up her mind and Adam realised that she was not going to come around.

"Listen," he said at last, "I have got to go to London to see Charlie. Can I give you a lift back?"

Well, that was that, thought Adam as he dropped her off near her house an hour later. He was probably not going to hear from her again. He headed towards Charlie's pad in a dejected mood, for he was not looking forward to seeing him again so soon. It was difficult to reason with Charlie; he had his own queer logic and it was never easy to dissuade him from a course of action he had made up his mind to follow. In this case he had probably decided to bare his soul to the police already, and Adam would have to watch him very closely indeed.

★ ★ ★

Charlie was in a foul mood when Adam reached his flat. He had been fretting all day while he had been waiting for Adam to show up. There were three cups of half-drunk coffee on the small table in the sitting area, which looked like a bomb site with things scattered all over the floor, unlike the neat little flat that Charlie normally kept.

Charlie had been a neat chap all his life; after all, he was a draughtsman and took pride in his work, but that was when he was actually employed. All of Charlie's belongings were tidily stowed away; each had a little place of its own and Charlie made sure that they stayed there.

Maybe that was the reason he was not very successful with women, Adam had surmised. He was much neater than they were and it seemed to put them slightly on edge. He never gave them the slightest chance to tidy up things, to put in their little touches. It was already done before they could even think of it. All their nesting instincts were thwarted in a stillborn effort, in the unease they felt in not being able to make the place their own.

But Charlie did not mind. He was normally at ease with himself, quite content to plod along with his daily routine. This mainly consisted of him getting on with the concocted series of rituals that was his life.

Still, neatness mattered to Charlie and it was a shock for Adam to see the place in such a state.

"What's up, Charlie?" asked Adam, a little puzzled.

"The police were here," Charlie almost shrieked.

"It's just routine, that's all, only because we were the last people to see him. They came to see me as well." Adam tried to calm him down.

"I am sure they suspect something." Charlie gave Adam a furtive look. "They suspect *us*."

"What's the motive?" asked Adam.

"You fancy his wife and I am jealous of his success. It's true, isn't it?"

"Now don't go making things up to give the police something to latch on to," Adam admonished him. "What happened was not our fault. We did not want to get rid of Dick. The pond got flooded and the crayfish have disappeared."

"You turned him into a crayfish and now he's disappeared," insisted Charlie angrily. "It's all your bloody fault! You planned it all."

"Don't talk nonsense. He asked me to do it. You heard him, you were there," Adam protested. "If you remember, he tried the spell on me first."

"You should have been more careful, and now you have gone and lost the book as well, so you can't even bring him back." Charlie looked at Adam disgustedly.

"I didn't lose it, it was burgled. You sound as if I organised the burglary." Adam was becoming angry himself.

"So what are you going to do about it?" asked a truculent Charlie.

"I don't know, do I? There's no guarantee that I could have brought him back even with the book, even if he hadn't disappeared." Adam shrugged. "Anyway, all this arguing is not going to help much."

"What are we going to do?" Charlie looked dismayed. "They want to see me again at the station on Thursday."

"You have got to keep calm and stick to the story. Dick left and you don't know where he is, and it is the truth," said Adam.

"Yeah, right, just conveniently forget the bits in between."

"You try telling them and they will lock you up for being mad. Who is going to believe you? Listen, I still can't believe it myself and I was there."

"Neither can I," agreed Charlie.

"Just be calm and stick to the story. Maybe the spell is only temporary and he'll change back on his own and turn up again."

It was a wild hope, and Adam knew it. He was clutching at straws, but there was nothing else he could do. At least if Charlie thought there was some hope of Dick coming back, it might stop him from cracking up. Charlie gathered up the cups and started washing them and even offered Adam a cup of tea, which he accepted gladly.

"You may be right," agreed Charlie. "We have to wait and see. Meanwhile I'll try my best to stick to the story."

Adam left soon afterwards. He felt Charlie had calmed down sufficiently not to be an immediate threat. Adam hoped Charlie's nerve would hold.

★ ★ ★

After leaving Charlie, Adam made his way to see Rachael. He had mixed feelings about going there. It was beginning to get too risky. Who knew what the police were up to? They could well be watching the house, but Adam decided it was early days yet and Dick had only been missing for a week. They would not be taking things too seriously if they had not gone and blown up Dick's car. But now they had to look like they were doing something and Adam and Charlie were in the frame, especially Adam. But, the police probably wanted to soften up Charlie as the easier target.

Adam parked his car around the corner and decided to walk, looking around with purpose and apprehension to see if he could spot any parked cars with occupants in them, watching the house. But he could see none, and decided he was getting a bit paranoid. So after a few further furtive glances, he was at the house. Adam rang the bell, hoping there were no neighbours watching him.

Rachael opened the door with a big smile. She was dressed casually in a sleeveless top and tracksuit bottoms, and was a bit sweaty, as if she had been working out.

"I have been doing a bit of packing," she said after a while when Adam had settled into the sofa. Adam asked if she was going somewhere. As a matter of fact, she was off on holiday. "I am off for a week to Spain tomorrow – got a special offer on the internet. I had already taken a week off work as my mother was supposed to come, so it seemed a shame to waste it. If Dick can go off by himself, so can I."

Adam was a bit stunned by her sudden decision, but he did not mind. At least he would get her out of his hair for a while, so he could concentrate on things at hand.

"It's not a bad idea," said Adam.

"I was hoping you could come with me. I think there are places still available."

Adam was sorely tempted, but decided to decline. He was mad to even think about it, he thought on reflection. What would the police make of it, not forgetting all the work he had to get on with as well?

"I have got too many things to do next week," he said. "Anyway, it's not a very good idea with the police breathing down my neck. I am taking a bit of a chance just to come here."

"What a ridiculous idea," retorted Rachael. "Surely they don't still think that you had something to do with Dick's disappearance?"

It seemed to Adam that Rachael, in whose mind was firmly entrenched the idea that Dick had run away with another woman, could not even contemplate the thought that somebody as innocuous as Adam could have anything to do with Dick's disappearance.

"Still, I have a lot to do at the house. I need to get it finished soon, so I can get back to work," Adam insisted.

"I thought you had a large stash of cash from the sale of your last house."

"Well, I haven't managed to sell the last one yet, and money's running out fast until I can refinance."

"It's a shame." Rachael smiled as she slipped her top off, revealing her delightful breasts. "We'd better make the most of tonight. You won't be getting any until I get back. Knowing your luck, Dick will probably be back by then!"

There was probably not much chance of any alternative fun, thought Adam to himself, and knowing his luck and the way Vera was behaving, Rachael was probably right.

Two intensive but delightful hours later, Adam fell back, exhausted. He felt he could get quite used to the lovemaking but was too tired to go back home. He decided to stay for the night, against his better judgement and much to Rachael's delight, who left him to get on with organising the evening meal while she got on with the packing.

In the event Adam decided he was too tired even to organise a meal, and he ordered a takeaway pizza and settled down to watch some television. As he was watching the local news a strange item caught his attention. It was a report on the weather around Ironbridge Spa. The weather predictions had gone completely haywire. There had been large amounts of sudden rain not predicted in the forecasts, taking everybody by surprise, especially the forecasters, and there had been a lot of complaints about the wrong forecasts being given out, especially from the farmers, and apparently there was going to be an inquiry.

Adam chuckled, knowing that it would be a complete waste of time, for he knew what had caused the rains. He always marvelled at the arrogance of the weather oracles. Obviously they thought their predictions could not be wrong, as if forecasting weather was an exact science, or at least that was what they would have people believe. It was one of those peculiarities of human nature, which led people to accept something as fact if it was repeated often enough to be so.

After a further exhausting session the following morning, Adam dropped Rachael off at Stansted airport en route to his house. The bargain deal she had got inevitably meant that the flight was at some ungodly hour in the morning. This of course meant that she had needed somebody to take her to the airport. She also gave Adam a spare set of keys and made him promise to look in at the house while she was away enjoying herself in sunny Spain.

"Don't forget to water the plants," she said as she departed towards passport control. "Oh, and one other thing: I am back next Sunday evening about five o'clock. Can you pick me up?"

"I will see what I can do," replied Adam, getting the feeling of being used, just a little bit.

"Well, if it's not too much hassle for you," she said tartly. "It's not as if you get up to much on Sundays."

It was on Adam's lips to ask how she would know that, but he did not see any point in saying anything, and with that she was gone.

She will be lucky if she sees me on Sunday, thought Adam, but she was of course right, for he never had much to do on Sundays.

It was uncanny how women latched on to such things. It was abundantly clear to Adam that in Rachael's eyes he was just a bit of fun, to be used for her amusement while it suited her. But why should he complain too much? It was not as if he had too many other offers.

He had always thought that his past lack of success with women was because they did not understand him. They failed to recognise the complexities of his life that he had to deal with, and the fact that it was only his tenacious, determined efforts that had hauled him out of the relative poverty of a hand-to-mouth existence to become a man of substance: a man with three properties, though still without much cash in the bank. But it was obviously not enough, and Adam did not know what was required of him to be thought more successful.

People just thought of him as somebody who had, because of good fortune, managed to wangle his way to owning a few properties, but that did not mean he was successful or well-off.

His image was that of a man who had clearly failed to have a successful career. They could not see the potential of the new house like he could. They did not know that he owned the flat outright now, or about his other house. In essence, his success was not visible.

Things just confirmed Adam's earlier conclusion that it had all to do with the image a man projected. Dick was perceived to be successful. He was tall, good-looking and had a good-looking wife. He had a big house in a good area, which meant that he earned lots of money, which meant he had a successful career.

Adam drove along, feeling a bit listless. He needed a change of image badly if he was going to feel successful. But how was he going to achieve it? Obviously he needed to change his car, but that was not enough. Though most successful people had good cars, any Tom, Dick or Harry could have a fairly good car as long as they did not mind the extortionate interest rates charged for a car loan.

No, he definitely needed something more to change his image. Then it hit him suddenly. He needed to change from being a teacher of English in a foreign language school to being the owner of one, or at least a partner in it, but he was rather strapped for cash. Vera was offering him a chance to become successful in people's eyes, and cash or no cash, he definitely had to go and see her at the school to discuss the matter with her. He would string her along until he could refinance and raise the cash, once he finished the house. He hoped she would be alone for their discussion, at least the initial one.

However, as he drove towards home a deep sense of foreboding filled him. How much money would it cost to buy into the business? Money was very tight at present. Could he trust Vera and her husband? Why were they willing to sell a share of the business if it was so successful? Adam would have to look at things very carefully. Was a successful image worth the price he would be required to pay?

He was a bit worried, however, in the way he had left things with Vera the day before. Oddly, it seemed like it was a long time ago and not just a few hours before, because so much had happened since then.

In fact, so much had happened in the last week. Most of it was beyond belief. In truth it had been like a dream, or a nightmare, and Adam could not quite decide which yet. He decided to pinch himself to make sure he was awake, and then decided against it; anyway, it was quite irrational to think that he could not pinch himself inside a dream.

In a bizarre way, life had actually become quite exciting for a change, compared to the humdrum existence he had led in the last few years. He was really sorry about what had happened to Dick, but he now decided he personally was not to blame for what had transpired. What had taken place was absolutely not his fault. In fact, it could be compared to a freak accident of nature, and it was most definitely not his fault that he had been burgled and the book had been stolen. There was absolutely nothing he could do about that.

Adam felt there was very little he could do to recover the book. Now that Rachael had departed on holiday, it gave him a chance to sort his own life out and he was going to take it. He felt somewhat selfish about the whole thing, but he could not afford to let things slide by having a breakdown about Dick. Now, he definitely needed a distraction, and that was going to be his change of image.

Adam felt a great weight lift from his shoulders as he came to a clear conclusion that it was not his fault. It was just one of those things and he had to get on with life and become successful at last.

He dropped the hired car back at the place of hire and collected his Skoda. Yes, he was going to change his car soon, but he was strangely fond of his little Skoda. Maybe he could just buy another car and keep the old one for his work, he thought. He needed a runabout to fetch things for his house until the work was finished.

CHAPTER 11

Daley was waiting for him at the door when he reached his house. The roofer had a big smile on his face, as if there was an amusing joke going on at Adam's expense. He reminded Adam of a shark which just had a good meal. Daley asked if Adam had found the book he had been looking for, which sounded strange, as if he knew something about it.

"No, I didn't," replied Adam.

"Did you lose it when you got burgled?" asked Daley.

"Yes, but how do you know that?" asked Adam.

"I don't," snapped Daley. "I'm just trying to put two and two together. Surely you don't think I had something to do with it?" He was suddenly on the defensive.

"Your scaffolding didn't help," said Adam.

"That's it, blame it on me," said Daley. "Let me just finish this ceiling off and I'll get out of your hair."

Irritated, Adam opened the door and let the man in.

"Was the book very valuable?" Daley enquired again.

"I don't think so." Adam tried to sound nonchalant. "A few quid, maybe. Not more than £20, I shouldn't think."

"Oh," said Daley, sounding disappointed.

"I've got somebody coming to put in a burglar alarm this week." Adam decided to let Daley know even though nothing had yet been arranged. He was suddenly getting very suspicious of Daley.

"There's hardly anything worthwhile here to bother with an alarm," quipped Daly.

"I'm putting a system in before I get anything expensive." Adam smiled.

"Right you are," said Daley, "especially if you are away a lot of nights."

It was a fact that had obviously not escaped Daley's notice. Adam did not reply. He left Daley to get on with the ceiling and retreated to the lounge to ring his mother. Adam was always apprehensive about ringing his mother whenever she left an urgent message. Last time there was an urgent message he had to fork out £6,000 to help her repair her flat. It had been a very expensive phone call. Adam did not mind too much, although he was sure she had a lot of money stashed away, but preferred to spend his money. Previously, he had even helped her buy the flat she lived in, when the landlord had offered it up for sale. His mother answered the phone.

"You left an urgent message, what was it about?" he asked.

"Somebody's been trying to get in touch with you. Guess who?" She laughed.

Adam was not in the mood for all this intrigue, and was impatient to know who it was. Off the top of his head he could not think who it could possibly be.

"Who is it?" he asked, irritated. "Everybody knows where I live."

"It doesn't look like it," his mother carried on. She was enjoying his discomfort.

"Come on, tell me."

"It's Linda. She was here to see me. Because you've moved house and left your job she can't get in touch with you."

"What does she want?" Adam asked his mother. Alarm bells suddenly started going off in his head.

"She wants to see you, she asked me for your number."

"You didn't give it to her, did you?"

"Yes, of course. Why not? She's such a nice girl. I don't know why you never married her," his mother carried on.

"She left me for an older man, Mother." Adam was livid.

"She probably had her reasons."

"I can understand her going after somebody younger, but an older man… He's in his fifties."

"That was probably your fault. You can never make up your mind about these things, can you? Anyway, you may be lucky; she probably wants to come back to you."

"I don't want her back," Adam replied angrily, and asked his mother if there was anything else. He put the phone down when she told him there was nothing more.

So now he was expecting a phone call from his ex-girlfriend. He was not sure what to make of it. Maybe she had had enough of this old bloke and was ready to come back to him. Well, she was in for a surprise. His hands were pretty full at the moment.

Adam decided to concentrate on matters in hand. After telephoning the plumber and the electrical contractors he normally used, he rang a firm who put in alarms. He then decided to go and check up on Daley, who had been making a lot of noise putting up plasterboards on the ceiling which had fallen in.

Daley informed Adam that he would soon be finished, and so Adam should have his money ready and waiting for him. So Adam went off to fix himself some brunch and think about his next move.

He had been wondering about what Daley said earlier about the book, and his suspicions were growing. Daley seemed to show an undue interest in the book Adam had lost, especially as he had not even laid eyes on it – or had he after all? He could be behind the burglary, for all Adam knew. But most likely there was nothing to it, so Adam decided to let the matter drop.

Adam decided that he had to get himself another car before he went to see Vera again; he was desperate. He thought he would visit the English college the next day to get an idea of how the business was doing, if he was going to invest in it. He wanted to spend some time there before Vera's husband came back. At present, however, he did not have the money to spare to buy a new car, so he needed a good financing deal.

Adam looked through the car section of the local advertiser which had been delivered to his door, and which he had been using earlier to ring electricians and plumbers for further quotes, before deciding on the ones he knew.

Adam finished his sandwich in a leisurely fashion while flicking through the paper. All the cars advertised seemed pretty expensive to him, but they seemed to be doing some good offers in one local garage.

He was just about to ring up the garage when he heard several cars pull up in front of the house, and then there was a determined ring on his front doorbell.

A little perplexed, Adam made his way to the door. When he opened it there were four policemen standing outside, including Officer Stevens. One of the policemen was carrying a battering ram with which he was getting ready to batter his door down.

"Hang on a moment with that," said Adam. "I've just had this door put in. What's all this about?"

"I've got a warrant here to search the house," said Officer Stevens. "Are you going to let us in?"

"No problem, but can I see a warrant first? What is this all about, anyway?"

"Don't pretend as if you don't know," said Stevens.

"What is it about?" asked Adam deliberately.

"It is about your missing friend, sir. The neighbours think that you are practising some kind of black magic rituals here."

"You must be joking!" Adam feigned surprise.

"Now stand aside, sir," said one of the other officers.

"Sure, sure," said Adam. "Come in." He moved aside and let them in. "Where would you like to search?"

"Two of them will search down here," said Stevens. "Officer Jones and myself will go upstairs. It shouldn't take too long. Don't try to leave the house. There are a couple of officers, who will be searching your back garden."

"I'm not going anywhere," said Adam angrily, and followed Officer Stevens up the stairs. As they reached upstairs they came across Daley, who was trying to make his way downstairs, to see what the commotion was.

Stevens immediately recognised Daley, whose face registered a huge shock.

"What is he doing here?" asked Stevens, blocking Daley's way.

"He's been putting on a new roof for me," said Adam.

"That's right," agreed Daley.

"Doing some honest work for a change, then?" Stevens smiled. "You'd better hang around until we finish, we may want to check your van as well."

"Why's that, guv?" asked Daley. "I'm just doing a job here."

"We know all about your jobs, don't we?" Stevens sounded sarcastic. "You two might be in league with each other."

"What am I being accused of here?" asked Adam.

"Well, you are associating with a known felon," said Stevens.

"I don't know anything about him," protested Adam. "I'm just employing him."

"I haven't been in trouble for a long time now," Daley protested angrily as well.

"You mean we haven't caught you lately." Stevens smiled. "Once a villain, always a villain, in my book."

Adam looked at Daley, who averted his gaze and went back to his work. Adam followed Stevens into his bedroom.

"You should be more careful about who you employ," Stevens said once they were out of Daley's earshot. "No wonder you've had a burglary."

Adam asked him if he was going to search Daley's house.

Officer Stevens informed Adam that Daley wouldn't have anything there now, and anyway, Adam hadn't lost that much.

Adam was about to say how valuable the book was, but stopped himself in time. He watched quietly as Stevens looked through his belongings in a methodical fashion. He finished in about twenty minutes without finding anything except Adam's building society savings book. Stevens commented that there was a fair bit in there.

Adam said it was all accounted for, and asked him what exactly he was looking for. A little bit of irritation was creeping into Adam's voice.

"We are looking for anything belonging to your friend that he may have left behind."

"Surely you don't think I had anything to do with his disappearance?"

"So he has disappeared, has he?"

"You tell me. So his wife says."

"According to your neighbour, she was over here to visit you. Are you having an affair with her?"

"Of course not." Adam denied it, and tried to sound convincing. "Aren't you supposed to read me my rights first?"

"You've been watching too many movies, sir." Stevens laughed. "When we want to arrest you or question you properly, we'll do it down at the station."

The other officers had all finished by this time and had not found anything suspicious, so they were ready to leave.

"We'll be back again tomorrow. You will be here, won't you?" said Stevens as he was about to leave.

Adam nodded. "What for?"

"To dig up your concrete patio," Stevens said with a little smirk. "A contractor is coming down with a digger."

"What's that for? I only just had it put in."

"Exactly. We want to check what is buried underneath."

"You're joking," said Adam.

"No, sir, we are deadly serious." With that, they all left. It was just as well that Adam had dumped Dick's car keys when he had. He could just imagine what they would think if they had found those in his possession.

"Bastards," said Daley. "Always sticking their nose into other people's business." He didn't seem overly fond of the police. He had just finished, and was watching the police leave. After inspecting the ceiling, which seemed to be a job well done, Adam paid Daley off.

"You don't think I've nicked your book, do you?" asked Daley before leaving.

"I don't know."

"I'm going straight, haven't been in trouble for over two years. He had no cause to tell you anything about me."

"He didn't," Adam answered. "But is there anything I should know?"

"No, no." Daley looked relieved. He left without further fuss.

The police had left without searching Daley's van, probably because they had not found anything at Adam's house. But something was beginning to bug Adam. It was Daley's attitude, but how could he follow up his suspicions? Daley would recognise Adam immediately if he ever saw him snooping around, but Adam had no choice; he needed to find out if Daley was involved.

At this stage Adam had already given up hope of ever finding Dick again. He had always been a practical man and could not afford to have remorse pull him down. He needed to get on with life as normally as possible so as not to arouse the suspicions of the police, but maybe there was a slim chance of recovering the book if Daley was indeed involved.

Before going to see the cars Adam rang his solicitor to make an appointment regarding the problem with the police about Dick's disappearance. He wanted to get some advice about the matter. After twenty minutes he eventually got through to them, and whilst on the subject he asked them if they could recommend a good private investigator. He was going to find out more about John Daley.

Next Adam concentrated on the matters in hand. It was already late in the afternoon and if he wanted to see a new car, he had to get a move on. However, he found he was not in the mood to do much about his image change. He decided the car could wait a bit, and that he would ring the college instead.

Vera's husband would be away for another week, she had informed him, and he wanted Adam back at work, if he wanted to. Rachael was also away for a week, so this was the perfect opportunity to do a bit of work on Vera, except that the police were coming back the next day to dig up his patio.

When he got through to Vera, she sounded a bit cool. There was no encouragement in her voice, as there had been previously. Adam wondered what could be the matter with her. Was the thought of Rachael still bothering her?

"I thought I would give you call, as you said. I could come back to work for you."

"That's right," she said unenthusiastically. "You can discuss it with my husband. He is coming back tomorrow."

"I thought he was away for another week," said a surprised Adam.

"So did I," Vera snapped. "But he is coming back on Wednesday."

"Well, I can't make it this week as I have a few things to sort out, but maybe I can come and see him next week."

"Suit yourself," she said. There was absolutely no chance any letter with an offer of employment was coming his way at present.

"I suppose there is no chance of seeing you tonight?" Adam asked, and regretted the question straight away. He had to be more positive in his approach, and not ask a question when he could put forward a suggestion instead. But it was too late. Vera said she had lots to do in the house before her husband came back, and that was that.

In his frustration Adam decided to ring the detective agency next. The name Ramsbottom & Ramsbottom did not inspire confidence in him, but the agency came highly recommended from the solicitors.

"I am sorry, Mr Ramsbottom is out in the field," replied an incredibly put-on posh, middle-aged female voice. Adam was just going to ask if the man was a farmer in his spare time when the voice carried on. "He is on an enquiry and out on an investigation, and won't be in the office until tomorrow."

Adam left his name and number. It was going to be a frustrating day; he resigned himself and opened a can of beer. But he could not relax. He decided that he would find out where Daley lived, because he did not want to hang around in the house any longer.

He had Daley's address from the receipt he had received. Adam decided he would go there and have a look around. He was not sure what he could achieve, but he had to try something. The electrician and the plumber were coming the next day and he would be rather occupied until the end of the week, but at the moment he had time on his hands.

★ ★ ★

Daley lived on the other side of Ironbridge Spa in the direction of Cambridge, in a hamlet called Bottoms End, which proved to be as exciting as the name sounded. It was just a row of houses on either side of a stream which ran though the middle. It was the same stream which flowed past Adam's house, but it had grown much wider. At one point the stream could be forded and a car driven across to the other side, where there were a couple of pubs and several more houses. There was also a public pathway for a short but good country walk around the village.

Adam popped into one of the pubs for a quick pint and to gather his thoughts. It seemed to him that the pubs were doing a brisk business. As it turned out, Daley actually lived on the road side of the village and there was no need to get one's feet wet to get to his house.

For a second Adam was tempted to see if he could find any crayfish in the stream, but this was a long way from his house and the stream was quite wide by now. Even if he found some crayfish it would be impossible to tell if one was Dick, so he dismissed the thought as crazy.

After finishing his pint Adam drove past Daley's house, which was at the far end of the village boundary. There was only one other house after it, and then just fields and open land. There was a narrow road just past the houses, which seemed to go behind Daley's house.

Adam noticed Daley's truck was parked in front of his house, so he drove on without stopping as Daley was at home. He would make a detour down another road to avoid going past Daley's house again.

As he made his way back to Ironbridge Spa, he got quite lost on the little B roads with their high hedgerows and shady glens. While he was negotiating the narrow bends and some big potholes, a mad scheme began to germinate in Adam's brain.

He first tried to dismiss it as a flight of fancy, but the idea had got hold of him fast and would not go away. After narrowly avoiding hitting a car coming the other way while he was grappling with the idea, he decided to stop and consider the merits of it.

The solution was to break into Daley's house and see if the book was there, and if so, steal it back. It was a mad but simple idea. Adam was desperate to get the book back, and desperate people needed desperate measures.

He tried to dismiss the other implications of such an action. What if he got caught, or if he had got it wrong and Daley was not the man after all? But one thing he was sure of was that he had to try, even if there was only a remote chance it was Daley who stole the book.

However, after a further few minutes of contemplation Adam decided that a break-in was too risky an idea to entertain, as the book might not even be there. Instead he would let things take their course and wait and see what the private investigator could dig up.

He drove into Ironbridge Spa and decided to go to a garage and test-drive a Mercedes. They seemed to be doing very good deals on slightly used demonstration cars. His next car, he decided, would be a sporty Merc or a BMW. He needed to make a statement, and this would be the first part of that new image.

The car of course drove like a dream, and at a mere £35,000 it was a snip, but it was a little out of his reach at present. So, still feeling a bit unfulfilled, Adam called it a day and drove home.

It had been that sort of a day; one of pent-up frustrations, when nothing had actually been resolved. Everything hung in the air, and it did not matter how much Adam wriggled, he was held fast in sticky glue, which was a slice of his life in which events were bent on taking their own course no matter how hard he tried to influence their outcome.

When he got back to Littledon, Adam thought he would go for a drink at The Three Witches and get plastered. Although he was probably too cautious a person to let himself go totally, he needed a good drink to feel more relaxed.

★ ★ ★

When he got to the pub it was still quite early and it was still daylight outside, so Adam bought a pint of beer and took a seat in the garden. It was late April and the weather had turned fairly warm in the last couple of days, so it felt quite pleasant.

As Adam sat quietly supping his beer, several people turned up and took up the rest of the tables near him, of which there were four. As the beer garden was situated on the side of the pub and not in the large garden at its rear, it was fairly small. Because of the close proximity of the tables Adam could hear the conversations that were going on around him. One of them happened to include a large, well-dressed Australian man who was saying that his grandfather had been an inhabitant of the village and he had come to find out where he lived, as he happened to be in England on holiday.

Adam's ears pricked up when the man said that a house had recently been sold in the village and his mother had received an amount of money in Australia as the sole surviving heir to the estate. The Australian was sitting with another man who Adam identified as a resident of the village. Though Adam did not actually know him, he had seen him around in the pub a few times. The man nodded to him as he looked his way.

Adam nodded his head in acknowledgement, and then the man said to the Australian, "I think this is the gentleman you are looking for. He recently purchased the house your grandfather lived in, I believe."

The Australian looked at him suspiciously and then broke into a wide grin. Adam looked at him more seriously. The man was brawny; large but athletic. He seemed to have a jovial face, but there was something in his eyes, a kind of coldness, which hit Adam for a split second and faded. The man was wearing a large, expensive watch; he was obviously a man of substance.

"Hello, I'm Bruce." The man smiled

"Hello, I'm Adam," said Adam, stifling an urge to laugh at meeting an Australian called Bruce, as he had recently come across an old *Monty Python* sketch where all Australians were called Bruce.

"Is it true you purchased the house recently?" asked Bruce.

"That's right," replied Adam. "It was in a bit of a derelict state when I got it. What brings you here, then?"

"Just plain inquisitiveness," said Bruce. "My mother never even mentioned my grandfather until she received the money from the sale, probably because she is only related by marriage. I actually thought he had died a long time ago."

"I see."

"Would you mind if I came around sometime to have a look at it?" asked Bruce.

Adam regarded the request as strange but decided there was no harm in it, so he went along with it and agreed that Bruce could come round the next day. He soon regretted the decision when he remembered that the police were coming round to dig up his concrete patio. But by then it was too late, as Bruce had seized on the opportunity and had offered to buy Adam a drink, disappearing into the pub before Adam could refuse.

While he was waiting Jack and Wendy turned up and decided to take up seats on Adam's table without even so much as a by-your-leave. Adam decided it would be too rude and unneighbourly to tell them to go somewhere else, even though he did not really want them there at that moment. He was more interested in finding out who the Australian Bruce was.

Jack went off to get drinks for Wendy and himself. He actually offered to buy Adam a drink for a change, but Adam had to refuse as he was already getting one from Bruce, and didn't want to look greedy.

"What were the police doing at your place today?" asked Wendy when Jack had left.

"Routine enquiry," Adam replied.

"They had an awful lot of police cars there for a routine enquiry," remarked Wendy.

Just at that moment Bruce came back with the drinks and happened to hear what Wendy was saying. His ears pricked up.

"You had police round your place today?" he asked, as if it was his business somehow.

"What is this, an interrogation?" Adam was piqued. "So they were round and they may be coming back tomorrow. It's none of your business."

"Sorry, mate," said Bruce. "As you say, it isn't really my business."

"Ever since his friend disappeared from the house the police have been coming round," Wendy piped up.

"You had a friend disappear from the house?" Bruce's ears pricked up again.

"He did not disappear from the house," Adam said vehemently. "Stop spreading false rumours."

"We didn't see him leave," Wendy insisted.

"That's right," said Jack, who was back with the drinks by this time.

"Alright, I give up," said Adam. "I murdered him and hid his body underneath the concrete patio. The police are coming round tomorrow to dig it up, so why don't you all come round and see for yourselves?"

A hush fell over the table, and they all looked at each other. They did not know what to say next. Were they really sitting there and having a drink with a murderer, or was Adam pulling their legs?

"According to rumour three other people disappeared from that house before. All girls. They say they were witches," said the man who had been drinking with Bruce, who had been sitting there quietly up to now, eavesdropping on their conversation. "In fact," he continued, "this pub is named after them: The Three Witches." The man seemed to have a habit of repeating certain words to emphasise what he was saying.

"My grandmother told me a story like that," said Bruce.

"If I think rightly, it was in fact during the time she was here, and they were her cousins."

"They did accuse my grandfather of doing away with them to get hold of the property, but there was never any proof of that," said Bruce.

"As there is no proof of Adam's friend disappearing from the house," said Jack, much to Adam's annoyance.

"He did not disappear from the house. He left to go somewhere," Adam insisted again.

"So was it his car at the station car park in Ironbridge Spa that had to be blown up when the Queen was supposed to be visiting?" asked Jack with a wink.

"How should I know, what makes you think it was his car?" said Adam. "His wife thinks he has run away with some other girl."

"The police mentioned it. They asked if we'd seen the car before, here." Jack's face lit up in a knowing grin.

"That's another thing," said Wendy. "What was his wife doing down here and all?"

"She came to look for him," said Adam. "Listen, I've had enough of this, I'm leaving." Adam finished his pint and got up. "Can't a man have a quiet drink anymore?"

"Oh, don't take it so badly, mate," said Bruce. "They accused my grandfather of all sorts of things. They made his life hell for a while. My grandmother even left him and went off to Australia to get away from the village. But he survived, didn't he? In fact, all this time."

Adam sat down again. He wanted to find out more about Bruce's grandfather; he was intrigued.

"I actually called the police in the first place to report a burglary." Adam tried to appease them.

"Did you get much stolen?" asked Bruce.

"No, just some personal items, nothing of much value," said Adam.

"He had a valuable book stolen," said Jack.

"Who told you that?" asked Adam.

"Daley, who else?" replied Jack. "He said you accused him of stealing it."

"No, I didn't," said Adam.

"Did you find the book in the house?" asked Bruce.

Now that was a very interesting question, thought Adam.

"There was no book. I lost some other stuff, but not any books." Adam felt determined to deter Bruce.

With that Adam decided it was definitely time to leave. He got up, and while Bruce gave him a strange look, he said goodbye and made his way home. When he got back the phone was ringing. It was Ramsbottom, who said he could come round next morning, which was Tuesday, to see him.

CHAPTER 12

The next morning Adam woke up with a jolt. It was nine thirty and there was someone knocking at the front door. For a moment he thought it was the police, and he jumped up and ran downstairs in fear that they would break his door down.

However, he realised when he was downstairs that he had an appointment with the private investigator Mr Ramsbottom at nine thirty, and obviously the man was a stickler for timekeeping. Adam had not had a very good night, as he had been thinking about Bruce the Aussie and this had kept him awake. There had been something odd about him and his interest in the book, but nothing Adam could put his finger on.

He let Ramsbottom in and apologised for his appearance. The man was a middle-aged gentleman, probably in his fifties, dressed in a pinstripe suit, and was wearing a bowler hat for some reason. He was built fairly stockily, with a good head of hair, which was greying. He looked like somebody who regularly worked out in the gym, and had been in some tight situations. Adam invited him into the lounge and went upstairs to get a dressing gown. When he returned, Mr Ramsbottom was sitting patiently in an armchair, looking relaxed. Adam offered him a cup of tea, which he declined politely. He was in a hurry, so if Adam would get straight to the point.

When Adam had finished telling him all about the burglary, Ramsbottom looked up.

"So let me get this straight. You have had a burglary and have lost a valuable book, which you wish to recover." He seemed good at stating the obvious.

"Yes," replied Adam.

"Well, normally I'd say that you haven't got a dog's chance in a Korean restaurant, but in this case as you actually suspect somebody, we can give it a try."

"Good," said Adam. "How much will it cost?"

"£100 per day, plus an extra £500 if we recover the book."

"That seems quite expensive," said Adam hopefully.

"Nonsense," said Ramsbottom. "Solicitors charge more than that per hour and sometimes they do nothing for you."

"I suppose so," agreed Adam reluctantly. He did not particularly like solicitors much, following his transactions with them whilst buying and selling property.

"It's agreed, then?" Ramsbottom asked.

"Okay," replied Adam.

"I myself or an associate will spend five days on the case at first, and if we don't turn up anything interesting we will call it a day. I will, however, need £200 in advance. The rest can be paid later."

"What will you do?"

"First we will follow him around to see what he gets up to. We will try to get an idea if he is our man."

"I'm telling you, he is."

"We'll see," said Ramsbottom sanguinely. "First I require the money and his details."

"I'll get them now, give me a minute."

Soon after that Ramsbottom left, with Daley's details and Adam's money. He did not seem very hopeful, and Adam had a sinking feeling that he was going to part with £500 without too much return. However, it had to be done.

A bit later as he was getting out of the shower, the doorbell rang again. This time it was the plumber. Adam led him upstairs to where the new bathroom was to be installed to have a look around and went to change.

Half an hour later the man gave him an estimate, which would have horrified Adam when he had first started out, but he was prepared for it this time and told the man to start work as soon as he could. The plumber left, after promising to be back the next day to start work. The electrician was due in the afternoon about one, and some time soon after, the man who was going to fit the alarm. Adam wanted them all there and working at the same time so he could get it all completed as soon as possible. He was a man in a hurry.

It was all happening today, though Adam was not quite sure if the police were actually going to turn up to dig up the patio. Adam decided he would make lunch as he had already missed breakfast.

★ ★ ★

As he was sitting down to eat his meal, Adam heard a lot of commotion outside and then there was a loud knock on his door. For a moment Adam thought it was the electrician, but it was the police. They had turned up with a JCB.

"You're not serious," said Adam when he was confronted by Officer Stevens.

"I'm afraid we are," said the policeman. "We will have to knock down your gate to the back garden to get through."

"Can you take out part of the fence instead? It will be easier to replace." Adam tried to maintain his *sangfroid*, even though he knew they were on a fool's errand. "Who's going to pay for the repairs when you don't find anything?" he asked.

"We will if we don't find anything under the concrete, that's for sure," retorted Officer Stevens.

The crew the police had brought along soon got down to the

job. Half the village, who had somehow heard about it, turned up to witness what was going on.

After dismantling part of Adam's fence, none too gently, the police started to break up the concrete. Soon big chunks of it were lying around the garden, as the police dug deeper and deeper.

After about four hours they finally gave up. Nothing had been found except Adam's discarded shoes imbedded in some concrete.

Adam insisted that they clear up the concrete blocks and take them out to the road, and he took several photographs and a video of the whole operation. The police also mended the fence after them, though not to Adam's satisfaction.

Adam smiled at Officer Stevens as they left. The officer looked grim.

"You'll be hearing from my solicitor soon," said Adam, probably a bit too smugly. "It's going to cost you a pretty packet in compensation."

"You will be hearing from us again soon too, sir," said the officer grimly. He did not seem to like Adam's tone. "We haven't finished this inquiry yet."

However, surprisingly, the villagers took Adam's side in the matter and started booing the police, who soon left. Maybe Adam was going to make some friends in the village after all.

"You weren't kidding then, when you said they were coming to dig up the concrete," said Jack, who was observing things all this time at a distance, along with Bruce the Australian and his friend, who had also turned up to the scene.

Adam decided to invite them in. This was as good a time as any to show Bruce the house and to find out a bit more about him.

"You're doing a lot of work here, mate," observed Bruce.

"Well, it needed it," said Adam. "The place was almost derelict."

"Don't forget: when you want to do the decorating, I'm your man," Jack butted in.

"Don't worry, I'll keep that in mind," said Adam, having no intention at all of giving Jack any decorating work.

As Adam was walking them around the house, he observed that Bruce was tapping the walls as he went along. When Adam looked at him questioningly, he laughed out loud.

"Just checking how safe the structure is," he claimed, trying to calm Adam's fears.

Adam knew that he was lying; he was looking for something else. It was as if he was checking for a secret passage or hidden compartment in the wall. *Curious*, thought Adam; how much did Bruce know that he was not letting on? What did he know about the book? was, without question, the uppermost thought in Adam's mind.

"I've heard reports that there has been a lot of peculiar weather here lately," Bruce put to Adam.

"Nothing unusual," Adam countered. "Weather is one thing which is very changeable in England."

"Maybe your friend disappeared after one of these storms, or during one," suggested Bruce.

"What do you mean?" asked Adam. "What has the weather got to do with my friend going missing?"

"Well, funny you should think that there is no connection," Bruce carried on, "but my grandmother told me that her three cousins disappeared after such a heavy downpour. It was a storm which appeared out of the blue on a sunny day and then disappeared as suddenly."

"Very strange indeed," Jack cut in. "Anyway, Bruce here was interested in the book you had. He thinks it belongs to his grandfather."

"I don't have any book," retorted Adam. "I certainly don't believe in all this nonsense he is going on about."

"Well, if you come across it," Bruce smiled, "I'd be willing to pay you handsomely for it."

"What does it look like?" Adam feigned innocence.

"I don't really know," Bruce admitted unhappily. "All I know is that it is written in German. My forefathers came from Germany."

"I'll watch out for it." Adam nodded. "I'll let you know if I find such a book." It was an odd coincidence, but his own forefathers were also from Germany, a fact he decided not to mention.

"You will be well rewarded," said Bruce.

"It sounds like a very expensive book," said Adam. "How much is it worth?"

"Well, let's say I can pay you a couple of thousand pounds for it."

"Phew," Jack whistled, "I'll have to tell Daley about it."

"What for?" asked Adam, irritated. He didn't want Daley to find out more about the book.

"He has a nose for these things," said Jack. "If we come across the book we can share the reward."

"Hope you find it," said Adam, trying his best to put Jack off. "But it sounds like a wild goose chase to me."

"Maybe you are right," Bruce agreed, "but be that as it may, there is no harm in keeping an eye open for it."

With that Bruce and Jack left the house, much to Adam's relief, though in his heart of hearts Adam knew Bruce was giving him the message that he did not quite believe Adam's disclaimers about the book. One thing was very clear to Adam: time was running out. If Adam was ever to regain the book he would have to get a move on, before Bruce got hold of it.

Good thing Bruce had failed to notice the cellar, which was probably what he was looking for when he was tapping the walls. Due to some misgivings and insecurity Adam had decided earlier to hide the new cellar door behind a dresser cupboard, which was attached to the door and covered it completely. The cupboard had wheels underneath, so it could be moved fairly easily to open the door and give access to the cellar. It was his secret room in the house, even though it felt like shutting the gate after the proverbial horse had bolted.

From what Jack had said, it was obvious to Adam that Daley was probably the key here. But what could Adam do? He had to wait for Ramsbottom to turn up something. He was sure that Daley must have the book, but he either had not met Bruce or was waiting for the right moment to sell him the book.

The next day Adam decided he would go up to London to the school and meet Vera, and probably her husband as well. Even though he had said he would be there the following week, Adam wanted to keep himself occupied. But before that he had to let the plumber and the electrician in to start work. He could trust them to be left on their own, as he had already worked with them.

It was difficult for Adam to concentrate. On the one hand the work on the house had to carry on and Adam had to get it finished as soon as he could. On the other hand he had to look for the book and find it if there was to be any chance of bringing Dick back. He was beginning to suffer a pang of conscience about the whole thing and choosing his own material interest over the wellbeing of his friend, especially when he thought of his little affair with Rachael.

Strange how things affected people, but it was much stranger how things did not actually affect them. Adam was horrified suddenly at how blasé he had become about the whole matter of Dick's disappearance. It was almost as if he was enjoying it in some strange, sadistic way.

He had to snap out of it and make an effort to find the book. Though he had to believe that it was not all his fault, he was still to blame partially for what had transpired. He should have not used the spell on Dick, even though he had asked for it.

Adam also did not want to believe that he was to blame for his affair with Dick's wife. But it was not easy to dismiss the thing as Rachael's fault because she had pursued him. He was still guilty, and he had to do something about it. He had to get Dick back before it was too late, but the details of the process escaped him.

★ ★ ★

Adam was still thinking of these things as he made his way to London the next day after letting the plumber in and getting him going on the work to be done. Without any major hitches the main work in the house would be finished soon, and Adam would have a lot of time on his hands.

He made it to London by lunchtime. Adam parked his car and decided to ring the college first and ask for Vera. He wanted to find out what lay ahead, and whether Mr Cruz, the husband, was back. He was informed by the receptionist, Lucy, that Vera was out to lunch and she had not seen Mr Cruz that day. Lucy asked Adam if he was going to come back and work at the college again. Adam decided to play it in a non-committal manner and said he was thinking about it, especially as he was missing her.

This made Lucy laugh. She had always liked flirting with Adam, along with everybody else who obliged. After the usual banter, she informed him that Vera might be at the pub with the new EFL teacher. She had just interviewed him and was thinking of employing him instead of Adam. Recently the student numbers had picked up again slightly, for they had been down after Adam had been dismissed in March. He thanked her for that information and decided to go down to the pub himself for a drink.

He knew the pub they would be in. It was The King's Head, the only pub near the college. However, when he got to the pub they were nowhere to be seen. He decided to order a drink anyway and settled down to enjoy it. Adam was a bit perplexed about the situation. He wondered where Vera had disappeared to with the new teacher. He decided that he would have to go to the college and wait for her, to find out what was going on.

After finishing his drink, Adam decided to walk back to the college at a leisurely pace. As he neared the college he saw a car pull up in front of him. He could see it was some sort of a flashy sports coupé. Before Vera got out the man grabbed her and gave her a big smacker full on the lips, which obviously caught Adam by surprise.

As Vera got out of the car, she noticed Adam was looking at her and mild shock registered on her face, but she managed to hide the expression quickly. She gave Adam a little smile as the car pulled away.

"That was my cousin," she said, but Adam knew she was lying.

"Lucy said you were interviewing him for a job." He smiled.

"That's true," she lied confidently. "He is not working at this moment. We were going to take him on temporarily, but only if you were not coming back, of course."

"He seemed to be awfully friendly," suggested Adam.

"He has not seen me for a long time." She edged closer and kissed Adam on the cheeks. "You're not jealous, are you?"

"Of course not, if you say he was your cousin. But he seemed awfully friendly."

"He is a bit like that, I'm afraid." Vera tried to gloss over the fact.

"There's nothing between you two, then?" Adam was not quite sure, so he grabbed Vera around the waist as there was nobody in the lobby on the ground floor of the building and gave her a big kiss. She didn't offer any resistance. But as Adam's hand moved up to her breast, she stopped him.

"Not here, please," said Vera. "Somebody might see."

"Where then?" asked Adam without letting go. "You didn't seem to mind your cousin."

"Come up to the office, let's talk," said Vera, trying to push his hands away.

Adam let go and followed her up to her office, past Lucy, who winked at him behind Vera's back. Adam grabbed Vera again after she closed the door of the office, and she gave in after a token struggle; in fact she was quite eager to kiss him. Adam's hand was wandering, and Vera didn't resist as he slid it under her skirt. However, when he started pulling her knickers down, she stopped him.

"Don't do that, somebody might come in." Vera resisted him. Adam gave up; he knew it was futile. He had a disappointed look on his face.

"Please, Adam." Vera smiled. "I don't want to disappoint you, so let me do something quickly for you to ease your pain." She grabbed the front of his trousers and pushed him back on the desk. As Adam let go of her she quickly unzipped his trousers and groped inside. Soon he was in ecstasy. However, about five or so minutes later as Adam was nearing the end of his resistance, the phone rang. Vera ignored the phone and carried on. A minute later the ringing stopped and Lucy opened the door on them.

"It's Mr Cruz…" she began, and then gasped at the situation. Vera had her back to Lucy, but Adam was facing her. A big smile began to form on her face.

"She can't talk at the moment," said Adam, trying to think of something more appropriate to say. He had his hand on Vera's head, but she didn't pull away.

"I can see that," said Lucy. "Leave it to me." With that she moved back out of the room, and before Vera could move her head back Adam let out a sigh of intense gratification.

Vera suddenly remembered Lucy and asked, "Did she see us?" She had pretended not to be aware of Lucy's presence, even though she must have heard her.

Adam nodded.

"You better have a word with her," said Vera.

"Why me?" asked Adam.

"Well, she could tell my husband," Vera retorted. "You are the one who caused the problem by insisting on things."

"Is he back?"

"Not yet," said Vera. "Maybe tomorrow, that's why he was ringing, probably."

"Give Lucy the afternoon off. I'll take her out for a drink and talk to her," suggested Adam.

"We need a new teacher after next week," said Vera. "Are you coming back to work?"

"We'll discuss that tonight at your house when I see you," said Adam.

"But I was going to go out tonight," protested Vera. She was blowing hot and cold again.

"Well, in the light of the situation, you should change your mind. I'll see you around seven," Adam insisted, trying to seize his opportunity.

"Alright," said Vera, giving in. "But you definitely must start in two weeks' time, mornings only."

Adam knew from before that she did not relish the thought of interviewing people. She had often roped Adam in to interview new teachers in the past.

"What about your cousin?" Adam asked.

"Oh! He can start as well, we have lots of students enrolling again," replied Vera.

I guessed as much, Adam thought to himself, but did not say anything aloud. He was going to have a good time that night, he thought. It was nothing less than he deserved, after all the hard work he had put in over the last few days.

"Don't forget to send me the offer of employment letter," said Adam as he left the room.

Outside, Lucy was sitting there with a big grin on her face.

"I think she said you can have the afternoon off," said Adam. "Come on, I'll buy you a drink."

There was another motive to Adam's making such an offer. He wanted to pump Lucy for information about the college. Before he parted with any money for a share of the college he wanted to find out all he could about what had happened during the time he had been away.

Lucy smiled and followed Adam, much to his surprise. He had been expecting her to refuse his offer point-blank, as she had done many times previously. His street-cred had shot up exponentially. When they were outside, Lucy asked him whether he had had a good time. Adam tried to make a joke of it and replied that he had no idea what had got into Mrs Cruz, and that he was as surprised as Lucy.

"Obviously she remembers you from the last college party," said Lucy, laughing.

"Maybe," said Adam. "Tell me, how has the school been doing lately?"

"It's picked up a bit in the new term. To tell you the truth, recently we were all a bit worried about losing our jobs."

"I didn't realise that, thanks for telling me," said Adam, suddenly realising that maybe it had all been an act by Vera and Mr Cruz to get rid of him, because of falling student numbers. He wondered then what she was up to now.

"Were you thinking of coming back, then?"

"Well actually, they are offering to sell me shares in the business."

"So obviously Vera was offering you some extra inducement back there in the office."

"Stop it," said Adam. "But you could be right."

"So you might end up as our new boss?" asked Lucy.

"It's just a thought," said Adam. "She's asked me to come back and teach in two weeks' time."

"Well, things have picked up a bit again," said Lucy as they entered the pub. Adam offered Lucy a drink and bought her some lunch, and pumped her for more information about the college.

"I think you will find Mr Cruz is setting up an English school in Malta," said Lucy. "That's where he comes from originally."

"Ouch, wrong again," said Adam. "I seem to have got everything wrong."

"Don't worry, just be careful with your money," said Lucy. "If there's anything I can do to help let me know."

Adam exchanged telephone numbers with Lucy while they finished their lunch. The pub was quite full and they kept getting interrupted by people saying hello to Lucy, and even one or two to Adam. They were people who had been his students when he was there last, and other teachers who had popped in for a drink after finishing work.

Adam felt quite encouraged that people had actually recognised him and wanted to talk to him, though it was mostly Lucy they wanted to see. He came away with a feeling that he should cultivate his friendship with Lucy more, especially as she was quite friendly. It seemed that instead of suffering for the incident in the office, his street cred had actually gone up in Lucy's eyes. It seemed strange to him that women always fancied him more when he was with another woman. It seemed to bring out the competitiveness in them. During the time when he had worked there Lucy had always, while flirting with him, thwarted all his attempts to become more friendly with her. He concluded that he was certainly not going to question his recent good fortune with women, or even attempt to analyse it.

He said goodbye to her a little later when she went back to work, much to his surprise. Adam had time on his hands so he decided to pop in to see Charlie, before going around to Vera again at seven that evening. It was probably going to be his last opportunity before her husband came back. Adam had to get on with things, and he saw no reason why he should not, before the other guy with the sports coupé got a foot in; that's if he was not already there.

Adam gave Charlie a call on his mobile and said he would be coming round in a short while. As it happened Charlie was also eager to see him. He had a controlled calm on the phone but there was a note of strangeness in his voice, some sort of manic detachment.

"I've been told to report to the police station tomorrow," said Charlie, as if resigned to his fate, like a man on the gallows. Adam had completely forgotten about that, though Charlie had mentioned it on his last visit.

"Don't panic," he said. "We'll discuss it when I come round."

"I'm not panicking," said Charlie. "I already know what's going to happen. They're going to put us away."

"Don't be so silly," Adam chided. "Wait until I come round." He switched off his mobile before Charlie could say something more incriminating. One could not trust the police not to listen in. He did not want to talk any more over the phone.

Adam cursed Charlie silently as he made his way to his flat. There was trouble brewing, and he could smell it. If he could not stop Charlie from spilling the beans he was probably in for it as well. Adam knew he had to silence Charlie somehow, but he could not think how he could do it. He wished he had turned him and not Dick into a crayfish. Charlie would not have been missed at all, and Dick would also have been more supportive in the last few days.

CHAPTER 13

An outwardly composed but nevertheless distraught Charlie opened the door. Adam could see the fear in his face, though he was trying hard not to show it. Charlie said he had been asked to report to Wood Green Station where an Officer Stevens was going to interview him about Dick's disappearance.

So it was clear to Adam that despite the disappointment suffered when he had dug up Adam's patio, Officer Stevens had not given up yet. The man was like a tenacious bulldog who did not let go easily once he had got his teeth into something, in this case Adam and Charlie.

"What am I going to do?" asked Charlie.

"What do you mean, what are you going to do?" retorted Adam. "Just tell him the bloody truth: Dick's disappeared and you don't know where."

"But that's not the truth," insisted Charlie.

"So what is the truth?" asked Adam, a bit exasperated. He could see that Charlie was beginning to go into one of his obstinate moods, when all reasoning went out of the window. He had seen Charlie go into one of these once or twice before, and when this happened there was no reasoning with him.

He remembered the time when they had gone on holiday together to Greece. One night after getting drunk Charlie had become obsessed with the notion that one of the locals had it in for him and was giving him the evil eye. It was just too weird to imagine, but Charlie was adamant. The locals were in fact quite friendly and maybe a little over-inquisitive, but certainly had no malevolent intentions toward them.

But try as Adam might, there was no convincing him. To top it all off, Charlie ate something which gave him the runs the following day. That was the last straw and he was off back to London. He went to see the holiday rep immediately for a flight back. By that time the rep was so fed up with Charlie that she was glad to see the back of him, and managed to get him a return flight the following day, which cost Charlie more than the holiday. However, there was no dissuading Charlie; there was no way he would wait two more days to get the regular return flight.

Adam had gone on the coach to see Charlie off at the airport, but had decided to stay behind and finish his holiday. That had turned out to be one of the best decisions he ever made. On the way back he had a good laugh about Charlie with Deidre, the rep, and ended up getting drunk with her that night. With Charlie gone he had the room to himself, and that came in really handy later on. After three memorable nights together Adam got back to London and related the story to Charlie, much to his disgust. In fact, he did not even want to believe Adam, until Deidre turned up sometime later to visit Adam for a weekend in London.

So Adam knew he was in trouble when Charlie started to go into one of those moods.

"Listen, Charlie." Adam spoke again. "We've been through this already. All you have got to say is that Dick left the house and you have not seen him since."

"They are not going to believe me," protested Charlie.

"They haven't got a choice. They have already come and dug up my patio and found nothing. So, unless you confess, they can't prove a thing."

"But I feel so guilty," Charlie protested again.

"Why the hell do *you* feel guilty?" Adam was getting angry. "We've been through this already. I'm the one who used the spell, and I don't think it's my fault. Dick wanted me to try it. We didn't know the bloody spell was going to work."

"But we've done so little to bring him back."

"Without the book we can't do anything. I'm not sure we could do anything even if we had the book."

"Oh God," said Charlie. "What a mess!"

"Well, I'm looking for the book." Adam tried to console him. "Maybe we will find it soon."

"Yeah, and how is that exactly?" Charlie did not believe him.

"I've employed a detective to trace it. I've got some hunches about who might have stolen the book." Adam did not want to tell Charlie, but it came out before he could stop himself.

"Well, I hope it works, and soon," said Charlie.

"Don't worry, it will. But meanwhile you must control yourself when the police question you." Adam tried to reassure him. "Don't tell them about the book."

He left Charlie in a better mood than he had found him and made his way to Vera's house. All the chatting made him feel frisky again and he was looking forward to seeing Vera once more. It was a spring evening and it was quite warm for the beginning of April, but there was a cool breeze blowing which made things feel quite pleasant.

Adam found a new bounce in his step that he had almost forgotten for a good while, as he approached the house after parking his car down the road. However, his joy soon turned into utter disappointment as he knocked on Vera's door. There was no answer. He knocked again but there was still nothing; then it occurred to him that Vera was not in. Adam's spirit sank. He realised that sometimes expectations can grow like an overblown balloon, and then when it burst under pressure, it left a bad taste in the mouth.

He had been looking forward to this meeting the whole afternoon and felt angry, as if he had been cheated out of a reward that was long overdue.

Feeling rather dejected Adam made his way back to his car and then made up his mind to visit Mary, his new tenant, to see whether she was ready to sign a new rental agreement. In his depressed mood Adam fully expected her not to be in either, but much to his surprise, she was.

To his further surprise, she seemed quite glad to see him. After a brief chat with her Adam found out that her friend was moving in that Sunday and they would be ready to sign the contract then. As Adam had cheered up a bit by this time he asked her whether she would like to go for a drink.

"What, socialise with my landlord?" She sounded a bit surprised.

"Officially I'm not yet your landlord. Not until the contract is signed."

"Well, alright then." She did not need any further convincing.

Adam asked her if she knew a place they could go to.

"What about The Rat and Gherkin? It's just down the road and it's a really great pub. Don't worry, Doug and Steve told me about what happened. I told them to leave you alone."

"Thanks." But he was not too keen to go back there.

"So you have a violent streak in you, then?" Mary seemed intrigued.

"I still don't know what came over me. I was having a bad day," Adam protested.

"I think they'll think twice about coming near you now."

Adam groaned inwardly. He remembered that was the pub where he had only just managed to avoid being pulped just a few days ago; in fact only the last time he had been there. However, Mary thought the pub was great, while he thought the exact opposite.

"It's not bad," Adam agreed out of politeness. "But you can go there anytime. Let me take you to another nice pub in Muswell Hill," he suggested.

"You're not trying to take advantage of me, are you?" Her face showed mock horror.

"What, me?" Adam feigned surprise. "A man who is about to become your landlord?"

"Alright then," she said again.

★ ★ ★

On the way to Muswell Hill they made small talk about things in general. Adam told her about the time he had lived in the flat a little while ago, and that it had been a real dump when he bought it.

Mary said she thought that it was not too bad now. It was quite spacious.

"I should really do it up better and charge more rent for it, but I can't be bothered." Adam was trying to size her up as he made conversation.

"Where are we going?" She avoided the subject.

"Here we are." Adam pulled up in front of a flashy-looking new pub called The Last Resort.

"Very nice," said Mary.

"Bit pricey, but hey, only the best on our first date, eh!" Adam hammed it up a bit; he was suddenly enjoying himself.

Mary groaned. "It's just a drink, not a date."

"I know, I know." Adam ushered Mary into the building and asked her what she wanted to drink. As there were a few empty tables scattered about he gestured to her to grab one of them. After getting served fairly quickly, as the place was not too full, he joined Mary with the drinks.

"Well, here we are, so what do you think?" asked Adam.

"I suppose it's okay," said Mary. "But I quite like The Rat and Gherkin."

Well, there's no accounting for taste, thought Adam as he cast his eye around the place, and then he suddenly spotted a very familiar face in a corner.

It was Vera. She was having a drink with another man who Adam thought also looked familiar. He was in fact the man in the sports coupé who had earlier dropped Vera off at the school. This was very interesting to Adam, who realised that Vera had ditched him for the other man.

Adam was just wondering what he should do when Vera looked up and saw him. She let out a little gasp of surprise, unseen by her friend, but recovered quite quickly. She smiled and nodded in Adam's direction and carried on talking.

"A friend of yours, then," quipped Mary, as the proceedings had not gone unnoticed by her.

Adam was on the point of saying that he did not know Vera, but then decided to come clean and admitted that he used to work for her and her husband when he used to teach.

"That's not her husband, surely?" said Mary with a tinge of sarcasm.

"I don't think so, but I don't know him," replied Adam, who was now very glad that he had told the truth when he saw Vera get up and start walking over towards him.

Vera smiled as she got nearer and Adam was compelled to smile back, even though he did not feel like it.

"Well, fancy seeing you here," said Vera. "How are you?"

"Fine," said Adam, acting nonchalant. "And you?"

"I'm having a drink with George, who, by the way, is going to become an investor in the college. I think you should meet him if you are still thinking of investing in the business. Why don't you come over and join us with your friend? You should introduce us."

"This is Mary," said Adam. "Mary, this is Vera." He was giving nothing away.

"You are thinking of buying a language school?" asked Mary after nodding to Vera in acknowledgement.

"Just a small share," said Adam.

"How interesting, maybe you can offer me a job. I'm a qualified EFL teacher."

Adam winced inwardly. Was there anybody these days who was not an English teacher? Outwardly he kept his composure.

"Why not?" he offered, as if he already owned part of the college. "Shall we join them, then?"

Soon he was being introduced to George, who seemed be an affable kind of chap, and obviously had no idea of the goings-on that afternoon.

"Vera told me that you are also interested in buying the college," George said in a very upper-crust accent, which sounded a bit phony to Adam. He had a broad smile on his oval face. Adam wondered what incentives Vera was offering him on the side.

"Well, only a part of it," Adam corrected him.

"Myself too," said George. "We should get together and have a chat sometime. You used to work there, so you must know a lot about it."

"Not too much," said Adam. "I left a month ago."

Adam could not understand Vera's interest in George at all. He was shorter than Adam and well rounded. His hair was thinning and he looked about forty. Though he had quite a jovial smile, not for the life of him could Adam fathom what physical attraction Vera would have to him, unless he was a really smooth talker. Vera was pretty, in fact not just pretty, but verging on beautiful, with a fantastic figure. In fact Adam did not understand what she saw in him either, and for that matter in Mr Cruz, who was much older than her.

Adam was obviously missing the point somewhere. There had to be a common thread running through. However, before he could work it out George interrupted his thoughts.

"I was toying with the idea of becoming an English teacher myself," George said again. "I've even completed a certificate in teaching English."

"That's how we first met," Vera cut in. "He came round looking for a job."

"But she's managed to convince me that I'm better suited to management than teaching, so she's going to offer a job to you."

"You are taking up the job from Monday week, aren't you?" pleaded Vera, as if she had been looking after Adam's interests all this time.

"Sure, but I'll see you next Monday about the other thing," said Adam, even though he felt everything had fallen into place a bit too neatly. He smiled and decided not to mention the fact that Vera had told him George was her cousin.

"Good. Maybe you would all like to come round to my place tonight for a coffee," said Vera. "Don't worry, George, we'll still offer you a job, if you really want to teach."

But disappointment really showed on George's face. He had obviously been expecting something else to happen, but Adam knew this was a classic Vera ploy.

"If you don't mind," said George after recovering a little, "I really need to be somewhere else later on."

"Oh," said Vera. "Maybe Adam does not mind dropping me off on the way back?" She gave Adam a big smile.

"Sure," said Adam, and looked at Mary, who shrugged.

"Don't mind me," she said, "I'm only here for a drink."

As they left the pub Vera gave George a big hug and a kiss on both cheeks, making him promise to ring her the next day. This seemed to cheer George up a bit, who duly agreed to phone her the next day at work. Adam was sure that George was totally besotted by Vera, who obviously had some use in mind for him.

Adam decided to drop Mary off first, disregarding Vera's objections, after promising to be back on Sunday to sign the contract for the flat.

When they were alone in the car Adam brought up the subject of their meeting earlier in the evening.

"He turned up at my door so unexpectedly that I did not have a chance to ring you before I left with him. I'm very sorry," she added, "but I'll make it up to you, don't worry."

"Tonight?" asked Adam.

"Don't be so demanding," said Vera. "I'm a bit tired tonight and my husband's coming back tomorrow morning. Be patient."

"I have been very patient," Adam insisted.

"And you got a big reward today." She gave him a little squeeze, teasing him.

"Of course." Adam nodded. "But I'd like to get to know you even better."

"I can't tonight. Make sure you come and see my husband on Monday."

And that was that – nothing Adam could say or do had any effect on her. She was resolute.

"See you're back driving your Skoda again," she remarked when she was getting out.

"I've had a slight problem with the other car," said Adam. "But I'm getting another new one soon."

"Well, you don't want to be seen in this thing too often, if you want to impress the ladies."

"Don't worry, it's only temporary. The next time I see you, I will have the new one."

When he got back to the house there was a single message waiting for him on the answerphone. It was Linda, and it was absolutely urgent. She needed to see him immediately. *Great*, thought Adam, after no contact whatever for months on end, he had to now see her immediately, because she required it. But then, Linda had been quite demanding. She had left him when she thought she could do better.

Well, damn you, thought Adam, who still felt hurt by her parting remarks when she had left him. He was not going to ring her back in a hurry, just to suit her.

But as he was ready to hit the bed, the phone rang again. It was Linda. She sounded almost angry.

"Why haven't you rung me back?" she demanded without so much as a 'how are you?' first.

"I've just got in." Adam tried to stay calm. He was not going to let Linda affect him again. "Anyway, what can I do for you?"

"Aren't you going to ask me how I am, first?"

"You're the one who is ringing me," retorted Adam. "How are you?"

"Too late," said Linda. "You don't really want to know."

"You didn't give me a bloody chance to ask you before. But you are right, though, I don't want to know." Adam was beginning to get a bit annoyed.

"You never cared for me at all, did you?" said Linda. "That's why I had to leave you in the first place." Now it was his fault, but it had always been so, and that had been her reason for leaving him. She had almost had him believing it.

"I thought you met a wonderful man, who was going to give you everything."

"The bastard, he just took advantage of me. You men are all the same." She started crying at the other end.

This was interesting, thought Adam. "What's happened?" he asked.

"Can I come and see you tomorrow?" Linda had recovered a bit.

"I don't think that's a very good idea." Adam was on the defensive.

"You said you would help me out if I ever needed help."

"Alright, you can see me on Friday," he relented. In reality he was intrigued and wanted to find out what had happened. Adam also realised that he had indeed made such a rash promise. It was more to sound noble and to stop her leaving in the first place, but he never imagined she would ever actually take him up on it once she left. However, he had a soft spot for Linda, but in reality, he realised he only wanted to see her to show her how well he was doing without her, even though it was going to cost him money.

Anyway, Adam regarded himself to be a man of his word, and he was also very keen to find out what had befallen Linda, so he decided he would see her. There had been some good times with her, after all. He was still fond of her.

"I'll pick you up at the station about one." He gave in. "It's called Ironbridge Spa. You can get a train from Liverpool Street station."

He said goodnight after that and went up to his bedroom, but it was not easy for him to get to sleep. Too many things were happening too quickly. It seemed like he was not in control of events anymore.

Linda did have her good points. She had introduced him to music and dancing. She had managed to get him to go salsa dancing with her on weekends. Adam had enjoyed dancing, even though he had been terrible at it initially. It made him calm down when under stress.

The trouble with Linda was that she just wanted what most people wanted: a nice, comfortable life. She had thought that Adam would be the person who would finally provide it, but had been surprised to find that he was embarked on a different path.

Adam lay in bed, wide awake, for most of the night. This was not his usual style, as normally he was an excellent sleeper. In the usual course of things nothing bothered his sleep. Problems had to wait; he gave them his best shot and if he could not solve them he still went to sleep and they waited until the next day. And the following day, refreshed from a good night's sleep, he found things were much easier to resolve.

To Adam problems were to be looked at as opportunities, because he always found that there was another angle. Things looked at another way always became more favourable, or at least that had been the way until now.

Because now, whichever way he looked at it, he could not think of a way to solve the problem of bringing Dick back. The problem was snowballing and he was not sure where things were headed. Especially as the police had become involved. It seemed Officer Stevens had grabbed the bit between his teeth and was hell-bent on achieving a result. And that would mean a very bad end to Adam's cosy little existence.

Adam had over the years grown fond of his lifestyle, such as it was. It was not much of a lifestyle in some people's eyes. Most people said that they thought he was always living on building sites, but recently Adam had started thinking that they envied him secretly and were out to undermine him, though this could just be an inferiority complex on his own part. For him it was steady progress, from being worth nothing to a man of substance. He still had some way to go but he was well on his way until this little problem had cropped up.

Adam liked his lifestyle, even though he was envious of Dick and didn't want to admit it; in a perverse way he was actually proud of it. But this book of magic had not been anything but a disaster for him so far. Even his leg-over with Rachael had not been enough to compensate for it, for that just made matters worse, leaving him with a huge feeling of guilt.

His thoughts moved on to Vera. What was going on there? She had been leading him on relentlessly, but he was always on the verge without actually getting there. Now George was on the scene as well, so what was her game? He decided he would find out soon enough, as he was going to see Vera on Monday, but by then her husband would be back. Adam decided he was past caring and he had to get some sleep.

He got up and put some classical music on. It always helped at stressful times. Finally, while he was trying to figure out why

Linda wanted to see him, which actually gave him some sense of satisfaction, he fell asleep.

★ ★ ★

Adam was picking up his new BMW on the day when he was due to meet Linda, and decided to do so when he picked her up. Well, it was almost new. It was an ex-demonstration car and they were offering a loan at zero per cent interest, and a substantial discount.

First he had to find out what Ramsbottom had discovered. As far as he knew Ramsbottom had been following Daley about, to find out what his movements were and to ascertain if he had indeed stolen the book. Adam was paying him a lot of money. The question was whether he was getting any returns.

As usual Ramsbottom was out in the field and his secretary, who Adam suspected was his wife, did not want to give him Ramsbottom's mobile number. Secretly Adam suspected that he in fact did not possess a mobile phone.

His idea was based entirely on Ramsbottom's appearance, as he dressed in a most peculiar fashion. It seemed to Adam that he was always dressed in a very old-fashioned way with a pinstripe suit, which looked slightly worn, a bluish overcoat and a bowler hat. Adam had initially thought that he was wearing one of the many disguises he had imagined a detective or investigator to have, but of course he was wrong. In fact it looked like it was Ramsbottom's standard attire, come rain or shine.

How did he know that? Well, he knew it because he had seen Ramsbottom lurking in the corner when he had a drink at The Three Witches, outside in the front beer garden. How Daley could fail to notice him all this time was a question which was still bugging Adam.

Anyway, his wife or his secretary told him that Ramsbottom

would be in touch with him soon, once she had informed him that Adam needed to talk to him. She had strict instructions not to contact him while he was out in the field. Ramsbottom, however, kept in touch by ringing in every so often. Adam was now more convinced than ever that Ramsbottom did not possess a mobile telephone. What had he got himself into, he thought – and he was paying £500 a week for the privilege. However, much to his surprise his phone rang the next morning. It was Ramsbottom.

"I've been trying to get in touch with you all morning," Adam lied. "I thought you were going to report in yesterday."

"That's precisely what I am doing," said Ramsbottom emphatically.

"Don't you have a mobile or something," asked Adam, "so I can keep in touch more regularly?"

"I find mobiles more of a handicap than a boon. I can't do my job properly if I am always answering calls."

"Right you are," said Adam in mock agreement. "Well, have you got anything for me?"

"Not a sausage so far, I'm afraid," said Ramsbottom glumly. "Do you want me to call it off?"

"You don't think he's our man?" asked Adam. It occurred to him that Ramsbottom was not exactly forthcoming with information.

"I didn't say that," Ramsbottom said. "In fact he is behaving very cautiously indeed, which makes me feel very suspicious."

"He has probably figured out that you are following him," said Adam. "One can hardly fail to notice you hanging around all the time."

"That may be so," said Ramsbottom.

"Can't you get a disguise or something?" asked Adam. "So he does not recognise you."

"It's no good – sooner or later they all figure it out that you are following them, but dressing like I do avoids confrontation.

They think I'm some sort of government official or the police and keep their distance."

"That's great," said Adam sarcastically. He did not buy this reasoning at all. "They are hardly likely to do anything if they think you are following them."

"Sooner or later they all crack under the pressure," came the sombre reply.

"Sure, sure," said Adam. "But can you tell me anything in particular that has happened?"

"Sorry, nothing unusual so far but it's early days yet," Ramsbottom replied. "But if you ask me, we'll catch him doing something sooner or later."

"So do you recommend that you carry on?" asked Adam, instantly regretting it.

"Of course. As I said, it's early days yet, and you did agree to five days at least," replied Ramsbottom.

"I suppose you are right," Adam agreed, groaning inwardly. "A few more days then."

"I shall expect a cheque in the post for the expenses for the five days as soon as possible," Ramsbottom said.

"Okay." Adam asked hopefully if he would get a reduction for the second week.

"Sorry," Ramsbottom replied. "But you won't regret it. I have a hunch something will happen this week."

"Yeah, I'm sure it will," Adam muttered under his breath as he put the phone down. He was not at all sure he was doing the right thing, but what was the alternative? He was determined to have a strong word with the solicitor if nothing came of Ramsbottom's stupendously overconfident machinations.

Thursday had gone by very slowly and Adam felt very frustrated, but the work was getting done. He was almost ready for the survey that would save him financially. He went to the pub once, but did not see anybody there he knew. He had quite forgotten that Charlie was due at the police station on that day.

He suddenly remembered that he had to be at the railway station by one. He was already running late and Linda was a stickler for timekeeping. When they were together she would always pace up and down every time he was late. He was sure to get a telling-off. It was another of his traits that she did not like. He had to admit he was a bit slapdash with his timekeeping, but it was not so bad.

He began to wonder again why Linda had left him, but decided that he preferred not to visit that place of self-doubt again. He had been through it already when she ditched him for an older man. In any case, now he was doing well with women and lately had been showered with attention not just by one, but several of them. Deciding there and then to play it cool, he got into his Skoda and drove off.

Linda hated his Skoda and he knew what her first reaction would be when she saw it, but he did not mind. In fact, he was quite looking forward to it. It was payback time in a small measure for the way she had treated him.

In the back of his mind he knew time was wasting away. However, as he was nowhere near getting hold of the book, unless Ramsbottom came up with something, he had time on his hands, for there was not much else he could do just then.

CHAPTER 14

In fact Linda was not at the station when he got there at quarter past one. As Adam was trying to figure out where she was, a train pulled up and she got off. She had caught the right train but it was late for some reason or other, which did not interest Adam, who had never liked trains much.

"Hope I haven't kept you waiting too long," Linda said as she greeted him like a long-lost friend.

"Not at all," said Adam, smiling. "I only just got here, I was late myself."

"That's alright then," said a subdued Linda, who somehow seemed to have relished the idea that Adam would be eagerly waiting for her at the station.

"Well, this is a surprise," said Adam. "I didn't think I would see you again."

"Don't say that – we parted as friends, didn't we?" Linda sounded a bit upset.

"I suppose you can call it that." Adam was cool. "The truth is, you left me."

"Well, it was a bad mistake and I'm sorry if I hurt you," Linda apologised; she smoothed her dress nervously.

"It's water under the bridge now." Adam said dismissively. "So what brings you here?"

"Can we go somewhere first for a drink or something?" asked Linda.

"Sure, I suppose I can buy you lunch," said Adam. He could see that she looked rather hesitant.

They walked in silence to the car park and Adam opened the door of his Skoda for her.

"Still got the old car, then," was all she said, and Adam nodded. Much to his surprise she did not make any further comments about it.

They parked near a little café which Adam knew. It was an inexpensive place as Adam was not particularly in the mood to splash out anything large on a meal for Linda at that moment.

She was homeless, or about to be so as the landlord had decided to throw her out on the street over the weekend unless she came up with two months' rent.

"How the hell did you get into such a state?" Adam was flabbergasted. Linda had always been one of those women who was very careful about money. When she had lived with Adam, she had always kept her own money to herself. In fact she had hardly contributed towards any of the expenses of keeping the house, except for buying some groceries occasionally. Even then, these were things that she wanted. She had saved her money, relying on Adam to spend on the household expenses. Not that Adam had minded very much, as most were expenses he would have had to pay anyway if he had lived alone.

"So how much do you need?" he asked finally.

"A couple of thousand. Jim has not paid the rent." Adam noticed that Linda was wringing her hands, but seemed not to be aware of it.

"What happened to all the money you had saved?" Adam asked, surprised.

"I lent him the £30,000." She looked dejected. "You see, we were going to buy a house together."

"But I thought you said he owned his house." Adam was taken aback by her naivety.

"That's what Jim told me also – well, it is a flat, but he said he owned it."

"So why did he need your money?" asked Adam.

"Deposit for a house. We were looking to move into a house and buy it in our joint names. We even found the house and went to see a solicitor. Originally Jim was going to remortgage the flat and raise the deposit, but two weeks ago he told me his money was being held up as there was not enough equity in the flat. It was for the initial deposit, you see, before the exchange of contracts."

"And you lent him £30,000? A man you had only known for less than a few months?" Adam was angry.

"I didn't see anything wrong with it," protested Linda. "I thought I was living in the flat he owned."

"Well, you wouldn't lend me five grand when I was trying to buy the last house, even though you had known me for more than a year." He felt his anger rising.

"It was different," said Linda. "Jim was going to buy the house jointly with me."

"And let you keep your money at the same time. Great, and you fell for that." Adam could not contain his anger anymore.

"Well, I thought we were going to get married and settle down," she protested again.

"I offered to buy the last house with you, but you came up with all sorts of excuses at the time."

"But I didn't like that house. It was such a tip."

"Sure, but it's worth twice what I paid for it," Adam said with some venom. "You could have been rich."

Adam was lying somewhat. The house was still hanging around his neck, which was the reason for the perilous state of his finances, but he couldn't help himself. He had felt such humiliation at the time and needed to get some satisfaction out of the current situation, even to the point of being petty.

"How was I supposed to know?" protested Linda again. "So then you must be doing well. How come you are still driving a Skoda?"

There it was at last; it had to come sometime, sooner or later.

"I'm going to rectify that as soon as we finish here," he said with a smile.

"Are you going to give me the money?" asked Linda.

"Give you? No. I'll lend it to you," retorted Adam.

"You were always a miser," said Linda. "I didn't ask you for anything when I left."

"But you never contributed anything," protested Adam.

"Well, I lived with you for over a year. Doesn't that count for anything?"

"That's why I am lending you the money, even though things are very tight for me at the moment," said Adam coolly.

"How's that? I thought you said you're rolling in it," said Linda.

"I would be if I had managed to sell the last house."

"So you've still got the house?" Linda looked interested.

"Well, I've just managed to let it, so I can help you out. I expect I'll be alright very soon – I'm going to remortgage the present house instead."

Inside he was hurt. Not so much by Linda, but his failure to impress women generally with his abilities. There she was, an example, lending – no, giving – £30,000 to a smooth-talking old bastard, but she would not part with a penny to him after living with him for a year or more.

But then, he thought, looking at it from another angle, if he had bought the house with her, he would only be worth half the money he was worth now. Even if she had lent him the £5,000 she probably would have insisted on half the profits. This certainly made Adam cheer up a bit, but he was still profoundly perturbed about his failure to impress women generally to participate in things that were important to him. It occurred to him then that either women didn't understand or were not interested in the intricacies of his financial machinations. They were looking for something more tangible, like what car he was driving.

Adam drove around with Linda to the garage to pick up his new BMW – well, almost new. He left his Skoda at the garage, promising to pick it up the next day. Linda was impressed, and for some reason she wanted to see Adam's new house. *Why not?* thought Adam. The house was beginning to look good and he wanted to impress her a bit more.

"How can you afford a new car, if things are so bad?" asked Linda.

"I'm getting a special deal, interest free for three years and a big discount," said Adam. "I'm fed up of slumming it."

On the way Adam went to the bank and withdrew the money for Linda, and then they made their way to his new country residence. As he pulled up in front of his house he saw Jack standing there outside his own house. When he saw the car he came over for a closer look.

"New car?" he asked.

"That's right. What do you think?" asked Adam in return.

"Very nice," said Jack. "New girlfriend as well."

"No, this is my ex, Linda." Adam rubbed it in as Linda was within earshot. "Meet Jack, my neighbour."

After the introductions were over, Jack said he was just on his way to The Three Witches to meet Wendy and asked whether they would like to join them. Adam was not keen, but Linda wanted to have a look around, so it was decided they would meet in half an hour at the pub.

"He seems a nice man," Linda said after Jack had left.

"A bit too nosy for my liking," Adam said deliberately.

"So you don't like him?" Linda remarked.

"I didn't say that, but he is always poking his nose into my business."

Adam could see Linda was very impressed with the house when they made their way to the pub.

"Your tastes are improving," she remarked. "I suppose you've done well lately."

"Yes, much better, since you left me." Adam threw in a barb.

Linda did not, however, take the bait. They entered the pub in silence, just in time to buy the next round for Jack and Wendy, who seemed to have timed their last drink with Adam's arrival to a tee. Adam did not mind, however. He also saw Bruce and his friends propping up the bar on the other side. Adam nodded in Bruce's direction and his face lit up in a very broad grin. Very soon he was at Adam's side, pumping his hand, and Adam had little choice but to buy him a drink also.

"Well, have you found your book yet?" asked Bruce after a while when pleasantries had been exchanged.

"No, have you?" asked Adam.

"What do you mean?" Bruce was a bit taken aback by Adam's direct question, and had a funny look on his face.

"Well, you are looking for it, aren't you?" Adam asked again without mincing his words.

"Well, I'd like to buy it, if possible," said Bruce, recovering by now. "After all, it is sort of a family heirloom."

"Well, I'll let you know if I find it," remarked Adam, knowing full well that he had no intention of doing so. He collected his drinks on a tray and made his way over to the others after saying goodbye to Bruce, who seemed eager to join the group but Adam decided against inviting him to do so.

"Been seeing a lot of your friend lately in this pub," remarked Jack as he sat down next to him.

"Oh?" Adam was interested.

"And guess who else?" Jack carried on without finishing, building up the tension.

"Who?" asked Adam.

"Your mate Daley," guffawed Jack. For some reason, he thought this was extremely funny.

"He is not my mate," Adam said, irritated.

"Well, they've been thick as thieves, those two," said Jack. "I'd say they are up to something. Wendy thinks so as well." Jack looked for confirmation towards Wendy, who nodded.

"Thick as two thieves," she said.

"Last time I overheard them, they were haggling about the price of something," said Jack again.

Adam's ears pricked up. This was news indeed. He had to get on to Ramsbottom as soon as possible, to see if he had found anything. All this time Linda had been listening intently to their conversation, without saying anything, so obviously the substance of their chat was not meaningful to her.

"Who are all these people? You seem to have got to know a lot of them in your short time here," Linda said exasperatedly.

"It's a long story," said Adam. "I'll explain to you later. Basically I got burgled and lost something and some other people seem to be interested in the object."

"Oh," said Linda, none the clearer.

"We'll have another drink and then go," said Adam.

Reluctantly Jack got up and got the next round in. But just when Adam was about to leave, Jack drained his glass and slammed it down in front of Adam, who then found it difficult to say no to buying the next round. Eventually when Adam staggered out of the pub with Linda, he was a bit the worse for wear and in no condition to drive. But for some reason Linda had been enjoying herself and had not wanted to leave either.

When they got back it was decided that Linda would stay on overnight and go the next morning. At this point Adam was thinking of warming up some food but as Linda was standing rather close to him, he was a bit perplexed.

"Would you like something more to eat?" he asked.

"I'm not that hungry." She smiled suggestively. "Would you like to do something else?"

"Are you sure it's a good idea?"

"Well, it's not as if you've been getting much lately." She smiled.

"Who told you that?" Adam was a bit irritated. She always assumed the worst.

"Your mum said you haven't had a girlfriend for a while."

"So you thought you'd do me a favour?"

"Why not? For old times' sake – we used to have great sex. It's not as if I'm betraying anybody," said Linda. She put her arms around Adam's waist.

"So your boyfriend's not only taken your money, but he was lousy in bed?" Adam threw that in for good measure, even though he had no idea of the man's prowess in bed.

"No need to get personal. I'm not thinking of moving back in with you."

"The last time I tried it, you said you couldn't betray his trust."

"The situation was different then. I was going to move in with him."

It was on the tip of Adam's tongue to say, "Well, I suppose for old times' sake…" He did not want to show any weakness, but neither could he see any harm in it. After all, she had just cost him £2,000 and there was some truth in what she said. After his recent disappointments with Vera, why not? But he surprised himself.

"Sorry," he heard himself say, "but my life is already too complicated at the moment."

Adam decided he could not go down that road again. He knew at the back of his mind that he had to make the break to forge his new life.

★ ★ ★

However, the next morning when they were ready to leave, he decided against getting her to sign a loan agreement, as he had originally wanted. Instead he decided to write the money off as a gift.

"Listen, if the tenancy is in your partner's name, why not move out and use the money for a deposit somewhere else?" he suggested to her.

"Well, it would be quite nice here," she laughed.

"I didn't mean that," he corrected her quickly. He was glad he hadn't slept with her. He remembered a quote from Søren Kierkegaard about how life could only be understood backwards, but had to be lived forwards. He had outgrown her.

"I know what you mean, but I want to stay there in case Jim comes back."

"Surely you don't think he's coming back, do you?" Adam was horrified at this woman's gullibility. "He's conned you out of thirty grand… you should go to the police."

"Well, people can have a change of heart, or he may have had a good reason for it," Linda said hopefully, more to convince herself than Adam. "In any case, I like the flat I'm in."

There was nothing more to be said. At last he had closure. Linda's leaving him would never bother him again. He even offered to help her to get her money back at a later date from Jim, if he could.

Adam called a taxi. He wanted to drop Linda off and pick up his Skoda. He had to get back in time for the people who were going to install his alarm.

When he got back after saying goodbye to Linda, in his old car, he found the people already waiting for him, having arrived a few minutes before him.

After setting them to work Adam wanted to have some breakfast and ring Ramsbottom. He was eager for some news from him. However, the police rang him first. It was Officer

Stevens. He wanted Adam to come to the station on Monday for an interview and to make a statement.

"I've got a business appointment on Monday," Adam told the policeman.

"You'll still have to come in," he insisted.

"But why? You've already dug up my patio and found nothing."

"Your friend has said some interesting things already. You know he is in custody?" the officer informed him.

"How do you mean? What's he done to be held in custody?"

"We are keeping him for psychiatric observation. He absolutely flipped during his interview and had to be restrained."

Oh no! Disaster, thought Adam.

He has accused you of practising black magic rituals," Officer Stevens said.

"What nonsense," Adam retorted. "I've got an appointment in the morning for a job interview. Tuesday morning would be better for me."

That seemed to satisfy Officer Stevens, who did not seem to want to push Adam too much, and they made an appointment for ten o'clock on Tuesday for Adam to present himself at the station. Adam felt Stevens was being more reasonable after the last two raids on his house had failed to produce any evidence.

But matters were worse than Adam had anticipated. Charlie had gone and spilled the beans. Adam had had a suspicion that he would crack, but had been hoping that Charlie would survive the police pressure somehow.

Well, it was much too much to expect of Charlie not to crack under pressure from the police. But what had he actually told them, and if he had indeed told them everything, would they believe his fantastic story? No wonder he was under observation.

Adam decided he had nothing really to worry about, as there was no evidence to the contrary. For a start, there was no body, and the police case desperately needed a body unless he confessed as well. In a way he found it all quite amusing, but he still was not looking forward to the police interview.

Adam had been feeling very disturbed all morning. He was a little worried about what Jack had said about Bruce and Daley. The more he thought about it, the more he was convinced Daley was the man. If he had not done it himself he obviously knew something about it. But what could he do about it? What could he do about anything? Well, he had done his best to help Linda out, but there was nothing more he could do for her. He was enjoying his newfound freedom too much to contemplate ever getting back together with her. It was finally over; he had closure and he was free of her.

Just now he was on a mind-blowing adventure and it was rapidly spiralling out of control, and this is what he needed to concentrate his mind on. How could he squeeze Daley to get the book back? That's if Daley had it in his possession in the first place. The next few days were going to be crucial.

Rachael was also coming back from holiday the next day. Adam was in two minds whether to meet her or not. The police were bearing down on him and he did not want to be seen with her. At the same time he wanted to show off his new car to her, to cultivate his new image. He was looking forward to seeing her on the one hand, and at the same time dreading the consequences if the police found out.

Adam decided he would make his final decision the next day, but meanwhile he had to get on with things. He decided he had to find out how much Bruce and Daley knew, and what they were up to. What were Bruce's plans, and how long was he in the country on his holiday? Adam thought he would go round to the pub that afternoon to see if they were there.

After pondering a few moments on the decision he had just taken, Adam went to check on the progress of the work being carried out. The man putting the alarm in had come back to finish off the job. It was nearly 1pm by now and as the work was going to take several more hours, he decided he would go and have lunch at The Three Witches and hopefully catch a glimpse of Daley or Bruce.

Adam was not entirely sure how he was going to broach the subject if he did meet Bruce at the pub. Anyway, he thought it would be an interesting exercise and marched down to the pub without any further distractions coming his way. At least the lunch would be good, better than the pre-packaged microwaved food that he lived on usually.

However, when he got to the pub Adam decided that instead of having lunch in the restaurant as he had previously resolved, he would stay in the bar and have some sandwiches. He was worried that if he was in the restaurant, he was likely to miss Bruce if the latter decided to drop in. After ordering his ham and tomato sandwich on brown bread and securing a pint of local beer, he sat down at an empty table and relaxed. He was still trying to decide whether he should meet Rachael the next day or not.

The next day was Sunday and he did not have a great deal to do except sign the contract with Mary and her friend and pick up Rachael, who was arriving back about five o'clock. This posed a dilemma for Adam, who had difficulty in deciding whether to see Mary before or after seeing Rachael.

Adam was just finishing his first pint when the sandwiches arrived, and then just as he was finishing his sandwiches, Bruce arrived. He saw Adam and asked him if he wanted a pint. Adam nodded and Bruce soon came back with two pints from the bar.

"So have you found your book yet?" asked Adam.

"I thought it was your book," said Bruce.

"You must have been talking to Daley," said Adam.

"Daley? Daley who?" Bruce was surprised. "Oh, I know who you mean – the roofer. No, it's my friend who is talking to him. He needs a new roof. In fact he is talking to him today."

"I see," said Adam. "So what happened to the book?"

"Like you say, I now believe it to be an old wives' tale. There isn't any book," Bruce said with a smile.

"So how much longer are you staying in the village?" asked Adam.

"I don't know why it's any of your business, but I am leaving next week," said Bruce a bit tersely.

"Just enquiring." Adam smiled. "That was an interesting story you told me the other day about your grandmother and your grandfather and his cousins being witches."

"Who knows?" said Bruce. "My grandmother got divorced and emigrated to Australia. She told many stories and that was one of them. It's really hard to believe, but I'm very glad I came here for a holiday. I've had a great time here."

"That's good to hear," said Adam. "Let me get you another drink."

"Why not?" Bruce looked happy. Adam went to the bar to get the drinks. He knew Bruce was lying. Either he had already got the book or he was about to get it. That was why he could afford to look so smug about it.

Adam had to confront Daley and offer him more money and get the book back at all cost. He had to be bold. All his life he had taken a cautious approach to things, even when he had been buying houses. However, now he needed to have a different take on life. He decided he would start with Bruce.

"So you think that the book doesn't exist?" Adam asked Bruce as he got back with the drinks.

"That's right," confirmed Bruce.

"What if I told you that it does, and I've still got it?" said Adam, smiling.

"I'd say you were having me on." Bruce looked him directly in the eyes.

"I can prove it to you." Adam's eyes met his full-on.

"Well, if you let me have a look at it, if it is the right one I'll buy it off you." Bruce had slipped up.

"So you do think there is such a book?" Adam laughed.

"I see. You are just playing games with me." Bruce looked at him angrily.

"Not at all," said Adam. "I will prove it to you, but I won't show you the book, because I don't want to sell."

"So how?" asked Bruce.

"What happens when the book is used?"

"It rains."

"That's what will happen tomorrow, though the weather forecast is for a dry day," said Adam. He was taking a desperate gamble but he was also sure Bruce did not have the book yet.

"I'll look forward to it," Bruce said, putting on a brave face.

"Then you will know that whatever Daley is trying to sell you is a complete con."

"If you've got the book it's better you sell it to me, if you know what's good for you. You don't know who you're dealing with," said Bruce.

"Is that a threat?" He looked Bruce in the eye, but he didn't say anything more. He knew definitely now that Bruce didn't have the book.

Adam stood up without a further word, finishing his drink in one swig and after nodding to Bruce, left the pub. On his way out he recited that part of the rain-making spell, the bit that he had read on the first day when he had found the book, which he still remembered. The lights started popping all around him, but it soon stopped and everything remained intact. Adam turned and smiled at Bruce, before he left. There was a look of terror on people's faces, but Bruce seemed very calm.

A desperate but bold plan had formed in his mind. He was going to summon Daley using the spell he had used on him the last time, for he had written down the spell on a piece of paper, and he still had that piece of paper somewhere.

When he got back, the alarm people were still hard at it. When they finished they showed him how to work the alarm, and gave him the instructions for changing the code. He promptly did so when they left.

CHAPTER 15

After much consternation, Adam decided that he would confront Daley directly and offer more money for the book than Bruce had. Adam was sure the only reason that Daley wanted the book was to make money by selling it to Bruce; otherwise the book meant nothing to him. He would summon Daley using the spell he had last used. He would thus be killing two birds, for once it rained he would also convince Bruce that he still had the book. Adam therefore started looking for the piece of paper which had the spell on it. He knew the spell worked because he had used it once before and Daley had turned up to finish the job at his house. The only problem was that Adam could not remember exactly where he had put the piece of paper.

Because he still possessed the book at the time, he had been less than careful with his notes, as they were superfluous to his requirements. Normally he put such bits of information in the top drawer of a chest of drawers he had in his bedroom. It was full of bits of paper with information that might one day prove useful; however, it seldom proved so. Usually he would rummage through the drawer once in a while and throw out the most useless and outdated papers, and occasionally he would dump the whole drawer load into a black bin bag.

But such occasions were rare as Adam was a hoarder by nature, and in fact all his furniture had been acquired by default when it was left over from the houses he had purchased. It was furniture which had been discarded by other people as they had moved on. All was kept by Adam, along with other artefacts and bric-a-brac. However, recently he had resolved to get shot of the whole lot and replace it with some brand new stuff to go with his new image.

Adam reluctantly dumped the contents of the drawer onto his bed and started to look through them carefully one by one, and have a clear-out at the same time. Unfortunately, as he had been fairly lazy with his paperwork following his move from the last house, there was a lot of it to sift through.

One of the problems of such an exercise was that every so often, one came across a piece of paper whose importance was very difficult to gauge. Suddenly a moment of indecision would grip Adam, and when this happened it would sometimes manifest itself as a slight pressure pain in the forehead region, and this invariably would involve a break for a cup of tea. Every now and then he would also come across a sentimental piece or a photograph which would cause his memory to drift back for a while, as he basked in the sunshine of some long-forgotten holiday for a few moments. But then it was back to reality and a mound of paper.

Adam woke up with a jolt. He had almost nodded off reminiscing over an old Valentine's card he had found, and he still had half the pile to go through. By the time he finished it was nearly 1am. The bedroom was ankle-deep in waste paper and he had not found the piece he was looking for.

He put back the bits he wanted to keep in the drawer and decided to go to bed. In the morning he wanted another quick look through the waste before throwing it away. But he was sure it was not there. What was he going to do? But not having an immediate answer, he decided to sleep on it.

★ ★ ★

Next morning Adam woke early. Desperation had gripped him, when he thought of a last place to look: the front pockets of his jackets where he often kept small pieces of paper which he could not find an immediate home for.

And there it was, in the pocket of his favourite casual jacket. Adam decided not to waste any further time, but to cast the spell. He then carefully folded and put back the paper where it had been and started clearing his bedroom.

Though the rain did not seem to follow any particular time frame after he cast a spell, by the time he had finished breakfast, there was a sudden outburst of thunder outside. Bruce would be pleased, or maybe not. Adam sat back and supped his tea as he watched the rain come cascading down, and he was suddenly glad that he had put the new roof on the house.

About lunchtime there was a knock on the door. It was Daley. He had his little terrier with him on a leash. The dog seemed quite friendly towards Adam.

"What brings you here?" asked Adam in mock surprise.

"I was just passing," replied Daley. "Thought I would drop in to see if you needed any more work done. The roof holding up well? When do you want the rest done?"

"Not for a few weeks yet, but the roof is holding up very well at present."

"Oh good, I'm glad to hear it."

"Yes, very well." Adam smiled. "You've done a sterling job. Come in for a second. As you are here I wanted to discuss something with you."

Daley came in slowly, looking around to see how the place was coming along.

"You've put an alarm in," he remarked. "The place is turning into a little fortress."

"Well, you know, an Englishman's home and all that," remarked Adam. "New front door and locks as well."

"What did you want to ask me?"

"That brings me right to the point. I want to recover the book."

"What book?" asked Daley, trying to show surprise.

"You know, the one Bruce wants to pay £2,000 for." Adam looked Daley in the eye. Adam was guessing, as that was the price Bruce had offered him in the pub. "I'll double it. £4,000, no questions asked."

"I don't know anything about it," Daley protested.

"But if you know somebody who does," said Adam, "remember: no questions asked. You bring me the book and I'll give you four grand."

"You have that sort of money?" asked Daley.

"I can arrange it," said Adam. "Say, by Tuesday?"

"I'll see what I can do," said Daley. "Mind you, I am promising nothing. I have a friend who might just know something."

"Great," said Adam. "Remember, I don't need to know anything. Just bring me the book and you can have the money."

"The book must be very valuable," remarked Daley.

"It's of sentimental value to me," lied Adam.

"Funny, that's exactly what Bruce said to me." His face lit up in an evil grin.

"Well, do you really need an explanation?" asked Adam.

"I suppose not," Daley agreed. "But remember, I'm not promising anything." He left.

Adam was feeling chirpy again. In an upbeat mood he decided he was going to meet Rachael after all. Maybe she could be his witness when he signed the contract with his tenants. With all that was going on, he was too late to see Mary before Rachael.

★ ★ ★

Adam left the house about four to head towards Stansted airport. The rain had cleared as suddenly as it had appeared and it was a bright day again, but the air smelt freshly washed with a hint of spring in it. Adam loved this time of the year. Probably like the other several hundred million people in Europe, he looked forward to the summer. Spring made him feel young and frisky, and today he was feeling especially so as Rachael was coming back. He reached the airport just before five and parked his new BMW in the short-term car park. Rachael would be proud when she saw it.

Adam made his way to the arrivals area. The plane was due at five thirty. Sure enough, at about ten to six Rachael appeared through the exit with her booty. She looked absolutely stunning as she had acquired a very lovely tan and was still dressed in her shorts and summer gear.

Adam waved at her, and when she saw him she came over to him, pulling her pink suitcase behind her. The thing looked really heavy, and Adam wondered how she managed to cope with the weight. But then she probably had enough people offering to gladly take the load off her.

"You look fantastic," said Adam, giving her a kiss on the cheeks.

"Thanks," she said. "Thanks for coming."

"Here, let me take that for you," said Adam. "Shall we go? I have my new car in the car park."

"New car?" She looked impressed. "No more Skoda?"

"Actually, I've still got it," admitted Adam. "It's useful for carrying things for the building work at the house."

"Of course." Rachael smiled. "Actually, Adam, do you mind waiting a bit? I have a friend who could use a lift as well. He's been stopped by customs but should be out in a minute or two."

"Sure," said Adam, putting on a brave face. "Who is he?"

"He was on the same holiday as me," said Rachael. "You'll love him, he is so funny."

Actually, Adam couldn't see the funny side at all. Well, it was only to be expected, a good-looking girl like Rachael, alone on holiday. It was bound to happen. There was no harm in giving the man a lift. But when Adam saw him he was sorry he had waited. The man was a large, good-looking Australian, who happened to be also called Bruce. Rachael introduced them and Adam heard himself agreeing to give the man a lift to London with Rachael.

This was typical of Rachael, thought Adam as he made his way to the car. He had been looking forward to meeting her again, but by herself and not with a strange man in tow.

"You should have come on this holiday, Adam," Rachael remarked, once in the car. "It was fantastic."

"I'm sure it was," said Adam. "But I've been very busy."

"You're a busy little beaver, aren't you? You are always busy," laughed Rachael.

"I suppose so," agreed Adam reluctantly.

"Too busy to enjoy the good things in life," said Rachael.

"That's a shame, mate," the new Bruce cut in. "Yeah, you should have been there on the holiday. Rachael told me all about you."

"Hopefully all good," said Adam, trying not to hate the man too much.

"Strewth, we had a really good time, mate," said Bruce again.

"I can see that," Adam retorted. "Where do you want to be dropped off?"

"Oh! Didn't Rachael mention it? She's putting me up for a few days."

Adam's worst nightmare was coming true, and the bloody Australian was also called Bruce.

"You don't mind, do you, Adam?" Rachael cut in.

"No, why should I mind?" Adam resigned himself to the inevitable. "It's your house. I'm only the driver, giving you a lift home."

"Ripper! You're a sport, mate," said Bruce. "Rachael told me you have been very supportive, since her husband left."

"I try to do my best to help." Adam kept his calm, but he was burning up inside.

"Don't worry, mate. She won't have to bother you anymore," said Bruce. "I'm here now." Adam did not require any better valediction.

That just takes the biscuit, thought Adam bitterly. Well, it was all probably for the best. He was sure he would have given in to temptation where Rachael was concerned, and would have been in more hot water if the police found out. Now at least he had no choice; she was off the menu and that was that.

A doleful Adam drove silently the rest of the way and dropped them off. Rachael remarked how nice his new car was, which rubbed salt further into his wound, but Adam accepted it all stoically. At least now he could feel less guilty, seeing that Rachael was off with another guy. He decided there and then that it had been no way his fault that he had this little affair with Rachael. Well, one could hardly call it an affair; it was an episode and that chapter was now closed.

★ ★ ★

He decided not to bother asking Rachael to be the witness to his rental contract, but to ring Lucy instead, to see if she was free.

To his great surprise she was very eager to help him out. She was supposed to go out with a friend that night, but she said she could cancel it as it was not too important. She would be there to meet him in half an hour.

Adam offered to buy her a meal, but she said she was not hungry. A drink would be fine, and that was that. In half an hour Adam was ringing the bell to Lucy's flat.

Lucy opened the door and asked him to come upstairs. She said she would be ready in five minutes, though she looked pretty ready, and Adam, who was getting quite used to seeing many women recently and was learning to gauge their moods, decided that Lucy had made a special effort to spruce herself up for the occasion. He suddenly had the idea that she was treating it more like a date than just a casual drink.

This was interesting, thought Adam; one door had closed but another was about to open if he played his cards right. But Adam dismissed it as a figment of his imagination. He was reading too much into it. She was just helping him out; after all, he was about to become her boss.

"You look great," Adam remarked as Lucy finished her ablutions and came out of the bathroom.

"Thanks." She smiled.

"I was just admiring your flat," he said. "It's got great views."

"It's only rented." She was forthcoming with more information. "I share it with a friend, but she is on holiday at the moment for a couple of weeks."

"Well, this is a nice area to live in and it's such a lovely flat."

"We were lucky," said Lucy. "Shall we go?"

They made their way to his new car, which impressed Lucy even further.

"You are going up in the world," she remarked.

Adam told her that he was trying hard but still had a long way to go.

"You sure are a quiet one," said Lucy. "I never guessed when you were working at the college that you were a property developer."

"Well, I'm hardly that," said Adam modestly.

"Vera said you have a beautiful house. Vera's been there, hasn't she?"

Adam mentioned that she came to see him to talk about the college, as she wanted him to buy into it. He hoped this would satisfy Lucy enough not to take this line of questioning any further.

"And that's all?" Lucy smiled.

"Of course." Adam tried to look convincing.

"What about the stuff in the office the other day?"

Adam intimated that it had taken him completely by surprise, and he hoped Lucy was not going to inform Vera's husband.

"Not if you treat me well." She beamed him a big smile.

"Of course." Adam smiled. *Here we go*, he thought. "What does your little heart desire?"

"I'll think of something, don't worry." She winked.

Very soon they reached Adam's flat. Adam rang ahead to Mary to let her know he was on his way. Mary opened the door for them, but she had bad news: her friend had decided at the last moment to drop out. Unfortunately her finances could not stretch enough for her to take on the flat by herself, so could Adam wait until she found somebody else?

It had been a somewhat frustrating evening but Adam decided he wanted to keep Mary, so he signed a temporary contract with her for renting a room instead of the whole flat. The contract would be replaced when she found somebody for the other room. After that was done and they'd had a little chitchat over a cup of tea, during which Mary and Lucy had got better acquainted, Mary asked them if they would like to go for a drink together. Adam guessed that she was a bit lonely by herself, and as he had no designs on Lucy, he agreed readily. Obviously she had some other plans in her mind, but tried not to be too put out by events and decided to play along with things.

"You were going to go out somewhere tonight, weren't you, before I rang?" Adam asked her.

"Only for a drink with George." She smiled.

"You don't mean…" Adam left the sentence unfinished, and Lucy nodded. "He doesn't waste much time, does he? When did he get a chance to ask you out?"

"Oh, he rang the office on Friday," said Lucy. "He had been chatting to me on the day he came to see Vera. You know the day?" Lucy laughed.

"Yeah, I remember." Adam almost blushed a little.

"Am I missing something here?" asked Mary, who had been listening to their conversation.

"Nothing important," said Adam quickly.

"Who's George?" asked Mary.

"He's trying to buy a share in the college along with Adam," said Lucy.

"Fancies himself as a bit of a ladykiller, I think," said Adam.

"Poor George." Lucy laughed. "He's alright when you get to know him."

"You stood him up tonight. Maybe you can ring him and see if he wants to make it a foursome."

"Probably be fun," said Lucy.

"Okay, let's give it a try. You don't mind, do you, Mary?"

"Not at all, you seem to meet such interesting people at the college. I think you should get me a job there."

"Mary's a qualified EFL teacher," said Adam.

"Well, why not?" Lucy was warming to Mary. She started fishing for her phone in her bag.

Adam had an ulterior motive for inviting George. He wanted to get to know him better, especially if he was going to become a partner in the business with him. He wanted to get him on his side if he was going to deal with Vera and her husband.

★ ★ ★

George seemed to have been just sitting at home, so he jumped at the chance of joining Lucy and Adam for a drink. After a fair amount of deliberation, it was decided that they would meet at The Last Resort in Muswell Hill for a drink and then go on to the local Chinese for a meal. It seemed George was also eager to have a chat with Adam about the impending purchase.

When they reached The Last Resort they found George already there holding a table for them, which made them happy as the place was much more crowded than last time Adam was there, being a Sunday evening.

"Very lucky," said George. "Somebody just moved out and I happened to be standing right next to it." George greeted Adam like a long-lost friend and went off to buy a round after inviting them to grab the table. After the girls were seated Adam joined George at the bar.

George seemed genuinely happy to see him, even though Lucy had earlier stood him up for Adam. Adam explained that it had been an emergency and he was grateful for her help. Of course Adam had no idea that Lucy was about to go out with George, but he was very glad of the opportunity this had afforded him to meet up with him. George accepted the explanation with good grace and grinned.

"Soon to be partners, then," he said as he got the drinks in.

"It does seem like that, doesn't it?" Adam agreed. "How do you feel about it?"

"I have my doubts about the business, but there is a lot that could be done. How much is she asking you for your share?" he asked.

"£30,000, for twenty per cent of the business," said Adam.

"That bitch. She asked me for £40,000."

"Well, you are richer than I am," laughed Adam.

"Yeah, right." George smiled. "And I'd like to stay that way. What I don't like is that they would still have control of the business. I don't trust that husband of hers any more than I trust her."

Well, this was good news indeed, thought Adam; when it came to business, George was not silly at all. He was worried about the same things as Adam was – that is, buying a minority share in a failing language school, but to have some control in running the business.

"I think we should ask her for fifty per cent and offer her the same price each," suggested Adam. Buying into the college seemed to be an ideal business opportunity. Adam had quite a few ideas how it could be run better.

Whatever else was going on with recovering the book, it still looked a very unlikely prospect. Adam still needed to pursue his original course in life and achieve his goals, in case he never recovered the book.

"Good idea, like £20,000 each?" said George gleefully.

Adam said it depended on how desperate the Cruzs were to sell. They could start with that and see how it went. Whatever happened, it was in their interest to stick together, he said in peroration.

George seemed to think it was a good idea. He wanted Adam on his side, because he did not trust Vera's husband any more than Adam, who hated the man for giving him the sack.

"We'd better join the girls," said George. "£20,000 each, then. We'll keep in touch."

"Of course," Adam agreed. "But let's keep it quiet from the girls for the moment. We won't mention our little deal."

"Absolutely not," agreed George.

Nothing further was mentioned during the evening, and after a very pleasant time together it was decided that George would drop Lucy off home and Adam would take Mary back to the flat. Much to Adam's relief, Lucy didn't seem disappointed by the arrangements. So he wasn't quite the ladies' man he was beginning to think of himself as – just as well, as in any case Adam thought it politic not to upset George unnecessarily. He was looking forward to seeing Vera's face when he made her the new offer.

They had been driving along mostly in silence when Mary suddenly asked Adam if he was trying to have a relationship with Lucy. However, when Adam assured her that she was just a work colleague and he had no romantic inclinations towards her, she perked up quite a bit, a fact which did not go unnoticed by Adam.

Adam decided not to complicate matters further by making any advances towards Mary. He had a lot on his plate already, and realistically he still needed the rental income from the flat to make ends meet while he was still out of a job.

He said goodnight to her at the flat and went to the empty room where he was going to spend the night, for he felt too tired to drive back home. He had told Mary earlier of his plan and she did not have any objections to it. If anything, she seemed quite happy about it.

★ ★ ★

That night when Adam felt quite thirsty he decided to get a glass of water from the kitchen, and when he came out of the kitchen he bumped into Mary coming out of the bathroom without a stitch of clothing on. It was as if she had timed herself to meet him.

"You look good," said Adam, not being able to think of anything better to say.

"I'm sorry." Mary blushed slightly. "I didn't realise you were about." However, she made no attempt to hide anything.

But Adam was too surprised to think of anything else to say at the moment. Witticism escaped him.

"I was a bit thirsty," he replied sheepishly.

"Well, goodnight again," said Mary, and disappeared into her room after throwing him a big smile.

"Goodnight," replied Adam, bemused, and as he walked back to his room he could not help feeling it was another lost opportunity. He consoled himself that he needed the rent.

CHAPTER 16

The next morning when Adam awoke, Mary had already left the flat. Adam got himself ready mentally for the day ahead. He had a meeting with Vera and Mr Cruz that morning about the purchase of the business. No doubt Vera was also meeting George, but she would make sure it was separately.

It made Adam smile, for Vera and her husband were in for a big surprise. He also had a meeting with Ramsbottom that evening, who had finally rung him on Sunday and who apparently had some news, but wanted more money. Ramsbottom always wanted more money. The expenses had been mounting steadily and Adam was beginning to regret that he had ever employed Ramsbottom in the first place.

Adam got ready and was just about to leave when Mary popped back in. She had been out shopping and was carrying a couple of bags with her.

"Thought you might want some breakfast." She smiled invitingly.

"There wasn't any food in the flat. I helped myself to a cup of tea already because I am in a hurry," said Adam. "I have to be at the college." But as Mary looked rather disappointed, he decided to offer her another alternative.

"How about lunch?" he said. "I'll be finished about twelve, so if you are free I'll come back and meet you."

"Sure." Mary perked up. "I'm not doing anything particular today."

"Great, I'll see you around one." Adam left the flat.

He made it to the college just after ten, the meeting with Vera being at ten thirty. He had had a horrendous journey by Underground and was feeling rather exasperated, but when he walked into the reception and saw Lucy he felt better.

She greeted him with a big smile, and offered him a cup of tea, which cheered him up. He told her the time when Vera and her husband were expecting him.

"But she's not in yet," said Lucy. "I believe just her husband is coming in this morning instead of her."

"Great," said Adam. "That's all I need. How are the student numbers holding up? Have I got a class next week?"

"They are not too bad," said Lucy. "I think you'll be okay. As you know, the numbers went down a little bit after you left." Lucy smiled.

"I knew the students liked me." Adam tried to sound a bit cocky.

"I'm not sure that you had anything to do with that." Lucy deflated his ego. "Get back alright yesterday?"

"Yeah, sure," said Adam, a little dented. "Stayed at the flat last night."

"Oh, I see." Lucy grinned.

"It wasn't like that." Adam smiled. "How about you?"

"George dropped me off and we had a cup of coffee, and then he left."

"Sure that was all? I saw the way he was looking at you."

"Can't a girl have any admirers these days?" Lucy protested.

"I am sure you've got many. I'm one of your big fans as well." Adam laid it on a bit thick.

But before they could continue any further, Mr Cruz, Vera's husband, walked in. Adam had wanted to pump Lucy further about the college, but this was not going to be the case. He would be seen in five minutes by Mr Cruz.

Soon Adam was being shown into Mr Cruz's office by Lucy, who winked at Adam as she walked out with her back turned to Cruz. Adam sat down and glanced around the room. The furniture had been somewhat shifted around since he had last been there, and there were some items missing as if there was a clear-out going on. Mr Cruz leaned back regally on his elongated throne of a chair and surveyed Adam for a moment, and then smiled broadly.

"So, Mr Smith, are you looking forward to having a share in the business? I'm sorry Vera could not make it today, but I thought I'd better deal with the matter."

"It depends on what role you want me to play, and also on the price."

"I thought the price had already been fixed." He smiled again.

"Not at all," said Adam. "A price was suggested but I did not agree to anything yet."

"What's on your mind?"

"Well, the business is currently not doing so well, I gather," said Adam. "It seems to have gone downhill since I left, so I'm willing to pay £20,000 for a twenty-five per cent share."

"That's ridiculous," said Cruz. "The business has been running for over ten years and it is doing fine."

"Well, that's my offer." Adam tried to look firm. "Also, I have to be made a director."

"I'm afraid we can't do a deal on that basis. You know there are other people interested in the business." Mr Cruz looked grim, but tried to smile.

"So I gather," said Adam. "Good luck with them." He called Mr Cruz's bluff, for he felt sure he knew full well who the other people, or person, concerned was.

"Well, I'll think about it," Mr Cruz said glumly.

"Will I still have my job next week when the new term starts?" Adam asked hopefully.

"Vera will be in touch with you about that." That was the end of the conversation.

Well, that was that, thought Adam, as he made his way out. He now had to wait; George would be in next and it all depended on what he said. Lucy was waiting for him outside and asked how it went, and Adam apprised her of the gist of his conversation with Cruz. She was not very impressed with the situation and said Adam may have blown it.

Adam replied that they would have to wait and see, trying to sound confident, even though he was not very sure himself. He asked Lucy what had happened to the furniture in the office, which had seemed a bit bare to him.

Lucy told him that they had been shifting some things out of the office in the last few weeks. The nice desk which had been in there, the pictures on the wall and any item of value had been removed. This struck Adam as very odd, but Lucy did not know anything further. Lucy wondered aloud if Adam was still going to start work there and Adam informed her that it depended very much on Vera, who was going to see him about that.

They agreed to keep in touch and Adam left after asking Lucy if George was coming in that day, but she did not know. Obviously they were not keeping her informed about these matters. He decided he would ring George later on to see how he got on.

Adam wanted to skip lunch at Wood Green with Mary as his mind was too full of other things, but in the end he decided to pay her a visit. He was not meeting Ramsbottom until five that afternoon, so there was no rush.

The next morning he was also due at the police station to see Officer Stevens, who wanted to question him again. No doubt he had found something out from Charlie, but exactly what, he did not know.

★ ★ ★

Adam got back to the flat about twelve and Mary was still there waiting for him. She wanted to cook him something for lunch but he did not have time to wait.

However, it was too early to go out and eat and Adam was not feeling very hungry. In the end, it was decided that they would drive out to Ironbridge Spa and have lunch there and then she would catch a train back later. Adam did not see anything wrong with it. It was only lunch and she seemed a nice girl, and Adam did not want to disappoint her.

When Adam came out of the flat with Mary to his car, he noticed somebody had put a long scratch down the side of it with a screwdriver or a key. This made Adam quite angry; his luck seemed be turning from bad to worse. He cursed an obscenity under his breath, but checked himself from saying anything aloud because of the presence of Mary. Adam was sure it was Doug and his friend, but didn't want to bring it up.

The drive back was uneventful and they soon reached Ironbridge Spa. Adam decided he would take Mary to a better restaurant than the one where he had taken Linda, and buy her an expensive lunch. He was in a lugubrious mood and wanted to cheer himself up much more than to impress Mary. However, Mary seemed quite impressed by his gesture and even appreciated the wine much more than seemed necessary. The wine was good, but not quite that good.

After they had polished off a bottle and finished the lunch in style, Adam suggested he should take her to the station before going back to his house.

"Oh, but I would like to see your house very much," interrupted Mary.

"I have to meet somebody there on an important business matter," protested Adam. But Mary was very persuasive and insisted that she would not get in the way at all, so finally he decided to let her come with him. He would drive her back later to Ironbridge Spa station.

When they reached Littledon there was still almost an hour left before he saw Ramsbottom, so he decided to pop into the pub with Mary for a quick drink and to see if he could pick up any further information on the book by meeting Bruce if he happened to be there.

"The Three Witches?" exclaimed Mary. "I've heard of this place."

"Oh, where?" queried Adam. He was suddenly feeling a tingling sensation on the back of his neck.

"I can't really remember." Mary checked herself. "Is it a nice pub?"

"Well, I have mixed feelings about it," replied Adam, thinking nothing further of it.

"Oh, why?" asked Mary.

"You meet some strange types in there, from the hostile to almost over-friendly."

As they entered the pub Adam could see straight away that Bruce was sitting there with his cronies. Among them he noticed a man called Ernie, with very deadpan eyes, who sent a little shiver down him. As Adam approached Bruce's eyes seemed to light up, almost as if there was a hint of recognition there towards Mary.

Adam quickly glanced at Mary, but there was no sign of any familiarity there. Adam said hello to Bruce, and as he introduced Mary to him, he again had the strangest feeling at the back of his mind that the two knew each other, but neither gave anything away. After the exchange of pleasantries was over Bruce offered them a drink, which Adam accepted.

"Every time I see you here, you are with a different girl," complained Bruce after getting the drinks. "Who's this one?"

"Oh, Mary? Just my tenant," said Adam defensively, instantly regretting giving him that information.

"So you have another place?" asked Bruce.

"Just a small flat in London." Adam gave in. "Anyway, how's things with you? Found the book?"

"You tell me." Bruce smiled in a mysterious way. "It rained again."

"So it did," agreed Adam. "Maybe it was just the weather."

"What, with the sky clear as a bell one minute and thunder and lightning the next? No, my friend, you are not telling me something." He was almost threatening.

Adam soon found it was time to leave. He made his apologies to Bruce and said he was in a hurry and would get him a drink the next time he saw him. Bruce seemed to accept things with good grace, and as they were leaving he gave Mary a wink, which Adam pretended not to notice. However, when they were outside the pub, he asked Mary about it.

"What was all that about? Why was Bruce winking at you?" he asked Mary bluntly.

"Was he? I didn't really notice." Mary denied it. "Maybe he was trying to warn me against you. You seem to have a reputation around here."

"Don't listen to gossip." Adam pretended to be annoyed, but actually he was quite enjoying his newfound reputation.

"Okay, if you say so."

"It's just that some friends have visited me here, and like you, they were interested in seeing the house." As they approached it he saw a figure was waiting for him there. It was Ramsbottom. Adam parked the car and invited them all into the house.

Mary asked to be excused after asking where the bathroom was. Adam had not bothered introducing Ramsbottom to Mary, and they just nodded to each other.

"Well, what's the big news then?" Adam asked Ramsbottom.

"I've found the book," said Ramsbottom.

"Where is it? Can I have it?"

"I haven't got it," was the bland reply.

"You said you've found the book." Adam was exasperated. The man seemed to annoy him more and more.

"Yes, it's in the shop Daley sold it to. I followed Daley there on Saturday," came the bland reply again.

"Was it still there?"

"Yes, sure. I don't know why Daley went around there, but it was still there after he left."

"So why the hell didn't you get it?" Adam was livid that Ramsbottom had eschewed the logical conclusion.

"They wanted £200 for it. I don't carry that sort of money with me when I'm in the field," Ramsbottom said tersely.

Adam couldn't believe his ears anymore, and he lost control.

"You fool! The whole purpose of employing you was to get the book back," he said in a raised voice.

"I'm not spending £200 of my cash," said Ramsbottom sounding cool to the idea. "If you want it you have to pay for it."

"I'll get it myself," said Adam angrily. "What's the address of the bookshop?"

"There's a little matter of my expenses first," said Ramsbottom. "I don't much care for the mood you are in."

Adam asked how much it was and was told that there was £350 outstanding. It was beyond Adam's understanding how that figure was made up and he knew it was hopeless arguing about it, but he made a pitiful try.

"Isn't that a bit too much?" asked Adam.

"Not at all," was the glib reply. "You'll get a detailed statement in the post. Don't forget you still need to pay me the extra £500 if you manage to get the book from the shop."

Adam fished for his chequebook, which he happened to have in his pocket, and wrote out a cheque for the amount. Ramsbottom then produced a piece of paper from his pocket and wrote out the address of the bookshop.

They exchanged items and Ramsbottom was about to leave.

"I don't think I will be needing your services any further," Adam told Ramsbottom rather tersely.

"*C'est la vie!* Well, goodbye then, sir," said Ramsbottom rather tersely. "Thank you for the work. I'm glad I could be of some help."

"Yes, yes," said Adam impolitely. He was a bit surprised by Ramsbottom's sudden penchant for French. "Thanks very much."

"Oh, before I go," said Ramsbottom, " – and I'll throw this bit in for nothing – I've seen that girl you are with before, with your Australian friend."

"You have?" asked Adam incredulously.

"Yes, but I can't recall where," came the exasperating reply. "Goodbye, sir."

And with that Ramsbottom was gone. Adam glanced up and saw Mary walking down the stairs. He had no idea how long she had been there and what she had overheard. Adam put the piece of paper in his pocket and decided to confront Mary.

"He says he has seen you before," said Adam, "with Bruce."

"Who is that man? I've never seen him before in my life." Mary denied the whole thing.

"Maybe he is just imagining things," said Adam tersely.

"I've got one of those faces which lots of people seem to recognise as somebody they have seen before," Mary said soothingly. "Anyway, what were you arguing about, some book or something?"

"Something like that," said Adam. "It's not important; he was trying to locate something I had lost."

"Has he found it?" she asked, concerned.

"I don't think so," Adam lied, thinking he had given away too much already.

"Oh, I see," said Mary, disappointed. "Listen, I've got a good idea. Why don't you put me up for the night and I'll cook you a meal? You've had quite a lot to drink and I don't want you to drive me to the station tonight."

Adam had a funny feeling about it but decided that he could not see any harm in it. There were two spare rooms in the house and to tell the truth, he did not feel like driving any more that evening.

"Sure, make yourself at home. I am not sure I have too much food, but we can always order a takeaway," he said, smiling, and excused himself to go to the loo upstairs.

Mary went into the kitchen as he made his way upstairs. He wanted not so much to relieve himself but to see what was on the piece of paper Ramsbottom had given him. Once upstairs he took the paper out of his pocket and read it. It said *University Bookshop, London Road, Cambridge.* That was simple enough. He decided to tear up the piece of paper and flush it down the toilet. This he actually found to be a much more daunting task than he had anticipated, as pieces of the paper kept floating back up.

He tried dumping more toilet paper on the small bits of paper, but this did not work. He then tried to push them down with the toilet brush, but that also failed. In the end he poured some bleach on the pieces of paper hoping to dissolve them, but this did not do the trick either. However, in the end, with repeated flushing, he finally got rid of all the pieces of paper.

Adam made his way down to the kitchen where Mary was busy preparing the food. She told him she had found quite a bit of food in the fridge, like eggs and bacon and other goodies, so a meal would soon be on the way.

How wonderful it was to have a woman around the place to take care of things, thought Adam. He got a can of lager for himself and one for Mary from the fridge and then made his way to the living room to drink in peace.

However, the phone started ringing just at that moment, and when he answered it, it was Vera. *Here we go*, thought Adam, but Vera was as nice as she could be and instead of telling Adam that he was no longer needed, she assured him that he still had a job at the college, whatever the outcome of the negotiations. Vera then asked him if she could meet him the next day.

"I'm doing something tomorrow morning," he said, thinking of the police interview.

"How about lunch then?" asked Vera, pleading. "I can come down there, I need to see you desperately." How could Adam refuse such a plea? So he agreed to meet her at the Ironbridge Spa railway station at one thirty the next day.

"Who was that?" asked Mary, popping her head around the door of the kitchen.

"Oh, just work." Adam said dismissively.

"You should relax a bit occasionally," suggested Mary. "Instead of thinking about what you have to do all the time."

"You are right," said Adam. "I'm not going to talk about work anymore tonight."

"Good," said Mary. "Dinner is ready. Clear the table. I've found some wine."

Adam came back into the living kitchen to do so. Soon they were tucking into the meal she had cooked out of almost nothing. It felt unusually good to Adam even though he had had a pretty good lunch. The wine tasted particularly good.

When he finished the meal he felt slightly light-headed, and was feeling unusually horny.

"Let's go into the living room and relax," Mary suggested.

Adam did not need any prodding. He picked up his wine and followed Mary into the living room, and they both sat down quite close to each other. Indeed, she was sitting so close to him that Adam reached out and stroked her hair and neck with his left hand. Before he knew what was happening Mary was sitting on his lap and he was trying to swallow her tongue. It felt wonderful, and as he kissed Mary back, there was no word of protest from her.

"Shall we go upstairs?" asked Mary after a while. Adam nodded, and as they stood up Mary grabbed him from behind around the waist, and after stroking his chest for a bit, she slowly put both her hands into his trouser pockets. Was she looking for something, he thought? And then he knew what she was looking for.

Within minutes they fell into bed together and virtually ripped each other's clothes off. Unfortunately it did not last too long, for within minutes it was all over and Adam fell back, feeling very disappointed. However, he did not get a chance to rest too long, as Mary didn't let him. Soon he was back on top and this time it went on for ages, and when they finished Mary had a very satisfied smile on her face. But now his eyes felt very heavy, and he could hardly keep them open. He saw Mary get up and she was doing something with his jacket, and then he fell asleep.

He was dreaming that he was having sex with Mary and it was fantastic, and then he woke up with a jolt and Mary was riding him again.

"I love you," he said. "I'm in heaven."

"Shh," said Mary, and she started kissing him as she kept up the action. Adam suddenly realised his hands and legs were tied to the four corners of the bed.

Mary went on and on. It felt like that night was never going to end. He felt almost delirious. She started whispering to him, but it wasn't about love.

"Where's the piece of paper that man gave you?" she asked.

Adam tried to concentrate. "What paper?" he tried to say, but the words would not come out.

"I flushed it down the toilet." He smiled weakly as Mary carried on.

She started to moan. "Tell me what was on it?" she asked.

"I can't remember," said Adam. He tried to concentrate on the pleasure as Mary's groans grew louder.

"Try to remember." She slapped him, but did not stop what she was doing. But Adam did not feel any pain, only more intense pleasure. He could die of too much pleasure. He tried to remember, but it was fuzzy.

"Universal Bookshop, Cambridge Road, London," he said finally, with great effort.

Mary arched her back and let out a massive moan and started shuddering, and then she was done and so was Adam. He nodded off to sleep again.

When he woke it was next morning. There was no sign of Mary, but mercifully his hands and legs had been untied. His body still tingled from the night before; he felt fantastic. He could not remember much except that he had had the most wonderful time ever. He was ready to face anything. He was ready for the interview with Officer Stevens. He should have felt totally enervated, but instead he was bursting with energy.

However, Adam slowly began to remember bits about the night before. How Mary had tied his hands and feet, and how she was asking him questions. She had been asking him questions about the book. It was all about the book. He was just a pawn in the great scheme of things. So Ramsbottom had been right: she was thick as thieves with Bruce.

Just when he thought his luck with women was changing, he was being let down yet again. She must have drugged him, the bitch.

CHAPTER 17

Adam collected the contents of his wallet from the bedroom floor. All his trouser pockets were empty, but he could not remember why. He had a quick shower and got dressed, as it was almost time to get down to the police station.

It was ten o'clock when Adam reached the police station. He went up to the reception kiosk and was told he needed to get a ticket and wait his turn.

The station was well secured, with only the reception area being accessible to the public. Even the reception desk was isolated with thick glass panels.

Finally his number came up and he was seen by an officer behind the glass panel. Adam told him he had an appointment with Officer Stevens at ten.

"You're late for your appointment, sir," said the man, who was a small, muscular person in uniform.

"But I was here on time. You told me to take a ticket and wait," Adam protested.

"That's the system, sir, you have to wait your turn," the man said uninterestedly. "You need to come early enough to take that into account."

"Sorry, I didn't know," said Adam. "First time in a police station."

The man picked up the phone and sent a message to Officer Stevens and asked Adam to wait again. Adam went back to the seating area to find all the seats had been taken. The place was filling up rapidly.

Officer Stevens appeared ten minutes later and greeted Adam, and motioned him to follow him through a side door, which led to an interview room. There was another man waiting there who was introduced as Detective Turnbull. The officer switched on a recording device.

"I will be interviewing you with Detective Turnbull present." Turnbull went through the police caution. He told Adam that he didn't have to say anything when questioned, but it would harm his defence if he forgot to mention something which he later relied on in court, etc. Things looked serious.

"You can request for a lawyer to be present, and we can call a duty solicitor if you do not have your own representative."

"Are you arresting me?" asked Adam.

"Not at the moment." Officer Stevens smiled grimly. "But this is a formal interview and it will be recorded. Now, would you like a solicitor?"

"Not necessary," said Adam. "I'm fine."

The interview carried on and Adam was first asked his name and address.

"What do you know about the whereabouts of Richard Drummond?"

"I don't know where he is," replied Adam.

"He was last seen at your place and we have witnesses corroborating the fact," said Officer Stevens.

"I told you before, he left that morning," said Adam.

"What is your relationship with his wife?"

"I don't have a relationship with her," retorted Adam.

"But she visited you and stayed the night at your place," insisted Officer Stevens.

"Who told you that?" asked Adam.

"We have our sources." The officer smiled, and Adam knew instantly who the source was: Wendy and Jack!

"Yeah, well, she came to look for her husband and it was too late for her to get home, and I have several bedrooms in the house."

"That's very convenient," said Detective Turnbull.

"I don't know what you mean," replied Adam, trying to keep calm.

"Your friend has already confessed," said Officer Stevens.

"To what? We didn't do anything."

"That's your story."

"Look, ever since you made fools of yourselves digging up my patio, you've been out to get me."

"We'll find the body sooner or later," said Detective Turnbull.

"So it's murder now, is it?" Adam tried to show disbelief. "What's the motive? He is a good friend of mine."

"You were probably jealous of him and are having an affair with his wife."

"Is that what Charlie told you?"

"No, but he said you fancied her," replied Officer Stevens smugly.

"Look, she is a lovely girl, but she is a friend's wife," Adam pleaded.

"You were jealous of his money and success," said Detective Turnbull.

"Is that why you did him in?" asked Officer Stevens.

"I didn't do him in. In any case, why should I be jealous of him? I've got more money than he has and it's all legit," snapped Adam.

"Your friend Charlie said you sacrificed him in some magic ritual," said Officer Stevens.

"So where is the body?" Adam smiled. "I'm sure my neighbours have already confirmed that I never left the house the day Richard disappeared – I mean, when he left the house," Adam corrected himself.

"He also said that your friend never left the house either."

"So where is he?" asked Adam.

"That's what we are going to find out," said Detective Turnbull.

"I think you'd better charge me or let me go," said Adam.

"Your friend Charlie said you turned him into a crayfish," said Officer Stevens, "using some magic spell." He was looking a bit unsure of himself at this point.

"And you believed him?" Adam squared his eyes on the squirming Officer Stevens. "So tell me, why didn't I turn you into a little frog?"

The two policemen looked at each other, and were finding it difficult to say anything further.

"Now, if you've finished with this cock-and-bull story, can we stop?" continued Adam in a belligerent tone.

"Interview ended 12.35pm," said Officer Stevens reluctantly. "You may go for now."

"Listen, why don't you check out Dick's wife? She's got some Australian staying with her in her house, who she brought back from holiday." Adam smiled and then added, "Would she be doing that if she was having an affair with me?"

Adam left the police station at twenty to one, feeling quite smug with himself. He had given Officer Stevens what he deserved. He had to rush because he had quite forgotten that he was meeting Vera at one thirty.

★ ★ ★

However, he made it to the station well before time. What he really needed, though, was to get to Cambridge fast, before the others worked things out. He decided he would get rid of Vera after lunch and make his way up to Cambridge. There was no way he could just give up on her.

The train was just pulling in as he got there and Vera got off the train looking fantastic as ever. She had a cute little suit on with slits in the skirt, which showed off her black tights with their little gold motifs which gleamed in the sunlight. As ever, she looked a picture and she knew it. She was out to make an impression, and she had Adam completely mesmerised. And he was not the only one, going by the number of whistles she was getting from the people doing maintenance on the side of the station. Adam limbered up to her and kissed her on the cheeks continental-style as if she was some long-lost friend.

"Wow," he said. "You can certainly dazzle if you wish to."

"Can I?" she asked sweetly. "Are you impressed?"

"Oh, more than impressed," said Adam honestly. "I can't take my eyes off you."

"So it was worth the effort," said Vera. "I'm so pleased, it was all for you."

"And what can I do for you?" Adam smiled.

"Shall we have lunch?" She smiled alluringly. "We can talk while we eat." That suited Adam very much, who was feeling rather hungry at the time. He decided to take her to another really fancy restaurant.

Once they had ordered the drinks after sitting down, Vera smiled at him. Adam smiled back, trying to keep his mind on the menu.

"You look like the cat that just had the cream," she said, still smiling.

"Not yet," said Adam. "But I would like to."

"Feeling very self-confident, it seems." Vera laughed.

"Not at all, I'm just wishing," said Adam. "Can you blame any man for that? Especially as you look the way you do."

"Thank you," mused Vera. "But there is really something very different about you today, I can't quite put my finger on it."

They ordered lunch and ate mainly in silence, but when their hands touched by accident, sparks flew.

"You know why I am here?" she asked finally.

"To see me," said Adam.

"Also that," said Vera. "I have missed you, but I also need to talk about something else."

"The sale of the shares," prodded Adam.

"Yes," said Vera. "Both you and George have offered the same price, so obviously you have ganged up together."

"Well, we are trying to strike a reasonable deal," Adam reassured her.

"I'm afraid the price is a bit low," said Vera. "Can't you increase it a bit? My husband can't open his other college abroad unless he gets more."

"But is the place worth it?" asked Adam.

"Sure." Vera smiled. "With his other venture, he will be away a lot and I'll be in London looking after the college with you."

"And George," Adam prompted.

"Yes, of course," agreed Vera. "But you know what I mean."

"How much?" Adam smiled.

"Let's talk about it later," Vera suggested. "Shall we go back to your village for a drink? I'd love to see your house again now that it's nearly finished."

It all felt like a sense of *déjà vu* to Adam at that moment. He seemed to have been down this path only two days earlier.

"Let's," he said. He was never one to question the taste of Manna from heaven. "I'd love to show you my house again and get your opinion on the final touches."

So as they drove back, Adam felt almost delirious. He had only one ambition at that moment and he was prepared to pay dearly for it. Cambridge would have to wait a little. He suppressed any thoughts of guilt.

"Why don't we go straight back to my place?" he suggested. "Get the business over with and go for a drink later? Anyway, I have plenty of drinks in the house." Adam desperately wanted to avoid any encounters with the locals, or Bruce for that matter. He wanted Vera to himself.

"Why not?" Vera smiled, much to Adam's relief, knowing full well what business Adam had in mind. There was a warning bell going off at the back of his head, but he ignored it. Surely tomorrow morning should be soon enough to get hold of the book, he thought.

★ ★ ★

Adam asked Vera what she thought when they had entered the house, after grabbing her around the waist and pulling her close.

"It still needs a bit of work," said Vera, as if it was a metaphor for herself. "Shall we have a drink first?"

"Sure," said Adam. "Before what?"

The thirst for her was quite overpowering, but it was Mary he really wanted. But Adam knew it was impossible; she was in some way connected with Bruce.

"Before getting down to business," replied Vera.

As Adam poured the drinks he turned towards Vera and asked her what was the price that Mr Cruz was prepared to accept. Adam knew he was being used, but it was an incentive he could hardly refuse, especially after the episode with Mary, whose real interest had only been to acquire the book for Bruce.

"At least 330,000 each," said Vera, "for twenty-five per cent each."

"Don't forget I'm not the only one who has to agree," prompted Adam. "George has a say in it as well."

"He'll agree whatever you agree." Vera was positive.

"Let's say £25,000," Adam said.

"Can I trust you to keep your word?" Vera smiled.

"Shall we seal the bargain?" asked Adam, and grabbed Vera; this was as good a chance as he was ever going to get.

"£25,000, then. Don't forget." She offered her lips readily. On the face of it he seemed to be paying a high price, but at that moment Adam was quite prepared to pay almost anything.

"You seem irresistible today," she said as he stripped her clothes off. "A bit more slowly, though," she commanded. "There's no hurry. There is something different about you today," she said again.

But Adam was in a hurry – a very great, urgent hurry. He had been waiting a very long time for this moment, and whatever was making Vera so agreeable, he wanted to utilise it before the effects wore off.

Finally they were in bed together, and it seemed to go on for an eternity.

"If I only knew how good you were I would have given in a long time ago," she said finally, much to Adam's surprise, but then added, "But it's almost five o'clock and I'll have to go. My husband will be expecting me. I think it was a bad mistake on his part to send me here today."

"Why don't you leave him?" asked Adam, hoping that his luck had finally changed. He was suddenly now even more besotted with her. He had thought he wanted Mary, but Vera was a surprise package he had finally unwrapped.

"You wouldn't understand – I have family obligations," said Vera, as if the whole thing was a mistake. "Normally I am very faithful to him. But today you were just irresistible. Don't ask me why."

"He's just using you," retorted Adam, but he knew it was futile. *It was just too good to last*, he thought. *She's only here to make the deal.*

"No it's not as simple as that," protested Vera. "Anyway, you got much more than my husband or I intended. Don't worry, I'm going to look after you. My husband is away a lot and I really like you."

"It was my lucky day." Adam let it go. He had an interesting idea; it had something to do with the night before, but he did not broach the subject. He knew he had surpassed himself for some reason. Something had rubbed off on him the day before, or he was on something that Mary had given him, and its effects had not yet dissipated. Anyway, he did not care anymore – he felt great, and what he needed was to get hold of more of the stuff that he was sure Mary had put in his drink.

As Vera was putting her clothes back on, he remembered about the book. He was supposed to go to Cambridge today to recover it. But it was too late already. It was past five and most of those sorts of shops closed soon. There was no way that he was going to make it there that evening.

CHAPTER 18

After dropping Vera off at the station Adam came back to the house. He felt very tired suddenly. Whatever Mary had given him was beginning to wear off, and tiredness was overcoming him. He wanted to get to bed early that evening and make a very early start the next morning, but he had a sneaking suspicion that a car had been following him all the way from the station. He remembered he had given Mary the wrong address, but still did not know how he had managed it. It had required a superhuman effort not to divulge the correct address of the bookshop. A great deal of willpower, which Adam had never before realised he had. It had been strong enough to survive the onslaught from Mary and twist the address around. But they would realise it soon as they tried to find the bookshop, and it was inevitable that they would then be looking for him, unless they could figure it out for themselves.

It dawned on Adam that maybe it was far too dangerous to stay in the house that night, and that he had to go somewhere else. But it was no good going back to the flat, for Bruce knew where it was also. He was now sure that Mary and Bruce knew each other and were part of the same team that was looking for the book.

As he was getting ready to go, a car suddenly pulled up outside. Adam could see from the window that it was Bruce and another man he had seen with Bruce before, and soon there was a knock on the door.

The squat gorilla of a man had a look of meanness about him generally, which was hard to quantify, but made Adam very apprehensive. Most of all it was his eyes; they just radiated coldness. They sent shivers down Adam's spine. He had met him before.

Adam was in trouble, for there was no way for him to get out past them. Not only that, they had parked their car in such a way that they had blocked both of Adam's cars in. So there was no use escaping through the back door, as they would soon catch up with him.

Adam put the alarm on, grabbed his jacket and car keys and made for the kitchen. The hidden basement was his only option. He remembered the last time Bruce was there, he had missed it.

Adam wanted the alarm to go off if they forced the door open. However, as he entered the kitchen, he could hear the front door being opened already, as if he hadn't even bothered to lock it. The alarm didn't go off either, for some reason. *They haven't had to force the door open*, he thought. There had been no sound of splintering wood, if a jemmy was being used.

"He must be somewhere," Bruce's voice boomed, as Adam squeezed in through the half-open cellar door. "Find him. His cars are still outside."

"I'll have a look upstairs," the other man said. "You look downstairs."

Adam just managed to get into the basement and close the door with the dresser unit attached to it, hiding it from view. Lucky for him the wheels underneath the unit didn't creak. He hoped against hope that they would not discover him, or he was in big trouble.

Either they had not found the address he had given them, or alternatively they had already been to the bookshop and not found the book. He didn't much care which it was just then. He just wanted desperately for them not to find him.

A few minutes passed and the man came back from upstairs and met Bruce again by the kitchen.

"He's not upstairs," said the man to Bruce. Adam could hear them talking, but they didn't bother coming into the kitchen, as they could probably see from the doorway that it was empty.

"He's not downstairs either," said Bruce.

"Maybe he's in the back garden."

"No, I've already checked. The back door is locked, so he hasn't gone out that way," said Bruce, who sounded hugely annoyed.

"He must have popped out somewhere."

"Well, the only places I can think of are the village shop or The Three Witches," said Bruce.

"Shall we wait for him to come back?" asked the man.

"You wait for him here and I'll go and check out the pub and the village shop," said Bruce.

"Okay," said the man. "Call me if you need me."

"Okay, Ernie, but watch yourself if he comes back. Mary told me he can be a bit of a handful, the way he beat up Doug."

"Don't worry about me, mate, I'll sort him out for you. He'll find out I'm not a wimp like Doug. Yeah, I'm lookin' forward to smashin' his bloody face in."

Bruce left, slamming the door behind him. So Adam had been right after all when he thought he had seen Doug's friend somewhere. It was at The Three Witches with Bruce. They were out to intimidate him into giving up the book, until Mary had probably persuaded them to let her have a go. Obviously they had resorted to their old tactics again.

Adam couldn't help smiling at the thought of such a mean-looking man being called Ernie, though he dreaded what he was hearing. Obviously they were out to do him bodily harm. This was his chance, though, at last; he needed a gateway plan, while there was only one of them in the house. Even though he didn't relish the idea of confronting Ernie at all, he had to make a move.

Adam heard Ernie move towards the living room and tiptoed out of the basement. He needed a plan, but could not think of anything useful.

Adam was desperate, and all kinds of thoughts criss-crossed his mind. Was it best to make a run for it after all and knock on the neighbour's door for help? Unfortunately he didn't hold out much hope of support from Jack, big as he was. One look at Ernie and he would shut the door firmly in Adam's face, after telling him off, in no uncertain terms, for not sorting his troubles out himself.

Adam thought of ringing the police, but was sure they would arrive too late to help him. Bruce would be back long before they would turn up, and meanwhile Bruce and Ernie would make mincemeat out of him.

No, he would have to tackle Ernie, before Bruce came back. What was needed was direct action, but he would have to surprise Ernie, otherwise he would stand no chance.

Adam remembered that the plumber had left behind a wooden mallet. It was still where he had put it, in the cupboard under the kitchen sink. Adam took it out as quietly as possible. It felt good in his hand.

He now needed to surprise Ernie, but how? He thought of tiptoeing down to the living room and hitting him on the head with the mallet. But that was never going to work. The chances were that Ernie would hear him or see him long before Adam reached him, and that would be that. Ernie had been driving and Adam needed their car keys, which Ernie had in his possession, to clear the way before he could drive off in his own car.

Adam decided on a plan, but he had to get to the front door without being noticed by Ernie. What he wanted now was a diversion. He took out his mobile and dialled his own house landline. The phone was situated in a corner of the living room, from where one could not see the corridor.

Adam's plan was to run out of the front door and bang it behind him. He would then wait for Ernie to come rushing out after him, whereupon he would ambush him. But would he come, and would Adam be able to go through with hitting him with a mallet? It was the sort of cold-blooded violence to which Adam was totally unaccustomed.

But time was ticking by, and his phone wasn't ringing. Adam looked at his mobile; in his haste he had dialled the wrong number. Adam could hear footsteps coming his way. Adam cursed himself and redialled. As his phone in his living room started ringing, the footsteps stopped and then reversed, whereupon Adam made a dash for the door. He ran out of the kitchen with his mallet, cutting short his call to make sure that Ernie could hear him. He slammed the front door behind him.

Adam took up a position on the right of the door as he went out. The door was hinged on the left-hand side and swung open inwards. It was therefore more natural for a person to look towards the left first when opening the door. At least Adam hoped this would be the case when Ernie popped his head out.

Adam didn't have to wait long before his prediction came true, as out popped Ernie's head, looking towards the left. As he was turning his head to the right Adam hit him with the mallet, but the blow was a bit tentative, for he didn't want to kill the man. Horror and surprise showed on Ernie's face as he staggered back and tried to close the door. Adam kicked the door hard and hit Ernie with the mallet again as he pushed his way in, but Ernie half-blocked the blow and still didn't go down.

Ernie was strong, much stronger than Adam had realised, as he headbutted Adam. Luckily Adam caught the blow on his own forehead and not his face. As he staggered back, he could see Ernie was also staggering a bit himself after the headbutt. Most likely the cumulative effects of the two previous blows and the headbutt were telling on him.

Adam hit him again, square on his forehead this time. He felt like he was trying to stop a bulldozer, however this time Ernie's eyes glazed over and he slumped to the floor. Adam hoped he hadn't killed him, but was almost past caring. He searched Ernie's pocket for the car keys, as he knew Ernie had driven the car which was blocking his own cars.

Adam soon found the keys in the right-hand pocket of Ernie's jacket. He ran out, closing the door behind him, jumped into Ernie's car and drove it clear of his own new car. He then ran to his own car and drove off with the keys to Ernie's car still in his pocket.

After he had driven clear, he rang the police and reported an attempted burglary at his house. *That'll teach them to break into my place*, he thought with great satisfaction, as he drove towards Cambridge and the bookshop.

Things were getting very exciting all of a sudden, but they were also getting very dangerous. Bruce and his mob obviously wanted the book badly and Adam was not sure how far they were willing to go to get their hands on it. Only they knew the real value of the book. But Adam also needed the book badly. He needed it to get Dick back, if indeed he could get him back, but that was the next stage, as he needed to recover the book first to even attempt it.

Adam booked himself into a cheap little hotel in Cambridge, not far from the bookshop. He had gone past it to see if it was still open, but he was not expecting it to be. He grabbed a bite to eat in a little Indian restaurant around the corner and then went straight to bed. He soon realised that it was always a bad thing to go to bed on a full stomach, because it induced nightmares. He was already mentally and physically exhausted after his amorous endeavours that afternoon and the night before, even before his run-in with Ernie.

He knew he was paying too much for the share in the English college, but he did not care at all that moment. He reasoned to himself that he could not better use the money to uplift his image and status, and the college had great potential if it worked correctly. His only worry now was whether George would agree.

Sleep came very slowly, for he was overtired and over-full, and it was very troubled sleep indeed. The nightmares began almost instantly; he found himself being chased by both Bruce and Mary. He wanted to run, but Bruce had him in a vice-like grip and he was pinned down.

"Leave me alone," he heard himself saying, but they just laughed at him.

"You've had your fun, and now you don't want to pay the price," said Mary.

"But I don't owe you anything," he protested.

"But you do," said Bruce. "You owe us a great deal for the fun you've had."

"You don't think I wanted to sleep with you out of choice, do you?" said Mary.

"I thought you liked me," pleaded Adam.

"But it's not true," sneered Mary. "I even had to give you something to make you perform. Otherwise you'd be useless in bed."

"I thought you loved me," said Adam desperately.

"All I want is the book."

Mary was still there. She was sitting on top of him as she had done when she had made love to him. Bruce had disappeared.

"Where's the book, Adam?" she was screaming at him. "Tell me where the book is."

"It's in a bookshop," Adam blurted out again. The dream was so real. He decided to push Mary back and get on top of her; after all, he was stronger than her.

That wasn't too bad, thought Adam after he had managed to achieve his objective. He had Mary pinned down for a change and she suddenly became quite submissive.

Sometimes all they needed was to know who the boss was, Adam decided as Mary started kissing him. At last he was beginning to enjoy his dream.

Adam relaxed and Mary started stroking his hair, and then started pushing his head down her body. Adam knew what she wanted, and after one or two stops on the way down, he got down to business. Then suddenly he heard Mary's voice and he looked up.

"You lied to us," rasped Mary again, and there was something gleaming in her hand. Adam tried to protest, but he knew it was going to be too late.

"We found the book anyway, so we don't need you anymore." Bruce appeared again.

"No, wait!" Adam tried to say, but it was useless. The dagger came plunging down on him.

Adam woke with a scream; his whole bed was wet with sweat. His clothes were soaked completely. It was still dark outside, and in the eerie twilight the room took on a spooky atmosphere. As the room had not come with its own bathroom attached, Adam groggily made his way down the hall to the communal bathroom to splash his face with water.

That had the effect of waking him up, and he made his way back to the room.

As he came towards the open door of his room, somebody came out of it, and without thinking, Adam made a grab for him. The man pushed him away, and as Adam was about to punch him, he realised it was the hotel manager.

"Just came to see what the commotion was," the man said. "People in the next room complained that there was a lot of noise coming from your room. I found your door open when I came up, so I decided to check."

Adam was not sure whether to believe the man or not, but finally he said that he had been having a nightmare.

The man laughed and left. Adam went inside to check whether his possessions were still intact, and they seemed to be, so he felt that the man was probably telling the truth. Adam had been growing very suspicious of everybody lately because of what was going on in his life.

He needed to calm himself down and get some sleep. He lay down on the bed, but sleep was not forthcoming. He felt quite tired, but he could not sleep, which had never been a problem of his. He decided he would get out of bed early and skip breakfast as he could not face the tedium of it, and then make his way to the bookshop. However, this was not to be as at about seven o'clock he fell into a deep sleep after dozing off for a moment.

★ ★ ★

Adam woke about ten thirty. He had missed breakfast already, but did not regret the fact. By the time he got downstairs it was ten past eleven.

"You're supposed to check out by eleven. I need to charge you for another day," said the man downstairs.

"You must be joking," said a shocked Adam. "It's only ten minutes after. I'm not paying any more."

"I'll have to report you to the police," the man threatened.

"Go on then," retorted Adam, who was by now in a foul mood indeed, and wanted to punch the man. This was of course not very practical as the man was much bigger than Adam. In the end Adam offered the man a fiver, which the man readily accepted and neatly put into his pocket straight away.

"Don't I get a receipt then?" asked Adam.

"Only if you want to pay the tax on top," was the tart reply.

Adam decided it was best to just let it go and look for the book. It had not been the best start to the morning he had hoped for, and he did not want to waste any more time.

Adam reached the shop after a short walk from the hotel. It was a small bookshop full of old books that belied its name of the University Bookshop. There was not a single course textbook that could be seen anywhere, and of course there were no signs of any students rummaging through the books or looking to buy course material.

"Why is it called University Bookshop?" Adam asked out of curiosity.

"We used to sell books to the students when we just opened, but that market crashed through the floor when a large bookshop opened around the corner. It would cost too much to change the name, so we left it."

"Why not?" agreed Adam.

"I kind of like the name," the man said.

"So do I," said Adam.

"Good," said the man, a slightly plump, balding, grey gentleman in his mid-forties most likely, who seemed to have a perpetual big smile on his face. This probably meant he really enjoyed his work. "Now, can I help you with something or do you want to know more about the history of the shop?" He smiled again.

"Well, I am looking for a book," said Adam.

"I can gather that," the man quipped. "This is a bookshop."

Wise guy, thought Adam, but he did not rise to the bait.

"There was a book in German, you had it in your window last weekend." But Adam did not have to describe the book any further.

"Funny," said the man, "we've been having a lot of enquires about this particular book."

"Have you still got it?" asked Adam.

"Sorry, no." The man smiled. "A guy only sold it to me about a week ago. On Saturday, he came back to buy it back, but didn't have enough money on him, then an older gentleman came and looked at it but did not buy it. Yesterday afternoon another man and a woman were asking about it, and now you."

Bloody Ramsbottom – he had had it in his hands and let it go. It must have been Bruce and Mary this morning. All was lost. Bruce and Mary had finally worked out where the shop was.

"Did you sell it to the couple?" asked Adam.

"No," said the man. "It had already gone, and guess who bought it?"

"Who?" asked Adam desperately.

"It was the man who sold it to me in the first place. He was back yesterday morning, before the couple," guffawed the bookseller, but it wasn't the least bit funny to Adam.

Daley, thought Adam, it had to be Daley. He asked the man for a description.

"Slightly taller than you, thin but muscular and he looked like bit of a wheeler-dealer. Funny thing is, we bought it for £20 from him and sold it back to him for £200." The man let out a little chortle.

He sold it for £20, thought Adam. If only he knew the value of the book. He supposed that now, of course, Daley had a better idea.

"What's more," the man continued, "he was happy to pay it. I think he has found a buyer for much more."

Adam of course knew who that buyer was. He thanked the man and said goodbye to him and left. He still had a chance. Bruce had not yet got hold of the book.

CHAPTER 19

Adam made his way back to Littledon, for he knew Daley would be looking for him and if he did not find him, he would be off to see Bruce pretty sharply. Adam had to be very cautious, especially as he was aware that now Bruce and Mary had found the shop. They had managed to work out the location of the shop but it seemed that he had probably delayed them enough for Daley to get hold of the book again.

He was sure that they had not worked out that it was Daley who had collected the book. That was why Bruce and Ernie had turned up at his house, and they would still be after him. However, he had to take his chances to get the book from Daley and if necessary pay him the £4,000.

Adam desperately needed some time to think things through, but that was one commodity that was in very short supply. He decided he would get back to the house and ring Daley and then play it by ear.

However, as soon as he had parked his car in front of the house, Jack and Wendy came rushing out.

"Come and see what they have done to your house," said Jack with astonishment on his face.

"Yeah," said Wendy, "you won't be very happy."

For a moment Adam thought the house had been broken into again, but fortunately that was not the case. Still, Adam was not happy with what he saw on the door. Somebody was clearly trying to intimidate him.

They had vandalised his front door and there was something spray-painted on it. To Adam it looked like some sort of a hexagon inside a circle with some other symbols on it. It was not graffiti. Adam had seen similar signs before during his research into magic.

"Bloody vandals," said Jack, not realising the significance of the sign that was on Adam's front door.

"It's a shame what people get up to these days," chirped Wendy.

Adam asked them if they had seen who had painted the sign.

"We saw a girl running away from the house, but we couldn't get a good look at her and that was before we had seen this," Jack said, pointing at the door.

"We didn't see her face," said Wendy quickly, almost too quickly. It was clear from her face and body language that she was scared. "It was very early in the morning and we were just getting out of bed."

"Would you like me to clean it up for you?" asked Jack. "It won't take me more than two minutes to do it and it won't cost you much."

"Not at the moment, thanks," said Adam. "I may have to call the police first."

Jack's expression changed to a scowl as he sized up Adam. "This used to be a nice, quiet neighbourhood before you moved in. Everything has changed since you've come here. First you have a burglary and now we have this," said Jack. "When is it all going to stop?"

"Yesterday the police were around here again, talking to those two men who had lost their car keys. Yes, we would like to get back to a peaceful, quiet life," said Wendy.

"I'm afraid we'll have to report you to the neighbourhood watch council if things go on the way they have," said Jack.

"Hey! I'm the victim of the crime here," shouted Adam, who did not really care if they reported him or not, though usually he preferred to keep the peace. He was both amused and annoyed at Jack's attempt to intimidate him into giving him work.

"Alright, sorry, mate." Jack became apologetic.

"You can probably paint it in a couple of days. Now I must go inside as I have a few things to do."

This seemed to have the effect of placating Jack, who said goodbye with a smile. "We'll catch the next lot who come along and try to do anything else to the house."

Adam of course had no intention of relying on anything Jack said, but nodded to him agreeably as they left. As soon as he got inside he wanted to ring Daley, but the phone was already ringing.

It was the police. Adam could guess what it was all about.

"What can I do for you, Officer Stevens?" asked Adam in the nicest tone he could muster.

"We apologise for the delay in getting back to you, but things have been very busy. Did you report a burglary yesterday?" the policeman asked.

"Two men had forced their way in and were attempting to rob the place," said Adam.

"That's not the story they gave. They said you had assaulted one of them."

"What would you do if they were trying to get into your house by force?"

"So you admit it," said Officer Stevens.

"I admit nothing. I had to run away from the house. That's when I called for your help."

"They said they came to talk to you, but you were just leaving when they showed up, and you got into an argument and assaulted one of them. By the way, there was no sign of a forced entry."

"Sure, I opened the door to talk to them, but they were trying to force their way in," said Adam.

"They said that you hit one of them and left. They had lost their car keys, so they were waiting for a replacement," said Officer Stevens.

"Very convenient, I'm sure," said Adam.

"Good thing they didn't want to press any charges. You would be in a lot of trouble otherwise."

"I'm sure of that," retorted Adam, even though he realised his comments could be highly deleterious.

"I don't like your attitude. We could get you for wasting police time."

"What about all my time that you have wasted? Not to mention damage to my property. If you're not careful, I'll sue for damages for police harassment."

"We're willing to drop the matter this time." Officer Stevens' voice sounded downbeat.

"I'm glad that's settled," said Adam. He was angry, but he was also quite enjoying facing down Officer Stevens.

Adam rang Daley and gathered from his answerphone that he was out. Adam decided not to leave a message but ring again later. He then decided he would ring Charlie to see if he was still in custody, but to his relief Charlie answered the phone in a voice that sounded quite calm and collected.

"Hello, Charlie," said Adam. "So you are out?"

"Yes, and it's no thanks to you," said Charlie. "Did they keep you in custody as well?"

"Of course not," said Adam. "There was no reason for them to do so."

"It's not fair," said Charlie. "They kept me locked up for two days and asked me to go through a lot of psychological evaluations. I don't want to go through that again." It was clear he was annoyed by his incarceration, but he seemed chastened by it.

"Well, if you didn't tell them that cock-and-bull story, they wouldn't have kept you in either," said Adam.

"But it's true, and you are responsible," protested Charlie.

"Now, now," said Adam, "you know that's not true and I'm definitely not responsible for anything." Adam denied everything bluntly, for he was never sure who could be listening to their conversation.

"They might want me back for more questions," said Charlie. "They kept me under observation for two days and they said it was for my own good."

"Well, next time be careful what you say," said Adam. "Or you'll end up in the loony bin." He was running out of sympathy very fast for Charlie. He had enough problems of his own to deal with.

★ ★ ★

Adam decided to have some lunch and ring Daley again later. He busied himself making a sandwich, and about an hour later when he had finished eating it, the phone rang. It was Mary.

"So you're back home at last," said Mary. "I've been looking for you."

"I bet you have," said Adam.

"What do you mean?" asked Mary. She seemed hurt by his response. "Don't you miss me? Did you not have a good time the last time?"

"Maybe," said Adam. "I don't remember much," he lied. "Where did you disappear to in the morning?"

"I had a call from a friend and it was an urgent matter, so I had to leave in a hurry."

Adam could sense she was not telling the truth. "But you could have told me, and maybe I could have helped," he suggested.

"I didn't want to wake you up; you seemed so peaceful in your sleep. But listen, I am free at this moment so why don't I come round and see you?"

"Where are you at the moment?" Adam heard himself asking. He was feeling an uncontrollable urge to meet her again, even though it was not prudent, such was her effect on him.

"I'm at the flat," said Mary, "but a friend of mine has lent me her car so I could drive down to see you. We could have a great time."

The urge was almost overwhelming to meet Mary, but Adam knew he must try and resist it. But if Mary was calling him it meant they thought he had the book.

"Actually, I'm coming up to London, so I could meet you," said Adam, though he had no intention of meeting her.

"But I wanted to see your house again," said Mary. "I had such a good time there."

"What about tomorrow, then?" said Adam. "I'm free tomorrow."

"I don't know if I can wait that long," said Mary.

"You'll have to," Adam insisted. "Tonight I must meet George to arrange things for buying the college."

"Always business first," quipped Mary.

"One's got to live." Adam tried to sound casual. "I could drop in afterwards at the flat."

"No, don't do that," said Mary sharply. "I'll see you tomorrow."

"Okay," replied Adam. He had the distinct feeling that Mary knew he was lying.

As soon as he finished talking to Mary, the phone rang again. It was Daley.

"Have you got the money?" he asked without the courtesy of exchanging any formalities first.

"Have you got the book?" asked Adam.

"I might," said Daley cagily.

"Then bring it round tomorrow and I'll give you the money. I'll have to go to the bank first, so say about twelve."

"Not so fast," said Daley. "I want half the money first, before I bring the book round."

"The arrangement was that you bring the book and I give you the money," said Adam.

"Well, it's changed," insisted Daley. "I want half the money first."

"How do I know I'll get the book afterwards?" asked Adam.

"You'll have to trust me," laughed Daley. "You haven't got a choice. I've got a better offer from another party."

"Okay, at twelve," agreed Adam.

"Don't worry, you can trust me," said Daley smoothly. "I won't take your money and not give you the book. You know you can trust me."

"I'll have to," said Adam.

The last thing Adam knew that he could do was trust Daley.

"Listen, have you still got the book?" said Adam again.

"Sure," said Daley.

"How much have they offered?" asked Adam.

"The same as you."

"Well, I'll give you two up front and another four when you deliver."

"You sure you can afford it?"

"I'll have the money here tomorrow. Two up front and four when you deliver."

"How about three up front and three when I deliver?"

"Sorry," said Adam. "Two and four, take it or leave it."

"Okay," said Daley, "tomorrow at twelve", and he rang off.

Somehow Adam was still not sure of Daley's intention to give him the book; he probably just wanted to take Adam for as much as he could get. It was quite clear that if he did not materialise with the book after collecting the money, there was not a lot Adam could do.

Adam needed somehow to get hold of the book while Daley was still thinking about it. A desperate plan was forming in Adam's mind.

Adam decided he would go round to Daley's house and case it out, and see whether there was a chance to sneak in there when

Daley went out. He opted to go in the Skoda as everybody had now seen his new BMW and therefore he would be much more conspicuous in it.

Adam made his way to the Skoda, which was parked in front of the house next to the BMW. He had not used it for a few days, but it started up alright. As Adam already knew where Daley lived he decided to make his way there.

It was already nearly five o'clock and he was not sure if Daley would be back yet. If he was not back Adam decided he would try his luck and get into the house. If only he could be sure that the book was there. He grimaced at the thought that he was now about to become a petty burglar.

However, as he approached the house he saw Daley's truck was parked outside, so he was in. Adam decided to drive on and park the car in the lane nearby. He wanted to find a way to the back of Daley's house if it was possible.

Adam drove down the lane to see if there was another road further up which ran parallel to the main road, and which went towards the back of the house. He was lucky, for fifty yards down the lane itself veered right and doubled back to the village, just behind Daley's house.

Great, thought Adam, there was probably a way through the back garden to Daley's back door. If he could wait hidden until Daley left, he could try and get in there.

He jumped across a little ditch that was separating the lane from Daley's back garden. There was then an overgrown hedge to contend with but after looking around Adam managed to force an opening, though in the process he scratched his face and hands as he got through. The garden was fairly long and there were some mature trees and overgrown brambles at the back. There was a long lawn area near the house and a patio area, which was quite well kept.

This suited Adam's purpose well, and he positioned himself behind some bushes and a large tree. From there he could see the house easily. There was a figure moving around the upstairs of the house and he could vaguely make out that it was Daley.

Adam decided to wait where he was, to see if Daley would make a move to go out. After waiting over an hour, it began to get dark. As he was thinking whether to leave or not, the back door opened and out came the little terrier into the garden. This was Daley's dog which always accompanied him wherever he went; he always left him sitting in the cab of the truck to guard it.

Adam decided it was time to move. He rushed towards the hedge as the dog came bounding towards him. Then the dog started barking as it ran in his direction. He just managed to scramble through the hedge, when he tripped and fell into the ditch. Luckily it was dry. He hauled himself up and legged it down the road, and as he went around the bend, he could hear the dog had reached the hedge.

He could see all the lights suddenly come on at the house, and he heard Daley shouting at the dog. Adam kept running until he reached the car, which he quickly opened and dived inside. He looked in the mirror and saw that he looked a sight. He had scratched his face even more, and as he had fallen into the ditch his face had brushed against some nettles and had come up in a rash on one side. His shirt was also torn in places. He decided he would wait until things quietened down before he started the car.

After about ten minutes he saw some of the lights go out and heard a door closing. He waited a couple more minutes and then started the car; reversing it around, he made for the main road. Once on the main road he gave Daley's house a wide berth, choosing instead to take the long way home.

★ ★ ★

Half an hour later he was home. After getting rid of the ripped shirt Adam decided to wash his face and put some lotion on it to lessen the stinging sensation. He looked a bit of a sight: one side of his face was still red and blotchy, but the cuts were not too bad. As he was just finishing he heard the doorbell ring. As he was not expecting anybody, trepidation filled him. He grabbed the baseball bat he kept beside his bed and crept downstairs to have a look through the peephole.

To his surprise, it was Mary. What was he to do now? Pretend he was not in? But his cars were parked outside.

"Come on, Adam, let me in," said Mary. "I know you are in there."

"What do you want?" asked Adam, not opening the door.

"I need to talk to you urgently. Open the door and let me in."

There was something in Mary's voice that seemed very convincing, so Adam opened the door. Mary came in and remarked that he looked like he had been in a fight.

"It's nothing," Adam said. "I'll be alright in a few minutes. Now what do you want? I haven't got the book."

"I know that," said Mary calmly, "but you have a bigger problem. Bruce means to kill you as soon as he has his hands on it."

"Why would he want to do that, if he already had the book?"

"He is a very vindictive person and you have been giving him the run-around. I was told to slit your throat the last time." Mary produced a long, curvy dagger from under her dress. Adam gave out a gasp and stepped back.

"Don't worry, I'm not going to hurt you." She threw the dagger onto the floor.

"You're not?" asked Adam in surprise.

"No, I'm here to warn you instead."

"Why?" asked Adam, quite flabbergasted.

"Because I think we can help each other," she said matter-of-factly.

"But you were in my dream, killing me," blurted Adam. "Was it some sort of a premonition of things to come?"

"Bruce is casting spells to frighten you, so that you'd be afraid of me. He practises the black arts," said Mary. "That's why he was able to open your door without the alarm going off."

"Great! And you're in with him."

"That's before I decided to change sides. Who do you think painted the sign outside your door?"

"Let me guess. You did, I suppose, to frighten me?"

"To protect you from Bruce, not to frighten you," said Mary. "He won't come in here to harm you while the sign is there. But I don't think it will be needed anymore."

"He's that much of a threat?"

"Believe you me, you've been very lucky so far. If Bruce had managed to get hold of you, you would've suffered very badly. He was alerted by somebody in the village as soon as you used the book, and made his way to London with us. He's done his research on you and probably knows more about you than you do."

"How did you come to be in my flat?"

"That was easy. Soon as he found out the flat was yours, he got Doug and his mate Steve to beat up your tenant and get rid of him, so he could plant me there. The plan was then to intimidate you to give up the book, but because you beat up Doug, he decided to let me seduce you to get hold of it."

"Which nearly worked, and there was I thinking that I had suddenly turned into something of a ladykiller because of the book."

"Well, you have done very well so far and you have managed to turn me to your side, so don't be hard on yourself. I'm convinced that with a little help you can stand up to Bruce. He doesn't suspect anything, that's why he sent me here to keep an eye on you."

"He knows what's going to happen to him if he comes here again."

"Bruce knows now that you don't have the book, so they're unlikely to come here, except for revenge."

It was very difficult for Adam to take it all in. He motioned Mary to come into the kitchen and have some tea while they talked. To think he was going to have the sign painted out!

"You poor dear," said Mary, and she approached him, putting her hand on his face. Straight away Adam felt a soothing calm where the nettle had stung him.

"So why are you helping me?" asked Adam.

"I told you, we can help each other," she said. "I felt a strange connection with you that night."

"You put something in my drink to make me feel so good," said Adam.

"But I didn't," protested Mary, "that's the whole point. You were great without any help. We have a natural connection. In any case, the real reason is that I want to get away from Bruce and you are my only chance to do so. I'm very impressed by the way you've been able to stand up to Bruce."

"Why do you want to get away from Bruce? What's the matter with Bruce?"

"He is a very brutal man, not kind like you. You don't know half the things he's done. Bruce is a warlock, but his powers are limited until he gets hold of the book. I dread to think what he'll be like then. All I know is that he's going to get much worse."

"I didn't think such people actually existed. Just my luck. So what do I do now?" asked Adam with slight trepidation.

"If you want to survive you must find the book first," said Mary. "Bruce hasn't got it yet. He can't harm you directly with his spells until he has the book. He's not strong enough."

"Why is that?"

"You have certain abilities, though you're not aware of them."

"Well, has Daley still got the book then? I was at his house earlier trying to break in so I could get my hands on it. But Daley was there. I fell into a ditch on the way back and did this to my face."

Mary gathered Adam by his waist and kissed him, and he felt a tingling sensation go right through his body.

"See what I mean?" Mary laughed. "We have a connection."

Adam nodded in agreement.

"Seriously though, Daley means to give the book to Bruce after he has collected as much money as he can from you. Daley is in his power. He's scared shitless by Bruce, so he won't give you the book. You've got to get it by other means."

"Are you sure?"

"Bruce is so sure of it that he's only coming here tomorrow. That's why he sent me here to keep an eye on you."

"But Daley's coming here tomorrow to collect an advance, before bringing the book," said Adam.

"Perfect," said Mary. "I'll meet him and say you have been delayed while you go round to his house to get the book."

"But he knows you are with Bruce."

"I'll tell him that I'm here to keep an eye on you. That's what Bruce thinks too. To make sure Daley doesn't give you the book," said Mary. "Bruce would've been here tonight, but he has some other commitments he can't get out of. But he's not worried."

"But you'll be in danger if Bruce finds out that you're helping me."

"Bruce probably already suspects that I have a connection with you because I didn't kill you, and because you managed to resist me and give me the wrong address. However, he's confident that I won't dare double-cross him."

"Have you killed anybody before?" asked Adam.

"No, but I would've probably killed you if things hadn't worked out the way they did."

"Ouch," said Adam. "Remind me not to cross you ever."

"You won't have to." Mary smiled. "When you get the book you have to cast a spell."

"Why?"

"You have to cast a spell to save yourself and me, as the book works for you. It doesn't work for everybody. Only a few people are born with that gift. That's why it's not possible for Bruce to control you."

"That is why Daley doesn't understand the value of the book." Adam was amused. "To him it's all gibberish." That explained also why the spell had not worked when Dick tried to turn him into a crayfish.

"Exactly; you're special," said Mary. "That's why Bruce means to kill you. He tried a spell to control you but it didn't work on you."

"That's good to know," said Adam. "But is that a good enough reason to kill me?"

"Well, that's the main reason, but he is also afraid that I may be drawn to you. But generally, you've just pissed him off."

"Then he is going to hurt you if he finds out you helped me," said Adam.

"He'll kill me as well." She smiled. "But don't worry, I am going to hypnotise Daley if necessary, so he won't remember anything. I know how to do that. All this time with Bruce; I've picked up a few tricks."

"So what is the spell I have to cast?" asked Adam. "Also, is there one that would bring my friend back?"

"What happened to your friend?"

"He disappeared from the pond outside, where I left him after I turned him into a crayfish. You know, when it rained after I used the book."

"So the rumours were true. You can try a lost and found spell that might bring him back to the pond, and then just reverse the words in the spell you used to turn him into a crayfish."

"You mean replace 'crayfish' with 'Dick' and vice versa? We tried that already, it didn't work."

"Sorry, can't help you then; my knowledge is limited, but Bruce told me that there is a spell in the book which would make everybody who knows about the book forget about it completely, except the person who cast the spell."

"But that means you as well," protested Adam.

"I'm afraid I may also forget you," said Mary, "as my only connection with you is because of the book. Our relationship may not exist in my mind anymore, only you will remember."

"I can't let that happen," said Adam. "I've only just found you."

"But to survive, you must. Cast the spell as soon as possible after you get the book to save us both."

"That means I may not see you again," said Adam.

"I'm afraid so," said Mary.

"That can't be," protested Adam. "It's not fair."

"Well, if you really want to see me you will have to come to Australia. But you will have to master the book first or you won't succeed."

"Because of Bruce, I suppose. Anything else?" asked Adam.

"Beware of the three witches."

"What three witches? That's just an old wives' tale."

"There's more to it, according to Bruce."

"So, let me get this straight. To be with you, first I must find the book, then I must cast a spell to lose you and then I must win you back, after I have mastered the book." Adam showed his exasperation. "Meanwhile I have to be wary of the three witches."

"That's correct," replied Mary very matter-of-factly. "The path to true love is never smooth, ha, ha."

Where have I heard that one before? thought Adam. Just when he thought he had finally met the right girl, he might have to make her forget that he ever existed.

"Hold on," he said, "there must be a selective spell which I can use."

"There may be, but according to Bruce to use a selective spell you must know everybody's real name. Bruce is not his real name and Mary isn't mine."

"Great," said Adam. "And I thought all Australians were called Bruce."

"Don't worry," laughed Mary. "I will leave you my address in Australia, just in case you decide to come."

"You must know their real names," protested Adam. "What's yours?"

"It's Alicia," said Mary. "The danger is, if you miss even a single person out and he reminds Bruce, he will remember everything."

"I suppose you are right," Adam agreed finally.

"Come, you must pack," said Mary, or Alicia. "You must not come back to the house for a few days after you cast the spell. I see great danger here. The sight of you may remind them of everything."

Adam decided he must remember to take his small garden pruner with him, and some gloves which he had forgotten the previous time. He was going to cut a hole through the hedge to make it easier for him to get through.

Suddenly he had an afterthought. "What happens if he brings the book with him?" he asked.

"Then I'll force him to give it to me," said Alicia. "But I don't think he will, because Bruce said he was going to meet Daley at his house, but I don't know when."

"We must make the most of tonight, then," said Adam, "if this is going to be our last night."

"I will delay Daley as long as I can so you can find that book," said Alicia, kissing him. "Are you sure you have enough energy for this?"

Why not? thought Adam. He remembered another of Kierkegaard's quotes: *Life is not a problem to be solved, but a reality to be experienced.* The man had been a genius.

CHAPTER 20

The next morning Adam woke early. Alicia was already up making the breakfast. She gave Adam a big smile. What a perfect night, thought Adam. If all his nights were like that he would die a very happy man.

They had breakfast in silence and just touched hands. It was electric. Alicia voiced her plan.

"Give me a ring around ten past twelve to check if he is here and then get to work. Don't ring again unless you have to. I'll be gone as soon as he leaves. Remember to cast the spell as soon as possible, and don't come back for a while."

"Got it," said Adam. "I hope I can find the book. Let me just make sure Daley comes here." Adam pulled out the piece of paper and cast the spell. He then gave Alicia a big kiss and left the house.

It was about eleven. He took the shortest route out of the village and made his way towards Ironbridge Spa town centre.

About twelve o'clock he went past Daley's house, and seeing his van was not there, he parked his BMW in the usual place, but facing the main road this time for a quick getaway.

Making his way to the back of Daley's house, he jumped the ditch after making sure nobody was around. He then clipped a few branches off with the pruner and made his way towards the house. He put the pruner in his pocket and called his own house number on the mobile.

Alicia answered the phone. "He's waiting for you here," she said. "Where are you?"

"In position," he said.

"Don't be long," she said, and put the phone down.

Adam put on his gloves and went to the back of the house. He tried the windows, but they were all securely locked. He tried the back door, but it was also securely locked. He tried to kick the door in, but that did not work either. The door opened outward, and it was impossible to kick it in. He had forgotten to bring a crowbar. He only had a screwdriver from his car, but it proved useless.

In his frustration Adam decided to try the front door. But as he went out of the garden door, the latch closed behind him because he had forgotten to secure it in the open position, so he could not get back into the garden.

There was nothing else to do other than to try and open the front door. Luckily for Adam he managed to wedge the screwdriver in and loosen the lock a little. A car went past. Adam tried to make it look as if he was knocking on the door. When he could hear no other car coming, he kicked the door hard and the loosened lock gave way. A few more kicks and he was inside. He had, however, wasted a lot of time.

The first thing he did was to grab a chair from the kitchen and jam it at an angle against the front door so it would take a lot more effort to open it this time. He then went to the kitchen door and made sure he could open it. The key was in the lock and the door opened easily. There was another door to the back garden from the living room, but he could not see a key, and before he had time to try it the phone rang. It was Alicia.

"He's just left, I couldn't keep him any longer," she said. "He is meeting Bruce at the house at one. I managed to make him tell me where the book is. He didn't suspect me – in any case I made sure he won't remember telling me. It's under the floor under the dining table. You'll have to hurry. Good luck and goodbye."

"I will," said Adam. "Goodbye, Mary... Ah, Alicia."

With that she was gone. Adam looked at his watch. It was twenty to one already; Adam ran into the dining room and pulled the dining table to one side. As he was pulling the carpet up he heard a car pull up outside. Was it Bruce and his cronies? He didn't have time to look.

Adam groped around on his hands and knees. For a moment he panicked; all the floorboards looked sealed, but then he saw one small section at the edge of the carpet which was not. He scrambled to pull it up and there it was: the book in a plastic bag. He grabbed the bag, replaced the floorboard and pulled the carpet down. Pushing the table roughly to where it had been before, he made his way to the kitchen. He managed to lock the door behind him even though his hands were shaking uncontrollably.

Adam ran to the back of the garden, and as he was doing so he heard Daley's van pull up. There was a commotion going on as they had discovered that the door of the house had been tampered with.

Adam threw the key into the bushes and pushed his way through the hedge. As he was doing so he saw a head appear above the garden gate, and soon somebody was trying to clamber over it. Adam was not sure the man had seen him; he ran to his car and jumped in. Throwing the book to the floor on the passenger side, he started the car and moved off towards the main road. The car reminded him his seatbelt was not on. Adam paused for a second at the main road to put it on, as it stopped him from concentrating, at which point he heard another car starting up in front of the house. There was also a man running up behind him with a gun in his hand. He clipped his seatbelt on and squealed onto the main road, narrowly missing a car on the right side and ending up in front of the car on the opposite side coming from the left.

The man fired, but missed him as the oncoming car from the right shielded him. Adam was away. He stepped on the accelerator, as the road was clear. They had seen him, but they would not catch him, or so he thought, but very soon he could see a car flashing its lights behind the car that was behind him. This was the car he had cut in front of earlier, so obviously they were going to give chase.

Adam put his foot down on the accelerator even more and nearly lost control of his car. His mind was racing madly. He was not sure how powerful a car they had, and though they had been delayed by the car that was behind him, very soon they would overtake it and would try to catch up with him. Adam could almost put money on it that their driver would be better than him. Not only that, they had guns, which meant they did not need to get too close to him.

Adam decided that he probably could not outrun them, so he had to lose them, and lose them quickly before they gained on him any further. There was a bend coming up to the left. As he had been down this road before he knew that there were three minor roads after the bend just before him: one on the left, one on the right and then another on the left, and then there was another bend on the main road to the right further up. He decided that he would take the minor road on the right as soon as he was out of sight after the bend to the left, and hopefully they would assume that he was still following the main road. In any case, because he had a choice of three turnings to choose from, if they realised he had left the main road, they would be confused as to which turning he had taken.

Most likely by then they would have gone past the turnings before they knew he had left the main road. Of course he was assuming that their knowledge of these roads was not as good as his own.

As Adam went around the bend he could not see any of the other cars. He slowed slightly and took the turning on the right, which was the second one. The little road curved further to the right, and his car was screened off from the main road by the hedges along the sides. He was sure they could not see him from the main road. He stopped the car and listened with the windows open. Very soon he heard a large car go past, followed soon by another car with an irritated driver also driving fast and tooting his horn.

Adam was sure it was them, so he turned the car around and came back up to the main road and turned left, which was in the opposite direction to the pursuing cars. This meant he would have to go past Daley's house to make his getaway, but he had no other choice.

Very soon he went past Daley's house, and Adam noticed that Daley's van was still there, but that there was no sign of him. The front door of the house was still open. Adam drove as fast as he could, and hoped they wouldn't see him. Luckily there was not too much traffic on the road during this time and he made good progress.

Adam decided that he would take Alicia's advice and make his way away from Littledon immediately. Instead of heading to London on his usual route he decided to bypass London and catch the M25 and then make his way to Brighton, or London by the Sea, as it was sometimes known.

Three hours later he was in Brighton. He drove past the Royal Pavilion and swung a left towards Eastbourne. He parked his car on a side road near the first hotel he could find near the seafront, outside the centre, and booked into a room. Unfortunately for him the summer season was just beginning and he had to pay for a double room, as the rest of the hotel was full. But Adam did not mind at all; he had the book!

He bought a bottle of beer and a bottle of water and went up to his room. The Brighton Belle smelled musty and had obviously seen better days in her youth. Her faded glory was still apparent in the old chandeliers which were hanging in the lobby, but she badly needed a change of attire. There was no minibar in the room, he was told.

He put his suitcase down, opened the bottle of beer and flopped onto the bed. He needed a moment's rest before looking up the spell. But immediately his mobile rang, and it was Alicia.

"Have you seen the news?"

"No," said Adam. He was shocked, even though he half-expected something like that.

"This is the first chance I had to ring you from a public phone. I'm back at the flat – Bruce was here earlier and he was questioning me about you. He even checked my mobile phone to see if I had rung you. He left half an hour ago and he was in a very nasty mood. He slapped me around a bit," said Alicia.

"The bastard," said Adam with fury. "I'll kill him."

"Never mind that," said Alicia. "The police may be after you. Your friend Daley is dead."

"No!" said Adam in surprise. "I only saw him this afternoon."

"Have you got the book?" asked Alicia.

"Yes, of course, thanks to you," said Adam.

"Better move from where you are. Especially if you paid by credit card. Don't use the car and switch off your mobile. Do the spell as soon as you can, tonight if possible, or Bruce might figure things out. Come and get me if you can. Take care." Alicia hung up.

Adam jumped out of bed and pulled out the little handbag he always carried in his suitcase, for carrying small essentials when not using the suitcase. He stuffed a couple of items of clothing in it, and the book, plus the dictionary he had with him. He then finished the beer and put the water in the bag and left.

The desk attendant asked him if he was going somewhere. Adam told him he was off to visit some friends and had a present for them in his bag.

On the way he drew out £250 from one automated cash machine and another £250 using his other card from another bank, then made his way to Brighton coach station and caught a bus to Eastbourne.

When Adam reached Eastbourne later that evening he booked into another hotel, where he thought he would be secure for the night, after paying in cash. Adam felt he would be safe, at least for a few days. If they managed to trace his credit cards to Brighton, they would still take a few days to find him. Meanwhile he had a job to do, which he could not put off any longer.

But he found after an hour of translating that he would require the use of a candle, which he did not have. He did not want to ask in the reception if they had a candle. They would think he was mad, and for that matter it was probably against the hotel regulations to light a candle in any of the rooms, in case it caused a fire.

It was ten to eleven. Was there still time to find a shop? Adam decided to stuff the book under the bed and go in search of a candle.

He saw some lights on down the road and decided to go there, but it turned out to be an off-licence which did not have any candles. However, they told him there was a store around the corner that might still be open. As Adam hurried around the corner he bumped into two people coming out of a pub who were more than a little bit drunk.

"Oi, watch it," said one. "Where do you think you are going?"

"Sorry, mate," said Adam, trying to appease him without stopping. He carried on towards the shop, which he could see now. The shopkeeper was trying to pull the shutters down.

"I need some candles and a box of matches," said Adam desperately.

"Sorry, sir, we're closed, come back tomorrow," was the reply.

"Come on, mister, it's a romantic dinner. I'll buy a bottle of wine as well."

"You'll have to spend at least £10," was the reply.

"Okay." Adam agreed readily.

The shopkeeper opened the door again and put on the lights. The only candles he could find were two oversized green ones. Adam grimaced.

"Well, you said it was a romantic dinner." The man smiled.

Adam chose a bottle of red wine, and the man wrapped it up in paper.

"That's £6 for the wine and £5.50 for the candles," said the man again.

"You're having me on," said Adam. "That's daylight robbery."

"So, do you want them or not?" asked the man sharply. He was still smiling.

Adam nodded and paid up in silence. As he was coming out of the store he again saw the two men he had bumped into hanging around in the street.

"Oi, we want a word with you," said one.

"What about?" asked Adam, keeping his distance.

"You just hit my friend earlier," said the other.

"I did no such thing," said Adam. "Now if you don't mind, I'm in a hurry."

"We want that bottle of wine," said the first man.

"Okay," said Adam, "you can have it." Perhaps he had agreed too readily.

"Look, he's got some fancy candles," said the other. "I want those."

"Why?" asked Adam. "Why don't you just take the wine and I keep the candles?"

"He said he wanted these candles," said the first man, "and I want your wallet." The two men came towards him; one was holding a small knife.

"Okay, okay," said Adam. "You can have them." He was getting a little bit desperate by now. Time was running out, and he had to do the spell tonight or things could turn nasty. He was also beginning to feel a bit angry. It had been a long day.

As the men approached him, Adam felt he had no other choice. After his little altercation with Ernie, Adam knew what he must do. He hit the man with the knife hard over the head with the bottle of wine. The man was caught by surprise as he had not expected any resistance, and went down like a sack of potatoes, dropping the knife. The bottle broke and half of it was left in Adam's hand.

He brought the broken bottle up to the other man's face, who cowered, putting his hands up. Adam kicked him in the groin and the man crumpled, and for good measure Adam whacked him on the head with the rest of the bottle. Adam stepped on the first man's hand as he reached for the knife and kicked the knife away.

He was now in a manic mood. He gave the first guy a kick in the ribs. "If you try to get up I will kill you," he said, and probably meant it. It had been a very long day indeed and he had had enough. The shopkeeper, who was watching all this, locked his door from inside and put the light off.

Adam made a run for it. He threw the stem of the bottle away into a nearby garden when he was quite a distance from the scene. It was still wrapped in paper.

He knew the pub was closing and there would be people spilling out soon onto the streets. He carried on running a little further and then slowed down. Looking behind him, he saw nobody was following him so he quickly dashed into the hotel. Adam adjusted his jacket and walked past the lobby, hiding the candles from the receptionist. The man gave him a knowing wink, as if he knew what was going on, but he did not really have a clue.

At last Adam was in his room. He looked around the room, which was a little better than the one in The Brighton Belle. There was a kettle and two cups with an assortment of tea and coffee and some biscuits.

Adam grabbed one of the cups and filled it with water from the tap in the bathroom. He then took off his shoes after setting down the cup. Adam removed the wrapping from the still-undamaged candles. He took his shirt off and lit one of the candles, which he placed upright on a saucer, which he then placed on the dressing table.

Adam took the book out from under the bed. After all that had happened that day he almost expected the book to not still be there, but it was there. He opened the book to the right page and held it with his left hand. He then took the cup of water with his right hand and recited:

"In all others, who claim the right,
And in whose memory this book burns bright,
May it be washed away by this water,
And the flame extinguished tonight."

He threw the cup of water on the candle. There, it was done at last. But whether it would work, only time would tell. It was one minute to twelve.

As Adam started to relax, the smoke alarm in his room suddenly went off.

Adam grabbed the two candles and threw them out of the window as far as he could. He stuffed the wrapping and the matches into his jacket pocket and the book in his bag, and hid it in the wardrobe. He was desperately fanning with his hands to clear the air when the alarm went off as suddenly as it had come on. But there was a loud knock on the door.

Adam opened the door reluctantly. A young woman stood outside.

"You've been smoking," said the woman.

"No I haven't," denied Adam.

"Can I come in?" she said, pushing past Adam, who did not try to stop her. He was past caring.

The young woman picked up the saucer and examined it. "You've been lighting a candle here," she intimated. "You some kind of weirdo or what?"

"Not at all," said Adam, holding out a £20 note; he was a firm believer in the power of persuasion held by cash.

"I suppose you threw the candle out of the window." She smiled, grabbing the note.

Adam smiled back, but did not say anything. He looked at the woman. She was not bad-looking, a bit too much makeup perhaps, a little bit tarty but not bad at all.

"Is there anything else I can do for you?" she asked finally, admiring his well-built torso. Adam was suddenly brimming with a new kind of confidence. It had been a long day, but he had made it.

"Maybe you'd like to scratch my back?" he said, smiling.

"I'll be back," she said. "You just relax." She closed the door behind her.

Adam did what the girl told him to do. As he lay back on the bed and relaxed, he thought of Alicia; she was still very fresh in his mind. He had not really got to know her that well after all, and it was all a bit too much to take in. Everything was happening so fast. It all seemed like a film he was watching, but he was the main character in it.

This was the first time he had relaxed in weeks, but it was still not over. He did not know yet if the spell had worked. If it did work then it was possible Alicia would not remember him anymore. He would not even be a distant memory to her. He would not exist for her, according to what she had said about the spell.

She did not even have time to explain how she knew about the spell, or the book for that matter, and what her connection was to it. She had come and gone in and out of his life like a few scenes in the film which he almost felt he was just watching and not actually participating in.

But she had been sure, immediately, absolutely sure enough to help him without any hesitation. It was so amazing, as he had never been that sure of anybody in his life. He did not know what he felt, really; it had all happened too fast. It had been just two nights with her, that's all he had had. Who could be sure of things that quickly? But Alicia probably was, or she was desperate to get away from Bruce.

"Come and get me if you can," were her last words to him, but would he be able to go? He had not really promised anything, and she had not demanded anything. Even if he wanted to go, she had told him to master the book first or he would not stand any chance against what was waiting for him there. No, it was probably best to let her go.

Adam drifted off and thought of the last few weeks. As soon as he got back to Littledon his first priority would be to get Dick back if he could. He had been told not to go back too early, and so he had time on his hands until he elected to go back. He decided Monday was soon enough. He would study the book until then to see if he could find a way to bring Dick back.

His main problem was that the crayfish were gone. He had to find a way to get them back to the pond. If he could do that, he was sure that the answer to turn Dick back to his original self was in the book. Tomorrow morning he would start his search for the answers, for he was just too exhausted today. His thoughts turned to the events of the last twenty-four hours, and he nodded off into a dream about Alicia. There she was, with her great smile.

Somebody was knocking on the door. Adam woke up with a start. He jumped out of bed and opened the door. The girl slipped past him.

"I told you to relax, not to nod off," she said.

"I'm sorry," he said, "I was dreaming. It's been a long day."

"I had to take care of some business first, but I'm all yours."

She came up and kissed him lightly on the lips and slipped her arms around him. She moved towards the bed and started to undress slowly, with deliberate effort.

"That won't be necessary," Adam found himself saying, much to his own astonishment.

"What do you mean?"

"You see, I said goodbye to a wonderful friend today and I may not see her again. It's been a very eventful day and I would like to savour her memory tonight."

"It's your loss." She was irritated.

"Oh, completely, and I will probably regret it tomorrow. Here's something for you." He fished out a £50 note from his pocket.

"I wasn't doing it just for the money. I thought we might have a good time."

Adam was beginning to regret it already. But there was definitely something different about him; he had the confidence to say no. "Call it a present."

As she was leaving there was a loud clap of thunder and it started raining like it was the Great Flood once again.

"Funny, I could have sworn that there was not a single cloud in the sky half an hour ago," she said.

"Don't worry about it," he said soothingly.

"But I saw the weather forecast," she insisted, "there is no rain for at least three days. The skies should be clear."

"It will clear soon, trust me," said Adam.

"How do you know?" she asked. "How can you be so sure?"

"I know," said Adam.

"Bloody global warming. You can never be sure of the weather anymore," she muttered.

CHAPTER 21

It was Monday morning and Adam made his way to Brighton and The Brighton Belle to pick up his things. He had been studying the book intensely for the last three days. He had stayed in the Salisbury Hotel in Eastbourne for the last three days and hoped that was enough time for the last spell to have worked, and that nobody could now remember anything about the book, including Charlie and Officer Stevens. It would be interesting to see what their memory of the events of the last few weeks would be.

He'd paid his hotel bill in cash at Eastbourne, and rang the college on his way to Brighton saying he would not be in until the next day. If they were not happy, well, they could sack him.

He had also bumped into one of the two men who had accosted him, on one of his walks near the hotel. He was not seriously hurt, but he had the good sense to cross the road on that occasion to avoid Adam.

When he arrived at The Brighton Belle, they were surprised to see him. His things were not there. The receptionist said the police had been there on Saturday and taken them. Adam did not offer them any explanation, but when they tried to charge him for an extra day he refused. He left the hotel and went to see if his car was still there.

He was pleasantly surprised to see it was still parked where he had left it. Obviously nobody had even tried to look for it. They must have thought he had taken it with him.

Adam got in and drove off to Littledon. He did not go to the local police station for his things, as he did not want any snags.

On the way he saw a car valeting place, so he got them to give the car a good clean inside and out, just in case.

He reached Littledon about three o'clock. Just as he was getting out of the car his neighbour Jack came rushing out.

"The police came looking for you on Friday. They said your friend Daley had been murdered," he said excitedly.

"He wasn't my friend," retorted Adam. "He worked on the roof for me and that's all. Why do people think he is my friend?"

"He was here on Thursday, the day it happened," said Jack.

"But I wasn't here, I didn't even see him. Probably wanted more work." Adam feigned surprise.

"He was in there with your girlfriend for a long time," said Jack with a dirty smirk on his face, trying to imply something.

"She must have kept him entertained then." Adam returned the grin. "Hope he had a good time." He knew perfectly well what sort of time Daley had had.

"Anyway, I painted your door on Friday after everybody left. Good thing the police didn't see that stuff on the door," Jack said, feeling he had scored a point.

"You did well," said Adam. "So how much do I owe you?"

"Call it £50 and I'll throw in the paint," said Jack.

"Here's £50 and here's another tenner, say for the paint, okay?" Adam eyed him.

"Very decent of you, old man," said Jack. "Tell me – where have you been the last few days?"

"Ah, well," said Adam, "that's my business. Since you seem to know everything, you'll have to work it out." With that he left Jack standing there and made his way into the house. Jack had done him a favour at last, though, painting his door.

While he was coming in, he got a call from George. There was something very funny going on. The Cruzs wanted to meet Adam before agreeing to sell George his share at the new price

Adam had agreed with Vera. Adam felt a little guilty, but he didn't want to change his mind. He had to convince George now.

"I think they want even more money," said George, who was far from being convinced that he should pay any more than £20,000 for his share.

"We've agreed £25,000. I think it's worth that."

"Have you seen the balance sheet?" asked George. "That makes interesting reading to say the least. They haven't got any assets to speak of, but a lot of goodwill apparently."

"I've got a few ideas," said Adam, "and I'm sure so have you. You were prepared to pay £40,000, and we did agree £25,000 would be our top limit."

"I suppose so," said George reluctantly. "Are you sure Vera hasn't been softening you up on the side?"

"Tut, tut, George." Adam tried to nip it in the bud. "She's a married woman."

"Oh yeah? Lucy told me a few things about you two."

"All good I hope," Adam said, without showing the slightest sign of compromise. "I thought it was you Vera was sweet on, at least according to Lucy."

"Alright," said George at last, "let's get something in writing before we part with the money, but I'm not paying any more."

"We can sort it out tomorrow," said Adam. "I'm a bit busy right at this moment, but I hope to be in London tomorrow. I'll meet you at the college after the lesson around 1pm."

George seemed satisfied with that. Adam could not be bothered with the college at that moment as he had other things to think of. The classes had started already, and though he had missed the first day, he intended to turn up the next day and teach his class, but so far that was all he had planned for.

It was nearly lunchtime, and he decided he needed to find out if Bruce and his cronies were still in the village, and if they were, if they remembered anything about the book. He decided he would visit The Three Witches for lunch and catch up on the gossip there. He was sure Jack and Wendy would be there, with the £60 flush in Jack's pocket. He needed to be sure Bruce was gone before he tried any more spells.

But first there was something else he had to do. He had to give his mum a ring and hoped the police had not been bothering her. He had not seen her for ages and had not spoken to her at all last week. But it turned out nobody had been in touch with her and she was blissfully unaware of any goings-on. He promised to visit her soon.

★ ★ ★

Adam got to The Three Witches soon after and ordered some lunch and a pint of beer. The pub was not that full and there was no sign of Bruce anywhere. Just as Adam sat down, Jack and Wendy rolled in. Jack even offered Adam a pint, which he declined as he did not want to get in a round with Jack. It was going to be a busy afternoon.

Jack and Wendy joined him with their drinks. They exchanged pleasantries and Adam asked Jack if he had the afternoon off.

"I don't get days off," said Jack, "I'm always busy. Just having a break." Jack intimated that he had a big project on, which turned out to be clearing his own back garden and building a patio.

"Maybe you can do my garden sometime?" said Adam, trying to be nice.

"Anytime you want me to." Jack leaned in. "Say, I could build you a nice patio where the concrete was at the back of your garden. That's what you put it down for, isn't it?"

"But one thing at a time," said Adam, trying to curb Jack's enthusiasm. "Let's just get the garden done first."

"Anything you say," said Jack. "I'll start on your garden in a couple of days. I'm just going to lay the foundation for a patio today."

"I think it may rain heavily later," said Adam, smiling. "It's probably not a good day."

"But the forecast is for a clear day," Wendy piped in.

"I just have this feeling," said Adam.

"Listen, there's not a single speck of cloud in the sky out there," said Jack.

"Tell me, Jack, have you seen that Australian guy around lately – what was his name…?" Adam left it deliberately unfinished.

"Bruce, you mean," said Jack. "He was always hanging around here with his mates, but they have all disappeared since Friday."

"Funny, that," agreed Adam. "Probably gone back to Australia. He wouldn't have anything to do with Daley, would he?"

"Interesting you should say that," said Wendy. "I was just thinking that. We will have to tell the police."

"I think it's definitely going to rain today," said Adam, and made his excuses and left.

As soon as Adam got back in he got the book out from its secure hiding place and set about casting a spell. He had researched it in the three days he had spent sitting in the Salisbury Hotel.

It was not a simple task, but he had found a spell, which he had adapted to his own purpose. Now he wanted to try it out to see if it worked. He held the book and cast his spell.

"Of all things lost and to be found,
I want the crayfish to come around,
Safe and sound from any attack,
To their original place, be back."

Adam closed the book and put it back in its hiding place. He then made himself a cup of tea and sat down to wait. He did not have to wait too long. He was just finishing his cup of tea when it all started. It absolutely pelted down. Adam made himself another cup of tea.

After the rain had stopped he could see from his back window that there was a clear flow of water running from the stream to the pond. Adam put on some rubber shoes and went fishing with a plastic bucket. It was really wet out there near the pond. At times he had to wade through ankle-deep water until he reached the pond. His feet were soaked but he did not care. His heart was thumping; would it work? He was not sure, as he had changed the spell to suit his purpose. He was experimenting already, but there they were, the four crayfish, one large one and three smaller ones.

Adam scooped up the biggest and put it in his bucket. There was no resistance, no attempt to hide. As if this was what it had been waiting for. Adam decided to carry it inside the house in the half-full bucket of water. His heart was still thumping. He felt elated beyond any level he had known before. He was sure both the spells had worked.

He went into the house and put the bucket down safely on the kitchen floor. He suddenly felt excited and exhausted. He was wondering about whether the spell to reverse Dick's situation would work when there was knock on the door. It was Officer Stevens. Adam opened the door and greeted him.

"What brings you here?" Adam asked.

"We've been looking for you." The officer smiled enigmatically. "Where have you been?"

"What have I done now?" asked Adam, feigning innocence.

"We wanted to question you in connection with a burglary at Daley's. He reported he had seen you breaking into his house."

"He was probably trying to get at me," said Adam, "for having a go at him for not finishing the roof. Really, I can't think of anything else. What would he have that could be of interest to me?"

"Well, he is dead," said Officer Stevens.

"So he's not going to press charges."

"I suppose you had nothing to do with that either."

"You're joking, aren't you?" said Adam. "We had an argument about the roof, but he was going to finish it, so why would I want to kill him? Now I have to find another roofer."

"Well, you were a suspect for a while after the reported robbery. However, forensics say he was strangled with bare hands, so that rules you out. It must have been a rather large man. I don't think you quite fit the bill."

Adam was quite prepared to put up with the putdown from the officer. "Do you suspect anybody then?"

"We're still on the case and are sure to catch somebody soon. Most likely it'll turn out to be one of his past associates. Villains always have people holding grudges against them."

"What about that Australian character, Bruce, he had been hanging around in the local pub with? He was rather large."

"We've ruled him out. Daley only met him a couple or so times, mainly because his friend was negotiating some work on his roof with Daley."

That was that; Bruce was off the hook. Adam couldn't go into any details about why the police should look for Bruce without raising suspicion about himself as well.

"Is that my suitcase you got there?" he asked the officer, who nodded.

"Tell me why you suddenly disappeared from The Brighton Belle?" asked Officer Stevens, handing him the case.

"I didn't disappear. I met a girl and went off with her. I'm sorry I can't give you her name and address. Anyway, if you've ruled me out, why are you still questioning me? The next-door neighbours have a theory about who murdered Daley."

"Regular detectives, aren't they?" The officer smiled. "They told me you were back. There's something fishy about you all the same."

Officer Stevens did not realise how close he was to the mark.

"Are we done?" asked Adam, a little annoyed.

"Yes, for now. Your friend still hasn't shown up."

"Oh, I think he is going to make an appearance very soon." Adam smiled.

"You know something we don't." The officer eyed him suspiciously.

"Only a hunch," said Adam. "Watch out for the rain on your way back."

"That's another strange thing," he added. "Since you moved here the weather pattern has been very erratic."

"What? You're blaming me for the weather now?" laughed Adam. "Goodbye, Officer Stevens, I hope I don't have to see you again soon."

"Goodbye," said the officer, and left reluctantly. He seemed sure Adam was guilty of something, but he could not put his finger on it just yet.

Adam closed the door behind him and went to the kitchen. He decided it was high time Dick made his appearance again. He produced the piece of paper on which he had written down the spell to bring him back. He did not want to show Dick the book again. He did not want to explain anything to him either.

Adam grabbed the large crayfish from the bucket and took it next door into the living room. He then put it on the floor and pulled out the piece of paper again and read out the spell. During his research, whilst hiding from the police, he had found the right spell for the purpose, or at least he hoped so.

> *"Those who have changed and don't know why,*
> *Time to change back is nigh.*
> *You, Dick Drummond, in the form you are there,*
> *Return from crayfish as the man you once were."*

For a moment nothing happened and Adam thought the spell had not worked. But then there was a flash and Dick stood there in front of him. His clothes smelled slightly of damp, but otherwise he looked the same as the day he had disappeared.

"Hello, Dick," said Adam.

Dick looked a bit shell-shocked, but recovered as he recognised Adam.

"Hello, Adam. Where am I?" he asked. "The last thing I remember is standing in your garden."

"That was a few weeks ago," said Adam. "You've just suddenly turned up here."

"I can't remember anything more," said Dick. "Except that…" He left the sentence unfinished.

"Except what, Dick?"

"Except for this strange dream that I was a crayfish and having a real good time with three female crayfish."

"Well, everybody's been looking for you," said Adam.

"I can't remember any more," said Dick. "How long have I been missing?"

"Over three weeks," said Adam.

"No! Really? Rachael must be distraught with worry."

"She went to the police and reported you missing."

"Oh my God! I don't even know where I was. She will kill me."

"The police thought I had killed you," said Adam. "They came and dug up my concrete patio at the back."

"Why would they suspect you?"

"They thought I was having an affair with your wife and that I wanted to get rid of you." Adam was feeling mischievous.

"You and Rachael? Ridiculous! Sorry to say this, but there's no way she's going to look at you. Imagine!"

"Yeah! Can you just imagine that?" laughed Adam.

"I'd better ring the wife."

He fished out his mobile from his pocket and dialled. But there was no answer. Her mobile phone was also switched off.

"Listen, Adam, I'll have to go London, I just don't know what's going on," said Dick, looking exasperated. "I also need to see a doctor about my loss of memory."

"Why don't you come down to the pub and I'll call you a cab from there to the station? Have you got any money?" asked Adam. Dick checked his pockets and yes, he had money.

"Good," said Adam again. He knew most likely Jack and Wendy would still be there, because of the rain. Their patio plans would be awash with water. He wanted them to see Dick. He wanted to see the look of surprise on their faces.

"I'll get my car from the station," said Dick.

"I'm sorry, mate, but the police have taken your car away," said Adam. He did not have the heart to tell him it had been blown up. "You'd better catch the train. Now let's go before it starts raining."

They just nipped into the pub when the downpour started again. Just as Adam had thought, Jack and Wendy were still there, looking very glum.

"Listen, Dick, one piece of advice," said Adam as they were going in. "Less of that crayfish dream if possible. They might assign you to the loony bin."

"Yeah," Dick agreed, "you're right, but it was so real."

Adam went up to the bar and ordered two drinks and asked them to order him a taxi. He then went up to Jack and Wendy. Dick followed.

"Guess who has turned up," said Adam to Jack and Wendy, whose jaws totally dropped in surprise. "This is Dick, everybody." Adam introduced him and said that Dick did not know where he had been for the past few weeks.

Dick nodded in silence and finished his drink. Jack and Wendy did not say a thing.

The taxi arrived and Dick left, saying goodbye.

"Bloody rain, it gets on your nerves," said Jack.

"Yes," agreed Wendy, "it's a nuisance. We can't start on the patio."

"The farmers need it," said Adam. "Anybody want a drink?" He was feeling in a generous mood.

As he was waiting for the drinks, Adam decided to give Dick's wife Rachael a ring again. This time she answered the phone.

"You haven't been answering your phone," Adam accused her.

"We were busy," said Rachael, squealing with laughter.

"I bet," said Adam.

"Aw, don't be sore," said Rachael. "Listen, while you are on the phone I wanted to tell you that we are off to Australia soon for an extended holiday. I am going to let the house. You know all about letting, Adam. Tell me: how do you get your tenants?"

"Sure," said Adam, "but before you get carried away, let me give you one piece of good news first."

"What's that?" asked Rachael suspiciously.

"Dick's back," said Adam.

There was a sudden long silence at the other end.

"Are you still there?" asked Adam.

"Yes," came an almost inaudible reply.

"I said Dick's back. He's on his way to you now," said Adam again.

"Where's he been all this time?" asked Rachael.

"I don't know," lied Adam. "He couldn't remember, but you can ask him yourself. He'll be there in an hour or so." Adam hung up. It would be interesting to see what Rachael did with Bruce.

Adam was feeling in an expansive mood, and quite pleased with the day's work – hell, the week's work. He collected the drinks and made his way back to Jack and Wendy. He was sure that the other Bruce was going to get short shrift now that Dick was on his way back. Rachael knew which way her bread was buttered and there was little chance that she would ditch Dick for Bruce.

"Where did he pop up from?" asked Jack as Adam got back with the drinks.

"I don't know," said Adam. "It's a complete mystery, and all this time you thought I had murdered him."

"No we didn't," said Jack and Wendy in unison.

"But that's what you told the police, didn't you?" said Adam.

"No we didn't." Wendy denied it. "We only told them that we didn't see your friend leave the house."

"Well, there you are," said Adam. "People always jump to conclusions. Perhaps you'll be good enough to tell Officer Stevens that you have seen him and you saw him leave this time."

"Oh yes, we will," said Jack. "We'll let him know tomorrow."

"Yes, we definitely will," confirmed Wendy.

"So how about that gardening job?" asked Jack. "Is it alright if I start tomorrow? With the way the weather is I don't think I'll get started on the patio for some time."

"Very good," Adam said, looking serious, but inwardly he was smiling. "But make sure you ring Officer Stevens tomorrow."

"We will, we will," they blurted out together.

Adam felt delirious, but still he felt a tinge of sadness for Daley. He had not deserved to die, even though he had put Adam through a lot. Bruce or Ernie must have strangled him in sheer rage at not getting their hands on the book. He wondered what had happened to his little terrier. He rang Charlie on his mobile to give him the good news.

"Dick's back. This morning… I don't know, he just appeared. Says he can't remember anything. Listen, I'm starting work tomorrow, maybe we can meet up for a drink later? Okay, see you tomorrow. I'll call you."

Bruce was a dangerous man. Adam doubted if the police would catch up with him without some help. He was bound to be found somewhere, wherever Alicia was, of that there was no doubt. Adam could send an anonymous note to the police with an address close to the place. But would he be inviting more trouble on himself if he did so? He decided he needed a period of tranquillity for the moment. He would think about it at another time, when things were more settled.

Alicia had warned him about Bruce and told him to come prepared. He was sure he would meet Bruce again if he went to get Alicia. However, the next time he met Bruce, would he be able to match him? Meanwhile, he had other things to worry about, but tonight he was just going to get drunk.

Adam got them all another round. Jack and Wendy were over the moon.

"I don't know why we doubted you," said Jack, who couldn't recollect anything about the book. "You seem like a very decent chap."

"I agree," said Wendy.

"Here's to Adam," said Jack.

"To Adam," said Wendy. They both held up their glasses and Adam raised his. Things were going well. He had the survey on Thursday and the house was more or less ready. After that he would have the money to invest in the college. He was looking forward to a new life of opportunities.

"To all of us," he said aloud, but his mind was already elsewhere. He had this curious idea gnawing at the back of his mind.

What would happen if he tried out the same spell on the crayfish still in the pond? Would they turn out to be human as well? His mind was racing. He would of course make some minor changes to the spell. For a start, he did not know their names.

"Does anybody know the names of the three witches?"

"What do you mean, know their names? Whose names?"

"The names of the witches after whom this pub is named."

"No, why should we?" said Wendy.

"Just wondered," said Adam.

"You'd better ask the landlord," said Jack.

"I think I will," said Adam. "Last one for the road?"

"I'll get this one," Jack offered.

"No, today all drinks are on me," said Adam. He beamed them a big smile. He did not really need to be rich anymore; he had just got lucky. But somehow in his mind he was just as proud, if not more, of his achievements without the use of magic. They were just as important.

CHAPTER 22

Adam woke early the next day, a bit worse for the hangover he was nursing. He tried gathering together all the teaching material he required for his class, a task he normally would have performed the previous evening. The euphoria of the day before had carried him away and led him to drink too much.

Adam had quite a busy day ahead of him. He didn't want to be late for his class, as he had already missed the first one the day before. He decided that he would drive to Littledon and catch the train, rather than drive all the way to London.

When he arrived at the school Vera was not there, only Lucy, who greeted him in a friendly fashion and told him which room his class was in.

"Vera asked you to take the Advanced class instead of the First Certificate."

"Why is that?" asked Adam, who didn't like sudden changes.

"She's got George doing the Intermediate class and Mike's moved up to do the First Certificate class. She didn't think that he would be good enough for the Advanced."

"So George is going to teach after all. Where is he?"

"He's not in yet, but he said yesterday's class went well."

"Good. I need to talk to him about the college," said Adam.

"He wanted to speak to you urgently as well," said Lucy. "Apparently Vera was not too interested in talking to him yesterday."

"Probably she's waiting for me to turn up first, then kill two birds with one stone, eh?"

"I don't know," said Lucy. "Vera was acting a bit funny yesterday. I suppose it could be because it was the start of the term, we were very busy."

"That's what I like to hear, especially as I'm putting money into this college," laughed Adam.

While Adam was chatting to Lucy, George rolled in. He greeted Lucy enthusiastically, which Lucy responded to very eagerly.

"You two look like an item," commented Adam, and Lucy blushed. "Things have been moving fast since I last saw you."

"Where the hell have you been? I've been trying to reach you for the last four days." George seemed annoyed.

"Sorry, there was something going on that needed my full attention," said Adam.

"You had your phone switched off, why?"

"I didn't want to be disturbed, but now I'm back and fully at your disposal."

"Great! Did Lucy tell you that Vera hasn't shown much interest in following through with the sale of the share of the college ownership?"

"Probably was waiting for me to show up and then do it all at the same time." Adam tried to soothe him.

"Somehow I don't think so."

"I tend to agree," said Lucy. "She's been in a very funny mood lately, ever since last Friday."

"Well, I'd better get to my class," said Adam, perplexed. "Catch you later."

Adam moved off to his class, which went fairly smoothly without any hiccups, and at around 1pm he saw George and Lucy again at the reception, but there was still no sign of Vera.

"She rang to say that she won't be in today," said Lucy. "She'll see you both tomorrow."

"Very strange," said George. "I came to meet her on Friday

and while I was seeing her she received a call, and it all changed after that."

"What do you mean?" asked Adam.

"Well, we were happily discussing the transfers to you and me and she seemed very happy about it all. Next minute there's the call and she told them that she couldn't talk then, but would ring them back in five minutes and took down the number."

"Then she asked George to leave the room," said Lucy. "And after that she was on her mobile, talking for quite a while with the door closed."

"When she came out of her room, she made out it was Mr Cruz that she was talking to," said George. "But we knew that it wasn't him. He had rung earlier, to say that he would be back on Monday. She then said that she couldn't discuss things further with me, but would talk to both of us when you came back, which is today."

"Did they come in yesterday?" asked Adam.

"They were both here yesterday, but there's been no sign of either of them today," said Lucy. "I wouldn't mind, but it's such a busy time at the moment."

"We could help you this afternoon," Adam offered.

"No need. Mr Cruz is coming in this afternoon. He rang earlier and George will stay until he comes."

"I see," said Adam. "I don't particularly want to meet him, so I'll push off. Let me know later what's up, if you will, George. And Lucy, can you please let me know when Mr Cruz comes in?"

"I will if I find out anything new," said George, and Lucy also nodded.

Adam left feeling very perplexed. What was going on? The Cruzs were taking time off at the start of the term, which was unprecedented. There was something very serious going on.

Adam had already resolved to go around to see Vera when the coast was clear, to find out more.

He decided to have some lunch and catch a bus to Winchmore Hill, where Vera lived. About two o'clock Adam received a call from Lucy to say that Mr Cruz had arrived at the college, so he decided to leave the pub he was in and walk around to Vera's house.

Vera opened the door and looked very surprised. "What are you doing here?" she asked him.

"I thought I'd drop in to see how you were, since I missed you at the college."

"I'm a little bit under the weather. I think it's the stress of starting the new term."

"Well, Lucy's under a lot of pressure today, but I wanted to talk to you about other things."

"She will cope, she's a good girl. I'm sure George is helping her. They seem to be very pally these days."

"Can I come in?" asked Adam.

"Oh! Sorry, forgetting my manners. Of course you can come in."

Adam followed her into the living room. There was no fond greeting from Vera, who seemed rather distant, almost cold.

"Where have you been? I haven't seen you for almost a week."

"Sorry, I had some things to do." Adam tried to sound apologetic.

"My husband was away, we could've had a good time, but your mobile was turned off. No answer from your landline either."

"Sorry, it was an emergency. I had to help out a friend in trouble, but I didn't realise you wanted to see me again so soon."

"I see. Anyway, what can I do for you?" Vera broke into a smile.

"I wanted to find out whether you had changed your mind about selling us a share of the college."

"Of course not – after all my hard work?" Vera laughed.

"I thought I did all the hard work." Adam grabbed Vera and gave her a kiss.

"There's no time for that now, I'm expecting some people. Anyway, my husband is having second thoughts about the price. Maybe he suspects something."

"Like what?"

"That you may have got to me."

"You don't seem to be too worried about it," Adam observed.

"Well, it was his fault that he sent me to see you," quipped Vera. "He's just interested in the money so he can move back to Malta."

"So he wants more money?"

"Of course. Anyway, leave it with me. I'll see what I can do to persuade him. I'm sorry, but you'll have to leave, I'm expecting some friends soon. We'll talk at the college tomorrow."

Adam said goodbye and left. He was slightly perplexed by Vera's attitude, for she had seemed quite cold earlier, but had relaxed after his explanation and even looked glad to see him. It seemed she genuinely liked him and it wasn't all just business. But he didn't want to worry too much about things, about whether he managed to buy into the college or not; he had other things on his mind. He was still not sure if Bruce had really forgotten about the book and gone back to Australia.

Adam decided he would go and see Charlie and find out how he was bearing up after his ordeal, and what his recollections of events were. It would be interesting to see if he had actually managed to forget about the book.

★ ★ ★

Charlie looked more like his old self when he opened the door of his flat. He was in a cheerful mood.

"Hello, Adam. I've been trying to reach you. You know Dick's back, of course."

"Yeah, he turned up at the house yesterday. Apparently he has no recollection where he has been all this time. Did he tell you anything?"

"Not a bean. Most probably was shacked up with some pretty young thing. Come in."

Adam followed Charlie in. Yeah, he was back to his old self, observed Adam. Everything was neatly folded away and there was nothing out of place, unlike the last time he was there.

"What do you remember about his disappearance?" asked Adam.

"Not a lot. I don't think I can clearly remember when he left us that afternoon. He seemed impatient to get back to his wife."

"Don't you remember? He left late afternoon, saying he was going to catch a bus to Ironbridge Spa to go back to London." Adam decided it was best to implant a memory in Charlie's mind of how and when Dick left.

"Strange he didn't come back all this time. The police thought you had done him in."

"Yeah, they dug up my new concrete patio, looking for the body. Of course they didn't find anything."

"I think they thought I was helping you. Apparently I said some funny things at the interview. They locked me up for a bit, as you probably know, for observation. But it's all okay now, in fact I got a call from Officer Stevens today. I'm not a suspect anymore."

"I don't think you ever were, they were just out to nail me. That Officer Stevens doesn't like me."

"Anyway, I'm really glad Dick's back. He rang earlier and said he was having a barbecue this Saturday and you're also invited."

"Great, thanks," said Adam.

Adam could hardly believe that Charlie had not mentioned the book even once. The spell was working well. In fact, he couldn't remember Dick being turned into a crayfish at all.

★ ★ ★

Adam left Charlie sometime later after a couple of teas and made his way back to Littledon. He felt quite happy; things were beginning to look up. After all, if Charlie had forgotten about the book, the chances were that Bruce must have as well.

He didn't mind that Vera hadn't played ball that afternoon; she had been friendly enough, really. That morning his remortgage had been confirmed, subject to survey, and the money was coming through soon, but he decided he didn't really want to pay any more for a share in the college. He was going to enjoy spending his money, even if Vera decided against him.

However, Adam had bad news as soon as he reached the house. Linda rang him – she was homeless. She had been desperately trying to get hold of him all afternoon. Adam was livid.

"What do you mean, homeless? I gave you the money for the rent."

"Well, my landlord didn't want it, he wanted me out instead. He has a court order and he's going to keep my deposit. He said he can get a lot more for the place than we were paying."

"So where are you staying now?"

"I'm staying with a friend temporarily, but I need to move my stuff by tomorrow from my old flat or I won't get it back. Can you put me up? You've got a big house."

"Sorry, I can't have you moving in here." Adam was adamant.

"Why not? It's not as if you have somebody else."

"Doesn't matter. I'm sorry, but you can't come here."

"What can I do, then?"

Adam began to feel a little sorry for her, when he remembered that the flat was empty. Mary, or Alicia – he was still having problems adapting to her real name – wouldn't be there anymore, so the flat would definitely be empty. He hadn't even had time to check.

"Tell you what, I'll let you move into the flat until you find something else, but only for a short while."

"Oh! You still have the flat?" She sounded surprised. "I quite enjoyed living there."

"I can meet you there around two o'clock after my class. The tenant has just left, so you can move in there for a while."

"Maybe you can let it to me."

Here we go again, thought Adam. No, he had to be strong.

"It's better if you find another place."

"Don't be mean, we'll talk tomorrow," said Linda cheerfully. "By the way, Rachael has invited me to their barbecue this Saturday. Are you going?"

"I don't know yet, I'm a bit busy at the moment," Adam lied. He didn't want to give Linda any false hopes. There was no way he was going back to her.

★ ★ ★

Instead of going for a drink at the local that evening, Adam settled down to study the book further after supper. He had come across some very interesting spells when he had been searching for the spell to bring Dick back. He wanted to make a note of them and commit them to memory. He was sure that they would come in handy sooner or later.

Though he had constructed a safer hiding place for the book in the hidden cellar, he was still not sure it was secure enough. Adam had constructed a false cover for the cut-out shelf in the wall where he had originally found the book. He had put a metal safe inside it, bolted to the wall, and a false brick fascia to match the wall.

However, he was still worried about losing the book, so he decided he would photocopy it in its entirety and then deposit it in a bank safe deposit box as soon as he had time.

After trying to memorise some of the spells, which was not easy to do in German, he decided to copy some of them onto a piece of paper so he could practise learning them. He needed to get better at casting them if he was ever going to match somebody like Bruce, as he had been warned by Alicia.

It was fairly late when he decided to put the book away and go to bed. He was not looking forward to meeting Linda again the next day, and especially letting her back into his life again, as she would be if she moved into the flat. He didn't even know what state the flat was in.

However, Adam resolved that there was no point in worrying about anything and he would just have to let things take their course. After all that he had been through, what he needed to do was to sit back and enjoy life a bit more.

CHAPTER 23

Everything was calm when he arrived at the college the next day. Vera was there this time, and exchanged quite friendly greetings with him. She intimated that her husband Mr Cruz would be in later, and would talk to him and George after their classes finished.

Around 1pm they were both shown into Mr Cruz's office. Mr Cruz was sitting alone, and broke into a broad grin when he saw them. He seemed in a very jovial mood and there was no stopping him showing off his large teeth, which were immaculately white. Obviously a liberal amount of dosh had been used to polish them.

"Well, gentlemen, good to see you both again," Mr Cruz said. "Vera said you wanted to talk to me." He sounded as if they were completely out of step with any negotiations that had preceded the meeting.

"We want to find out what's up," said George, sounding very impatient.

"I'm sorry we can't accept the price you want to pay us."

"I thought we had a deal already," said Adam.

"I'm afraid we received a much higher offer yesterday."

"You must be kidding," snapped George, "if you think we're going to fall for that."

"I'm telling you the truth," said Mr Cruz.

"I didn't know that you were advertising the business. Vera, I mean Mrs Cruz, assured me this was not the case."

"That's correct. But it seems that word has got out through the grapevine. We've been offered £200,000 for the college."

"I thought you only wanted to sell a share in the business."

"We did initially, but if we get £200,000, I'm happy to sell the lot." Mr Cruz smiled.

"What about Vera? She wants to sell up as well?" asked George.

Mr Cruz looked puzzled, as if it was too much to expect Vera to have a mind of her own. "She's in complete agreement with me. I don't know why you think she would oppose the sale."

"How do you know that this offer is genuine?" asked Adam.

"They put down a non-returnable deposit of £5,000 yesterday. But I'll still sell you fifty per cent if you can pay £100,000. I think that's fair, don't you?"

"You can leave me out," said George. Disappointment showed on his face.

"Is there a chance of meeting the other party?" asked Adam.

"It may interest you to know that the other party is quite eager to meet you," said Mr Cruz, much to Adam's surprise.

"How do they know about me? Or do you mean the both of us?"

"No, just you," said Mr Cruz, which surprised Adam again. "Vera will arrange it for you. I'm about to go off to Malta to finalise setting up a school there, so I can't give you more details at present."

"That's alright," said Adam.

With that, they left Mr Cruz, but it was far from alright. Adam was highly perturbed at what was going on. Who was this mystery buyer who wanted to see him? He wanted to see if Vera would be more forthcoming. They left Mr Cruz sitting there, grinning from ear to ear, revelling in his good fortune.

"How can they find somebody like that without advertising the college?" asked George, sounding annoyed, once they were outside the room. His dream of becoming part-owner of the college was fast disappearing.

"I don't know. Let's ask Vera and see what we can find out. She might be more forthcoming."

"They want to meet you, but not me, which means I'm for

the chop. My career in teaching English will be rather short-lived," said George pessimistically.

"Don't be so downhearted, the college hasn't been sold yet. In any case, I don't really know why they want to see me. Look, there's Vera." They walked up to her.

"What the hell is going on?" asked George. "I thought we had a deal."

"Well, I was quite happy with it," said Vera. "But yesterday morning we got a deposit of £5,000 from this gentleman who has promised to pay £200,000 within the next two weeks. I'm afraid my husband won't listen to me. He wants to grab the money and go back to Malta."

"And you? What do you want?" asked Adam.

"I was quite looking forward to working with you. I think we could've made a good go of it."

"I see. I suppose you must return with him."

"Well, I'll have to stay behind and sell the house and then follow him there."

"I have a good mind to chuck the job in," George remarked.

"You should wait at least two weeks to see if the buyer comes up with the money first," said Vera. "He said he's transferring the money from Australia."

"So he's an Australian, is he?" Adam sucked in a breath.

"You didn't hear it from me," said Vera. "We're under strict orders not to divulge anything until he meets you."

"When is that going to be?" Adam was perturbed. What was going on? No, it had to be a coincidence.

"He wants to arrange a meeting at my place this Sunday lunchtime. He will meet George later."

"Is he a large Australian called Bruce?" Adam couldn't contain himself any longer.

"No, his name is John and I can't tell you any more," said Vera. "My husband will kill me if this deal falls through because of me."

"Well, I suppose we'd better hold fire for a couple of weeks," George said, very disappointed.

"I think so," agreed Adam. "Listen, I've got to run as I'm meeting somebody at the flat, but we could meet later if you wish to discuss things."

"Okay. I'll ring you later," George said.

"And I'll ring you later, Adam, about the meeting." Vera winked at him, without being seen by the others.

★ ★ ★

Adam left the college and took the Tube to Wood Green station. He hoped he wouldn't run into Doug and his friend, whose name he couldn't remember. He was already running a bit late for his appointment with Linda.

On his way to the flat Adam had a feeling that he was being watched, but he couldn't nail it down to anybody in particular who might have been following him. He decided that he was being a bit paranoid and tried to relax.

When he got near the flat, he could see that Linda was standing outside on the pavement with a whole load of her possessions in plastic bags and a couple of large suitcases.

"Where have you been? I've been waiting over half an hour for you. I thought you weren't going to show up."

Adam winced and wished he hadn't shown up. "Emergency meeting at the college, I couldn't get away earlier. Sorry."

"Well, at least you've turned up, though your timekeeping doesn't seem to have got much better," Linda complained.

Adam did not bother replying. He knew Linda from old; any reply whatsoever would have brought on a verbal torrent, which could last several minutes at least. It was better to keep quiet and let her calm down. As he opened the flat door there was a set of keys lying on the floor. He took a large suitcase and carried it up the stairs. On the whole the flat was in a good state, ready for the next tenant.

After finishing lugging Linda's stuff up the stairs, Adam wanted to get away, but Linda wanted to go for lunch, so Adam obliged. He took her to The Rat and Gherkin, as he had a particular reason for going there. He wanted to see whether he would run into Doug and his friend.

However, there was no sign of them, much to Adam's relief, and he started to relax and enjoy his lunch.

"Thanks for putting me up," said Linda. "Are you quite sure you can't rent the flat to me?"

"I'm quite sure." Adam was firm. "This is an emergency measure."

"Okay, I'll look for a flat, but it'll take time. I suppose you want your money back."

"If it helps, keep the money, but I want you out within a month. That should give you plenty of time."

"Why are you being so horrible? It's not my fault I was chucked out of my flat," protested Linda.

"Whose fault was it, then? How can you be so gullible?" retorted Adam.

"I didn't know that Jim was going to cheat me like that."

"Okay, okay, let's not go into why it's not your fault. I don't want a long bloody explanation." Adam was still smarting from the way Linda had left him.

"Do you think you can help me in any way to get my money back?"

"Who? Me? Why don't you go to the police?"

"I don't want to land him in jail."

"Still got a soft spot for him, then? Even after he's swindled you? Great. He's not going to jail if he gives you your money back."

"I don't want the police involved." Linda was adamant.

"So what do you want me to do, break his leg?" Adam asked sarcastically.

"No, no, I don't want any violence."

"There's nothing I can do. He's not going to give your money back if I ask him nicely." Adam felt the whole situation was getting exasperating, and he wanted nothing to do with it anymore. There was no way of helping people if they didn't want to help themselves.

"You can still have a word," she pleaded.

"Okay, okay. Send him a message to come here and I'll have a word with him," he said finally.

"But he'll just ignore my message."

"Well send him a text anyway with this address, if you've still got his number."

"I think his number is still in use."

"Okay, good. Now write down his full name on a piece of paper for me and I'll see what I can do."

Adam already knew what he was going to do. He was going to use the same spell he used on Daley to call him, however he was not sure what course of action he could take after that. It would all have to wait until the following week, though, as he had the survey the next day and then he had to chase Vera to find out what was going on. It was going to be a busy few days this week.

"Are you going to Rachael's on Saturday?"

"Maybe, I'm not sure yet. Why?"

"Can you pick me up?"

"You're going to have to make your own way there, I'm afraid. If I go I'm going to bring a friend along." Adam was thinking of Vera. The time had come to boost his self-image again, and who better to do it than Vera? Adam could just imagine the look on people's faces when he walked in with Vera. Yes, they were in for a surprise.

After leaving Linda, Adam decided to go back to Littledon. There was nothing further to be gained by discussing the matter again with George, until he found out more about the situation. His time was going to be better spent brushing up on some of the new spells he had discovered.

★ ★ ★

As Adam was getting out of his car, Jack and Wendy came out of their house. They came up to him and asked him if he would be at The Three Witches later on. Jack said they were going to be celebrating Wendy's birthday and would like to buy him a drink. This was such a pleasant surprise for Adam that he readily agreed. He was definitely not going to miss it if Jack was buying, but he had other things to do first.

He needed to inform Vera that he would have to leave work early the next day, because of the survey of his house. When he rang Vera she said that her husband was leaving early on Friday morning, so he could spend some time with her that night and there was no problem in him leaving a little earlier the next day. Adam was quite surprised to hear this. Vera seemed to be opening up to him suddenly, and didn't seem worried about the risks too much.

Adam retrieved the book from its hiding place as he wanted to brush up on a couple of spells first, and also cast them to see if they worked. First he looked for one particular spell that he had come across earlier. If it worked there would be no further rain when he cast other spells, and nobody would be any the wiser if the book was being used. He had already worked out that it only rained once he had closed the book properly for a time, after casting a spell. No rain fell while the book was still being used.

Adam cast the spell, and he then cast another spell, but only after putting the book away safely. Just as he finished there was a loud knock at the front door. It was Jack.

"Are you coming to the pub?" he asked. "We were expecting you earlier."

"I was busy," said Adam. "What's the rush?"

"They're going to bring out a cake for Wendy. I just thought that it would be nice to see you there."

"Okay, sure. One minute," said Adam as he turned the alarm on and went out. Really he wanted to do something else, but what was the harm in having a quick drink first?

When they got to the pub, he was surprised to see the man from the village who used to hang around with Bruce, sitting at a table. Bruce's friend nodded in his direction. Adam nodded back, as really there was no reason why he shouldn't be there. After all, he lived in the village.

Adam went to the bar with Jack and the man came up behind them. However, before he even reached the bar Jack offered to buy him a drink.

"This is John," said Jack. "He just offered me a very big job to tidy up his back garden."

"So that's why you're buying drinks for everybody. Hello, I'm Adam," he said to John. There was no harm in finding out if he had any news of Bruce.

"I know, Bruce mentioned your name when he was here."

"Oh! And where's he now?"

"Gone back to Australia, as far as I know."

"Did he find what he was looking for? He left rather suddenly." It was a deliberate trick question from Adam to see if the man remembered anything about the book.

"I don't know that he was looking for something," said John. "He didn't tell me anything."

Adam felt slightly relieved. He was also glad that there was no sign of any rain so far, though there could be two reasons for that. One was that the spell had worked, and the other was that the second spell he had cast hadn't worked.

Jack had been served, so they decided to head for the table where Wendy was seated. She beamed at them when they got nearer.

"The cake's coming soon," said an excited Wendy. "You're just in time, isn't this fun?"

Adam had just wanted to have the one drink and get back to the house, but in any event this proved to be impossible. After Jack's round he had to buy a round, and then when he was about to leave, Bruce's friend John bought him a drink, much to his surprise. Maybe he was telling the truth and he really didn't know anything.

The cake had already been eaten, but the party carried on and soon it was almost closing time.

"Well, I must thank you for a jolly good evening," Adam remarked to Jack, and he half-meant it, though it was said in a jocular fashion.

"I can't take all the credit," said Jack, showing surprising candour. "It was really John's idea."

"Oh! Really?" Adam was surprised, and a little alarm bell suddenly went off in his head.

"Yes," said Jack. "I happened to mention to him the other day that it was Wendy's birthday today and he suggested that we should have a birthday party in the pub. He even gave an advance on the job. I start next week."

It was really high time for him to get back to the house, thought Adam, suddenly feeling a bit apprehensive.

"I've got to go," he said. "There's a lot going on tomorrow, so I can't have any more to drink."

For some reason Adam rushed back to the house fearing the worst, but everything was just the same as he had left it inside. He couldn't quite put his finger on it, but there was still this niggling feeling that something was not quite right. He had a feeling that somebody had been inside the house and had conducted a thorough search, but put everything back just as Adam had left it.

Adam looked high and low for any signs of an intruder, but could find nothing. In the end he went to the cellar to check on the book, which was still there. Adam convinced himself that he was just imagining things.

However, logically it was still possible that somebody had been there, as Bruce had managed to get in the previous time without setting off the alarm. In which case the last spell had worked, for he had placed a charm so the cellar would remain hidden from anybody searching the house. Adam was now worried that they would come back when he was inside the house.

Adam was in the grip of paranoia; the last thing he wanted was to confront Bruce and Ernie again. Panic gripped him, and he now regretted giving Jack permission to paint over the sign that had been painted on the front door by Alicia to keep Bruce out.

Try as he might, Adam could not sleep that night. He decided that he needed another spell to make the house impregnable to any outsider not invited in by him. He had seen such a spell being used in a fantasy drama on television, so he decided to look for it in the book.

It was quite late when he found the spell he was looking for, but it was specific to guard against people trying to gain entry using charms or magic. Though the night had passed without incident so far, Adam cast the spell and fell asleep. He had also found a spell to open locks and untie knots. Adam noted it down as it was a general spell to open things, so it could come in handy.

Early in the morning Adam was woken suddenly and felt as if the house was shaking gently, but it was over in a moment and he fell asleep again soon after, thinking nothing of it.

CHAPTER 24

The next day whizzed by. Adam left half an hour early to get back to Littledon for the survey, which went without a hitch and on time. The house was valued at almost double what Adam had paid for it, and it made him immensely happy. The main thing, though, was that he would now get his refinancing and his financial crisis was over.

Adam cooked himself a little meal and sat down afterwards to go through the spells he had been learning and a few other ones besides. He was not quite sure which of the new ones he had tried were working, as the rain that followed was now absent.

Adam tried his hand at conjuring up things, but found it next to impossible. Huge amounts of concentration were required, and this Adam found difficult to achieve. After twenty attempts he finally managed to conjure up a teaspoon, which vanished as soon as he turned his head to look at something else. Adam was, however, elated with his success, and decided to practise concentrating harder.

Vera rang him shortly afterwards and asked him if he would like to meet up with her the next day, as her husband would be away. It was hardly a request Adam could turn down, as he wanted to learn more about the mystery buyer.

The evening passed unspectacularly and Adam concentrated on his conjuring trick instead of going out to the pub. He was determined to master conjuring up small items, and also one or two other spells he had learnt.

Finally, exhausted, Adam went to bed. Sleep wasn't long in coming. He dreamt about Alicia, and her life in Australia. He was there to meet her, after a long, exhausting flight to Melbourne, but she wasn't there. Instead it was Bruce who was waiting for him.

Adam woke with a jolt, for he nearly fell out of bed. The whole house was shaking violently, along with the bed. It was as if the house was resisting something that was trying to get in.

Adam rushed to the window to see if he could see anything outside. He thought he could make out two silhouettes in the dark, but he couldn't be sure. Then he heard the voices in his head.

There's no use resisting, I know you're in there. Open the door and let us in. Very ominously, the distant voice sounded like Bruce. There it was again, urging him to open the door.

Adam resisted with all his might and pulled out the piece of paper with the repelling spell on it. He desperately repeated the spell, not knowing what else to do.

Things quietened down as suddenly as they had begun, leaving Adam to wonder if it had actually taken place. The house stopped shaking and he couldn't see the two figures anymore.

Adam then began to wonder if all of this had actually taken place and he was in big trouble, or had he just imagined it all? A shiver ran through his body. He tried to go back to sleep, but found it impossible to do so. Still, he felt jubilant; his spells had most likely worked.

So how long could he hold Bruce off, if he was still here somehow? The house had only shaken slightly the night before, but this night it felt like a raging earthquake. If it really was Bruce, would he get stronger and be able to make his way into the house again?

He could not stay there to find out; he had to move the book. He decided to take it with him the next day and put it in a safe deposit box. He had looked up just such a place on the internet earlier as he had been toying with the idea, but would Bruce's men be watching him and follow him to where he wanted to go?

Adam left the house very early, hoping to avoid traffic and avoid being followed. If there was not much traffic on the road, it would be difficult for somebody to follow him without being noticed.

He put the book in the boot of the car, after making sure that there was nobody about, and drove all the way to London. He wanted to make some photocopies before he went to his class to teach.

Adam knew that the cleaners would be there at the college and would let him in, as they knew him. He wanted to photocopy the book before anybody else got in, or at least a substantial part of it.

Adam was three-quarters of the way through it when he heard the door being unlocked. The cleaners had already left, so it had to be somebody else. Adam decided to put the book and the photocopies away and take out a course book, but he was in luck – it was Lucy. She was surprised to see him.

"I woke up early and decided to come in, I had some photocopies to do. I know the cleaners, so they let me in."

"Don't mind me, carry on. I'm going to make some coffee, would you like some?"

"Yes please," said Adam, and went back to photocopying the book as Lucy went off to make the coffee. He finished in a little while as it was getting near opening time, and joined Lucy in the office.

"Can you do me a favour? Don't mention this to Vera."

"Photocopying your own stuff, then?"

"It's something important and I need it in a hurry."

"Don't worry. You were almost going to be a partner in the college a little while ago."

"So George told you the bad news then?"

"Yes, sure. Very strange, though, this guy coming out of the blue and making such an amazing offer. Is the place worth that much?"

"Not to us," said Adam. "We'll wait and see if he goes through with it."

"It's just bad luck. Let's hope it falls through. I'm not looking forward to working with some complete stranger."

"When did he come to see the college?"

"As far as I'm aware, he's never been here. I certainly haven't seen him."

"According to Vera, I'm supposed to be meeting him on Sunday," said Adam. "It's all very mysterious."

"Vera said he's an Australian."

Alarm bells started ringing in Adam's head again. He was almost convinced that Bruce was still around. What if it was him after all? Adam needed to be prepared for the event. He had to safeguard the book at all cost.

"You know, there was a bunch of Australians hanging around in the village I live in. Maybe I mentioned something to one of them."

"Maybe it's one of them," laughed Lucy. "Where are they now?"

"Well, they've all recently left the village, so I don't know where they are now. But I hope it's not one of them."

"Why?"

"I didn't get on too well with them."

"Well, you needn't worry too much. After all, he's specially requested to meet you. He'd hardly do that if he didn't like you."

"I suppose so," said Adam with resignation, but for all he knew, Bruce was still around.

★ ★ ★

When Adam came out for his mid-morning break, Vera was there.

"My husband has left for Malta this morning, so I hope you're coming round tonight."

"When is his plane leaving?" Adam wanted to make sure.

"I think in two hours' time, but I think he's meeting John to collect some more money before flying out."

"You mean this guy buying the college? You haven't told me much about him. Can you describe him to me?"

"There's not much to tell. He's slightly taller than you, thin, and hasn't got much of an Australian accent. If you didn't know him, you'd think he was English."

Adam was relieved. "He's a bit keen, isn't he?"

"He seems quite nice. Anyway, more importantly, ring me first before you turn up." Vera winked.

"I will be there," said Adam. *Why not?* he thought; he didn't want to spend another night in the house until he had found an explanation for what had transpired the night before. He was also pleasantly surprised that Vera was still keen to see him, even though he was not going to be a part-owner of the college anymore. There seemed to be a definite change in her attitude towards him.

Adam wanted to go directly to the safety deposit box company, but he was a bit worried that he was being watched, so he decided to drive around aimlessly for a while and then pop into a pub for lunch, to ascertain if he was being followed. As far as he could make out, there was nobody following him around.

Adam decided to relax and had a leisurely lunch.

After finishing his pint, he made his way to the nearest Tube station, which happened to be Highgate, and headed for Covent Garden.

When he reached his destination it was nearly four, but he was in for a disappointment. He was told that he needed to come back the following Monday after making an appointment and filling in a form online. It was too late to go back to Littledon by the time he got back to his car, as Vera was expecting him shortly. He decided to call her as it was already past six o'clock.

"What time are you getting here?" she asked. "Can you bring a bottle of wine with you? I'm cooking a meal."

Adam decided to hide the book under the spare wheel in the boot, but left the photocopies in his briefcase as he wanted to have a look at them later on, if he got the chance.

As he was making his way to Vera's after buying a nice bottle of Pinot Noir, he was surprised by a call from Rachael.

"Are you coming to the barbecue tomorrow?" she asked.

"Yeah, sure," said Adam.

"Can you please not mention Bruce, or any of the stuff that happened between us?"

"I already told Dick," joked Adam.

"You didn't, did you? He didn't mention anything."

"Relax, I'm just joking. However, I did tell him that the police suspected me of having an affair with you."

"Why did you have to mention that?"

"Don't worry. He just laughed at the thought of it. There's no way he could even think of it being possible."

"He can be a pompous ass sometimes, but please don't mention it again."

"My lips are sealed. In any case, I have other fish to fry."

"Things are looking up then, I see. All you needed was a bit of confidence."

"Thanks. I'll see you tomorrow."

★ ★ ★

He reached Vera's ten minutes later. She was still busy cooking, but asked him in and got him to open the bottle he was carrying so they could both have a drink.

"I didn't know you could cook," said Adam. "You're full of surprises."

"I was brought up to cook from a very young age."

"So what's the occasion? Are you celebrating the sale of the college?"

"Not really. Believe it or not I was looking forward to working with you. It would have been fun. Tonight I just wanted to surprise you."

"You could stay on for a while. You still have to sell the house."

"I don't know if the new owners or my husband would like that, though I must say, I'm getting a bit tired of following what my husband wants me to do all the time."

"Well, at least you don't seem to be worried much about your neighbours anymore," said Adam.

"I don't really care anymore," said Vera. "My husband is hardly going to be here and we're going to sell the house. I don't really want to go back to Malta."

"We'd better make the most of it in the meantime," said Adam, grabbing Vera. He needed no further prompting. "Your mood has certainly changed."

"Did I tell you that I was married when I was really quite young? My husband is twenty years older than me. My life has been one of duty to him for nearly twenty years now. A girl needs a bit of fun sometimes."

"Why did you marry him?"

"He rescued my family from penury. My father's business failed and we were going to be destitute, but he saved my family."

"You were the prize?" Adam looked slightly disgusted.

"It wasn't quite like that. He was a very handsome man and I was quite happy to do it. I was very grateful, I suppose; maybe I even loved him a little as well."

"I suppose time takes its toll on all of us."

"Well, we never managed to have a family, so it's more of a strain, but I still have a sense of loyalty to him. However, let's not talk about him anymore now."

"Good idea. I might start feeling sorry for him." Adam smiled and pulled her closer. In truth he was feeling a bit sorry for Vera. She was not really the voracious man-eater Adam had previously imagined her to be, but a beautiful woman who was a little lost, and was looking for consolation in a little distraction.

★ ★ ★

When Adam left the next morning, he asked her if she wanted to go to the barbecue at Dick's and she agreed readily to do so.

Adam wanted to go around quickly to his flat and see Linda before going back to Littledon. He wanted to make sure that Linda was indeed making an effort to relocate elsewhere, though he knew from previous experience that she was unlikely to have done anything yet. In any case, he wanted to have a word with her and also let her know for sure that he definitely couldn't take her to Dick and Rachael's party.

Adam was half-expecting her not to be in, but she opened the door and let him in.

"Am I glad to see you," Linda said excitedly. "There was a man knocking on my door this morning, who claimed to be the last tenant's boyfriend. According to him, the woman had left some things behind and he wanted to have them."

"You're joking?" Adam was furious. "Hope you didn't let him in." Why was he getting so worked up, he thought suddenly? It was quite possible that Alicia had another boyfriend. After all, he had only known her for a very short while.

"He was most insistent, so I had no choice but to let him in, in the end," said Linda. "However, he was quite a gentleman and left after a quick look around to confirm that nothing had been left behind."

"Was he a big Australian?" asked Adam suspiciously.

"No, he was a little Englishman, about your size," said Linda.

Adam did not much like the reference to him as a little man, but let it go. He was relieved that it wasn't Bruce. He was beginning to get paranoid about Bruce. It was typical of Linda to put him down like this, and he was beginning to wonder what he had seen in her; enough to actually think of settling down with her.

"I'm here to find out if you've started looking for another flat yet." He wanted to be blunt.

"Give me a break. I haven't even finished unpacking all my stuff yet."

"Probably best if you don't unpack everything. It will be easier for you to move," retorted Adam.

"I thought you were here to see how I was settling in." Linda sounded hurt. "Are you picking me up later for Rachael's party?"

"I'm taking somebody else." Adam felt like being brutal. "You'll have to make your own way there." He was fed up with the whole situation, and found it difficult to hide his frustration at what he perceived as Linda trying to squirm her way back into his life.

★ ★ ★

Adam left soon afterwards and made his way to Littledon. When he got to the house, he found the alarm was ringing.

Adam opened the door and switched the alarm off. He could see straight away that somebody had been inside, as things were scattered all over the floor everywhere. The place was in a mess alright; however, he was relieved to see that the intruder had not discovered his cellar door. The charm he had placed on it was still working. Almost immediately, there was a knock on the door. It was Jack and Wendy.

"Where have you been?" asked Jack. "Your alarm went off early this morning and we saw a bloke running away when we looked out of the window. We were too late to stop him."

Adam grimaced. He knew that there was only a slim chance of Jack actually running after a burglar.

"Anything stolen?" asked Wendy.

"I haven't had a chance to look yet," said Adam, irritated.

"Have you informed the police?" asked Wendy.

"Not yet," said Adam. "Have you?"

"Not yet," said Jack. "We were waiting for you."

"Good," said Adam. "I'll inform them if I have to. Now, if you don't mind, I need to check and see if anything's missing."

"This used to be a decent neighbourhood, until you came here," protested Jack, as they left reluctantly.

Adam went around the house. The back door had been forced and Adam cursed himself for not having fitted a more secure door earlier. It was the weakest point in the house.

Nothing had been stolen as far as he could see. They were obviously looking for something in particular, but they had missed the cellar. In any case, the book had been with him.

So there was confirmation the spell didn't keep anybody from physically breaking in, thought Adam. It was meant to stop people like Bruce from coming in without using force. Was the burglar working for Bruce? In which case, Bruce was still around. Therefore, he hadn't imagined what had taken place the night before that.

Adam decided not to bother with the police. It was unlikely they would be interested if nothing was missing. They would only waste his time and his house insurance would definitely go up.

He rang the local locksmith to come and fit a more secure lock on the back door, and in the end settled for two locks, which cost him a packet. It was a waste as he decided he would have to get somebody in the following week to put in a more secure door anyway.

Adam rang Vera a couple of hours later, just before he was ready to leave for London, to pick her up for the barbecue, but was informed that she couldn't make it. She was a bit worried that her husband had not rung her yet and would probably ring later, so she had to stay at home.

Adam wondered why her husband never called her on her mobile, but surmised that it was a way for him to make sure she stayed at home.

"You can come round afterwards if you like," Vera said. "I'll be right here."

"I'll do that," said Adam. "I should be there just after eleven."

"Okay, see you then." Adam thought he detected a hint of anxiety in Vera's voice, but put it down to her worry about Mr Cruz not reporting back to her.

That was that, thought Adam; at least he had a place to stay for the night in London. He did not really want to stay in his own flat, with Linda there.

CHAPTER 25

Adam decided the best place for the book was in the cellar, until the safe deposit box was available. He decide to hide the photocopies amongst his other paperwork, by dividing them into three sections which he put in plain-cover files, with some lesson plans at the front and back of them, to confuse anybody searching for them. This was safer than having all the photocopies together, which would have been a lot thicker and more obvious to prying eyes.

He took the middle section, which contained most of the spells he was looking at, and put it in his briefcase, along with his teaching notes and books. He wanted to have a look at them the next day, which was Sunday, at Vera's, if he got the chance. But knowing Vera, he was sure that he was going to be otherwise occupied.

After buying a bottle of good wine in a nearby shop, Adam made his way to Dick's house.

He was greeted by Dick and Rachael at the door, and then by Charlie, who was already there. There were not too many people there as yet, but Adam recognised some other familiar faces. Things were back to normal.

"Where's Linda?" asked Rachael. "I thought she was coming with you."

"Sorry, I had some other things to take care of, so I told her to get here by herself. After all, I'm not her boyfriend anymore."

"I thought she had moved into your flat. We thought it was the start of a new relationship with her," said Dick.

"No chance of that, I'm just doing her a little favour, as the flat was empty and she needed somewhere to stay urgently."

"Well, she seems keen to get back with you. Maybe you should reconsider. We all make mistakes sometimes." Rachael smiled.

Adam smiled back. Was that an oblique reference to her own little dalliances? Was she maybe trying to put them behind her, and that was the closest she could come to admitting anything?

"I didn't make any mistakes," said Adam, to push his point home. "In any case, as far as I'm concerned it's over. I'm occupied with other things at present." His smile conveyed more.

He wished he had managed to bring Vera along, as that would have killed any suggestion of a reunion very promptly.

"I'm sure Adam has other fish to fry," said Dick. "Can't you see he's completely changed his image? That's some nice gear you're wearing for a change."

Well, at least Dick had noticed his new, well-fitting clothes. He was looking quite dapper in them, even if he thought so himself.

"Yeah, looks like you've been spending some money on good clothes at last. He's got a new car as well," said Rachael.

"I've still got the Skoda," said Adam. He was fond of his old car; it had given him very little trouble.

"You've got two cars then?" Charlie spoke up.

"Only temporarily, but now the house is finished, I'll probably get rid of one." A statement which was probably untrue, he thought.

"About time you followed Adam's example, Charlie," commented Dick.

"He's got lots of money, or at least plenty enough to get a new car," cried Charlie.

"I borrowed the money. So you can do it also, but first you've got to learn to drive."

"I suppose so, but I need to change my career first. I've already enrolled on a part-time IT course. After the last few weeks, I need to get a hold on things."

"Good, good," said Dick. "Let's have a few drinks and enjoy ourselves tonight. It's good to be back." He was not too interested in Charlie's life, as he knew too well that nothing much ever changed in it.

"So where have you been?" asked Charlie, as they poured themselves some more drinks.

"I wish I could remember. Everything is a complete blank until I suddenly turned up at Adam's. I didn't realise that I've been away so long. Must've been awfully hard on you, darling." Dick looked at Rachael. Rachael blushed as Adam was also looking at her, but recovered quickly.

"Well, it's never easy with disappearances, is it? I was going out of my mind. Adam was very supportive," said Rachael.

"Glad I could help," said Adam. "I was sure you'd show up soon. Are you sure you can't remember anything?"

It was amazing – neither Dick nor Charlie remembered anything about the book. The spell had really worked on them. Had Adam been imagining the weird stuff that had been happening around him in the past few days, then? Were they just nightmares he was having, and the break-in a coincidence where the burglar ran away because of the alarm, before he could grab something? Or maybe Adam didn't have anything valuable enough to be worth stealing.

Dick didn't answer, and Adam moved away. There were some interesting women standing around on the other side of the garden, however there was no sign of Linda. Dick followed him.

"I told you already, I had a very strange dream that I was a crayfish and was having a good time with three other crayfish. But I've taken your advice and haven't told anybody else."

"That's a very good idea. Do you know they had Charlie under observation for talking silly to the police, during the time you went missing? I'm surprised that they did not certify him," said Adam.

"Yeah, really?" Dick was surprised. "I definitely don't want to go through anything like that. Especially as I'm due to get a promotion shortly."

"Oh yeah?" It was Adam's turn to be surprised.

"Yep. Apparently they really missed me the weeks I was away. They believe I was trying out another job. Ha ha!"

Adam also couldn't stop himself from laughing. Funny how things played out. Most likely he was just getting a bit paranoid about Bruce, and needed to relax a bit more.

★ ★ ★

Adam made his way to Vera's; it was nearly half past eleven. There had been no sign of Linda at the party. He had tried ringing her mobile, but there had been no answer. He decided that he would look in on her the next day. Most likely she had the hump, because he did not give her a lift. With another bottle in one hand and his briefcase in the other, he rang Vera's bell.

Vera opened the door, but there was no smile on her face. Her eyes were trying to tell him something, but Adam didn't understand. He was used to her sudden changes in mood by now and most likely this was one of them, so he decided to ignore her signals.

"Hello, Adam. Come in," she said.

Adam said hello and handed her the bottle, and took a couple of steps into the house before he realised there was somebody behind him, who had been standing on the other side of the door.

He heard the steps, but before he could turn around, he felt a sudden blow to his head. He then felt a very sharp pain engulf him and everything went black as he slid to the floor.

When he came to he was sitting on a chair. His hands were tied securely behind his back to the chair, and his feet were tied together to the feet of the chair. His head was throbbing very badly where he had been struck, and he could feel the lump without touching it with his hand.

"Ah, the sleeping beauty awakes." It was Bruce's voice. Adam looked up to see that he was standing there next to Ernie. "I was afraid you might've killed him, Ern."

"Naw, it was just a light tap. He's tougher than he looks," said Ernie. "Anyway, I'm just getting my own back for what he did to me." Ernie laughed loudly.

Adam looked around. Vera was sitting on the sofa, and her hands and feet were tied as well. So this was what she had been trying to warn him about.

"Sorry, Adam, couldn't warn you. They got my husband," said Vera.

"Not only that, we got your little girlfriend Linda as well." Bruce smiled.

"Girlfriend?" asked Vera, surprised.

"Oh! Didn't he tell you?" Bruce laughed. "And all the other naughty things he's been getting up to."

"She's not my girlfriend, she's my tenant," protested Adam.

"Try telling that to Linda," said Ernie. "She's a feisty one, though, put up a good struggle. We had to sedate her in the end."

"She's my ex. I was just helping her out," Adam complained.

"Don't matter, we've got her. So shut up and listen. If you want her back alive, we want the book, so tell us where to find it."

"So you were in my house earlier," said Adam, looking for confirmation.

"That's right, but we couldn't find it there."

"Well, it's not there," said Adam.

"So tell us where it is. Make it easy on yourself, all we want is the book. Tell us where it is and we'll let you and your friends go once we get it." Bruce smiled.

"That's right, all he wants is the book," echoed Ernie.

"I haven't got it," said Adam.

"Here we go again," said Bruce.

Ernie slapped Adam hard across the face. "If you think we're joking, think again."

Adam winced; his face really hurt.

"I'm telling the truth. It's in a bank vault," lied Adam. "I deposited it there yesterday. You can't get it from there without me." Adam tried to laugh, but nothing came out.

"Where's the receipt for the safe deposit box?" asked Bruce.

"It's back at the house. So what do we do now?"

"I'm thinking," said Bruce.

"I thought you'd be back in Australia by now," said Adam. "Alicia told me you'd forget all about the book."

"That's what I told the silly girl, in case you got hold of the book, but I'm the direct male descendant. That spell does not work on me, but she's forgotten all about you and gone back to Australia. I made sure of that. She thought she was too clever and I didn't suspect anything. I haven't finished with her yet; she's going to get what's coming to her when I get back."

"You're one sick bastard," said Adam.

"Not at all," laughed Bruce. "Just protecting what's mine, and that means the book as well. That also belongs to me."

"Well I can't give it to you if I'm sitting here, can I?"

"So what should I do?"

"Let me go and I'll get you the book tomorrow. You've got the hostages. You can release them when you get the book."

Adam meant what he was saying. A desperate plan had formed in his mind. He had the photocopies, so why not give Bruce the book and be done with it?

"I'm still thinking about it," said Bruce. "If I let you go tomorrow morning, Ernie will go with you to make sure."

"Sure thing, no problem," said Adam. He was now almost resigned to giving Bruce the book. He could not see a way out of his present predicament, though Alicia's warning about what dire fate would befall him if Bruce ever got hold of the book still rang fresh in his mind. However, there were other people's lives at stake. Adam was already sure that Bruce had killed Daley, even if the police thought otherwise. Bruce held all the aces.

Bruce picked up Adam's briefcase and had a cursory look through it. Adam's heart was thumping. He was sure Bruce would discover the photocopies, but Bruce just threw down the case on the floor in frustration.

"Don't you think we should look in his car, boss?" suggested Ernie. "He's probably lying about the bank deposit box."

"Yeah, I forgot about the car."

"I don't have the book in there," said Adam. "So go ahead and check if you want to."

"I'll go down and check it out, just in case," said Ernie. "Where are the keys?"

"They should be in my jacket pocket," volunteered Adam.

Ernie dug the keys out from Adam's pocket, but as he was about to go, Bruce stopped him.

"I think I'll go and check the car," said Bruce. "I could do with some fresh air. You stay here and make sure he doesn't escape, Ern."

"There's no chance of that happening. It would take a magician to get out of those knots I've tied him with."

"If it's not in the car, I'll bring his car round and we'll go round to his house and give it a thorough search first, before you go to the bank with him tomorrow. Watch him, he's tricky."

"Don't worry, boss, he's going nowhere," said Ernie gleefully.

Bruce left, after asking Adam for the directions to his car, which Adam readily supplied. Adam was glad that he had left the book in his house, even though it didn't help his present predicament. Vera, who had been quiet all this time, spoke up. She seemed perplexed and angry.

"Sorry, Adam, they came with John, the buyer for the college, and surprised me."

"Where's John now?"

"He's left already."

"I can let him have the book tomorrow, if he lets me go," said Adam to Ernie in desperation.

"What's this book you keep going on about?" Vera asked. "You people are not interested in buying the college, are you?"

"'Fraid not. The meeting later today was a ruse, just to get hold of him, but then the boss thought it was better to surprise him tonight, because we had a suspicion what you two have been getting up to behind your husband's back." Ernie chuckled.

"You're going to let us go tomorrow if you get this book, aren't you?" Vera pleaded.

"If you're lucky and you behave, Bruce will probably let you and your husband go, but he's got other plans for him over there, after he gets his hands on the book." Ernie pointed at Adam. "Oops, I shouldn't have mentioned that."

This was beginning to sound more and more ominous, thought Adam. He needed an escape plan desperately.

"Why is this book so important?" asked Vera again.

"If I tell you, I'll have to kill you," laughed Ernie.

"Do you think I could have a glass of water?" asked Adam.

"If you say pretty please," said Ernie.

"Pretty please," said Adam.

When Ernie turned towards the kitchen, Adam cast his spell to spring the ropes around his hands. He then quickly freed his legs.

Adam put his finger to his lips, motioning Vera to be quiet, who was about to exclaim in surprise. Adam now needed a weapon, but could not see anything handy and began to panic, when he remembered the conjuring spell. He cast the spell, wishing for a mallet.

Adam concentrated hard on the image of a mallet and repeated the spell as Ernie appeared at the doorway to the kitchen. Adam still had the ropes around his legs, though the ropes were untied. His hands were behind his back so Ernie couldn't see them.

"Didn't you want some water as well?" Adam asked Vera. There was something in his voice which made Vera take notice.

"Yes please, I could do with a glass as well," said Vera.

"You can give her this one. I can wait," said Adam.

"Make up your bloody mind," said Ernie.

"Ladies first," said Adam.

"I suppose so," said Ernie, trying to sound chivalrous.

As Ernie turned towards Vera, Adam sprang. The mallet was already in his hand and he hit Ernie square on the forehead. Ernie staggered and gasped in surprise and tried to make a grab for Adam, who hit him again. The glass went flying and shattered.

Ernie dropped like a sack of potatoes on the floor, but he was clutching his heart for some reason. Adam searched Ernie quickly and found a small gun and bits of paper, which he ignored. He tucked the gun in his belt and moved a stone-cold Ernie to the chair and tied him up.

"He doesn't seem to be breathing," said a freed Vera. "You've hit him too hard."

"It was either him or us. You heard the plans they've got for me, it's not very pleasant."

A car pulled up in front of the house, which drew Adam's attention.

"That must be Bruce," said Vera.

Soon the bell rang.

"Okay, we need to get him inside the house," said Adam.

"What are you going to do?"

"I don't know yet, but we need to find out where they're holding Linda and your husband."

"What should I do?"

"You can open the door and step back, then let's see what happens." Adam couldn't think of any other strategy on the spur of the moment, and which would work better. He had to somehow disable Bruce.

Adam got ready behind the door; he had the mallet in his right hand and the gun in the other. He was not sure what exactly he was going to do, but had to do something.

Vera opened the door and stepped back out of Bruce's reach as best as she could.

"Where's Ernie? Who let you go?"

"He's in the living room with Adam. Something's happened, so he sent me to open the door."

"Is that right?" asked Bruce. He slammed hard against the door, and the mallet went flying out of Adam's hand as the door slammed into him.

Adam still had the gun. He pushed back hard and cleared the door. Adam pointed the gun at Bruce, and he stopped and glared at him. Adam thought there was an expression of amusement on his face. He had the car keys in his hands, and Adam grabbed them. Bruce didn't resist.

"What have you done with Ernie?" growled Bruce.

"He's in the living room, so get going. Don't try anything or I'll let you have it."

"You're really scaring me," exclaimed Bruce in a tone which belied his feelings, however he moved towards the living room, calling out for Ernie.

"I'm here," came a feeble reply from the living room. Ernie was waking up, so he wasn't dead after all. Bruce moved towards him.

"Stop," shouted Adam, but Bruce wasn't listening. Instead he walked up to Ernie and pulled at the ropes, which gave way immediately, as if Ernie wasn't even tied up. Adam pressed the trigger, but the gun just clicked.

"That gun isn't loaded. Now what are you going to do?" asked Bruce.

"Better run," said Adam to Vera, who didn't need a second prompting. She ran for the front door.

"Aren't you going to run?" Bruce smirked, and an evil smile formed on his face.

"I don't think I'll get very far somehow."

"That's right," said Bruce, laughing.

"I can't open the door, Adam," he heard Vera cry desperately from outside the room.

"I'll teach you to monkey around with me," said Bruce. "You may have the book, but I can still teach you a few tricks."

Ernie was still struggling to get up.

"Tell me where the book is, or I'll first strangle her, then we're going to kill you very slowly, and make it look like you two lovers committed suicide together."

"Tell me where you're holding Linda and Mr Cruz," said Adam in a desperate attempt to keep Bruce talking, while he thought of a way to escape.

"It's not going to help you much to know, where you're going," Bruce laughed. "But you'd be surprised if you knew how close you were to them yesterday."

"So you got them in Littledon, with your man John."

"How do you know that?" Bruce was surprised.

"He fits the description of the man who was pretending to buy the college."

"He hit me with a mallet again, boss," complained Ernie. "I just don't understand how he got free."

"I'll hit you with a fucking mallet next time," shouted Bruce. "Now get up and let's get him. There's going to be no escape this time."

"I thought you had a heart attack," said Adam, desperate to gain time. "Be careful about moving."

"Naw, it was just indigestion." Ernie smiled. "You're the one who's going to get a heart attack."

"Let's beat him to a pulp," said Bruce.

Ernie was beginning to get up. Adam knew he had less chance than a cornered rat in front of a ferret. He had to find a way out.

"What are you waiting for?" shouted Bruce, and as he turned to look at Ernie, it came to Adam in a flash of inspiration. He threw the gun as hard as he could and caught Bruce squarely on the head. A desperate plan had formed in Adam's head.

As Bruce staggered back, Adam cast his spell.

"Though as men you now stand,
Ernie and Jack, your hour's at hand.
Transform yourselves at my command
Into a creature, that I demand.
Turn into crayfish, now, where you stand."

Nothing happened for a moment. Surprise showed on Bruce's face. He was trying to resist the spell, but he was hurt, stunned by the blow to his head, and struggling to concentrate.

"Yes, I know your name, Jack Smith," said Adam. "Now obey my command." It was very a strange coincidence that he had the same surname as Adam himself, or was it a coincidence? Time itself seemed to slow down, as it felt like an eternity while Adam waited.

Then there was a sudden clap of thunder and there were two crayfish wriggling on the carpet; it had only been a couple of seconds. As Adam picked them up, he felt a sudden surge of energy through his arm into his body from the crayfish Bruce. It felt strangely exhilarating, but Adam didn't take too much notice; he wanted to get them out of the way before Vera came back.

Adam took them into the kitchen and found a bucket to put them in with a little water. He then opened the back door and made his way through the side gate of the house to his car. He put the bucket in the boot of the car, and after securing it, came back the same way into the house.

Adam found Vera upstairs, hiding inside a wardrobe in the foetal position. He pulled her out.

"You can come out now, they're gone," he said. She shivered as she clung to him.

"Where did they go?" asked Vera.

"I gave them the book and they left through the back door," said Adam.

"You had the book with you?"

"It was in my briefcase all the time, but Bruce missed it," Adam lied. "Come downstairs; let's have a cup of tea."

"I think I'll need something stronger than that," said Vera. "Are you sure they're gone?"

"Yes, they're definitely gone, and I've locked the back door. You're safe now." Adam led Vera downstairs, where they found a bottle of Mr Cruz's brandy and took a couple of shots each.

"What about my husband?" Vera asked. "Should we ring the police?"

"I'm sure they will release them tomorrow. They've got no use for the hostages now that they have what they were looking for. Involving the police will only complicate matters. I should get going – there's a man I need to see in Littledon."

"You're going nowhere tonight. You're not going to leave me alone in the house, in case they come back."

"They're not going to come back."

"Wait till the morning," said Vera, and grabbed him around the waist. "I can't face being alone here tonight."

What the hell, thought Adam, he had time on his hands. As Sartre had said once, everything has been figured out except how to live life.

CHAPTER 26

"I suppose we're not going to be able to sell the college now. My husband will be disappointed," Vera said the next morning, as an exhausted Adam was leaving.

"You've still got us."

"Well, for myself, I much prefer you as a partner." She grinned broadly. *She looks even more radiant than before, if that were possible*, thought Adam. She was opening herself up to him, and she was one beautiful woman.

"I'd better get going," said Adam. He did not really want to leave.

"Will my husband be alright?" asked Vera. It was back to reality; she was still someone else's wife.

"Logically, I think he should be back very soon," said Adam, and left.

Adam felt great, both physically and mentally, even though he was tired from the night before. He drove back slowly, taking in the beauty of the countryside in spring. A great burden had been lifted, and though there was still work left to be done, he felt he could achieve anything.

On the way, he took a detour and drove past Daley's house. He found a spot to stop by the river near the house and brought out the bucket from the boot of the car. After getting down to the bank, he emptied the bucket into the river.

"Have a good life," muttered Adam, as the crayfish disappeared. It was fitting, he thought, to put them in the river here, in memory of Daley. He had been a rogue, but Adam had a soft spot for him.

After having a leisurely shower and changing into some casual clothes, Adam sat down to study the photocopies of the book. He wanted to revise some of the spells he had learnt, but in reality he was trying to plan the next step he should take. In the end he cast the spell to summon John to the pub and decided to make his way to The Three Witches half an hour later. He had to confront John directly if he was there.

Adam saw John as soon as he entered the pub; he was standing at the bar and having a drink. Adam walked up and tapped him on the shoulder. Adam could see that John was trying to hide his surprise, but no matter how hard he tried, John could not keep it from his face. He looked very apprehensive.

"Hello, John. Surprised to see me?" Adam looked squarely into his eyes.

"No, no," he protested, "I'm always glad to see you."

"I have a little message for you, John. Bruce and Ernie aren't coming back."

"What do you mean, they aren't coming back? I thought Bruce was back in Australia."

"Come on, John, we both know that's not true, but what is true is that you won't see them again."

"I have nothing to do with them. Now leave me alone."

Adam jabbed a forefinger into John's chest. "I have some unfinished business with you. Be afraid, John, be very afraid. I'm going to hold you personally responsible if something happens to Mr Cruz and Linda."

"Get away from me," John almost screamed, as he tried to push Adam away.

Adam placed a hand on John's chest to stop him from pushing, and a strange thing happened. He could feel John's heart suddenly begin to pulse very rapidly, through his own hand. John was having rapid palpitations. Adam was not sure if it was the effect of his words or his hand on John's chest that was causing John's discomfort, but he could feel a strange tingling sensation in his hand.

"Be very afraid, John, do you understand me?" said Adam, and John nodded. His face was rapidly turning ashen with fright. Adam felt John's heart was about to race completely out of control. The last thing he wanted was for John to have a heart attack. John had turned completely white with fear.

"Don't even think of trying to get away from me," said Adam. He was in a fierce mood, and wanted to really drive the message home. "I can have you back here anytime I want, whether you wish it or not." He removed his hand.

Jack and Wendy entered the pub at this point and came up to them to say hello.

"I owe you a drink, John," said Jack. "Can I get you one as well, Adam?"

"I'm afraid I've just remembered something that I have to do," said John. "Sorry, got to go." He left without even trying to finish his drink.

"Very strange," said Jack. "I've never known him to refuse a drink before."

"Yeah, and he didn't even finish the drink he already had," said Wendy.

"Never mind him. I was just going to order a drink myself," said Adam. "What would you two like?"

★ ★ ★

Later that evening, Adam got a telephone call from Vera. She had heard from Mr Cruz that he was on his way back home after being released, along with Linda, near Dagenham. Mr Cruz even had all his money returned to him, before being set free.

Soon after that, Linda rang. She spent more than half an hour on the phone telling Adam about her horrible experience in the hands of the brutes who had blindfolded her after sedating her and kidnapping her. Then very unexpectedly, she was released along with the other gentleman, and they didn't have a clue what it was all about and where they had been held.

When Linda finally finished her story, Adam almost wished he hadn't asked for her to be released. It was his fault, she said, for putting her up in the flat in the first place, instead of his house. When finally he managed to get a word in, he asked her about Jim, her last boyfriend.

"Have you contacted Jim yet?"

"Not yet," she said, which exasperated Adam even more.

"Send him a text with the address now. I have a feeling he'll turn up when he finds out where you live."

"How do you know that?"

"Just do it, will you?" said Adam, getting even more frustrated, being unable to confide in her. "I can't get your money back if you don't tell him where you live."

Adam was relishing meeting up with Jim and trying out his new abilities again. He could only surmise that he had come to possess them since he had felt the surge of energy when picking up crayfish Bruce the first time. Somehow he had absorbed some powers from his vanquished foe, and he wondered what else he was capable of.

After putting the phone down Adam sat back in a daze for a while, reflecting on the things that had taken place in the last few days. Soon exhausted, he made his way to bed for the first uninterrupted night's sleep for a while.

★ ★ ★

The next few days went by quite slowly. Mr Cruz was back at the college and Vera was back to being a dutiful wife, without there being any chance of any extracurricular activity with her. Adam was frustrated, so he even visited Linda and played badminton with Charlie. He decided that even after the very eventful weekend, Vera had reverted back to type and there was no chance of her leaving her husband for him. Especially now, as there would be no move to Malta.

There had been no further mention of any share sales, and Adam thought it would take Mr Cruz a while to climb down from the heady heights of the last offer. Adam was in no hurry, even though he had already received the money from the remortgage.

Finally it was Friday, and Adam was wondering what to do when he got back to Littledon after college. The day was not finished yet, and Adam decided he had one more task to complete. He took a bucket from the kitchen and made his way to the pond in the garden and came back with a crayfish.

He had three names: Phyllis, Evelyn and Cynthia. He had been reliably told that they had been the names of the three women, allegedly witches, who had gone missing from the house. Adam wanted to find out if there was any truth in the story, and he wanted to know for sure if the crayfish in the pond were in fact the three witches.

Adam had already deposited the book in a bank deposit box and placed the photocopies in the cellar as a precaution, but was still very apprehensive about trying the spell on all three crayfish. Instead he was going to try the spell on one of them.

He took the bucket into the living room and took out the little crayfish and laid it on the floor. He then took out the piece of paper on which he had written out the spell.

He had already decided that he wanted to go for Evelyn first, as opposed to the other two. He liked the name, as it had been his grandmother's name. The idea was that he would try the spell, with that name, on each of the crayfish in turn and see if it worked.

Adam had left the other two crayfish in the pond, as he feared that he might inadvertently restore all three to being human. He could not even begin to comprehend the amount of trouble he would be letting himself in for, if they were all transformed into humans and ganged up on him.

Though he had wanted to try this out for a while, there had been so much going on and he had had to put it off until now. This was the first real opportunity to test his theory, even though he was unsure of what he would do if it actually worked.

Adam read out the spell, inserting the name 'Evelyn' in the appropriate place, however nothing happened. It had to be one of three possibilities, thought Adam: either the names were not correct, or he had the wrong crayfish, or the crayfish were just that: crayfish.

Adam was a bit disappointed, but felt relieved at the same time. He was quite sure that the spell worked, as he had previously used it restore Dick to his former self. However, maybe the crayfish were just crayfish. He needed to try out the other crayfish, but felt too lethargic to go out to the pond in the dark to get another one.

Adam put the crayfish back in the bucket and opened a cold can of lager and sat back on the sofa to relax. He switched on the television to catch up on the latest news. He was especially interested in the local news to see if there was any mention of the missing Bruce or Ernie.

As Adam sipped the lager, his thoughts were suddenly interrupted by a noise, which sounded like a knock at the back door of the house. Adam dismissed it and continued sipping his cold lager, which he was particularly enjoying. However, there it was again, and it was much louder this time; there was no mistaking it.

Who could it be now, and why were they knocking on the back door instead of the front door? He decided to pick up his trusty mallet from the kitchen and make his way to the back door. The knock sounded again, more impatient this time, so Adam decided to unlock the door.

He was ready with the mallet, in case of any trouble, but he was astounded to find a naked young woman standing there, with a very impatient look on her face.

"Who are you?" asked Adam, recovering.

"I'm Evelyn," said the young woman. "Who in the blazes are you?"

ALSO BY MAX NOWAZ...

The Arbitrator

MAX NOWAZ

"Was there a pang of remorse for his actions in his mind? Possibly, but what choice did he have? If he wanted to survive, he had no room for weakness."

Max Nowaz's science fiction novel, *The Arbitrator*, follows the story of 153 year-old Jim Brown, a former highly successful administrator who is now rotting in jail, for tax fraud. However, in reality, he is there for taking revenge and killing several people on the planet Levita, after meeting the beautiful Narissa...

In prison, he has acquired a drug habit, which is killing him slowly and his only chance of survival is a very expensive renewal process, which will make him young again and cure his drug habit. After ten years in jail, he is suddenly given a reprieve and offered a chance to redeem himself. He is sent as the 'Arbitrator' to 'Pirrus' in another solar system, to try and stop a rebellion and bring matters under control. Will he complete the mission successfully to earn enough funds for his regeneration? Only time will tell.

Just when he thinks he has accomplished his task, he meets Gina, the daughter of a rebel, and finds out that there is a plot by foreign powers to invade the planet... The plot thickens when Brown also discovers that there is a mole in his organisation who is undermining his efforts to succeed. How will Brown react to the devastating news?

"The Arbitrator is an action-packed epic science fiction novel encompassing love, betrayal, treachery, revenge and discovery," comments author Max."